I0597974

Shadow Lane
Volume Eleven

The Venus Club

A Novel of Sex, Spanking and Modern Love

by
Eve Howard

CCB Publishing
British Columbia, Canada

Shadow Lane Volume Eleven: The Venus Club
A Novel of Sex, Spanking and Modern Love

Copyright ©2012 by Eve Howard
ISBN-13   978-1-927360-53-8
First Edition

Library and Archives Canada Cataloguing in Publication
Howard, Eve, 1953-
Shadow lane volume 11 : the Venus Club,
a novel of sex, spanking and modern love / written by Eve Howard – 1st ed.
ISBN 978-1-927360-53-8
Also available in electronic format.
I. Title. II. Title: Shadow lane volume eleven.
PS3608.O824S543 2012   813'.6   C2012-902253-5

Cover artwork by Tarsis: www.briantarsis.com

Publisher: CCB Publishing
              British Columbia, Canada
              www.ccbpublishing.com

Contents

Chapter One

Things to Do with a Ponytail

Going to Europe the summer after freshman year of college had been one of Amanda Sands' most cherished dreams and the boyfriend she chose to accompany her, Colby Hodge, was an experienced traveler who could easily carry her extra bag. Colby wondered why Amanda even needed two suitcases, arguing that they ought to be traveling lighter, with backpacks instead of suitcases on wheels, but Amanda looked at him with a steely expression in her pale blue eyes, and said, "I'm going shopping in Paris and Rome." Colby shrugged and accepted her will. They were both spoiled only children, but he was less spoiled and more willing to compromise, whereas she was more determined to get exactly what she wanted at all times.

They were examining designer mark downs in the luggage department at Bartlett's department store in Woodbridge, Mass, the little village adjacent to Random Point, where Amanda was spending the month of June working in her father's antiques' shop and pre-reading required books for sophomore year at Harvard, which she and Colby both attended. Colby was about to depart to work in his family's winery for a month on the opposite coast. They had agreed to meet in London on July 1st and spend the entire month in Europe together.

"Babe, I've reached my saturation point. I'll be in the pub across the street," said Colby, disappearing in a flash of long khaki shorts and lean, muscular boy torso under a white t-shirt before she had a chance to protest that it was only three p.m.! Amanda thought he must have a very convincing fake id to get served alcohol in any bar in the commonwealth at age nineteen.

"If I may make a suggestion," came a silky voice from around the corner of an aisle, as Pamela Bartlett suddenly appeared before Amanda. "One of these will pack as much shopping as you can afford to do in Paris and Rome," Pamela showed Amanda a smart medium tall piece on wheels.

"If you say so," said Amanda.

"It's the nicest sale piece we have too," Pamela confided.

The two young women had modeled together and walked in the same in store fashion shows at Bartlett's several times and Pamela was well equipped to judge exactly the type of shopping Amanda would be doing on the summer streets of Europe. What Pamela didn't know was that Amanda's anticipated shopping spree was to be financed by a sexual encounter Amanda had engaged in with Pamela's husband Ambrose Bartlett, several months before Pamela and Ambrose had wed.

Pamela still worked in the *Damaris* boutique on the third floor, much to the annoyance of the tall, slim and fashionable brunette. She had fully expected to be relieved of all clockable wage-earning duties upon her marriage to the wealthy owner of Bartlett's department store that spring. She had planned to work solely on dress design from now on, along with her partner Damaris, who put out a smart little line of tailored ready to wear suits and dresses and now possessed two shops in the commonwealth, but had been summarily told by her husband that the boutique at Bartlett's was still her responsibility and that he had no intention of hiring another clerk at that time. It had been Pamela's first disappointment as a bride, but she hadn't argued, then. However, she brooded on the subject every hour of every day. She was currently on her lunch hour and prowling around the store restlessly when she ran into Amanda.

Pamela wasn't sure if she was happy that Amanda was in Random Point for the summer because even though she was in almost total ignorance about what had transpired between Bartlett and the then college freshman Amanda in the winter and spring, she somehow guessed that her husband had been and probably still was immensely attracted to the willowy blonde daughter of Hugo Sands. The fact of seeing Amanda together with her tall, broad shouldered jock boyfriend was a comfort to Pamela, who was as yet unaware that Colby was about to depart and leave Amanda alone for the next month betwixt all the men of Random Point.

Pamela feared Amanda yet also felt attracted to the polished blonde Ivy League girl. Amanda was lithe, lovely and as interested in apparel as she herself was. Pamela had no close female friends and was beginning to long for a companion to whom she might reveal all her inner thoughts. It should have been Hope Lawrence, but Pamela was aware that her husband had sent Hope good coats and dresses as tips on top of paying her allowance for spanking sessions. Pamela's jealousy of Hope was endless and while yet she loved her husband, Pamela and Hope would never be dear friends. Laura Sands was very nice, but Pamela had still not gotten over being in love with, being toyed with and then being summarily rejected by Hugo Sands, therefore she had no desire whatever to closely consort with Hugo's new wife. Everyone knew that Hugo had wooed Laura relentlessly for seven years before finally capturing his prize and this type of romance gave Pamela a pain in her flat stomach to contemplate, because no one had ever shown her such devotion.

"Do you want to have lunch some day?" Pamela asked Amanda impulsively.

"Yes! Tomorrow?"

"All right, meet me at the café upstairs at noon," said Pamela, unconsciously looking at herself in a mirror to make sure she was still absolutely thin. Food in itself meant very little to her, but she knew that eighteen year olds were always hungry.

Amanda was thrilled as she wheeled her Kenneth Cole suitcase out of the store. The warm, sunny streets of Woodbridge were thronged with the first wave of summer tourists that balmy afternoon and Amanda was so momentarily dazzled by the colors and movement around her that she almost walked into Ambrose Bartlett, who had in fact just been in the pub across the street where Colby now awaited her.

"Amanda, so nice to see you. Have you been shopping?" Mr. Bartlett extended his hand to shake hers, though she had been somewhat more inclined towards exchanging hugs, considering the last time they had seen each other he had made fairly expert love to her, but she realized that they were in a Pamela and Colby danger zone and so only returned his handshake with a squeeze.

"Yes, Pamela steered me towards this for Europe," said Amanda, smiling at him warmly to let him know that he was now completely forgiven for their first meeting, during which the department store owner had not endeared himself to her. But that was now ancient history, dating back to the previous winter. Their more recent history was much more agreeable and had left Amanda the richer by five thousand dollars. "By the way, congratulations, Mr. Bartlett," Amanda said.

"Oh, thanks," he replied vaguely, knowing she meant on his marriage but appreciatively taking in Amanda in the white halter top, beige capri pants and chunky wedge sandals that did remarkable things for her already beautiful arch.

"It looks like Pamela and I are going to be friends," Amanda told him, hastening to add, at the instant wrinkling of his brow, "But don't worry, I won't tell her what we did."

"Good girl," said Bartlett, momentarily pressing her hand, then leaving her to return to his store. Amanda watched the sleekly groomed Bartlett enter his store by one of the gilt edged revolving doors with a smile, but when she turned back to continue on her way, she saw Colby standing in the pub window across the narrow cobbled street glaring at her.

Slamming down his mug of ale he folded his arms and frowned heavily at her. Letting go of her suitcase pull for the moment she looked defiantly back at him over her own folded arms. But there were too many tourists passing back and forth in front of them to continue this pantomime for very long so Amanda crossed the street and motioned him out.

"Are you going to be horrible just because I exchanged pleasantries with Mr. Bartlett?" she demanded, as he took the suitcase from her and they began walking towards the village street where he had parked his car, which instead of being borrowed, as in the past, was now his own, having been allowed him by his parents upon having successfully completed his first year at Harvard with top grades. It was a fifteen-year-old jeep and he was happy to have it. The mere act of Amanda's climbing into the front seat soothed Colby's unease at having seen her with her wealthy admirer and being of a cheerful and optimistic nature, all hostile thoughts were at once replaced by the happy expectation of their last night together before separating for a month.

Amanda had invited Colby to stay with her these past several days at her father's house and he had also shared her bed. In fact, for many weeks together Colby had enjoyed the signal privilege of holding Amanda in his arms every night, their handsome young bodies pressed close, with rapturous sexual interludes only interrupting periods of peaceful repose.

Since Colby refrained from quarreling with her about Ambrose Bartlett, Amanda took great pleasure in first shopping at the village co-op and then graciously preparing a meal of pasta primavera for her young lover in the kitchen of her father's house. Colby opened one of Hugo's excellent merlots and Amanda sliced crusty French bread and summer fruit. After eating heartily, they went for a long walk down Shadow Lane until they came to the cul-de-sac where the Randoms lived. Behind their house was a wooded path that lead to the beach and Amanda led Colby thence to watch the sun go down on the water. They had brought sweaters and blankets and thus comfortably sat in each other's arms, kissing and hugging as the waves rolled gently in and the cool evening breeze blew through the cove.

Amanda suggested they return to the house, promising a surprise upon their arrival there. Beguiling the long walk back, Amanda produced a joint and they each had a couple of pulls on it, which brought the stars above them into much sharper perspective. Once they reached the house Amanda led him up to the attic via a narrow stairway at the back. This long, dark wood planked, skylight room was Hugo's playroom and well equipped as such with furniture conformable to B&D, along with fetish toy chests, wardrobe armoires and a quantity of mirrors to reflect provocative tableaux. A large box sofa which had just been reupholstered in cocoa and cream brocade with a equally imposing round pouf to match dominated one side of the room while the dungeon furniture ranged about the other, with ample space around each post, bench, "horse" or bondage bed to swing an implement. The light mocha walls were surmounted by cream crown molding a foot wide. Architectural wall sconces held fat ivory candles that Amanda now lit, instructing Colby to turn the lights off. Now the bewitching room was bathed in a lambent glow as they wandered from object to object, opening doors and lifting lids to explore the leathery or hickory scented contents within.

Shedding her light cotton cardigan, Amanda regarded her image in a mirror, wondering if she should have worn a sexier outfit on her last night with Colby before a month's separation. She was dressed in khaki shorts, a sleeveless, cropped white shirt that exposed two inches of sleek, flat midriff, high collared urban walking boots and white socks. Behind her she glimpsed Colby seizing on a jar of pomade, cream or oil from an open armoire shelf and said, "What's that you've got there?"

"Nothing," he said, sliding it into the pocket of his own khaki cargo shorts.

"Is that some sort of anal lube?" she demanded.

"Why should I tell you?" he countered evasively.

"Humph!" she said, her hands unconsciously going to her hips as she prepared to lecture him on preparing to take liberties she had not formerly granted him. But he cut her off and surprised her by taking her by her elbow and summarily pulling her over his lap with the large pouf under him.

"What do you think you're doing?" she sputtered. "And why do you have a hard on?" she added, wriggling across his muscle corded thighs.

"I just want to have a conversation with you," he explained, winding her long ponytail around one hand while pressing his other down around her waist. Amanda found being taken by the hair so exciting that she decided against expressing any additional indignation and simply caught her breath and waited.

"You saw I saw you talking to that old geezer today," Colby said, stroking the bare skin between the middle of her back and the waist band of her shorts mildly, then slipping his hand up under the back of her shirt to unhook her bra.

"I did see you glower at me," Amanda replied, turning her face back towards him.

"That was the exact millionaire who bought your favors last winter. Wasn't it?"

"Mr. Bartlett did court me at one time, but he's married to Pamela now and she's enough for one man."

"Oh, is that so?" Colby switched from holding her by the hair to capturing her wrist and folding her arm back, holding it to her impossibly small waist. "Then why was he eyeing you as if you were a red velvet cupcake? Huh?" Colby brought his palm down on the seat of her shorts smartly two or three times.

"I can't help it if that man likes me," she protested.

"Yes, you can!" he insisted, reaching under her to unsnap her buttons and loosen her shorts in order to yank them down to her knees. This operation revealed fine, thin, white cotton bikinis tightly girding her slim but jutting bottom cheeks. "I told you to stay away from that ancient metrosexual and you defied me!" Colby scolded, smacking her vigorously for one or two minutes.

"Humph!" she grunted but was determined not to give him the satisfaction of hearing her sob or feeling a tear fall from her eye. "I will always defy you!" she returned stubbornly, though the increasing impact and velocity of his descending palm had caused her to begin kicking her legs.

"Then I will always spank you," Colby advised her, yanking down her panties and finishing the punishment with an enthusiast volley of several dozen resounding smacks across the swelling center of each shapely bottom cheek. Then he held her in place and massaged her hot pink buttocks, rubbing her in circles with the palm of his hand until she began to squirm across his thighs in excitement rather than pain.

Pulling off her panties entirely, he made her sit on his lap facing him and in seconds flat had his hard, throbbing, condom sheathed, vein corded cock poised at her suddenly moisturized pink pussy slit. Remembering the lube, he used it to coat his shaft and her slim aperture before encouraging her to take him in her hands and guide him into her deepest recesses, while gently easing herself down on his cock. Halfway through this endeavor of patient concentration, Colby grabbed Amanda by the waist and pulled her abruptly the rest of the way down on his truncheon like stem, filling her so deeply as to evoke a yelp of indignation from Amanda, who then slapped Colby across the face.

"Ow!" she cried. He grinned at her and kissed her on the mouth while pulling her forcefully against his chest and throbbing inside the entire length of her vaginal canal. In a moment she had grown accustomed to his turgid penis thrust inside her at this acute angle and had begun to tentatively bounce up and down on her personal maypole. His own muscular arms doing most of the work, Colby propelled Amanda's lap pogo with a viselike grasp on her waist until the excitement was too strong to withstand another instant whereupon he pulled her hard against him one final time while exploding into orgasm deep inside her. She wriggled against him throughout the entire throes of his eruption, grinding her blonde fuzzed Venus Mound and by now almost painfully throbbing clit, against his groin with a genuine sense of urgency. As Colby squeezed her still warm, well-spanked bottom cheeks in his hands and lightly probed the cleft between them with his fingertips, Amanda grabbed onto him hard and reached her own shuddering climax.

"How am I going to do without you for a month?" he murmured into her ear.

Chapter Two

Amanda Persuades Pamela to Bob her Hair

When Susan Ross brought Anthony Newton his coffee on that balmy June morning, she found him leaning on the railing of his balcony looking out over the cove, the blue of the sky deep above them, the air warm and perfumed with summer.

"Is that Amanda Sands doing yoga on our beach?" asked Newton, of the slim blonde girl far below them going through her sun salutations in a white top and white yoga pants.

"Yes. She's going to walk up the stairs when she's done," said Susan, referring to the extremely long and steep stone steps that climbed up the cliff to the back of Newton's house. "Then we're going swimming," Susan added. Newton grabbed a pair of binoculars off the patio table and focused in on his best friend's eighteen-year-old daughter.

"Damn near perfect, isn't she?" Newton commented. "Who's going to be spanking *her* while she's in town for the next month?"

"I'm not sure," said Susan, curling up in a deck chair with her own coffee to regard her attractive older lover in the strong morning light. "Why? Would you like to?"

Newton put down the binoculars and shook his head with a smile. "Me? Want to spank such an obviously good girl? Certainly not."

"Do you have time to meet her today?"

"Of course, she can join us for lunch."

"She'll be on her own here, so I expect we'll be seeing a lot of her."

"Lovely," said Newton sincerely; for he had understood from Susan's reports that Amanda was a most agreeable girl.

"I have to admit, I'm crazy about her," said Susan of her newest friend.

"I'm glad you're going swimming. There's a present I've been meaning to give you down at the pool."

"Oh, really?"

"And just in case you're wondering, it's not the pool guy, though you might think so."

Susan went down to the kitchen to let Dennis know that Hugo Sands' daughter, whom he had heard much about from his employer, was to join them shortly. Anthony and his servant had recently returned from a long sojourn in London and this was the first time Susan had spoken to the young Englishman, with whom she shared such a long and vivacious history, since their return. She and Dennis had been studiously avoiding each other for a number of months, since a quarrel, harsh words and more had seemed to rend for good the delicate fabric of their complex ongoing relationship. Now both Susan and Dennis appeared shyly ready to put their antipathy behind them and begin afresh on a new footing of tentative politeness and respect. And yet, Susan knew him too well not to smile at the thought of how the hitherto romantically submissive young man would react to being introduced to one as obviously goddess-like as Amanda Sands.

Dennis was unpacking the provisions he'd just purchased in the village and Susan noticed his handsome brow wrinkle when Miss Sands was mentioned.

"So I'll lay out a lunch for three, shall I?" he asked mildly.

"Yes, please." said Susan.

"Mr. Newton mentioned she shot a video in Random Point over Christmas," Dennis ventured.

"Yes, she's in the scene."

"Susan –"

"Don't worry, Dennis, I won't mention anything about your orientation to Amanda. I'll never do that again. I give you my word," said Susan hastily, remembering how mortally offended he had been the last time she'd hinted to a pretty young woman about Dennis' innate submissiveness. Because the fact was that he was no longer the tame foot slave he had once been and Susan herself was in part responsible for his transformation from submissive to switch to… dom? It was possible. He had turned her under his arm and spanked her, without preamble, to demonstrate his indignation at her outing him as a former sub to William Random's pretty nanny.

"Thank you!" he breathed, his brow uncreasing.

"However, when you see this babe you'll want to go down on your knees just like in the old days," Susan added irreverently. "What are you making for lunch?"

"Salads and light sandwiches. And I got pounds of these Rainier cherries," Dennis displayed a bowl of the exquisite peach and crimson colored fruit.

Just then Amanda knocked on the kitchen garden door.

"Hey Babe," Susan said, hugging Amanda.

"Hello, my goddess," said Amanda, returning her slightly older friend's embrace and smiling at Dennis over Susan's bare shoulder. The petite twenty-five year old commercial artist had swathed her small, slim, curvy form in a pair of blue denim capris and a red and white check midriff halter-top. Her hair was arranged in a thick, long blonde braid down her back and her tiny feet were shod in mahogany penny loafers and white cotton anklets.

"This is Dennis," said Susan. Dennis smiled at Amanda shyly and nodded his head in greeting.

"Hi Dennis," said Amanda, disengaging from Susan.

"Let's go check out the pool, Anthony said he left me a present down there," said Susan, relieving Amanda of her rucksack and pulling her after her by the hand.

"Who's Dennis?" Amanda asked, happily allowing herself to be lead through the halls of the luxuriously decorated and richly furnished house belonging to Susan's wealthy lover.

"He's Anthony's personal assistant. He drives, valets, shops, even prepares some meals. He's terrifically useful."

"Handsome too," Amanda commented.

"Yes."

"But I have a boyfriend now so I shouldn't even be looking," Amanda chided herself.

"Oh, so you intend to be well behaved this summer in Random Point?"

They exited the house from the rear and took a garden walkway to the tennis courts and indoor pool. Susan noticed upon entering that the flat roof had been replaced with a clear dome of a glasslike material and the moment she entered the hitherto unremarkable pool building she saw that it had been transformed into a tropical hothouse in her absence. The pool still ran down the middle of the hall but it now bisected a lush garden.

"This place has been completely transformed," breathed Susan, delighted with her new private paradise.

"It smells delirious," Amanda commented, inhaling the heavy scents of blossoms permeating the warm, moist air within the long, sun drenched room.

"It seems to have everything," said Susan, noting with approval a large, deep, tiled Jacuzzi off to one side, a mist filled steam room opposite it and a dry sauna beside that. There were also fountains surrounding cupids and goddesses, cabanas for changing clothes, a wall of rolled towels and a wet bar. "We'll make this our summer party headquarters. Come over whenever you can," Susan invited Amanda.

A few minutes later, when introduced to Anthony Newton in the dining room, Amanda received a second invitation to make the house her own from her host. Seated at the head of the table, with Susan on his right and Amanda on his left, the affable Newton began handing around dishes of salad and the dainty plates of sandwich quarters that had been lovingly prepared by Dennis.

"I'm sorry it's taken so long to get around to meeting you in person," said Newton, "but I've been following your progress with interest this past year."

"How much do you know?" Amanda asked, in slight alarm.

"Oh, he knows everything," said Susan, with unconcern, "but don't worry, he's cool."

"I meant I'd seen your clips," Newton said to reassure her, though he did in fact know about all of the scandalous things she had done with Ambrose Bartlett the previous winter.

"Not only that, but financed them too," said Amanda with a grin. "Thank you for that."

"Susan said you've already paid her back for the model fees. I'm impressed by that."

Amanda said, "I was lucky that Hugo told his customers to go watch my clips. That started me off. Now he says they'll buy whatever I put up. If I ever have time to shoot again."

"Well, you can shoot here next time if you like," Newton offered.

"Thank you, you're so kind!" Amanda cried, certain that nothing would be required of her in payment this time.

"I've always patronized the art of spanking," he replied. "It's my hobby."

"I would like Susan to be the star of my next round of clips," said Amanda.

"Do you think I should?" Susan asked her lover. Her one previous experience making a fetish video had produced a result so awkward that Anthony had felt compelled to buy the master video and lock it away to save his darling any future embarrassment. So far she hadn't ventured in front of a camera again, but had faith that if anyone could create a charming vehicle for her, it was Amanda.

"I do," said Newton. "I would love a perfect video of you."

"But who would you want to sub to?" Amanda asked, selecting a piece of honeydew to sink her white teeth into.

"I don't know. Pick someone out for me. I trust your judgment," said Susan.

"Maybe we can do it when I come back in August," said Amanda.

"Okay, I'll try to get under the skin of one of the locals between now and then so they'll be some spark when we shoot," promised Susan. Meanwhile Anthony and Amanda were smiling at each other.

"May I ask how you met my father and how you came to be such good friends?" Amanda asked.

"We met at an estate sale about sixteen years ago. I was just hitting on Broadway and had money to buy things with. I liked the taste he showed at the auction and invited him to lunch. After which he showed me his shop. Naturally, what caught my attention above all was the rare erotica, and how much of it was corporal punishment oriented. Because I've been into it all my life."

"Right, the notorious collection that's always the tip off that Random Point is a spanking friendly zone," said Amanda, remembering how electrified Colby had been to discover the vintage spanking books in Hugo's print collection under glass and the readily available trove of spanking erotica placidly reposing on the third floor of Marguerite's bookshop. It was just too large a concentration of B&D material in a one-block radius of a quaint New England village to be coincidental. A true enthusiast would know at a glance that more than one of his or her own dwelt in Random Point or its immediate environs.

"Yes," agreed Anthony. "It's a dead giveaway. So of course we began to talk about it and I made no secret of my interest. Then he showed me his own magazine, which I'd never heard of before but absolutely loved. So in one day I became a customer, a friend and a fan."

"And patron," Amanda said, with gratitude, for she knew how many generous acts Newton had performed for his scene friends.

"Get to the part about me," said Susan, helping herself to Dennis' array of pretty, wholesome dishes.

"Oh yes, how could I forget," said Newton, "Hugo gave me Susan. It took a while for me to get disentangled from all of my various wives and become free to actually date a girl in the scene. As soon as that happened, Hugo said he'd like to introduce me to a cute, little submissive so I could really start living my fantasies."

"How many wives were there?"

"Five," Newton sighed.

"Didn't you play with any of them?"

"Not in that same satisfying way you can with a girl who's really into it," Anthony replied. "So he sent Susan over to me and I don't know about her, but for me, it was love at first sight."

Susan started, looking at Anthony in surprise, as he had never uttered any phrase as blatantly, sentimentally romantic in her hearing since they had met.

"So, we started seeing each other right away," he continued, "even though I was busy as hell and she was in college. Somehow it worked out okay. Then she stuck with me through design school in New York and then she started working at Chipper Knight about two years ago and we're still together."

"He says that like I'm doing him some favor," said Susan, her heart swelling with affection for her lover, who obviously still valued her so highly. "The truth is he's been spoiling me, my sister and half my friends rotten for years."

"You're a very good girl," Newton assured her. "You make me smile."

"Anthony made it so comfortable for my sister Laura after her settlementless divorce, that she was able to keep Hugo at bay for years," Susan reported. "Hugo will confirm that."

Anthony smiled and told Amanda, "I love how Laura draws. Of course I've been happy to patronize her. I'd probably do it even if she wasn't Susan's sister."

"I need to get to know Laura," said Amanda, thoughtfully. "But I don't think she likes being around me."

"Give her time," said Susan. "It was a shock suddenly having to share Hugo's attention with another girl. And then your appearance triggered his trip out west to see your mother for the first time in nineteen years, during which visit they played and made love. And on top of that, you introduced that crazy slut Thalia into our group and she wasn't happy until she scored with Hugo. Laura intercepted one of Thalia's emails to me and found out."

"I didn't know that," said Amanda, shocked and blushing with embarrassment. "I don't think Thalia does either."

"No," Susan said, "Hugo probably didn't think it was worth making Thalia feel guilty about once the damage was done. He knows girls kiss and tell. The end result was him finally insisting that Laura marry him, if only to prove that he had no intention of chasing after nineteen-year-olds for the rest of his life."

"Laura probably blames me for both the incident with my mother and with Thalia," Amanda mused with a troubled expression.

"Well, if you hadn't popped up all of a sudden, this far distant part of Hugo's past would never have become an issue. But here you are, an extraordinary creature of the scene, with this still hot hippy chick of a mom hanging out casually on the opposite coast and slightly sexually frustrated from not getting any BDSM love in twenty years, not to mention any number of bouncy young girlfriends ready to be intrigued by your newly discovered and singularly dashing father."

"I'm horrible," said Amanda with conviction.

"Never think that," Susan reassured her friend; "What's happened since you've come into Hugo's life has simply taught my sister to take nothing for granted."

Several days later, Amanda accepted Anthony's invitation to come and swim again, but this time Susan was away from home. It was after six in the evening but still quite light and Amanda had just come from the shop. She donned a white two-piece swimsuit with blue anchor accents and white Lycra swim cap in the cabana and dove in at the deep end. The water seemed colder than on her previous visit and Amanda shivered at the end of the lap. A lean, young Latino gardener in low rider jeans and a sleeveless white ribbed undershirt that set off his tanned, muscular torso to advantage, looked up from his Birds of Paradise and smiled.

"Is it too cold?" he asked.

"A little."

"Go in the hot tub for a few minutes and I'll turn up the pool," he suggested.

Amanda warmed up nicely in the Jacuzzi beside the Aphrodite fountain for several minutes, then dove back into the pool and began swimming laps. After a few laps she floated on her back, looking up at the cloud dotted deep blue sky through the clear dome of the greenhouse. The water was perfectly warm and Amanda felt suddenly restless. It had been a week since Colby had gone back to California. She'd spent every night alone in Hugo's house, in the guest room that looked out on the woods, a charming room, but it felt very empty without Colby there.

Amanda rolled over and over in the water, arching up her bosom and stretching out her long legs. She began stretching and twisting her lithe, small waisted form around and about in the water, staring up at the flowers and vines that intersected in a fragrant bower above the pool where she floated and dipped.

Then, the Latin boy came back into view, pushing a cart of soil and pretending not to look at Amanda. Amanda halted her shadow flirting display at once and felt herself flushing pink at having been seen behaving in such a manner by the good looking gardener. Then she swam a lap or two and covertly looked for him over her shoulder. He was pretending not to notice her but she could tell he was tracking her every stroke.

"I was just missing my boyfriend," Amanda explained, swimming up to Jaime.

"Lucky boyfriend," he said, with no trace of an accent.

"Thank you," Amanda replied.

"Well, have a good swim," he said, reluctantly attempting to avert his eyes from her lissome form in the well-behaved and thus completely obscene nautical two-piece.

"Aren't you hot? Don't you want to cool off in the water?" she asked absurdly, but so there could be no mistake. She patted the water with a graceful hand and pulled off her swim cap, allowing her long, blonde hair to tumble down in a single braid. She tossed the cap up on the deck and smiled at him. A second later he was in the water and she was in his arms. They clasped each other tightly, looked into each other's eyes and kissed. He cradled the back of her head in his hand and devoured her ears and throat with his lips, his hands going from her waist to her bosom, then down to her bottom and inner thighs. There was no part of her he didn't want to handle.

"So, are you a nice girl or a crazy bitch?" Jaime asked her.

"Nice and crazy but not a bitch. Oh please, just slip it in me for a minute, right here," she insisted, her hand sliding across the bar of iron that had emerged to tent the front of his shorts. Jaime freed his cock with impressive speed and while doing so, slipped his finger into the front of her bikini bottom to probe her tight, velvety slit.

"You really want me to? Here and now?"

"Please! But first, tell me your name?"

"Jaime."

"Amanda."

Jaime pushed Amanda up against the side of the pool and pulling her bikini aside, thrust his cock into her pussy. Reaching down to spread her labia, she helped him to cram his manly member up inside her.

"I'm not a slut," she protested, allowing his tongue into his mouth. "But it's summer, I'm 18 - " she added, clamping one of his hands to her bottom under the bikini. " - And you're such a pretty man."

"Tell me how you want it," he murmured against her throat.

"Just like you're doing, slow and deep," she urged him, pressing her bosom hard against his chest as he thrust into her under the water. She closed her eyes, but he kept his open to watch for intruders. This went on for two or three minutes before she moaned against his ear with a full body shudder and the spasmodic clenching of her vagina heralded her climax. He pulled out of her a second before his ejaculation and thus spared her a month of anxiety.

They held each other close for a couple of minutes, shared a final kiss and then he got out of the water and disappeared into one of the dressing cabanas. Amanda backstroked up and down the length of the pool until the throbbing in her clitoris began to ebb.

As she switched over from the pool to the sauna she told herself, "Who am I kidding? I am a slut."

On the following Sunday afternoon, Pamela invited Amanda to come over to her house for lunch and to watch *Pandora's Box*, which Amanda had never seen. They were sitting in a deep, butter soft camel colored leather sofa in Pamela's bedroom suite, slowly savoring a simple meal of French rolls, cheese, fruit and wine while mesmerized by the image of Louise Brooks on the large screen opposite.

"You should cut your hair like that," said Amanda to Pamela of Lulu's shingle bob.

"Ambrose wouldn't like it," said Pamela reflexively. Her new husband was a stylistic perfectionist who clearly preferred long hair on younger women.

"Don't you like giving him excuses to spank you?"

"No. He spanks too hard when he's irritated."

Amanda knew that.

"You would look adorable. It would change everything," said Amanda "I'll go with you and cut my hair as well," Amanda offered impulsively.

"Are you serious?"

"Of course I am. I'm just dating a jock and he couldn't care less about my hair as long as I let him fondle my breasts. I could get an Annie Lennox cut," said the fair-haired, soon-to-be sophomore.

"Are you insane? Cut off a beautiful head of straight, long, naturally blonde hair?"

"It'll grow back. And it'll be so much easier to take care of."

Pamela looked at Louise Brooks.

"I see what you're saying. That cut would suit my face," Pamela said decisively.

They decided to meet on their next afternoon off, which was the following Tuesday. First they lunched at the Café in Bartlett's, then walked out into the village. Ambrose Bartlett happened to be at the window of his office three stories above Main Street, Woodbridge when the girls exited the building. His heart contracted with a mixture of anxiety and excitement as he noticed his wife with the girl he had been so enraptured with earlier in the year. Why were they together? Where were they going?

They entered the village salon, each with long hair past their shoulders, Pamela's silky jet black and Amanda's ash blonde, and exited two hours later respectively sporting a geometric bob and a razor short crop. It was a late summer afternoon and the street was brightly dotted with tourists. Amanda was curious as to whether men would look at her with the same interest as formerly, when her hair was luxuriantly long. The first male to walk past them who was not the head of a vacationing family was a strikingly handsome young man in his early twenties, accompanied by two good looking girls.

"Did you see that Pamela?" Amanda whispered. "It was like the head of Ian Astbury on Danzig's body."

"That was Raphael Price," Pamela whispered back.

As though he had heard his name, the tall, muscular young man in the low-rider jeans and white tee was suddenly behind them, his girls behind him.

"Excuse me, ladies," he said, extending a strong, long fingered hand with a card. "You look like you need to go to an after hours party at an art gallery tonight." And then, he was gone, leading one girl with each hand. Amanda turned to look at them and noted that one of the girls had a long, thick, light russet French braid down her back and the other had long, rippling, shiny, jet black Mediterranean hair down hers. Both were slender, with tiny waists and slim hipped torsos in cut off shorts and ribbed tank tops, their feet in high cork platform sandals. They'd passed by too quickly for Amanda to retain a complete imprint of their faces but she had registered two flawlessly clear complexions, one ruddy, the other olive toned, behind their sunglasses.

Amanda looked down at the card. It said Raphael Gallery with a Woodbridge village address. She showed it to Pamela who said, "That's right, I just remembered, there's a showing of Pascal Robbins' photos there tonight."

Amanda got a little thrill, remembering the handsome photographer who had shot the fashion spread for the *Damaris* shop in Boston that Amanda and Pamela had posed for in the winter. She had liked Mr. Robbins a great deal and had seen him around Random Point recently as well. He had, in fact, come into the antiques shop while she was tending the counter to ask her to pose for him that summer if she would.

"He shot a whole book of my pictures a few years back," said Pamela, "I wonder if any of the photos will be for sale at the showing."

"Should we go?"

"Oh yes!" said Pamela.

"But what's this rock star of a gallery proprietor like?" Amanda asked, deftly leading Pamela into an ice cream parlor.

"Are you serious? Ice cream?" Pamela tried to pull back in horror.

"We were so good through our haircuts. We didn't even cry. Don't you think we deserve a treat?" Amanda asked, pulling Pamela by the hand deep into the cool, sweet smelling shop.

"I hope you're not going to be a bad influence on me," Pamela said, reluctantly ordering a cherry vanilla wafer cone.

"How late is an after hours party?" asked Amanda.

"Ten, I should think."

"Won't Mr. Bartlett mind your not being home?"

"I don't think he'll notice. He pays very little attention to me," sighed Pamela, fascinated by her own reflection in the mirror behind the ice cream bar with the silky, well cut bob. "As to Raphael Price, I do know he just moved here from New York a few months ago. His family owns half the Cape. And I think he bought a house on Shadow Lane pretty close to Hugo's."

"Is he married? Who were those girls?"

"I think they work for him at the gallery. I've seen the three of them shopping at the store together."

"Oh, I wish I hadn't cut my hair now!" Amanda almost sobbed, regarding her Jean Seberg cut in the mirror. "Did you see how long their hair was?"

"I begged you not to get it so short," Pamela exclaimed. Amanda accepted a butter pecan wafer cone from the teenaged counter boy, who smiled at her with ardent admiration.

"Your hair looks great," he said sincerely.

"Take my picture," Amanda said to Pamela, handing Pamela her phone and licking her ice cream cone provocatively. "I want to send it to Colby."

Pamela took the photo and Amanda sent it to her boyfriend, who was at that moment sitting in the bookkeeping office in his parents' vineyard in Northern California filling out quarterly tax forms and thinking of Amanda and how happy he would be to rendezvous with her three weeks hence, as they had planned. Colby Hodge's heart gave a little jump when he saw the return number was Amanda's. She didn't call him often and he was always startled and elated to hear from her. He didn't recognize the girl in the photo immediately. Five seconds later, Amanda's phone rang.

21

"Yes?" she answered as they continued walking down Main Street, enjoying their ice cream cones on the warm, June afternoon.

"Babe, what did you do?"

"Do you hate it?" Amanda asked.

"No. It's cute as hell. I can't wait to see you, Amanda," said Colby in his husky voice.

"It's very charming of you to mask your shock and repulsion, Colby. I didn't credit you with so much gallantry."

"I love you, Babe," he said before hanging up.

Amanda shut her phone with a smile and said, "So that muscular metal god lives next door to me, on Shadow Lane?"

"Amanda, have you fallen in love with him already?" Pamela laughed.

"Well, I am on vacation."

Chapter Three

Gallery Party and its Aftermath

Agreeing to meet at the gallery at ten that evening, the young women separated, Amanda to do some shopping in the village and Pamela to drop in on her husband at the department store. Young Mrs. Bartlett did look very smart in a straight skirted, chunky belted, sleeveless cherry red cotton shirtwaist and a pair of snub nosed black patent leather stiletto platform pumps, as she nodded to her husband's secretary outside his office and waited until she had been announced over the intercom before walking in. Ambrose had been studying the bank of security cameras on the far wall that monitored every department in his large and well-stocked store. But he looked up sharply on her entrance and gave an immediate start at the change.

"Oh my god, you cut your hair?" he ejaculated, getting up from behind his desk to take a closer look. He was a tall, lithe, dark haired man in his early forties, well favored, impeccably groomed and as fashionably tailored as a luxe department store owner should be. He took her by the arm and turned her around. "So that's the mischief you were getting up to with that bad Amanda Sands," said Bartlett disapprovingly. But she could easily perceive from his tone and expression that the sleek bob did not displease him. "Very becoming," he unwillingly complimented her. "But, you should have asked me first!" he added so sternly that she blushed.

"Why do you call her bad?" Pamela asked.

"Never mind."

"I told her I'd meet her later at that new gallery that Raphael Price is opening tonight."

"Fine. I'm working late tonight anyway."

"Could you meet me at the gallery?"

"We'll see," Ambrose said, by way of dismissal, before turning back to his spy cams.

Amanda called Susan to ask her to go to the opening but found her fair friend was in Manhattan for the next several days. Susan helpfully suggested to Amanda that Anthony Newton might escort her to the event and offered to call him and arrange this. Amanda flushed with pleasure at the notion of arriving at the party with a celebrity collector in tow. For even at her tender age she knew the value of introductions and counted on making a big impression on Raphael Price that night. And besides, she had a shy crush on Newton, having liked him very much on the first day they had met.

Anthony Newton cruised by Hugo's at ten pm to pick Amanda up. She had Hope Lawrence with her and both girls wore cotton halter dresses and strappy, high-heeled sandals, Amanda in white, Hope in pale blue. Hope was another one of Amanda's slightly older scene girlfriends, a sophisticated, sunny natured blonde in her middle twenties who could answer questions on every aspect of BDSM from hobble skirts to straight jackets with equal acumen. By walking into Raphael Price's gallery flanked by both a Broadway luminary and an exquisite second babe, Amanda knew that she would be not only noticed but also taken seriously. What had happened in the pool with Jaime so recently had been sweet, but it had hardly taken the edge off the crazily insistent itch of sexual frustration the sudden absence of Colby had left her with.

Dennis drove them to the gallery in the Bentley and went in with them. Amanda thought Anthony's young English driver looked very smart in his gray sharkskin suit and narrow tie and told him so with an engaging smile. Dennis blushed and melted for Amanda. Newton was in a lightweight putty-colored suit, white shirt and no tie. As always, Newton's pockets were stuffed with cash and he was ready to buy things. Cape Cod was Newton's home away from home and he felt it his duty to patronize its shopkeepers as much as he could. A stylish new art gallery was just the sort of place where he was likely to spend. And he was particularly well disposed towards the photographer whose work was on display that evening. Pascal Robbins was not only a sensitive lens man, but his wife, Phoebe, a well trained stage actress and gifted chanteuse, was one of Newton's friends. In fact, the Robbins were spending the summer in Random Point, as they had done several years before, so that Phoebe might perform at the Cape Cod playhouse with a repertory company she often toured with. The company was staging a revival of *Kiss Me Kate* this summer. Anthony Newton was producing, directing and accompanying the orchestra on piano and Phoebe was going to play Lily. Which was why Newton was spending almost the entire summer at his house in Random Point that year.

The Price Gallery was very large, taking up the three storefronts on the end of the last commercial block of Woodbridge village. The first storefront, towards the middle of the block, was given over to inexpensive prints, old-fashioned toys and novelties, sweets and stationary. The second store in was filled with moderately priced framed reproductions and mirrors, calculated to appeal to discriminating tourists and tasteful locals. The third room, at the corner end of the street contained original art, photographs, lithographs, signed numbered prints of the works of known artists as well as costly art and photography books.

Even though she was very new to Random Point and Woodbridge, Amanda ran into several people she knew in the outer courtyard behind the gallery, where there was a fountain, colored lanterns and several tables laid out with hors d'oeuvres and other refreshments. She first saw Dru Baxter, the young man who tended the coffee bar at Marguerite Alexander's bookshop on the days when Hope was off duty. He was about to be a sophomore at Vassar and they had spoken at length about academic subjects and life on their respective campuses when she came in from the antiques shop to get her mid morning coffee. He was having as hard a choice picking a major as she was and they had already gotten into deep discussions about books. She liked him and had no idea, as yet, that he was in the scene

Then she saw Marguerite Alexander, the proprietor of the bookshop, who was engaged in conversation with Pascal Robbins. The photographer regarded Amanda with shock, left speechless by her new haircut.

"It's adorable," Marguerite assured her, giving her a hug.

"Is the cute man here?" Amanda whispered to Marguerite, looking about her.

"There are several, but who did you have in mind tonight?" Marguerite asked, taking the greatest pleasure in the natural vivacity of Hugo's newly sprung offspring.

"The owner," Amanda disclosed. "Raphael."

"Oh! Raphael. Yes. He's inside, with the photos on exhibit."

"Don't you think he's an exceptionally well favored young man?" Amanda asked her worldly friend.

"He's a god," answered Marguerite whole-heartedly.

"Do you know anything about him, what he might be like?"

"I'm afraid he's a complete mystery to me," Marguerite replied. "He's only just moved here recently."

"Those two beautiful girls he walks around with, are they his slaves?"

"He walks around with beautiful girls?"

"Quiet, well behaved ones," said Amanda sagely.

"I don't know that he's in the scene. We can't assume that," Marguerite pointed out.

"Even if he isn't, I want to fuck him," said Amanda with complete candor.

"Go and lead Mr. Newton to him," Marguerite encouraged her young friend.

Amanda hastened to take Anthony by the arm and lead him into the corner store, which featured the Pascal Robbins showing. Sure enough, one of the most prominent blown up photographs was a moody black and white of Pamela, standing on a windswept cliff, in a simple black bodice dress, her long black hair blowing out behind her, with the look of a Bronte heroine, bad and wild. The photograph was from the book of dramatic editorial shots that had featured Pamela in a variety of stunning outfits and evocative settings.

Raphael Price's eyes widened when Amanda walked in with Anthony Newton. He knew exactly who Newton was and when he saw

Amanda immediately remembered handing her his card that afternoon. Amanda introduced herself and Anthony, explaining that her friend Pamela, whom he had invited along with herself earlier that day was due to arrive momentarily. Price was overwhelmed, not knowing who to fawn on first, the well-heeled patron or the dewy teenaged goddess.

"In fact, that's Pamela's photo," Amanda said.

"Really? The Louise Brooks girl you were with this afternoon is her?" Raphael looked at the blow up with interest.

"Yes, we both got our hair cut today. Mine was down to here," Amanda indicated the middle of her back.

"Oh? I wish I could have seen that," said Raphael sadly.

"I looked like this," said Amanda, showing him a photo of herself from the previous day on her cell phone.

Raphael smiled, "Should I cut my hair in solidarity with you brave women?"

"Oh no! Please don't!" cried Amanda. "Not until we've had sex at least once."

Raphael looked at her in complete fascination.

"Okay!" he agreed, a wide smile lighting up his already extremely agreeable features.

"I like this one," Anthony said of a portrait of Phoebe Robbins in one of her theatrical costumes from a Shakespearian play. Phoebe had the proper waist and bosom for a low cut velvet bustier gown.

"What a delicious young woman," Amanda observed, to cover her embarrassment at having thrown herself directly at the dashing young gallery owner.

"That's Pascal's wife," Newton explained to Amanda, handing Raphael his card. "Send it to my house tomorrow if you can," he said, not asking the price.

"Of course!" Raphael said, delighted.

Then Amanda handed Raphael a card from Hugo's shop.

"See, I brought you business. Now you have to come visit me at my shop," said Amanda. Raphael looked at the card.

"You work for Hugo Sands? I've always wanted to meet him. Is he here tonight?"

"No, he's on his honeymoon in Italy. I'm his daughter. I'm watching the shop for him this month. Then I'm going to Europe for the rest of the summer."

"And after the summer?"

"Sophomore year at Harvard."

Raphael raised his expressive brows at this disclosure.

"Lovely," he said, looking at her with doubled interest.

"I heard you just got a house on Shadow Lane. I'm staying on Shadow Lane too, in Hugo's house. I'm house sitting. All by myself."

"Are you?" Raphael continued looking at her with a bemused smile.

"Who were those two girls I saw you with today? Are they here?"

"Oh yes. That was Tori Allston and Luz Martinez. They're working at the gallery this summer. Then they go back to the Art Students League," Raphael explained while drinking in every inch of Amanda as she stood before him in the white a-line dress that flattered her slender body while exposing her satiny white shoulders and slim arms, clinging attractively to her deep, well developed bosom.

"You should come visit me," Raphael told her, producing yet another card to write his address on. "There's a path that leads directly from the woods behind my house to the beach."

"Are you inviting me to visit you at your house?"

"Yes! Come by anytime."

"I don't know," Amanda demurred. "Having already been so forward, perhaps I should take a step back now."

"By all means, allow me to court you a bit," Raphael agreed, pressing both her hands between his momentarily.

His touch wrought the exact effect upon her she had anticipated, her chest and stomach filling with butterflies.

"I'll come visit your shop tomorrow," he promised.

Amanda made a small bow to her host then fled to the outer courtyard to look for Pamela and report her success at attracting Raphael Price's attention. As she searched the tiled enclosure for her new friend Amanda found herself resenting the fact that Pamela was married to the problematical Ambrose Bartlett. It would have been so much nicer if Pamela had been currently single and free to come and spend the night with Amanda, so that they could watch black and white movies together and discuss sex long into the night. Amanda was still young enough to never think of wanting to spend any time alone, no less a whole night in a large house, empty except for the resident cats. The cats were kind enough to sleep with her, of course, but they weren't the exact equivalent of a human.

Amanda had decided that she could no longer keep a diary. With Colby now become so close, it was far too dangerous to commit every naughty thing she thought or did to print, for at any moment her lap top might repose unguarded in her room and in the midst of an innocent Google, he might inadvertently stumble onto her confessions. Her heart might have been his, but her favors and affections were still bestowed rather freely around and about everywhere that she went. So it was doubly important to her that she have her confidant close at hand to help her analyze her adventures. Pamela was so like her, in form and stature, in taste and sensibility, even in sexual orientation, that the smart brunette was the happiest choice for a new female friend that Amanda could have made. Pamela was even a few years older and had been about the world as a model and professional fashionista, which enabled her to give Amanda highly specific advice and provide excellent counsel on the subject of accepting jobs, for example.

According to Pamela, Mr. Pascal Robbins, the photographer whose work was being exhibited at the gallery that night, was one of the best friends a model could have. Pamela had traveled with him for a year as he photographed her for the fashion book, in which she had portrayed historical and fictional characters in rich outfits, and he had never once made a pass at her, honoring his marriage vows to the bewitching Phoebe Casper to the letter. Pamela held Pascal in high esteem for his fidelity and courtesy and never hesitated to introduce him to a lovely female friend. What Pamela couldn't know was that even Pascal Robbins now and then encountered temptations he couldn't resist, and Amanda was about to become one of them. For Pamela was ever Pamela, exquisitely chic but remote as a somnambulist and tense as a wire, whereas Amanda was glowing with warmth and bursting with animal spirits, the kind of girl Pascal truly admired on top of being stupefying beautiful.

Of course, Pamela was not blithe in the manner of a Hope Spencer Lawrence or a Susan Ross, two friends who were completely secure in their power over their men and their friends. The Parsons educated young designer was insecure and ridden with self doubt, jealous and suspicious, perpetually distressed and upset at being less than perfect on any given day and at any given moment. She never let herself relax long enough to enjoy the happiness she had as the fashionable young matron she thought she had longed to become above all things. She knew what happened when her husband's first wife had relaxed enough to let herself swell to a size 8 or 10 with cappuccinos and cream tortes. Mr. Bartlett had fallen out of love with Paula and began to look at Pamela instead. And Pamela had not only her social x-ray figure to maintain, but much more. She also ran the *Damaris* boutique at Bartlett's, while continuing to design dresses and suits for the *Damaris* label, in which she had become a partner with Damaris Perez Random several years before and which had just acquired its own factory in Puerto Rico to supply its numbers, another enormous pressure weighing on Pamela's mind. She took pharmaceutical amphetamines to maintain the size 2 that she wore and that contributed to Pamela's high-strung eccentricities and obsessive compulsions. Amanda suspected Pamela was doing this daily and had resolved to try to get Pamela to practice yoga instead but their relationship hadn't gotten quite close enough for even gentle criticism. Though Amanda was quite sure that coming from another slim, though more athletic girl, her advice would resonate.

"Oh my god, you went Mia Farrow?" cried Ambrose Bartlett as Pamela led him towards the girl he only just recognized as Amanda. Smiling shyly back at her new best friend's husband, (who had now spanked her twice, once to orgasm, unbeknownst to Pamela), Amanda recalled the fuss Bartlett had formerly made about her hair, which had reached to the middle of the back and was of a nature pale, ash blonde hue that always attracted attention. In addition to possessing the fine hair color, the texture of Amanda's hair had always been silky and straight, with plenty of body and the tendency to fall back into place with the slightest shake and finger comb. It was very good hair. And

Amanda could see on Mr. Bartlett's stricken face the exact degree to which he felt she owed her peculiar charm to it. "What the hell got into you?" he finally sputtered. "I mean, Pamela's cut is cute, so I won't fault you for suggesting it, but what you did to yourself…" Bartlett let his thought trail off as he lit a cigarette and looked at her.

"I thought you'd quit," she said, causing Pamela to wonder how Amanda would know such a thing. In point of fact he had quit the previous winter, but had lapsed back during their honeymoon in Paris in the spring, an end result of waiting for Pamela to try on clothes in various salons while parlaying with their owners.

Ambrose ignored Amanda's reproachful statement, though inwardly pleased that she seemed to care about him to this extent, and took Pamela's hand. "I hope *someone* spanked you for doing that," Bartlett said by way of farewell, leading Pamela away.

"I do like your hair," he said to his wife, suddenly quite interested in getting her home immediately. "It would look even better if you put on a silk satin chemise." Pamela owned many of these handsome, bias cut slips, along with the garter belts and panties to match, each ensemble luxuriously embroidered or smartly piped.

It was a good night for Pamela, one of the first in which she began to feel truly like a bride. Knowing she had a true Louise Brooks hair bob, she envisioned that silver screen goddess in her mind's eye as she changed into the requested shimmy in her enormous, cedar lined walk in closet. Smiling into the middle segment of a triple mirror at one end of the room, Pamela fancied she saw a glimmer of Brooksian mischief sparkle from her normally serious dark eyes. The haircut really suited her!

Then she frowned, wondering how Amanda had known that Ambrose had quit smoking, fairly sure she had been present all the previous times Ambrose and Amanda had met, these being during fashion shows at the department store, in which Amanda had several times walked as a model. Had Bartlett seen Amanda some other time, alone?

Ambrose was already undressed and in bed when Pamela joined him and allowed him to enfold her in his arms, pressing her satin wrapped back against him and instantly feeling his full bodied arousal freshly sprung to life against her oval bottom cheeks.

"Did you really hate Amanda Sands' hair or were you just teasing her?" Pamela asked, stretching her head up and back and exposing her throat to his lips.

He nuzzled her smooth neck for a moment before replying, "How could you let her do that?" he asked, caressing and squeezing Pamela's small, pert, upstanding bosom while remembering Amanda's voluptuous breasts with pleasure. His wife had an elegant body, but Amanda was a goddess.

"She said she'd cut her hair if I cut mine. I didn't take her seriously. Then when they started on her, I tried to stop her from letting them go so far. But she was determined."

"You're older than her and have better taste, you should help her make better decisions."

"I know," said Pamela, relieved that Bartlett wasn't opposed to a deeper friendship between herself and Amanda.

"I noticed that Anthony Newton bought that photo of you before he left," said Bartlett, allowing his fingers to graze Pamela's small triangle of dark pubic curls.

"That's very flattering," Pamela murmured, pushing her bottom back against his rigid cock, which was nestled between her satin clad cheeks. Ambrose reached down and pulled up the slip to bare her.

"It was a lovely photo," Bartlett assured her; contentedly guiding his engine to her portal's opening without inserting it. Reaching around in front of her again, he began to drum upon her Venus mound with his fingertips and then to slowly and delicately manipulate her to wetness before plunging deep inside her vagina to the hilt. Thus the beauty and her husband came together, as a newly wedded couple ought to do, though each one's thoughts were focused on Amanda Sands.

Amanda got dropped off at Hugo's house by Anthony and readied herself to enjoy the somewhat guilty pleasure of sleeping in Hugo's bed. She had a perfectly pleasant room given over to her for her use at the top of the house, but Hugo's master bedroom featured a large television screen connected to all the servers necessary to import every form of visual entertainment into the handsomely appointed room. Amanda had recently visited the vintage video store at the edge of the village to begin researching films for a course she planned to sign up for in the fall term called *American Culture in the Depression*. The helpful collector-owner of the shop with the walrus moustache had assured her that he possessed a viewable version of every preserved film from the 1930's ever issued, though many of these rarities were only available on videocassette. Naturally Hugo still had a working VCR in his media set up so Amanda had asked the film expert at the shop to guide her in her cinema journey with suggestions, stressing an interest in pre-code productions. Enchanted to be charged with this duty, the shop owner sent her home with *Dodsworth, Little Caesar, She Done Him Wrong, Professional Sweetheart* and *Five and Ten*.

After tending and feeding Hugo's three demandingly affectionate cats, Amanda changed into a white cotton wrapper, made herself a snack of tea, fresh peaches and buttered toast, and took the tray up to Hugo's room, where she crawled in between the smooth sheets of his large, mahogany bed and began to watch the 1931 Marion Davies, Leslie Howard drama *Five and Ten*, from the Fanny Hurst novel. Amanda had only ever seen Leslie Howard in *Gone with the Wind* and had not quite liked the character of Ashley Wilkes, but the younger and more cynical Howard as the Manhattan book publisher who is pursued by the spoiled rich girl Davies was much more interesting and Amanda sat up and took notice, especially when he threatened to spank Davies. The movie had also virtually begun with a small, slapstick style-spanking scene on a train, wherein her older brother Kent Douglass as a finale to some mutual horseplay spanked Davies.

The two small spanking startles triggered immediate longings in Amanda and she felt her pussy throb to life under the bedclothes. But it had been a very long day and as much as she wanted to dwell on the thought of the beautiful young man with the beautiful name whom she had met at the gallery, she fell asleep before she could even complete a fantasy in which he featured.

The next morning dawned warm and overcast, with a summer thunderstorm about to begin. Amanda awoke, hastily remade Hugo's bed, fed the cats and cleaned up after them, then quickly prepared a breakfast of coffee, granola and blue berries. She soaked briefly in a Caswell Massey peach bubble bath in the antique copper bathtub in the second floor guest bathroom, thinking all the while of Raphael Price, whose attractive image had filled her mind from the moment she awoke. He seemed a confident yet infinitely polite man, just the type who would know exactly how a young woman of sensibility might enjoy being treated. And she dared hope he was dominant too. After her bath, she showered off and shaved her legs in the thickly beveled green glass shower stall beside it. Finally she lavished a peaches and cream scented skin toner all over her taut, smooth bare skin, breathing in its delirious essence with delight. This is what she would smell like to Raphael Price if he took her in his arms and held her close that day. Back in her room she selected a sleeveless peach and white cotton seersucker shirtwaist dress with a chunky belt of the same material to accentuate her extremely small waist, a full skirt and notched lapel collar, which she artfully paired with pale green leather clog sandals that displayed her white tipped French pedicured toes flirtatiously. Around her neck she wore a golden locket on a gold chain and in her ear lobes hung small, gold-wired pearl drops. She frowned into the mirror at the image of a girl in a dainty dress with a boyish haircut. "Pixie do," she told herself positively.

"Very smart. Very Jean Seberg," the nice man at the vintage video shop had told her on seeing her thus shorn, while remembering having seen her earlier in the week with a gloriously full head of blonde hair. While on a clear day she would have walked the mile into the village or ridden Laura's bike, the threatening storm called for more protection and Amanda drove Hugo's old bottle green Jag into town.

Once she got to the shop she had to unlock the doors and put on all the lights, play the answering machine back and return any business related calls. There were none. Then she went back into Hugo's office and stroked on his Mac to view any emails from customers relating to both his antiques business and his sideline publishing business, which was responsible for the New Rod Quarterly, a spanking magazine originally co-edited by her mother with Hugo approximately twenty years before. The mode of publication of the journal had changed over twenty years, but the content was still concerned with high quality corporal punishment fiction, photography and art, augmented by articles and letters, advice and reviews, referrals and the type of ads which could only be of interest to spanking enthusiasts. Hugo had instructed her to reply to none of the antiques related queries and all of the spanking ones, trusting to her instincts as a self confessed practitioner of the spanking arts to provide the right answers even to questions she had never considered before. She was "into it" and she was his daughter. She already had spanking boyfriends, had written, shot and directed spanking video scenes, had done professional spanking sessions. As far as Hugo was concerned, Amanda was as qualified to handle his spanking business in his absence as anyone could have been. He had always been an active booster of female initiative in the scene, discovering new artists and writers and helping them to get their work in print and in Amanda's modern case, on video.

It had been through Hugo's offices on her behalf that she had worked out a deal with Ambrose Bartlett to shoot her video spanking scenes at Bartlett's department store the previous Christmas Day. Amanda's new best friend Pamela knew nothing about the subsequent consequences of this privilege granted Amanda by Bartlett, which had been to submit to a hard, nude, tear-provoking corporal punishment session at his hands, in his executive office at the store. As far as Pamela knew, Bartlett had only permitted Amanda and some of her college friends to shoot some video footage at the store as a favor to his friend Hugo Sands.

Amanda had a phone number to contact Hugo in Italy and ask him any questions she couldn't figure out the answers to herself. So far she had not called him. His computer files were meticulously organized and she was fully capable of doing searches and digging up information for readers and subscribers by herself. And if she couldn't figure something out for herself, she called Susan Ross or Marguerite Alexander for advice, as these two friends of hers and long time protégées of Hugo were immensely conversant with scene minutia, from professional referrals to the various availabilities of books, movies and supplementary erotic publications, along with support groups, party hosts world wide and related websites. Hugo had told her to make herself as helpful and useful to the scene as she possibly could and the scene in turn was sure to make itself helpful and useful to her.

Amanda saw there were several orders for subscriptions to the New Rod Quarterly to process. Hugo had quickly taught her how to put through a charge card order and how to postage envelopes using his postage machine and she had agreed to fulfill the important duty of shipping out new and back issues to readers during the month of Hugo's absence. This process involved packaging, postaging and taking the orders into the post office to be mailed. Amanda had an excellent memory for routines and with a little help from Sloan Taylor, the co-owner of Marguerite Alexander's bookshop across the street, she got everything to work and managed to start processing orders almost immediately. Just as she was printing out address labels, the doorbell tinkled on the outer door of the shop.

Amanda rushed out to the floor to greet the first customer of the day and to her surprise she found herself confronting Raphael Price at ten twenty am. He was dressed in a black long sleeved shirt and black jeans. His long brown hair was pulled back in a ponytail and he had a sexy two days' growth of hair on his chin and upper lip. Amanda now noticed that his eyes were nut brown and his hands long and graceful as he put one out to shake hers.

"Hello Amanda. Remember me from last night, Raphael?" he asked, holding her slim hand between both of his for a long moment as he smiled at her.

"Of course I do," she replied, self consciously pulling her hand away to run it through her half inch of hair.

"Not used to the haircut yet?" he smiled.

Amanda shook her head abstractly, suddenly happier to gaze into his kind, friendly eyes than to worry about her hair.

"It suits you. Gives you even greater power."

"Thank you. But why would you think I wouldn't remember you? I practically propositioned you!" she exclaimed, because it was a warm, wet June day, she was almost nineteen and the blood was coursing through her veins.

"You did proposition me. It gave me chills."

"I think you get propositioned all the time," Amanda accused him, daring to survey him from the golden chest vee emerging from his open collared shirt to the smart shine on his black urban walkers.

Raphael shook his head and lied, "No, of course I don't."

"May I bring you some coffee?" she asked.

"I get coffee too? Thank you," he smiled, and began to cast a practiced buyer's eye around the shop. She left him to browse in the front room while she made her way to the galley next to Hugo's office to start the coffee. When she returned to him she found that he had moved a large, ornate, gilt mirror away from the wall against which it had been leaning and dragged it towards the main counter.

"I definitely want this," he said.

"Oh, how nice!" Amanda cried. People who spent money in the shop were rare. Then she remembered the rich, fancy customer she had brought Raphael the previous night and realized that she was receiving quid pro quo! This was classic economics in action. Colby would appreciate this anecdote, she thought gleefully, then pulled herself up short and realized that the magnetic Raphael Price ought never to be introduced into a conversation she might hold with her distant sweetheart, but should be in fact a closely kept summer secret. The first really loud clap of thunder sounded above them and Amanda gave a start. "How do you like your coffee?" she asked, noting that he had pulled a perfectly preserved walnut telephone table and matching upholstered chair from the 1950's away from the wall.

"With a little milk, thank you. And you might as well get your tape, I'm seeing a lot of things I need for my house," Raphael delighted her by saying. She ran behind the counter and got a roll of pink tape out to mark the pieces he picked out.

"Did you say that you just recently moved into the area?" she asked.

"Just this year. And my house is half empty. Maybe you can point out some of the nicest things? I know you have excellent taste."

"Well, I just started working here, so I'm not exactly familiar with the stock, but let's stroll up and down the aisles together and see what there is," she suggested.

"That sounds great."

Amanda went to pour his coffee, her heart beating with excitement. Hugo was going to be over the moon. She knew how much Harvard was costing him and it weighed on her conscience. If she could deliver the goods during the month she was to work at the shop, she would feel less guilty about what an expensive newly found daughter she had become.

They went down the rows together and Amanda told Raphael what she herself would buy if she were the shopper. She picked out pictures, chairs, dressers, a vanity, china cupboards and armoires, an enormous carved bedstead, with a complete suite of bedroom furniture to match and finally, a pair of teak bookcases. Everything she said she liked, he had her put a pink tape strip on. And when he was done, Amanda felt unequal to attempting to add it all up on the spot.

"You'll have to let me call Hugo and ask him if there are any discounts with such a large purchase," she finally decided to say.

"That would be lovely, Amanda," said Raphael. "Meanwhile, just make an inventory today and I'll send my guys with a truck to pick everything up tomorrow. And maybe you can visit me on your next day off and help me decide where to put all of this."

"I would adore that," she murmured, remembering what he had said about the path to the beach through the woods behind his house.

They were standing in one of the side rooms of the shop, a long, narrow room, rather on the dark side, and crammed with heavy wooden chests of drawers topped with ornate mirrors on either side of the aisle. Perfectly alone in this secluded nook when the rain started to pound on the roof, they found themselves staring into each other's eyes and shyly, softly smiling. Raphael put out his hand and Amanda put hers into it. Then he surprised her by bringing it to his lips.

"You're a Venus," he said, sinking to his knees before her. Amanda looked down at his upturned face in wonder and he looked up at her, wonderstruck. For a long moment, she didn't move, keeping her arms relaxed but close to her sides as her brain raced to interpret his actions.

Was he simply a romantic or had she found her first slave? Either way, he was still the most beautiful young man she had ever seen and she imagined that they would be waking up together sooner or later.

Now Raphael dropped his head to her feet and placed one reverential kiss on each high, leather strapped instep. She reached down and pulled him back up to a kneeling position and pulled him against her, so that his chest was level with her thighs. She placed one hand on each side of his head and stroked his hair. He wrapped his arms around her hips and she pressed his head against her flat stomach. With only her thin cotton dress and a scrap of panty between his jaw line and her Venus mound, Amanda shuddered with a sudden thrill.

Then the bell tinkled on the outer door of the shop and Raphael sprang agilely to his feet.

"That'll be another customer," she said in a rush. "I have to go and greet them."

"Do that," he encouraged her. "While I think of some way to make this hard-on go down."

Amanda grinned at him and said, "Save it for Sunday afternoon. On the beach."

Raphael had to get back to his own shop and departed a few moments later, leaving Amanda to number and record all his purchases, then arrive at a preliminary total. According to her calculations, which she checked and rechecked four times, her customer had spent over nineteen thousand dollars in less than one hour.

Amanda went back to Hugo's computer and Googled international time to find out if it was a decent hour to phone her father in Italy. She found it was still early enough in the evening to place a call and opened the desktop file with his itinerary. He and Laura were in Florence that night, staying at The Grand Hotel Cavour. Amanda found its website and phone number and punched in the number. In a few minutes she was connected with Hugo's suite and he answered the phone himself.

"Hugo, I'm so glad I found you in," Amanda said in a rush.

"Is everything okay, Amanda?" Hugo asked with concern, for she was not the type to casually phone him.

"Everything is fantastic. Hugo, you'll never guess what happened. I just made a huge sale."

"Really?" he replied. She could envision his face breaking into a wide smile. "What did you sell?"

"I sold almost twenty thousand dollars worth of your best furniture. To a Raphael Price."

"No kidding! That would be Randy Price's nephew. He just opened an art gallery in Woodbridge, right?"

"Yes. I brought Mr. Newton over there for the opening and Mr. Newton bought graphics from him last night."

"So, you've attracted Anthony Newton's attention too, have you? How many millionaires do you plan to collect before sophomore year?" he laughed.

"He knelt down to me and kissed my insteps."

"Wow."

"Do you think he's submissive?"

"I wouldn't be surprised."

"Should he get some sort of discount for spending so much?" asked this child of several shopkeepers.

"Sounds like he's more interested in you than a discount."

"At first I thought he was just returning my favor from last night, bringing him Mr. Newton. But now I think he's interested in me."

"Yes. I'm sure he is. I hear he's a nice young man. Well educated. Cornell, I think. As far as the discount goes, cash gets him 20% off," said Hugo.

"Well, I won't keep you. I just wanted to let you know."

"By the way, you also get a five percent commission on the sale, Amanda. So you'll have some extra pocket money for Europe next month."

"I don't need that. You're already paying me to work here," she protested, ever mindful of the large tuition bills Hugo was coping with. He had insisted on paying her to working in the shop that month and had arranged for her to charge all her groceries at the local food coop, which her mother had adored and had situated her original psychic shop opposite so many years ago.

Laura emerged from the consummately modern Italian bathroom, clad in a sumptuously embroidered white cotton eyelet batiste gown set that clove to her curvaceous bosom and small waist and swirled romantically about her legs. She came and sat on his knee, stretching out her graceful legs to show off the white satin pearl sewn slippers they had chosen to match the gown. He put down the phone receiver and locked his arms around her waist.

"In 20 years of doing business I never sold twenty thousand dollars worth of wood off the floor in one day, and Amanda does it her first week at the shop," he revealed with wonder.

"Oh how wonderful! How did she manage it?" she demanded, unconsciously bouncing on Hugo's lap with the shared euphoria of the big sale.

"I guess Raphael Price is pretty taken with Amanda."

"I've never met him, but I've heard he's very good looking," Laura said, winding her arms around Hugo's neck and breathing in the scent of expensive Italian soap. "Does she like him?"

"If he's that good looking, I'm sure she likes him."

"It sounds like poor Colby is getting cut out," said Laura.

"Oh, I don't think he's in any real danger," Hugo laughed. "He'll have her to himself in Europe and then they'll go back to school together. And if she's as good at keeping secrets as her mother, he'll never be the wiser about Mr. Millionaire."

Chapter Four

Pascal Punishes Amanda for Cutting Her Hair

"Amanda, how could you?" Pascal Robbins accused her, striding into the shop mid-afternoon and arousing her from a Lord Byron induced reverie she had been indulging in while curled up in a comfortable rocker in the main room of the shop. She sprang to her feet and let the gold leafed volume fall into the seat of the chair as she reflexively put her hand up to the mere feather cap of ash blonde hair that now adorned her head. He shook his head at her in grave disappointment. "I thought that was you at the gallery last night but was hoping I was mistaken. A woman's hair is her crowning glory," the photographer harangued her mercilessly. "Now how can I shoot you in a Renaissance gown, or any gown except the one you get to wear in a lunatic asylum?"

Amanda lowered her eyes and bit her lip. Sooner or later someone was going to scold her for cutting her hair, it might as well be Mr. Robbins. And yet, he was rather a new acquaintance to adopt this degree of proprietary familiarity with Amanda and her proudly independent personality balked at his impertinence. So instead of apologizing for her mistake, Amanda serenely conceded, "I *would* make a terrible model at the moment."

"Not terrible," he grunted, "but problematical."

"I heard your wife is playing the lead in *Kiss Me Kate* at the local theatre this month," Amanda changed the subject. "I can't wait to see it!"

"Really? Are you a Cole Porter fan?"

"Of course. Plus, there's the famous spanking scene."

"Don't tell me you're into spanking too?" Pascal wondered when he'd stop being surprised by discovering spanking enthusiasts in Random Point.

"Can you have the slightest doubt?"

"What's with Random Point? Is it some sort of cosmic magnet for spanking people?"

"It's not a supernatural phenomenon. It's because of Hugo having his publishing company here for twenty years. The name Random Point has become synonymous with spanking, in the fetish world, like San Francisco and leather."

"Tell me about this famous spanking scene," Pascal growled. He vaguely remembered a spanking scene from the movie of *Kiss Me Kate* he had seen once long ago. Was his wife to play the character who got spanked? Again? When she'd starred in *A Doll's House* at the repertory theatre in Woodbridge two years before, she had contrived some spanking business that had never been in the play before. The little devil, he thought. No wonder she was more than over the moon about getting this part. The play was booked for a month of performances. She would get spanked numerous times on stage. Not to mention all the rehearsal spankings, during which she would be manhandled by her co-star, a buff, hearty, bullet-headed British baritone of unassailable masculinity. Pascal fumed.

"The spanking occurs during the play within the play, with Fred and Lily playing Petruchio and Kate. She takes a swing at him and he says, 'The name of the play is *The Taming of the Shrew*, not *He Who Gets Slapped*.' Then he spanks her on stage. It's a great scene. Probably the high point of 20th century musical comedy."

"Humph!" brooded Pascal. Then he turned his attention back to Amanda's head, looking at her critically from every angle. "I could shoot you as a tomboy, or a leatherwoman."

"I think I'd look good in skintight latex," Amanda said helpfully.

"Good point. Then no one will be paying any attention to your hair. Do you have any latex?"

"Not at this point. It's pretty expensive. I've been thinking about it."

"Go on line and pick out two latex outfits, send me the links and I'll buy them for the shoot."

"Yay!" Amanda jumped up and down.

He cocked his head at her, "Will you let me shoot you nude?"

"Skintight latex is just like nude. Especially in a light, transparent color."

"True," he conceded.

"Tasteful nude is fine," she told him. Pascal smiled. "But all your work is tasteful," she corrected herself.

"You're a very nice girl," he said gruffly. "but I still think you did a bad thing cutting your beautiful hair. Someone should spank you for that."

"Not you, Mr. Robbins. You're not even into it."

"Who said I'm not?" he demanded, taking her by the arm. "What man worthy of the name isn't into spanking?" he asked, pulling her over to one of the glass counters, bending her over and before she could process what was happening, smacking her slim oval cheeks over her skirt six times, bestowing three smart slaps to each before letting her up. A deep blush suffusing her face at this unexpected assault, Amanda unconsciously put both hands back to her bottom, now radiant with heat and a certain sting.

"How... dare you!" she sputtered indignantly.

"God, you're adorable," he cried, taking her face between his sensitive, long fingered hands and kissing her lightly on her rosy mouth just once. "But you're naughty," he added, causing butterflies to flutter in her stomach.

"You can't just bend someone over and spank them!" she charged, placing her hands on her hips.

"You're my model, aren't you? That means you have to be submissive to me," he casually informed her.

"Really?" she sputtered.

"Of course."

"Huh!" she retorted, now over folded arms. "I don't need to model that badly!"

"Oh yes you do. You like to see yourself in photos."

"Well... maybe I do," Amanda grinned, dropping her arms to her sides.

"Don't forget to send me the latex links," he told her, breezing out the door as though he had remembered an appointment.

"I won't," she called after him, imprinting his dashing image in her mental photo album. It would be charming being one of Pascal Robbins' models and to pose for shoots specifically tailored to her look and personality. This would be extra curricular work of the highest caliber and fit to be exhibited in any resume. Amanda was well pleased with the opportunity and in reality took only a little umbrage at the liberties the photographer had taken with her. However, mindful of his marital status, not to mention the fact that his wife was a lovely young woman also in the scene and apparently extremely jealous of her handsome husband's affections, Amanda decided she would let him go no further with her, no matter how adorable he found her to be. At any rate, between Colby, Jaime the gardener and very shortly, Raphael Price, she already had two or three too many boyfriends.

"Pascal Robbins spanked me," said Amanda to Pamela in the sauna at the Random Point health club that night. They were clad in two-piece swimsuits after just having done a yoga class as well as a number of laps in the pool.

"That's not like him!" Pamela replied with surprise.

"He never spanked you for cutting your hair?"

"He's never taken any kind of liberty with me."

"He was so fresh."

"It's so typical of the disrespect these dominant men show us," huffed Pamela, adding, "but then, Pascal is not exactly in the scene, so he doesn't quite know the etiquette."

"That doesn't make what he did any less impertinent," Amanda pointed out.

"Still, he knew he could get away with it. Even as innocent as he is, he can peg you for a submissive who isn't going to fuss if someone smacks her."

"He kissed me too. On the mouth."

"Really!"

45

"Do you know how long I made Colby wait for our first kiss? Months!"

"What is that like, being totally in control of a man?" Pamela wondered, leaning up on her arm to regard her younger blonde friend across the cedar box in which they reclined.

"Oh, Colby's not a man, he's a jock," replied Amanda carelessly, then added with more interest, "Why? What do you mean? What's Mr. Bartlett really like?"

"Oh, he's the worst offender imaginable when it comes to abusing his rights as a dominant," Pamela declared candidly.

"Is it... getting on your nerves?" Amanda asked delicately.

"It is," Pamela sat up entirely and folded her slender arms across her small bosom. "This whole business of keeping me working at the store, for example. When what I should be devoting all my time to is designing for the line and then promoting it!"

Pamela had been brooding about this all day, while fulfilling the many tedious duties of what amounted to an assistant store manager position at Bartlett's with neither a title nor salary to match. Instead of inspecting new inventory and conferring with department managers about summer clearance merchandise, she longed to be seated comfortably behind a drawing board in the airy design studio that occupied the second floor of the *Damaris* shop in Random Point. It was in this sky lit room with windows looking down on the main street of the village that she and Damaris created suits and dresses, sharing the same aesthetic and happy in each other's company.

"I've been to college, grad school and design school. I've worked on the floor. I've modeled. I'm a partner in a rising design label. And I'm told I'm a millionaire's wife. When am I going to be able to do what I want?"

"What would Mr. Bartlett say if you insisted he let you go?" Amanda asked with extreme interest.

"I'm not allowed to insist on anything. I'm supposed to be submissive."

"So, you're finding your marriage oppressive?"

"Not the marriage, but my work load."

"He's working you," Amanda observed.

"They all do. They all make me their bitch, Amanda," said Pamela with heartfelt exasperation. It was the first time she had fully unburdened herself to another woman in the scene and she suddenly felt as if she'd been let out of a Victorian waist cinch after wearing it for six hours. "Hugo was even worse than Ambrose," she added sensationally.

"You mean, when you worked for him?" Amanda prompted, already well aware of how cavalierly her newly discovered parent had used Pamela from his own confession of the episode.

"Oh yes, he was positively gothic with his impossible demands and relentless perfectionism."

"He was fucking with you for some reason, right?"

"That's true enough," Pamela admitted. "I was engaged to Sloan at the time and was jealous of Hope Lawrence working under him at the bookshop. Hugo attempted to distract me by working me to exhaustion every day and eventually beginning to spank me for mistakes."

"Why did you even let him do that?" Amanda marveled, as shocked and disconcerted at her father's inappropriate behavior towards Pamela as when he'd originally revealed the same details about the episode, which had concluded with Hugo's simultaneously firing Pamela and ending their brief dominant/submissive love affair.

"Oh, because I'd fallen madly in love with him by that time," Pamela smiled, even though the experience had caused her many tearful moments. "I must be a genuine masochist, I always love the man who is the meanest to me," she concluded.

"But, Mr. Bartlett isn't really mean to you?" Amanda asked with concern.

"I don't think he thinks he is," said Pamela.

"Pamela, it seems to me you could easily get your own way with him if you put your mind to it," Amanda suggested.

"What would you do?" Pamela asked with interest, almost to the point of open rebellion.

"Well, first I'd ask myself what would be the worst thing that might happen if you just stopped going into work."

"He might very well beat me."

47

"So let him beat you a few times. Just be stubborn and don't give in."

The girls were silent for a moment, thinking about Ambrose Bartlett. Then Amanda said, "Let's go eat!"

"Really?" Pamela looked doubtful.

"I found a great little vegetarian place in the village. The food only tastes sinful, it's really healthy," said Amanda, leading Pamela out of the hot box. "Don't tell me you were planning on skipping dinner?" Amanda demanded of her obsessively weight conscious friend.

"Well, yes. I had a big lunch."

"But you just worked out."

"I know, but..." Pamela quickly donned a white lace under-wire bra and matching French cut panties and briefly regarded her image in the locker room mirror before stepping into a pair of khaki capris, beige laced espadrilles and a fitted, open collared white cotton shirt.

"Pamela, you shouldn't let yourself get so thin. Let yourself gain ten pounds. Men in our scene like curves."

"Not Ambrose," said Pamela, running a brush through her smooth black geometrically cut bob. "He insulted his first wife into leaving him because she gained weight."

"Seriously?" Amanda got into a tailored black cotton bra and panty set, pulled a sleeveless black vee neck top over her head and tied a tan wrap skirt around her small waist. She sat on the wooden bench to strap on black cloth platform sandals. "The more you reveal about Mr. Bartlett, the more of a complete piece of work he sounds like."

The girls emerged on the street under a full moon, put their gym bags into their cars, then relocked their cars and began walking arm in arm into the heart of the village of Random Point.

"You've been a model, you've been in a book, and you design half the clothes in the line. You should be going on talk shows promoting yourself," said Amanda.

"I think so too, but I don't have time."

"I can see you on Project Runway in a heartbeat," said Amanda, who would seldom pause to watch television, unless a fashion show was on.

"Stop Amanda, you're agitating me."

"I'm sorry."

"If Ambrose knew you were steaming me up like this he'd be furious," Pamela observed. She knew her husband that well. "But what you say makes sense. Except about gaining weight. I'd die."

"Whatever you do, don't make Mr. Bartlett furious at me," Amanda begged. "I like walking in the shows at the store."

Pamela Bartlett had become even more tired of showing up for work at her husband's department store than she had admitted to Amanda and did in fact feel cruelly ill-used by her husband to the point of fully considering open rebellion even before Amanda suggested it.

That morning, after showering and perfuming herself in the black and pink tiled art deco bathroom that joined the master suite of Bartlett's house on the cliff, Pamela in a slate blue cotton wrapper, gazed long and hard at the perfect size 2 pencil skirted suit she had laid out. Summer inventory clearance was going on all over the store that day and Pamela knew she could look forward to hours in designer dresses deciding mark down percentages on various numbers and assigning personnel to retag them. She picked up the smart pair of four inch tapering stacked heels in black suede she had been going to wear with the suit. The notion of hours on her feet in those shoes suddenly oppressed her mightily. Swallowing the lump that rose in her throat, Pamela deliberately rehung the chalk gray suit back up, replaced the shoes in the area of her connecting shoe closet reserved for pumps, and then pulled out a navy a-line skirt and sleeveless white open collared shirt along with a pair of navy flats to wear instead. This outfit she slipped over a light, lace trimmed white cotton bra and panty combination.

Thoughtfully she brushed her gleaming black bob while looking in the mirror, realizing that Amanda was right, she was very thin. Pamela was not the victim of body dysmorphia, but she was never the less actuated by all the typical anxieties of the modern cosmopolitan woman, first and foremost of which was the imperative to stay thin. Had not the immortal Anita Loos, creator of Lorelei Lee and surviving beauty until age 90, murmured, "Fat is death?" Didn't Wallace

Simpson say, "A woman can never be too rich or too thin?" "One should eat to live, not live to eat," came from Molière. "Eat not to dullness," Ben Franklin had advised, as well as, "To lengthen your life, shorten your meals." Pamela didn't know who had said, "Nothing tastes as good as being thin feels," but had read that even Thomas Jefferson had observed, "We never repent of having eaten too little." These adages had been her law since a teen and they had served her well in maintaining the figure that had always gotten her noticed. But she saw Amanda's point just as well at that moment. Amanda was her same height, 5'8" and Amanda claimed to be all of a hundred and twenty five pounds. Pamela hadn't allowed herself to get above 110 in years. Amanda appeared slender to a fault but she also looked strong. Through the application of scientific exercise joined to a conscientious effort not to skip meals anymore, she too might allow herself to gain a healthy ten to fifteen pounds without appearing any less sylphlike. Perhaps it would be easier to stand up to her tyrannical husband if she were more robust. Possibly regular meals and the subtraction of the pharmaceutical amphetamines, which had been supplying her with frantic energy for so many years, would result in an overall relaxation of tension and stress in her day-to-day existence.

Pamela went to the medicine chest and looked at her bottle of Ritalin. She opened it. Ten left. Almost time to call in a refill. She took the bottle off the shelf and tossed it into the wastebasket, a sensation of relief passing through her frame. She hadn't taken one yet that morning.

She sat at her vanity mirror and reddened her wide, full lips with burgundy lip-gloss, just to the point of moist rosiness. Instead of applying any more make-up, she left her smooth, soft, faintly olive toned skin clean and ignored even her eyeliner, shadow and mascara. Her dark and wide set almond shaped eyes were naturally long lashed and she was determined not to expose them to any chemicals that day to enhance what was already lovely. Hanging small gold hoops in her ear and a thin gold chain and pendant around her neck, she felt herself to be adequately adored to greet the summer day.

Calling in sick, Pamela packed a white and navy leather tote with gym gear and a change of lingerie, as well as her Kindle, on which she had recently placed *The Ladies' Paradise* by Zola and deliberately left her phone on her dressing table before going downstairs.

Pamela was happy that her husband always left for the store an hour before she herself arose. He was never very cheerful in the morning before work, so it was best not to encounter him at that time if one could possibly avoid it, especially on a day when one looked far too good to seem in the slightest off color, no less to call in sick. In the kitchen she brewed coffee, poured whole milk over a half cup of fruit and nut granola and ate one entire quarter of a rapturously sweet honeydew melon, all the while watching one of her favorite HBO dramas, which she had dvr'ed on the kitchen TV. It was ten am before she left the house, got into her BMW and drove into Random Point to spend the morning at the gym and spa and then meet Amanda for lunch at the wonderful vegan café that Amanda had discovered earlier that week.

After lunch, Pamela drove over to the *Damaris* shop, climbed the polished wooden staircase to the pleasant design studio above it, and surprised her partner at her drawing board under the window.

"Pamela," cried Damaris. "I didn't expect to see you here today. Isn't there a big sale going on at the store?"

Pamela regarded the petite proprietress of the shop and co-designer of the *Damaris* line with affection as she announced, "My love, I'm here to stay. I'm never going back to Bartlett's. Never, never, never!"

Damaris got up to throw her arms around Pamela's waist and danced up and down the studio with her willowy friend.

"What changed?" Damaris asked.

"Today I awoke from my dogmatic slumber," Pamela declared, "and suddenly realized, with Amanda Sands' prompting, that being married to Ambrose Bartlett hasn't benefited me one iota, unless you count being mistress of the pretty house, which is nice, but doesn't equal the lifestyle upgrade that marriage to a millionaire once promised."

"You're not saying you've quarreled with Ambrose?" Damaris asked, concern flitting across her expressive face.

"Not yet. But that's inevitable," Pamela sighed, letting her charming friend go. "Because I am in full rebellion mode."

Chapter Five

The Venus Club

"Hello Ladies," said Marguerite Alexander, rising from her seat at the large round table in the private party room at The Owl Inn of Woodbridge, and addressing nine of her female friends. "Thank you for coming and welcome to the first assembly of The Venus Club." The tall, voluptuous redhead, clad in a full skirted, white portrait collar dress with black ribbon trim returned the smiles that went around the table at the disclosure of their new society's name. "Looking around the table, we all know we have much in common. We're all in the scene, we're all players and most of us have played with each other's men." A general murmur of laughter greeted this statement, followed up by several suspicious glances from one girl to another. "I'll get back to that in a second," promised Marguerite, "But first let me thank you all for dressing in black and white, as suggested in the invitation. It will make the photos ever so attractive." She paused as two waiters arrived with four bottles of wine and showed them to Marguerite for approval. She nodded and they busily began uncorking the two whites and two reds, then went around the table to fill each guest's glass to preference. One paused when he came to Amanda, but Marguerite fixed him with a penetrating gaze and thinking both of his tip and not offending the beautiful hostess, he poured Amanda a glass of white wine without murmur.

As soon as the waiters departed, Marguerite continued. "To continue, some of us know each other very well, there being less than one degree of separation between us, due to our playful natures and said men. Others barely know the group at all, having joined us more recently. I hope this society of Venus will become a regular part of our lives, encouraging us to meet and celebrate every happy event that may occur for us here on the Cape and out in the bigger world." Marguerite paused to sip her red wine with appreciation. "I'll have a word more to say on the precepts of our new society in a moment. Meanwhile, we're here tonight to commemorate both the engagement of Alison Albrecht to Freddie Johanson," Marguerite raised her glass to the slim brunette in a smartly cut white summer suit worn over a white open collared shirt, who smiled and blushed, not being used to this type of attention. "And to formally welcome Amanda Sands to our ranks."

Amanda looked startled and her blue eyes sparkled with pleasure. This had not been on the invitation! Amanda wore a short, white, form fitting, straight skirted, sleeveless, double breasted shirtwaist with a wide white fabric belt that emphasized her tiny waist. "I love your hair, Amanda, by the way," Marguerite beamed at her young friend. All the women around the table complimented Amanda on her pixie cut and said how well it became her. "And we also love Pamela's new hair cut," Marguerite added, starting another round of pleasantries. Pamela smiled with simple pleasure, enjoying the wave of admiration that swept over her from her faultlessly groomed and sweet smelling companions. She hadn't experienced much female comradery in her young life. She had always chosen one best friend, but had never felt the sensation of being well liked by an entire group of females at the same time. Pamela was too self-absorbed and hyper critical to realize how well liked and much admired she had become at Bartlett's by the mostly female staff. Pamela was dressed in a narrow lapelled black silk suit with a nipped waist, a pencil skirt and a scrap of white cambric lace camisole peeking out at the cleavage. A black pearl on a pendant matched her black pearl earrings and her hair also gleamed like a black pearl.

"What I propose is the strengthening of sisterly support in our own little rarified sector of the larger scene," said Marguerite. "We are all drawn to a certain type of male. Which makes us highly vulnerable. But we also have our pride. More than one of us has set a dom straight."

"Am I in the rebel camp?" Amanda thought with excitement, thrilled to be included in this deliciously grown up group.

"All of us have taken control at one point or another in our scene lives, to save our honor and our souls," said Marguerite. This pronouncement struck Pamela to the heart, for had she not been obsessing on the same dilemma, of choosing, only the previous day? "All of us," continued Marguerite, "have asserted ourselves from time to time, without abandoning those romantic notions that have motivated us since we first became aware of the opposite sex."

"In short, we're already so empowered that our tops are the ones who need safe words," triumphantly interjected Hope Lawrence, a divine natural blonde in her middle twenties, her slim, shapely form complimented to perfection by a black and white checked seersucker dress with a wide, black, patent leather belt.

"Thank you, darling, I'll remember that one," Marguerite beamed at her special pet. Hope had been running the coffee bar at Marguerite Alexander and Sloan Taylor's bookshop for several years now, and that young lady's charismatic personality and ravishing demeanor had been a draw for the little café within Marguerite's shop since Hope first put her cherry red apron on behind its counter.

"Now, here is what I propose, my dearest ladies," said Marguerite. "That first we order our lunch. Then, while we are waiting for it to arrive, we go around the table in round robin fashion, each speaking a few words about how we came to find ourselves in the scene and Random Point, sharing experiences we feel comfortable in revealing and pledging to keep any disclosures made during our meetings private and inviolate."

"I'll have a martini too," said Paula Taylor to a passing waiter. The thirty-something prep school guidance counselor, a well proportioned size eight beauty with pale blonde hair and large blue eyes was dashingly clad in a black skirt and fitted black silk brocade vest over a long sleeved white shirt, with a pink pearl on a gold chain encircling her smooth throat and pink pearls in her earlobes.

"Might not a full account of our experiences be dangerous?" asked Polyxena Guzman, in her faint Dutch accent. The European gym and spa owner, of the spectacular body and white blonde hair was clad in a full skirted, black and white toile patterned cotton halter dress that displayed her sculpted torso with both glamour and taste. She was the only woman who had come into the group as a dominant and had but recently gone over to the opposite side of the scene, unaccountably attracted to several of the more affably masterful Random Point males she had met since moving to the area.

"Ladies," said Marguerite indulgently, "please feel free to keep your lovers' secrets. But also, feel free to confide. So long as we all agree not to reproach our men with any ancient history that might be revealed or harbor any ill feelings toward each other, why should we not feel free to share our histories with one another?"

"I'll have a Long Island Ice Tea," said Phoebe Casper with ill-suppressed excitement to the other waiter. The petite, chestnut brown haired stage actress had dressed her nip-waisted but voluptuous little body in a white dotted Swiss tea dress with a fichu neckline that drew attention to her full, creamy bosom. Of all the women present, she was the least experienced and perhaps the most romantically inclined. And yet regarding the enchanting prospects offered by her second sojourn in Random Point, even she already had secrets which she dare not reveal.

"I think we must also assume that if any lady present has done anything scandalous with any man not belonging to herself, that it was the man who initiated the episode," said Marguerite. "Except in the case of Susan Ross."

Susan Ross, sitting at Marguerite's right hand in a short sleeved white cotton shirt and a round black cotton skirt with a wide black belt tossed her long wheat blonde pony tail and grinned at her older friend.

"But how do we know that if we reveal a secret that we won't be inadvertently hurting someone's feelings or creating needless insecurity?" asked Damaris, seated on Marguerite's other side, in a sleeveless black zip front jump suit with a beautifully defined waist and glove tight pants that pegged just above her slim ankles. The dress designer, retail entrepreneur and shop owner, like Marguerite, was the mother to a baby girl who was currently being well tended by a nanny at home.

"That is a question we must all ask ourselves before speaking," Marguerite agreed. "Personally, I must admit that I'd be surprised if even three of you haven't done everything with my own husband that it is possible to do in our scene," she remarked with surprising cheerfulness. "In fact, I go about pretty much assuming that Michael has had or will have had you all. So frankly, nothing you can say about him will shock or distress me and I'd love to hear the details. I'm just the type of person who enjoys collecting information. But you can trust me absolutely never to throw it back in his face. However, some of you may feel differently on this subject."

"Not me," said Phoebe, "I'd love to know if Pascal has been up to anything with anyone here after guarding me so closely!"

Amanda nearly jumped in her seat on hearing this pronouncement and wondered whether it would be worse to reveal or conceal Phoebe's husband's recent advances to her.

Susan raised her eyebrows at Hope who said to Marguerite, "May we be excused for two minutes, Mistress?" Then Hope took Amanda by one hand and Susan by the other and led them out of the inn by the back door and into the garden, which led to a small wooden bridge that spanned the Woodbridge brook. They crossed over the bridge to the woods in the golden red June sunset and Susan lit a joint.

"Do you think she knows I played with Michael?" Amanda quickly asked her friends.

"Yes, of course she does. You did that shoot at his bar," Hope reminded Amanda.

"I know she knows about that, but that first time he spanked me, when Hugo took me to his house," Amanda said.

"We can assume Marguerite knows everything," said Susan. "And if she doesn't yet, you heard what she said. She won't freak out if she hears something new."

"What about Pascal? What he did the other day?" Amanda said, taking a hit off the joint and passing it back to Susan.

"Pascal Robbins did something with you the other day?" Susan asked in surprise.

"He spanked me and kissed me!" Amanda revealed sensationally. The three blondes looked at each other and smoked thoughtfully for a moment.

"That's not like him," said Hope, with concern for Phoebe's feelings.

"That's true. And Phoebe's so innocent in the scene. She's done practically nothing," said Susan. Though in point of fact, she rather suspected Phoebe Casper Robbins of having an extremely large crush on her lover and patron, Anthony Newton, who was producing, directing and playing piano for the *Kiss Me Kate* revival at the repertory theatre that summer, with Phoebe in the lead role. "Amanda, I wouldn't say anything about that today," Susan counseled.

"Especially if you want to pursue some photography with him this month," Hope added. "I have a feeling he'd be peeved if you told on him."

"Huh!" Amanda grunted, refusing a second hit of the strong grass. "So he's allowed to make a totally unsolicited advance towards me and receives not the slightest censure?"

"Did you dislike it so much?" Hope asked, taking a final puff herself and offering Susan one more before extinguishing the spliff in a silver case.

"I didn't dislike it at all," Amanda laughed, "But I don't think he behaved like a gentleman."

"Well, Phoebe doesn't know that he isn't a gentleman at this point and it might break her heart," said Susan, while thinking to herself, "or drive her straight into Anthony's arms!" She didn't like that thought.

"And then there's Pamela," Amanda remembered, "She and I are just becoming friends. I daren't mention anything about Mr. Bartlett in front of her!" The others paused to turn and look at her.

"Does she even know he let you shoot at the store?" asked Susan.

"She may know that, though we haven't discussed it, but I can't let her find out why he really let me do that."

"I think she does know about that shoot," said Hope. "But she thinks Ambrose let you do it as a favor to Hugo."

"I mean, they weren't married yet ..." Amanda began to say when a familiar female voice interrupted her, saying, "What's this about Ambrose?"

They all turned to see Pamela standing on the bridge behind them, regarding them through narrowed eyes and over folded arms.

"Why don't I ever get invited to smoke pot?" she cried. Susan hastily produced the joint and lit it for Pamela to take from her. "It's time to come back and place our orders," she told them, after exhaling the buzz giving smoke. "And by the way, you all look stunning," she said, critically shifting her gaze from Amanda's short, figure molding white shirtwaist to Susan's inexpressibly charming figure in the classic white blouse and full black skirt to Hope's graceful slender torso set off to advantage by the light, crinkled, checked summer dress.

"We got all our clothes at your shop," said Susan soothingly.

"Yes, yes, but what about Ambrose?" Pamela demanded of Amanda. "What did that bastard do to you?"

Amanda jumped back at the vehemence of Pamela's loyalty to herself rather than her husband. Since she already knew her husband so well, Amanda saw little harm in admitting one thing to Pamela, and that a thing which might quiet her new friend's curiosity as to probing deeper into Amanda's relations with the owner of Bartlett's department store. That man, Amanda knew, was half in love with her. He had never stopped sending her gifts, even after paying her the five thousand dollars in cash for allowing him her favors for one hour one night.

"He...broke me!" Amanda admitted finally, and both Susan and Hope nodded their approval of her confession, both having been made aware of her first and most unpleasant session with Pamela's new husband.

"Yes, he does that on a first date," Pamela grimly observed, but then smiled and linked arms with Amanda as they started back. "You might as well tell us all the story together when it's your turn to speak," said Pamela to her new and dearest friend. Pamela knew that her friendship for Amanda was becoming deep and pure, something akin to love, for she felt no jealousy or hostility towards the eighteen year old for attracting the attention of her capricious, decadent and self-indulgent man. Of course he must have Amanda after he had seen her and after being informed that she too was tinged with the propensity to play hyper erotic games. To be told that the libido of this tall, slender, young and ivy league Aphrodite was as steeped in dominant-submissive fetishism as those of both his current and previous wife, would present an irresistible opportunity to a handsome and affluent man who had come to the world of playing somewhat late in life and wished to waste no more time in storing up such memorable experiences.

Plainly, Ambrose Bartlett enjoyed punishing girls. Of all the men in their circle, he was the coldest fish, the most sadistic spanker, the least gallant or courteous, the least perceptive, the least caring. And yet he knew how to get into a woman's heart and soul with clothes. He always choose women who adored clothes and it was a minor fixation with him to present his favorites with the most stylish numbers that passed through his ultra high end emporium. This was possibly the only way in which he was able to express generosity, but it happened to hit just the right note among the women he favored. They did feel like whores, but they always kept taking the clothes, which bound them ever in some degree of submission to this man.

"He's a villain," thought Pamela, and yet a wave of comfort and joy swept through her slender form as she contemplated her second whole day of no speed and no Bartlett's department store.

The four young women rejoined the group in the paneled private dining room, that same room that Amanda had peeked into on the night she had done her second session with Bartlett, the much more pleasant one, and had been shocked to see a group of jocks, feasting post-pond hockey game, with her Colby among them. But that was not a story that Amanda planned to tell. As she regained her seat and consulted the gold tasseled menu, she whispered to Susan Ross, "Gee, if I've only just come to Random Point within the last year and I have so many secrets, I can only imagine what you might be admitting to."

"It would take way too long for me to admit to everything I've done," said Susan. "Oh look, they have roast lamb."

"I'm trying to eat more vegetarian, but it's very tempting," said Amanda.

"I'm a vegan," said Phoebe Casper. "For ten years."

"I'm so happy to meet you," said Amanda, shaking hands with Pascal Robbins' small, fresh-faced wife, with her long, chestnut brown hair down on her peaches and creamy shoulders, which were exquisitely molded and flattered by the delicate, low neckline of her semi-sheer white dress. "You're Mr. Robbins' wife, I think? He shot me once."

"Yes, he's said he'd love to shoot you again this summer. I can see why," said Phoebe, feeling a definite pain dart through her stomach while contemplating Pascal photographing this young divinity, possibly fully undressed. No wonder he had barely mentioned her. Though he had mentioned the other night his great disappointment at Amanda having abruptly cut off all her hair, just prior to posing for him again. It was true that Amanda hadn't much hair left, Phoebe though, peeking at Amanda's funny little cap of fine, soft, straight, beige blonde hair, but this did not detract from her beauty in the slightest and rather emphasized her good bone structure and very blue eyes.

"I'm so excited that you're doing *Kiss Me Kate*," said Amanda, eager to turn the conversation away from the unpredictable photographer to whom Phoebe had been married but a few years and continued to adore. "And with Mr. Newton directing. That must be sheer heaven!" Amanda said, with the enthusiasm of a connoisseur. "That was one of my favorite albums as a child," Amanda continued. "My mother had a vinyl copy and a stereo to play it on. I would stare and stare at the picture of Alfred Drake enclosing Patricia Morrison in the lash of his whip. And then I loved the music so!"

"Bless Anthony for choosing this project," said Marguerite, raising her glass to their local luminary, who was in one way or another, the patron of so many of the women present and all of them drank to Anthony Newton's health.

Each woman haven chosen a dainty lunch, they allowed their glasses to be refilled and encouraged Marguerite to recommence.

"We'll start with our first honoree, Alison Albrecht," said Marguerite. "Alison, please tell us something of your history in Random Point?"

Alison took a sip of white wine and began, "First of all, thank you, Marguerite for making me feel so welcome. I've never done well with BDSM support groups, but I'm thrilled to be included in this obvious upgrade of one of those." Several of the women nodded sympathetically, having recoiled from the sometimes creepiness of such groups on more than one occasion.

Alison turned to Amanda and said, "I'm so happy to meet you, Amanda. I wasn't one of Hugo's original readers, but like you, my roots in Random Point and the scene go back a long way." Amanda smiled back at Alison.

"I grew up in Random Point," said Alison, "as did Freddie, my fiancé. And strangely enough, we both know that our parents used spanking for foreplay before we were born. Freddie found some diaries his mother kept when she was young and they detailed a number of spanking specific incidents.

"My father wasn't lovable and I wasn't fond of him. He was an elementary school vice principal, organically authoritarian and harshly critical to such a degree that by the time I was six or seven, he had completely lost credibility in my eyes. My mother's obsessive perfectionism kept him from picking on her and she managed him better than any other woman could have done. My mother was a true friend to me, and shielded me from my father's grumpiness as much as possible. Corporal punishment was only a small part of my traumatic childhood, mainly because I was too terrified of my father to ever get caught being less than well behaved.

"And yet, I grew up with a desire to be spanked by some strict male. Not my father, but someone who loved me instead of desiring to totally control me. I tried the BDSM groups and discovered an acute lack of symmetry in the scene in that half the men I met wanted to be spanked and the other half wanted the same thing. They'd always try to introduce the old "turn around is fair play" axiom, which I soon figured out was male submissive code for, 'Don't make me admit that I want to be your bitch.'

"I played with the personal ads for a while but so many people would lie about their age. Even the photos they sent were misleading. The dead give aways were those little triangles still glued to the corners of the black and white snap shots they'd pull out of their albums to answer my ad with.

"Then there were the ladies who wrote to my ad who turned out to be guys. And while I'm on the subject of pussy envy, is there anyone else as heartily sick as I am of listening to men dreamily confide that what they most want to be is a lesbian? The best joke is when two girly men wind up writing to each other and finally meet. I wonder, where do they go from there?

"Then there were the masters," Alison continued, deadpan as the women around the table giggled, grinned and cheered her on in this unexpected routing of the men. "Have you ever met a master who wasn't an asshole? The mean ones are scary psychopaths and the benign ones are as oppressive as Jewish relatives."

"Don't you love the ones who want to boss you over the phone?" Alison continued, "with their, 'Pull down your panties, kneel on beans, insert ice cubes into your pussy, hop on one leg, sit on marbles, shove your butt out a window, put on red stockings and masturbate for me. You agree to everything of course, while placing orders on-line.

"Or what about those liberal doms who will allow their submissives to be handled by others, provided they can sagely supervise? What the hell is that about?" Alison asked.

"They'll claim it's for the safety of their darlings," explained Marguerite, "but they just like to watch."

"Yes," agreed Polyxena, "and also to make sure the other man doesn't do too good a job and charm their girl away."

"Well, to make a long story short," said Alison, "My father finally died, making it safe for me to return to Random Point. Now I could finally enjoy the beautiful house he left me! I got a job as assistant comptroller at Braemar. There I met Paula and David." Alison nodded at the polished blonde who during the period Alison was thinking of, had been Paula Rohan, soon to become the first Mrs. Ambrose Bartlett, only to subsequently divorce him and finally end up the wife of Sloan Taylor. David Lawrence was the Braemar English teacher who had brought Hope out with him from California several years before.

"I overheard Paula and David talking about spanking and demanded to be let in on their secrets, admitting that I was one of them," Alison went on. "They told me about Hugo's magazine, and encouraged me to place an ad in it. I took their advice and was amazed that one of the first people to answer my ad was Freddie Johanson, who actually worked at Braemar, as the network manager. At first he didn't seem like my type. Too nice for me, I thought, too sweet to be capable of actually spanking a girl. But we worked it out between us," Alison smiled. "And, well, he turned out to be a very good spanker."

"Yes, he did," thought Polyxena Guzman, regarding Alison with an innocently benign smile.

"May I ask a question?" Hope addressed Alison.

"Yes," said Alison, who in the next breath forestalled the question by turning to Marguerite and saying, "but can we review again, are we supposed to be totally frank or delicately diplomatic here?"

Marguerite replied, "Ladies, what do you think? Shall we speak the truth here for our mutual edification?"

"If we all told all our secrets," said Susan, "we'd be here all night."

"You would at any rate," said Marguerite.

"I haven't misbehaved in years," said Damaris serenely.

"You also have the steadiest and most reliable partner," Susan pointed out, speaking of her once brother in law, William Random, to whom Damaris was now happily wed.

"I'm conflicted on this issue," Hope admitted, "though I myself was about to pose a volatile question to Alison. The problem is one of female comradery vs. loyalty to our various men."

"Perhaps we should agree to disclose only the data we feel comfortable about revealing," suggested Paula Taylor.

"For my part," said Phoebe Casper Robbins, "I'd want any information available about my husband." All the others looked at her with interest, for this was the second time she had expressed suspicion of Pascal's fidelity that night. She squared her creamy, half bare shoulders and added with some warmth, "He's always snooping around for information on me!"

"I like the idea of frank disclosure," murmured Polyxena Guzman. "And I love the idea of a society of women in our village. We should be loyal first and foremost to each other!" the mostly dominant, partially submissive Dutch siren declared.

"I would love to know what my husband gets up to," said Pamela sincerely, "but I have the feeling that he gets up to so much that no one could ever know it all."

"But might not full disclosure breed jealousy and resentment?" asked Amanda, not forgetting that she probably had the most to conceal from Pamela if she wanted to retain her budding friendship.

"I'd still rather know the truth," said Pamela, then turning the question back on Amanda, adding, "wouldn't you?"

"You mean about Colby?" Amanda grinned, trying to imagine Colby even thinking about approaching another girl while they were apart. She simply knew that he would not. She owned him that year, brain, body and soul. He was living for the moment, approximately once month hence, in the London airport when they would reunite after their June separation and spend the next month traveling Europe together. And except for a few local distractions, she was living for that moment too. Because for all the attention she was getting from wealthy Raphael and Jaime the pool boy, it was the hand written post cards from Colby that made her heart contract with joy.

"All right, Hope, ask your question," said Alison.

"Did David play with you that first month you came out?" Hope asked immediately.

Alison hesitated for just a moment, before admitting, "Yes, but let me explain. He only did it to make me feel better after I found out that Freddie had been playing with Polyxena."

Every eyed turned on the fair Netherlander in the bosom hugging toile halter dress. Blushing and sipping her white wine, the thirty something beauty gave a little shrug and stammered, "I was curious."

"I find that statement reasonable and I am satisfied," remarked Hope.

"There's something I should add," said Alison. "About Freddie. Because it's brought me to a curious emotional pass that most of you have probably never experienced. You see, shortly after I started seeing Freddie I found out that he's not a top but a switch."

Eyebrows were raised all around as a hush fell over the room.

"Yes, I was surprised too," said Alison. "He wasn't ever going to tell me, but it was how he justified having played with Polyxena while dating me." Polyxena Guzman looked puzzled, so Alison hastened to explain to the fair-haired spa owner, "You see, everyone thought you were a dom when you came to Random Point, including Freddie, who apparently thought you were flirting with him in a mistressy sort of way and became extremely excited by the prospect of subbing to you. When he discovered he had misunderstood you, he pressed his inner reset button and topped you instead. And if I'm not mistaken, satisfactorily?"

Polyxena blushed and nodded.

Alison sighed. "When Freddie told me all this I was doubly upset. First because I was jealous of suddenly having to compete with a blonde goddess for the attentions of my man," said Alison, without rancor, for the hurt had long since been healed by the constant attentions of her loving and loyal fiancé. "But also because I had to confront the fact that that my man is a switch, which didn't shock, but confused me. I needed to ponder how I really felt about this revelation, so I pretended to be angry only at the fact that Freddie hadn't trusted me enough to tell me the truth from the beginning. In the interest of fairness and political correctitude, I also felt I had to man up, if you will, and offer him the erotic release he had sought with Polyxena. After all, he is the man I love and I'm sophisticated in the ways of the scene, so why should I want to deprive him of his chosen foreplay? Using his betrayal of me with Polyxena as an excuse to punish him. I became the dominatrix from hell over that poor, hapless man. I thrashed him and told him I would keep on doing so, forever, but that he could never dominate me again," said Alison before pausing to take a sip of wine. "Well, this unnatural state of affairs went on for a couple of weeks, with me becoming bossier and more brittle every day and Freddie visibly chaffing under my draconian rule, but too miserably abject at having been found to have cheated on me, to protest. Then finally it all came to a head when he found out that I had consoled myself briefly with David, as I said." Alison nodded somewhat apologetically to Hope, who blew Alison a kiss of forgiveness. "As soon as Freddie found out he had something on me, he shook off the yoke of domestic oppression I had been submitting him to and gave me to understand that my days of domming him were permanently at an end. And he was right. As a dom, I was a tyrant. I became my father. Was I truly mean, or merely resentful at having been forced into the dominant role? (Even though I was the one who forced myself into it.) So my question is this, should we ever try to change our roles?"

"Going over to the other side can be interesting," said Susan Ross, "but going back and forth too much can backfire. It happened to me with a submissive young man. He swore he was there to serve me, and at first it worked out well. I spoiled him by letting him take care of not only me, but my girlfriends too. I thought I had him so thoroughly under control that one night I taught him how to spank me. This short-circuited his emotions and I think may have caused him to morph from a sub into a switch. In due course, he wound up thinking he had the right to lay hands on me in return the next time I well and truly pissed him off, which of course, I inevitably did, since I found it hard to forget the good old days when he was my meek and adoring foot slave. We quarreled bitterly and our once beautiful relationship will never be the same again. I think Freddie is right. You should choose one role and stick to it with a feeling and sensible man."

At that moment, the doors into the room opened and the waiters began to deliver the various entrees ordered up by the ladies. Passing by one of the open doors on his way from the bar to the front lobby, Pascal Robbins looked casually into the dining room and paused when he saw the many beautiful women in their coordinated black and white outfits ranged around the long table. Catching a fleeting impression of the faces of his wife Phoebe, Pamela Bartlett and Amanda Sands among the fair, his heart contracted sharply. Guilt at the sudden remembrance of having seized, spanked and kissed Amanda causing a flush to burn across his attractive face, he hesitated before moving away from the open door, torn between embarrassment at the idea of confronting what appeared to be ten or a dozen ladies at once and curiosity as to what they were all doing there together. Phoebe had mentioned nothing about a ladies' night out. She appeared to be keeping many things to herself lately, since becoming engaged to perform in Anthony Newton's production of *Kiss Me Kate* at the repertory theatre that summer. He fancied she'd been distracted and secretive and jealously suspected her of harboring a wild infatuation for the handsome Broadway composer, who was, incidentally an experienced spanker of ladies in the scene that she loved and that he himself was only beginning to comprehend the power of.

What if Amanda revealed to Phoebe the liberties he had taken with her during their last meeting? Phoebe would never trust him again and she might also use the discovery as a carte blanche to go adventuring on her own across the laps of the many interesting male players in the village that summer. As all of these troubling thoughts flashed across the photographer's mind, Amanda Sands chanced to look towards the door and immediately caught his gaze. She looked at him meaningfully and without smiling, which expression again triggered an involuntary contraction of his heart. He saw at once that she was piqued at him for having grabbed her in her father's shop and smacked her bottom, not to mention kissing her on the mouth. He had done so on a whim and perhaps a bit more. In spite of possessing an adorable wife whom he ardently loved and still jealously desired, Amanda was appearing increasingly in his daydreams.

Pascal Robbins gave the slightest lift of his chin and nod of his head to one side while holding Amanda's gaze. Amanda took the gesture to mean that he wished an immediate audience with her and suddenly informed the table, "I just saw Pascal Robbins outside. Shall I go and ask him to come and take our picture?" This suggestion was greeted with a chorus of approval and Amanda also noticed a warm blush suffuse Phoebe's face as she realized that her husband was near and would be joining them shortly.

Amanda jumped up and ran out to the corridor outside the dining hall, where Pascal was poised, as though ready to take flight.

"What the hell's going on in there, Amanda?" he demanded.

"Garden Club," Amanda replied without hesitation. "Will you come and take our photo?"

He looked at her for a moment. "Come with me a second while I get my cameras," he said. They walked out the front door of the Owl and into the small parking lot beside it. "What's really going on in there? Why are Phoebe and Pamela there? Some sort of perversity party?"

"I'll never tell," said Amanda breezily.

"Can I count on you for that?" he returned, taking two cameras from the trunk of his SUV and hanging them around his neck.

She looked at him steadily, understanding his meaning at once.

"With the liberties you took you certainly don't deserve my discretion."

"When are we going to shoot together, Amanda?" Pascal said, skipping the previous subject like a puddle on an April day.

"I don't know, Mr. Robbins. Do you think you can keep your hands off me if we do?" Amanda asked with steel in her sweet, mellifluous voice. He stared at her, becoming ruffled, though he knew she was entirely in the right.

"Of course I can... try," he said, adding quickly, "I'm sorry, Amanda."

"I just don't understand you, Mr. Robbins," Amanda said, as they made their way back to the dining hall. "You have the prettiest wife in the world. How could you possibly betray her trust in you by coming onto your models?"

"Not models, model. You're the only one."

"Why do I alone merit the honor? As I understand it, you're not even in the scene."

"Who says I'm not?" he bristled. But they were now at the door to the dining room and their conversation came to a necessary period. Pascal assessed his subjects with a practiced eye and briskly ordered them into position for his first shot, ranging them in a row before the mantelpiece, with half the group leaning left towards the center, and the other leaning right. Next he had them take their seats again and photographed the table as a whole and then each facing side separately, all the while using his flash. Finally, he took a head and shoulders shot of each woman separately. In fifteen minutes, he had taken all of his shots, was handed a glass of wine, which he downed in a couple of gulps, given a kiss by his wife and graciously encouraged to depart without further delay.

Damaris was the next to rise and address the company. She herself had tailored her jumpsuit for her doll-like body. Her lustrous, long black hair was pulled back in a gold barrette and she wore other heavy gold jewelry to match. She was dark eyed and olive complected, with dark red lips and nails, a small Puerto Rican girl from New York who had made a home for herself in Random Point for over seven years.

"When I first came to Random Point to be William's secretary, I was a tense, high functioning speed freak, full of insecurities and the desire to be perfect, and of course, very much into spanking," Damaris freely admitted. "The only reason I had decided on the Cape over Manhattan after business school was because The New Rod Quarterly was published here. I had been a reader for just a few months when I actually saw the secretarial position advertised in the classifieds. I wonder how many submissive girls applied for that job? I'll have to ask Hugo. He forwarded William the responses. Anyway, I did a lot of bad things that first year, but we don't need to go into all the details. It's enough to say that Michael Flagg married me in order to reform me. Most of you know Michael pretty well so you can imagine that being married to him was not a huge hardship, but I always sensed that he was much more in love with Marguerite than he could ever be with me. So when I found out that he was secretly seeing Marguerite, I freed him by leaving him. It took a couple of years for William to forgive me being the worst secretary ever, we don't need to go into the details of that either, but eventually he did and since Laura was no longer with him at that time, he and I got together and finally, we got married."

"You forgot about The Keep," Hope reminded Damaris.

"That's right," Damaris said, "you worked there too, didn't you?"

"So did I, for one day," said Susan.

"When I first found out that Michael was still seeing Marguerite," said Damaris, "I ran away to Hollywood to do drugs in peace and work at a B&D club, which was The Keep. Michael came and found me there and insisted on buying an hour in the dungeon with me. And yes, he did beat the hell out of me. But later he also did finally let me smoke a joint in the bathtub." Damaris sighed. "I'm sure we all have Michael Flagg stories, except maybe two or three of you." She looked around and decided that perhaps Alison and Paula were as yet innocent of her ex husband's large hand and muscle corded thighs. "But we must all acknowledge, as I did long ago, that he is Marguerite's finally and at last, now and forever. To Marguerite Alexander Flagg," said Damaris, raising her glass to the suddenly wet-eyed redhead.

The salads and half grapefruits arrived. Amanda, her senses enhanced and appetite piqued by the buzz she had obtained on the bridge, sprinkled a teaspoon of sugar on her pink grapefruit. Pamela watched her in astonishment. Knowing that Pamela was as stoned as she was at that moment, Amanda boldly sprinkled a second teaspoon of sugar on Pamela's grapefruit. "Eat it, bitch," Amanda whispered seductively. At first Pamela regarded the temptation in stubborn refusal. But Amanda lifted the grapefruit dish to just under Pamela's nose, so the brunette could inhale the sweet, tart organic infusion of pink grapefruit and sugar.

"Oh, all right!" said Pamela, digging out a wedge of grapefruit with a silver spoon and popping it into her mouth. "Oh my god, that's good!" she said a moment later. All the women now fell to their first course with busy attention and most of the wine glasses were refilled.

Then Marguerite stood up and said, "Shall I go next?" Everyone nodded and assented. "Very well then. Hugo Sands came into my life, let us say, a number of years ago. We met at a BDSM party in Boston and within a month he had turned me out. I began severely corseting and embarked upon a short but highly profitable career as a pro dom. In a few years I was in a position to buy the shop across from Hugo's. He was already publishing The New Rod Quarterly and I was already writing for him. I decided to open a bookshop with the best collection of fetish erotica available in the world. Romantic that I am, I located it in the highest gallery, at the top of the spiral stairs."

Hope Lawrence smiled to herself, thinking, "I wonder how many of us have managed a seduction up there."

Just at that moment, another young lady arrived. She was a pretty, clean scrubbed brunette of medium height and attractive proportions, smooth skinned and in her early thirties and wearing a shirred, sleeveless black cotton a-line dress that displayed her curvy shape handsomely. "I'm so sorry I'm late but I had a hell of a time shaking Marnie."

"Bring the young lady a salad and a cocktail," said Marguerite to one of the waiters, who had come in with a pitcher of iced water. "Jane, you're just in time. We were relating a bit of each other's histories and you are very much a part of mine," added the tall, bosomy, creamy skinned redhead in the portrait collar dress.

"Yes, I'll have a martini," said Jane Eliot to the waiter and specified her salad choice. "Let me sum my part up in a sentence," said Jane, looking at Marguerite without a hint of real resentment, "that evil enchantress cast a spell upon my man and took him from me in the space of time that it took for her to undulate up her gallery stairs and back down again."

"Oh, there is more to your part than that," said the knowledgeable Susan Ross. "I remember when you became Hugo's protégée and worked for him in the shop."

"Yes," Jane smiled, "he taught me to how to dress and I became a little spitfire who demanded to be spanked, just to feel a new sensation."

"And you had a crush on Hugo," Susan reminded her.

"Yes, of course I did," Jane's eyes crinkled in another smile at the agreeable memory. "I imagine that's the only reason I've been invited to join this most exclusive of clubs."

"That and Michael Flagg," said Susan, "and also, being adorable."

"Thank you, Susan," said Jane. "The truth is that I was engaged to Michael Flagg when we moved to Random Point together a little more than seven years ago. But I was a militant feminist with a consciousness raised to the highest degree. He didn't dare bring up alt. sex perversity when we were together. He was happy just to sodomize me and leave it at that. Then he met Marguerite and everything he wanted out of sex fell into place. I got dumped and rightly so. As Susan pointed out, Hugo Sands ever so kindly picked me up, shook me out and made me into someone new. That someone turned out to be more than a little bi, and as a consequence, my boyfriend for the last five years has been the jockiest girl in Random Point, Marnie Price. Michael was always too much man for me, but Marnie is just the right amount. I am still a feminist, but now I realize, so are all of you."

"To Jane Eliot," said Susan, raising her glass to Jane. "Who proved in her own lifetime that even an ardent feminist can play in the scene without losing her self-respect."

All the women drank to Jane, who beamed on them. Then Susan raised her glass to Marguerite. "And once more please, to Marguerite, the best erotic writer in the world. We've all thrilled to your novels for years and more than anyone else, you taught our men how to properly seduce us. You corseted us, tied us ever so tightly and showed us what dungeons are for; you pampered us when we felt neglected and built up our self confidence when we were shy. You make the scene a more lovely, a more welcoming and most importantly, a more female-friendly universe and we salute you for all this and more."

Marguerite's health was drunk.

Marguerite turned to Hope and said, "Your turn, darling."

The slim, longhaired blonde in the black and white checked seersucker shirtwaist took a sip of white wine before commencing her speech without rising.

"I've only been in Random Point for a few years, but I would never live anywhere else," said the schoolteacher's wife with an affectionate glance around the table. "I first met my husband, David, when he came to The Keep to do a session with me. It was love at first sight for the both of us, though I made him woo me for many months. When he got the offer from Braemar to come out to the Cape and become a prep school instructor he felt that it would be more respectable to bring a wife than a girlfriend and we married. Right from the start we knew that we were both sluts. I knew that he was still interested in spanking other submissive women and he knew that dominant men would continue to pursue me and bribe me with allowance to play with them. So we've both been keeping scorecards, just to make sure of a continual balance between us. Some people might think it a strange way to conduct a happy marriage but it seems to be working for us." Hope took another sip of wine before continuing, "I knew at once that the bookshop was the very heart and soul of the village and I love it very much. I've been running the coffee bar at Marguerite and Sloan's shop for several years now and I'm thrilled to announce that I've just been invited to become a full partner in the shop."

This was perfectly true. And in return, Hope was investing some twenty thousand dollars in enclosing and decorating the patio to accommodate more coffee drinkers and snackers at Marguerite's shop.

"Well done!" said Susan, raising her glass to Hope. "We love Hope for the glamour she has brought us and the cheerfulness she sheds like California sunlight wherever she goes."

Hope blushed with pleasure as she smiled on her many female friends, some of whom knew very well that their men paid her for sessions. Susan knew that Anthony had patronized Hope, Marguerite knew that Michael had engaged her and Pamela knew that Ambrose similarly employed the former video star, but none of them blamed Hope too severely for seducing their men. Her beauty was too perfect for a lover of beauty to resist and her personality too charming to make resistance desirable. One surrendered to Hope in order to obtain the rarified pleasure of mastering her and one paid whatever tribute was asked without complaint, merry in having obtained the privilege.

At that point the artfully plated entrees began to arrive and all the ladies paused to regard them.

Meanwhile, Pascal Robbins had driven directly to Michael Flagg's pub and had gone in for a pick me up. Michael's pretty blonde barmaid Carmen was assisting Michael in filling mugs and pitchers for the thirsty summer visitors when Pascal took a seat at the bar. Michael greeted him with a smile and immediately began to mix a martini for the photographer.

"They're all over there at the Owl," said Robbins, downing the first drink quickly.

"Who is?" Michael asked with interest.

"Our wives and all the other good looking women in a twelve mile radius. Susan, Pamela, Amanda, Hope, someone called Jane…"

"Really? Jane as well? I used to date her."

"They had me take their photos. It's some sort of club. They were all dressed in coordinating outfits."

"Interesting!" Michael commented.

Back at the Owl, Paula Rohan Taylor was the next to speak. Pamela was taken aback by just how attractive her husband's ex-wife's figure appeared in the fitted vest and blouse, bringing just the right emphasis to a dainty waist. Pamela felt sure that Ambrose still loved Paula and deeply regretted allowing her to divorce him and now she could see why. Paula was a luscious blonde, still in her early thirties, fresh, creamy and classically feminine.

"I wasn't aware of The New Rod Quarterly when I first began working at Braemar. But David Lawrence sensed I was in the scene right away, made me admit it and then put me onto the magazine. I thought about placing and ad, but I didn't have time to. When Hope noticed her husband mentoring me a little too enthusiastically, she wasted no time in appealing to Hugo to hook me up with a local dom who wasn't already taken," said Paula, somewhat apologetically in Hope's direction.

"It felt like the right thing to do," Hope explained. "I'm sorry it didn't turn out as expected."

"I'm not, darling," Paula assured her. "Ambrose Bartlett is an attractive and elegant man and I liked the way he topped me, right up to the end. But he was just a bit too much of a perfectionist and I could never live up to his standards. I craved a more relaxed partner day to day and somehow, Pamela and I decided to trade men. I got her Sloan and she got my Ambrose, though she rather had him for awhile, I suspect," Paula now smiled at Pamela. Pamela felt Paula's well wishes but was still embarrassed at the memory of having been accessible to Ambrose Bartlett while he was still married to Paula and while she was still ostensibly Sloan's lover.

"I can only add that while I'm probably one of the few women here who hasn't played with Michael Flagg," said Paula, with a smile for Marguerite, "he did flirt with me once and I valiantly resisted. He wasn't married to you yet, Marguerite, have no fear, and it was very tempting. But I was married to Ambrose at the time and my sinning came more in the form of indulging in hot fudge sundaes than extra-marital spanking scenes."

"My story can be told the fastest," said Phoebe, standing for her small oration and looking the flower of peachy perfection in her diaphanous, nip waisted, full skirted, tea dress. "I've always been into spanking, but I never knew a scene existed until that summer two years ago, when I first came to Random Point and we stayed at the home of William and Damaris while they were on vacation. My husband is naturally dominant, but he had never spanked me until that summer, when I became so inflamed on finding out about the scene, that I pushed or pulled him into it. I too rather flirted with Michael Flagg, I'm afraid," said Phoebe with some abashment, also looking with regret towards Marguerite, who again demurred with a smile. "But I've never been spanked by anyone other than my husband," she reported with the satisfaction of the pure in heart. She didn't add that she'd been thinking about being spanked by Anthony Newton every day since returning to Random Point and beginning to work under his directorship on *the Kiss Me Kate* revival. "In conclusion I would like to thank Marguerite for inviting me to join The Venus Club. I am honored to be a part of this delightful society. I wish I never had to leave Random Point, but I hope it will always at least be my summer place."

Amanda observed with some relief that Phoebe had nothing more to say about her husband and indeed seemed blissfully unaware of the fact that she had married a wolf. A large pasta with pine nuts and a tomato cream sauce was placed before her and she began to eat. Noticing that Pamela had ordered only a Caesar salad, Amanda transferred a third of her vegetarian capellini to a bread plate and presented Pamela with it. "Eat that or I'll hurt you," ordered Amanda affectionately. Pamela felt extremely hungry at that moment and did not argue with her new best friend. Rather she happily luxuriated in having a new best friend. Meanwhile, Amanda had drifted off on a mental raft with Raphael Price, where it suddenly struck her that she ought not to give him any sex at all, being that he was so submissive, but rather dole out tiny favors in miniscule increments over perhaps the next four or five years before finally granting him any real intimacy. And then the raft landed on that small strip of beach that Raphael appeared to have sole access to, but instead of the beautiful rock and roll star art gallery owner, she visualized Pascal Robbins fussing with his reflectors and setting up a shot. Amanda was aware that she was frowning as she remembered the tedium of a photo shoot, but for some reason, the thought of the photographer scolding her "not to look dead" or to "give him *something*" raised the corners of her mouth.

"I'm thinking I won't let Raphael have me after all," Amanda confided to Pamela between savory bites of the flavorful dish before her. "I'll only let him fetish parts of me, like my shoes and waist."

"It's a good idea," Pamela agreed, not feeling guilty about eating a real dinner and loving the taste. "After all, you'll probably know him for the rest of your life. There's plenty of time to try him out in stages."

Polyxena, the Nordic gym owner, ate about half of the roast chicken and dumpling dish she had ordered before taking the floor without rising. She refreshed herself with a few sips of white wine and then began, "I visited Random Point some years ago to attend one of Hugo's parties and thought it would be lovely to live here. You needed a good gym and I think it's been a perfect match, don't you?" All the ladies agreed, everyone being a member in good standing and regular attendance. "And yet moving here has also turned my life around in a way I wasn't expecting. I'd been dominant all my adult life. I came here with my slave and partner, Deiter Brandt. Some of you look surprised, yes he was my slave, for years. But soon after I began living here, I found myself becoming attracted to some of your men. They were different from the masters I knew back home, much more playful and relaxed, though still competent. I felt I had to try the other side and bottom a few times, to feel what it was like and whether it was something I'd been craving. I played at little bit at one of Hugo's parties and my Deiter chanced to see me being flogged by Michael. In that moment our relationship crumbled. My lover, friend and partner of many years became completely disenchanted with me and left me that same night. Therefore I agree with Susan, it is a potential_y dangerous thing to switch up one's orientation before the very eyes of a man who has been used to relating to you in the opposite way. The men simultaneously feel wounded and as though they now possessed new rights. I've been with Deiter again just once since all of this happened and he came onto me like a rude, careless dominant, even spanking me and forcing me over a table to submit to him." Polyxena smiled and paused to sip her wine. "That was pretty hot, I will admit," she continued, "but except for that one time, he's been indifferent to me since glimpsing my submissive side."

"Do you want him back?" Hope wondered. Like most of the women at the table she had felt the benefit of Dieter's massaging fingers and exercise wisdom.

"I want my sweet, good Deiter back, not this harsh stranger," said Polyxena. "but failing that, I must find a new lover." The women nodded in respectful agreement. "But let me ask you something," continued the luscious immigrant, "you all seem to be equal_y enamored of your spanking men and yet none so far has spoken of a classic master slave relationship. Do none of you serve?"

The question rendered all of the women momentarily silent as they considered their answers. Damaris laughed and said, "Most of us serve dinner."

"You raise an interesting point, Polyxena," said Hope. "To wit, are we all simply bedroom submissives?"

"Even if we are," said Susan, "there's nothing simple about it."

"Polyxena made a fair observation," said Paula Taylor, "we're all comfortable with a more playful form of submission than women who style themselves slaves."

"I've played slave games in dungeons. And they can make a pussy wet. But they're not for everyone and certainly not for everyday," murmured Marguerite.

"But there is something romantic about the notion of a perfect master, isn't there?" Amanda wondered aloud. Last year she almost thought she was ready for one. Listening to her new friends she began to wonder whether the concept of patriarchal mastery was not completely outdated and inappropriate for a woman of spirit.

"If a master is someone even more bossy than my husband, he certainly does not fit my definition of perfection," said Phoebe, draining another glass of wine.

"I'm suspicious of any man who insists upon being in control 100% of the time," said Jane firmly. "But I match the textbook definition of bedroom submissive. I can take and even relish a hard spanking, but to be punished for misdeeds? That would be ridiculously undignified at my age and as hard as I work."

It was Pamela's turn, but whatever she had inhaled on the bridge had made her introspective and her own reflections at that moment seemed a bit too jumbled to share, so she begged Susan Ross to go next instead. The small blonde girl stood in her place to address the table. "The one person missing tonight is my sister Laura, but as you know, she's on her honeymoon with Hugo at the moment, or she would certainly be here. It was Laura who brought me into the scene as soon as I turned eighteen. She had gone to college with Marguerite and when Marguerite met Hugo and discovered the scene, she got Laura interested as soon as she could. Laura's ten years older than me but we've always both been into it. Well, Marguerite had started writing for Hugo and she encouraged both Laura and me to start selling him artwork for his magazine. He liked our style and guaranteed he'd buy whatever we drew for him, so we started putting out spanking illustrations like crazy.

"Laura jumped into a hasty marriage with William while I began college at the Art Institute in Boston. I became infatuated with Hugo and he took advantage of that in just the way I wanted him to, but it was always Laura who was on his mind and he had to wait a long time to finally get her.

"Well half way through freshman year, Hugo introduced me to Anthony Newton. I say introduced but "gave me" to him would be a more accurate way of putting it. Of course, at the same time he also gave Anthony to me and for that I will be forever grateful," said Susan, pausing to refresh herself with a sip of wine. Phoebe almost felt a rush of envy as she heard the pretty illustrator complacently claim complete possession of their powerful patron. Did Susan Ross even know how remarkably lucky she was?

"Over the ensuing seven years I completed my education and got a job at Chipper Knight. My scene adventures in all that time would take too long to describe, but you can see little glimpses of them in my cartoons."

At last it was Amanda's turn to speak and the two glasses of wine she had drunk during the long meal seemed to encourage self-expression.

"Thank you, lovely ladies," she began, smiling at her friends, "As young as I am, I belong here with you. For I too, am a spanking enthusiast. And not just in my fantasies. I have a big, hunky, 19 year old boyfriend who is also in the scene and who would love to spank each and every one of you. Especially you, Marguerite."

Marguerite smiled and flushed, saying, "Don't you dare encourage him."

"No, I wouldn't think of it," Amanda replied. "I bring my boyfriend up to illustrate that I am far from innocent. I've been provoking boys into spanking me since grade school. My high school boyfriend spanked and sexually dominated me because I demanded it. In freshman year at Harvard I initiated four spanking relationships, the last of which took, with Colby Hodge. During that time I also indulged in a scene affair with a man I met at a support group in Boston and here in Random Point I've been spanked by (Amanda looked around the table, counting) four of your husbands."

Marguerite and Hope knew that their husbands had spanked Amanda. Pamela had just discovered during the break outside that Ambrose had done the same. Phoebe Robbins innocently finished her dinner, unaware that she was the fourth in Amanda's quartet.

"Talk about that more," urged Pamela, drinking wine and recklessly contemplating desert. She admired Amanda's strong curves as she stood beside her at the table in the well-fitted white cotton dress. Perhaps Amanda was right about *her* body too, that Pamela would appear even handsomer if slightly more luxuriously upholstered.

"All right, I will, because my encounters with the husbands of some of you have been highly instructive. The first was Michael Flagg. I met him on my second day in Random Point. I'd met Hugo for the first time the day before and had fallen instantly in love. Can you imagine being eighteen and meeting your father for the first time and he's Hugo Sands? I was well disposed to love him of course, having read the magazine for years. But I was also perversely sexually excited. I really wanted my long lost father to spank me! I had tricked him into doing so the previous day, by pretending to be an agency model sent for a shoot. But the truth came out before my skirt came up and I wound up getting only the briefest of spankings from Hugo that day. So the next day, I was all over him to do it again. Just for my enjoyment. Hugo's solution was to bring me over to meet Michael Flagg. So I got a patented Michael Flagg spanking, then and there. And it was lovely." Amanda took a sip of wine and continued. "The next time I was back in Random Point, Hope was kind enough to lend me *her* husband for a thrilling half hour of correction on a chilly winter day. David Lawrence, English teacher that he is, was an especially convincing disciplinarian. He chose an actual fault to punish me for as well, my having an impossible crush on my own English teacher, Mr. Keen. I *loved* your husband!" Amanda stressed to Hope.

"I'll bet you didn't love *my* husband," Pamela encouraged Amanda. "Tell about that!"

Amanda sighed, "No, I didn't love your husband. He spanked me as part of a deal Hugo brokered for me. In return for me being allowed to shoot a spanking video in his store on Christmas Eve, I was to take a spanking from Mr. Bartlett. He told me the shooting fee for the location is normally ten grand, I guess to prepare me for how hard he was going to spank me. I'd never experienced a cruel spanking before. Needless to say, I began to cry immediately, and not cathartic tears of deep emotion but 'Waaa, I feel sorry for myself tears of pain!' Besides which, he required me to be nude, which I thought crude, me being only eighteen and the daughter of his friend. Though it turned out that he didn't really believe I was really Hugo's daughter or that I was really going to Harvard at the time."

"To be fair to Mr. Bartlett," Susan put in, "Hugo wasn't acting like anyone's proper father at that point. He turned you out."

"Well, yes," Amanda agreed, "but I came as a complete surprise to him, showing up full-grown and model-ready. He would have behaved quite differently towards me if he'd actually raised me. He would have felt it a point of conventional morality to keep me well away from every aspect of spanking in so far as he could. The feeling Hugo has for me is sincere, but not typically paternal. I've simply become his latest protégée. He took on my college expenses without a murmur and was delighted when I finally settled on a respectable boyfriend of my own age. I know he felt guilty when he discovered how stringent Mr. Bartlett had been with me," Amanda explained to Susan.

"Who is the fourth husband?" asked Jane Eliot of Amanda.

"Oh, well, I suppose it hardly counts, as it was only a very small encounter," said Amanda, glancing at Phoebe Robbins, "but Mr Robbins spanked me for getting my hair cut so short last week."

Phoebe looked up in astonishment.

"It was only a small spanking, but he took a liberty in administering it, I thought," said Amanda with sudden decision. "I suppose he was cross because he had been counting on photographing a long haired blonde. And then I did this," Amanda gestured at her beautiful trimly cropped head. Phoebe flushed dark pink and felt faint as the heat mounted from her chest to her cheeks to her brow. "Where the hell did he get off???" the chestnut haired thespian thought angrily.

"What do you think about what Mr. Robbins did to me?" Amanda asked the others.

"When you say small spanking, what exactly do you mean?" demanded Phoebe, her heart pounding with jealous anxiety to realize that her husband had spanked this stunning young girl.

"He bent me over a counter and swatted me six times over my skirt."

Phoebe subsided in her chair at this, relieved that at least it had not been a protracted, over the knee, bare bottom affair, but rather a seemingly spontaneous display of masculine assertiveness over a naughty model.

"Did you flirt with Mr. Robbins?" Damaris asked Amanda.

"Not that I was aware of," Amanda replied candidly.

"Then he was out of line," Damaris said.

"I agree," said Jane at once. "The spanking was nonconsensual."

"How hard was the spanking?" asked Susan.

"Not very," grinned Amanda. "But enough to leave five minutes of residual warmth behind."

Phoebe didn't like the sound of that and felt her face grow warm again.

"That sounds like a mild enough spanking," said Susan. "But, did Pascal have the right behave so familiarly towards Amanda?"

"No, he did not," said Polyxena Guzman with certainty. "The rule is look but don't touch, unless invited."

"And when I think of how jealous and possessive he has been about me and my scene friends..." Phoebe fumed, breaking breadsticks violently. Hope Lawrence refilled Phoebe's wine glass. "And now," Phoebe went on, "he has the nerve to lay hands on an eighteen-year-old girl!"

"Mr. Robbins lives among us without being truly one of us," said Hope. "He needs a course in scene protocol."

"People who aren't really in the scene but hang around players can pick up mixed messages," observed Alison, who only vaguely knew who Phoebe and Pascal Robbins were but had encountered bad form before.

"Everyone agrees Mr. Robbins behaved inappropriately towards Amanda," said Marguerite, "the question is, is he cute enough to get away with it?"

"I know Pascal Robbins," said Pamela. "He's not a wolf. I think he was genuinely peeved at Amanda for cutting her hair and being the old fashioned male chauvinist that he is, he expressed himself in classic retro style. His behavior was improper but also in character."

"Perhaps I shouldn't have even brought it up," said Amanda, appealing directly to Phoebe, "you won't say anything, will you?"

"I won't," Phoebe promised.

"That's right, young ladies," said Marguerite, "whatever is discussed at The Venus Club should be held in strictest confidence."

As all of them agreed to this, Phoebe's mind was whirling. Hope patted Phoebe's small hand and said encouragingly, "This is like money in the bank."

Phoebe looked at her with dawning interest. The blonde girl was right, thought Phoebe. Now she knew one bad thing Pascal had done. Perhaps this entitled her to do one bad thing as well. The pressure to reveal herself to Anthony Newton as an ardent spanking devotee had lately become relentless. He was her director and she had a developed a very pressing crush on him. He was handsome and allegedly a masterful dominant. She worshipped his music and was honored to the point of ecstasy that she had been chosen to headline in his revival on the Cape that summer. In short, although she still adored her husband, she was experiencing a painful longing for a physical relationship with Anthony Newton. Was this sudden revelation about Pascal's bad behavior with Amanda her get out of jail free card with respect to Mr. Newton?

Amanda felt immediately guilty for betraying Mr. Robbins' inappropriate behavior to his wife, but at least she had withheld the more sensational conclusion to the affront, that being the kiss. The spontaneous spanking a male chauvinist joker could shrug off, even if confronted by a miffed wife who blushed so beautifully, but a kiss could never be satisfactorily explained away.

Chapter Six

The Girls Close Michael's Pub

After the dinner broke up, Pamela and Amanda decided to finish the night at The Dutch. First Pamela took Amanda with her to the shop in Random Point so she could change into a different outfit. This neat little dress and suit shop, owned by Damaris Random, had furnished the outfits for all the women at the dinner that evening. Pamela quickly shed her black suit for a sleeveless party dress in cream tulle, with a full skirt over a crinoline. Exchanging her black heels for beige ones, Pamela touched up her lipstick in a mirror while Amanda lingered admiringly over the racks of summer markdowns.

The girls drove directly to Michael's pub in Pamela's luxury sedan and found it fairly packed with youthful revelers from Boston and raucous townies. Michael saw them come in and waved them to a booth with a smile. The juke box was loaded with New Wave and Alt from the 80's and 90's, making the bar a popular dance destination in the summer months. Five or six couples were dancing to The Bangles when the girls walked in, among them gleamed the attractive Raphael Price with one of his female clerks from the gallery.

No sooner had Pamela ordered a white wine and Amanda a lemonade from Michael's bar girl Carmen than Raphael Price came over and asked Amanda to dance. A Beck song had begun to play and Amanda went out onto the small dance floor with the handsome, long haired gallery owner, who was clad in black jeans, black high collared urban walkers and a long sleeved, white on white textured dress shirt tucked out. Raphael took her in his arms to dance with her, looking deeply into her eyes.

"I thought you were coming to see me?" he asked, smiling.

"I will," she promised. "Soon."

Pamela had only had a sip cf wine before a shadow fell across the booth and she looked up to see Dru Baxter, the college boy who was working at the bookshop coffee bar this summer. Tall and lithe, with fair, collar length hair and a fresh, open, intelligent face, Dru was dressed in light chinos and a white, short sleeved button down shirt that was attractively fitted to his lean torso. Pamela had chatted with him on several occasions while stopping at the bookshop for an espresso and thought him laid back and charming. But being asked to dance by the nineteen year old greatly surprised her. He didn't take no for an answer, however, and extended his hand to lead her onto the floor. Pamela was even more surprised that Dru could really dance and never attempted to pull her hands away from his. Watching all of this from the bar with interest, Michael punched in the next song on the jukebox to see what Dru would do next. As soon as *Loser* ended, *I Only Have Eyes For You*, by the Flamingos began. Dru never let go of Pamela's hands as the beat remained slow and rolling, spinning and back twirling her until she wound up before him, her back pressed to his front, her arms crossed in front of her, and her hands pressed to her sides, each one still clasped in his. Abandoning herself to the sensuality of the moment and quite enjoying the gallant attentions of her young admirer, Pamela allowed herself to melt back against him, lost in the moment and unaware of anything except the pleasurable warmth of being gently seduced by the dance. It was this image that met Ambrose Bartlett's eyes when he entered the pub a few minutes later in search of a nightcap before going home.

Amanda had lead Raphael back to her booth to sit the next dance out when she noticed Bartlett enter the pub and walk up to the bar after casually nodding at Pamela, who still locked in Dru Baxter's strong, youthful arms, had finally opened her eyes and looked up.

Raphael impulsively seized Amanda's slender hand and kissed her palm. "Why wait until that phantom day sometime later when we can be together tonight?" he asked.

"You're very handsome, but I have a boyfriend who will use a strap on me if he finds out I cheated on him," Amanda amazed her admirer by admitting.

"Someone dares treat you like that?" he cried, now clasping her hand between both of his.

"Of course he does, he's my top," Amanda replied, ruthlessly crushing Raphael's hopes of having found the ultimate mistress in the exquisite young blonde.

"Oh! Well, in that case…let's make sure he never finds out," Raphael rallied instantly from the shock of discovering Amanda's true orientation and resumed flirting in spite of the revelation.

"Doesn't Pamela look stunning tonight?" Amanda asked, staring at her friend, who had not yet ceased to dance in Dru's arms, in spite of her husband's sudden presence.

Raphael followed her gaze and lingered on Pamela's svelte form in the princess dress and tantalizing high heels with a connoisseur's appreciation. "Yes," he replied, going on to observe, "She's seems to be channeling Louise Brooks."

"You noticed!" Amanda replied joyfully. "Oh you are a smart man. Don't you agree that Pamela's a princess?"

"Yes, certainly I do."

"Her husband treats her like a shop girl," exaggerated Amanda. "I'm talking about Mr. Bartlett, who just walked in."

"The one who owns Bartlett's?"

"Yes. He doesn't appreciate Pamela and it's making her ill."

Raphael looked again at the fashion designer/model/boutique manager still out on the dance floor with the tall, fair-haired college boy. "She's beautiful," Raphael murmured.

"She's ripe for adoration. And her shoe collection is dazzling."

Raphael smiled at Amanda, amazed at her instantly honing in on his most secret obsession. "How do you pick up on these things at your age?" he wondered.

Amanda said, "I've always known them. It's in my blood."

"Amanda, I can't bear to think of anyone using a strap on you."

"You could gallantly not seduce me," she suggested, pretending not to notice him lightly squeezing her upper thigh through her dress under the table.

"I promise to do nothing more seductive than feed you chocolate."

"Can we watch old movies on cable?" asked Amanda.

"Of course we can," Raphael agreed enthusiastically.

They took Raphael's large, shiny, red pick-up, stopping at the all night bakery to purchase fresh bagels, crumb donuts and apricot tarts. It was the mildest of clear June nights, with a light, exhilarating breeze wafting the ocean air across Random Point.

"Can we go to Hugo's house instead of yours? I need to feed the cats," said Amanda, remembering she hadn't been home since the late afternoon. Raphael agreed and they proceeded to the grey stone house at the edge of the woods on Shadow Lane.

Surrounded by three tabbies of various stripes the instant they walked in, Amanda led Raphael by the hand to the kitchen. Tripped up by swishing tails and nudging kitty faces, she suddenly realized how tired she was, it having been a very long day. Raphael took over the procedure of opening cans for the friendly felines and filling their three terra cotta dishes set beside the large, old-fashioned kitchen hearth. Amanda took a jug of milk from the double sized stainless steel refrigerator and poured them each a tumbler full then set the baked goods out on dishes along with butter and cream cheese. Raphael cut and buttered a half bagel for Amanda and put it on a dark red china dish alongside a half donut and half apricot tart. Amanda smiled at his instinctive knowledge of the way in which girls like their snacks prepared at one in the morning. Consuming all of the other halves himself, Raphael watched his lovely new friend enjoying her treats with wholehearted pleasure. Cats climbed up on each of their laps to rub against the young people and preen with self-admiration as they were petted.

"I'm so sleepy now," she admitted, "I don't think I could be bad even if I wanted to."

"Do you want me to go?" he asked kindly, taking her hand and lightly kissing it on the back.

She looked at him, considering. "Not really," she said. "I don't like being alone in the house."

A wide smile lit his handsome face. "I'm trying to guess whether you sleep in pajamas," he said playfully.

"I do when I'm trying to be good."

"Why don't I clear off down here and you go put them on? And find the old movie you want to watch and get in bed."

"Really?" Amanda was charmed at his solution to the potential awkwardness of undressing together before having actually decided that they were going to be intimate that night.

"Yes!" he said, letting the cats out the kitchen door as they were all mewing before it simultaneously.

Amanda exchanged her day clothes for a pair of white cotton Capri pajamas with embroidered hems and collar and was delighted to discover that an airing of the 1934 Cecil B. De Mille *Cleopatra* was just beginning on TCM. She decided to entertain Raphael in Hugo's suite, the single bed in her own room being large enough for slim young lovers to share, but she still hadn't decided if that was the way the night would conclude.

Raphael came in and dimmed the lights to the barest illumination.

"Wasn't Claudette Colbert a goddess?" he said, stripping off his outer clothes unselfconsciously and getting into bed beside her in a pair of black and white plaid cotton boxers. She eyed his bare, muscular torso admiringly. His gym-trained body was hard and lean in all the right places, and as symmetrical as a Greek statue. As soon as he climbed into bed beside her, she found her way into his arms, rubbing her cheek against the light fuzz of dark hair that covered his well-developed chest and ran down the middle of his torso to his abdomen in a straight line. This affectionate gesture was more eloquent than words in conveying the comfort Amanda felt in Raphael's company. He locked his strong arms around her slender shoulders and pressed a light kiss to her brow.

"Speaking of goddesses," she said, her eyes riveted to the screen, which showed Colbert in the famous bath of asses' milk. "in my opinion, Random Point has three."

"Three including yourself?" he asked, caressing her velvet earlobe between two fingers.

"Oh no, I'm too young to be a goddess. I was thinking of Marguerite Alexander Flagg, Hope Spencer Lawrence and Polyxena Guzman. Now, the first two I mentioned are happily married to good-looking men. But Polyxena Guzman, the owner of the gym, is without any man at all."

"There's a lady in this town named Polyxena?" he laughed.

"She's a Dutch beauty and a former mistress. But she's been abandoned by her long time lover and slave and at the peak of her beauty and charm, appears to be alone."

"I remember now, the blonde Venus at the gym. I've seen her there swimming. She wears a white suit like a forties pin up girl."

"She once had her own dungeon in the Hague."

"That's fascinating," said Raphael with unfeigned interest.

"But if I were you, I'd mix it up. Top Mistress Polyxena and bow down to Submissive Pamela. They both seem ripe for a change."

"Only eighteen and already manipulating your friends' sex lives. You're so precocious, Amanda," said Raphael, caressing her face and throat. She took his hand and brought it to her breast. His fingertips traveled under her pajama top and enclosed the full, round left globe of her bosom in his hand. She shivered with excitement against him.

"You can squeeze me," she encouraged him, leaning back against his chest and throwing her head back, consciously exposing her throat to his lips.

"Thank you," he murmured and kissed her neck and shoulders.

Then he stopped and looked at her, murmuring, "You're so delectable. If I stay here I'll undoubtedly ravish you. Should I go home and let you be good?"

Amanda had just been starting to grow comfortable in his arms and had also taken note of an interesting development under the covers.

"Don't go," she said definitely, leaning back against him more heavily and replacing his hand on her bosom. With her other hand she casually dimmed the light by the bed and then turned to bury her face against his lightly fuzzed, gracefully muscular chest. He smelled of sea soap and his entire well-groomed body was glowing with health and strength. Her hand strayed down to enclose his throbbing, ramrod cock as it pulsed under his shorts against her long thigh line under the crisp white pajama pants.

A couple of minutes later they were both completely nude while Amanda sat astride Raphael's pelvis, his bulky, lengthy penis buried in her sex to the hilt, their pubic curls grinding together as she rode and pumped him continuously until she had achieved a splendid climax, her shapely bottom cheeks clutched firmly in his hands. Having felt her orgasm, Amanda's newest and possibly most courtly lover, pulled out, rearranged their position so that he now straddled her, took himself in hand and rained an admiring benediction down upon her voluptuous, cherry tipped breasts.

Amanda was debating whether she should shower when Raphael brought hot washcloths back from the bathroom and gently patted her breasts clean.

"You're very thoughtful," she said when he climbed back into bed next to her and pulled the sheets and coverlet up over them. He put off the small remaining light and took her in his arms.

"Why do you love a man who beats you?" he murmured against her hair.

"He's not a man, he's a boy and he doesn't beat me, we play."

"But you said he'd strap you if he found out you'd been with me."

"Well, he is my lover."

"What do you mean by play?"

"Never mind. Stay as innocent as you are. It suits you."

Chapter Seven

Ripples and Reactions

Ambrose Bartlett had just ordered a second shot of whiskey when Pamela alit on the empty bar stool beside him, flushed from having danced twice with the tall, blond college boy.

"Glass of white wine Pamela?" Michael Flagg asked from behind the bar after delivering Bartlett's drink.

"Should I?" she asked her husband demurely.

Bartlett shook his head, downed his drink in one pull, left some bills on the bar and rose to leave.

"Good night," said Pamela to Michael, slipping her arms into her cream satin bolero before following her husband out.

He held the door of his Mercedes sedan for her and cast her a reproachful look once behind the wheel.

"What?" she asked defiantly.

"You're looking very well for someone who's called in sick to work three days in a row," he commented, throwing the car in gear and gliding quietly from the parking lot of the Dutch onto Shadow Lane.

"I've never felt better," Pamela confided carelessly.

"Pamela, are you being recalcitrant on purpose?"

"No."

"No?"

"Not exactly."

"That's a charming outfit by the way."

"Thank you."

"But you ought to be spanked for dancing that way with that boy in front of me."

"I accept that," she smiled.

In a few minutes they turned onto the winding cliff road and began ascending towards Bartlett's house.

"You are looking amazingly well tonight," he added, not being able to quite define the subtle change that seemed to enhance her beauty that night. He had never seen her skin tone so fresh or her shoulders so softly relaxed.

"Thank you. I've been taking better care of myself."

"So the three days off was about spa treatments?"

"No, Ambrose."

"Well, aren't you going to explain your unaccountable behavior to me?"

"I'm not coming back to work at the store. I'm going to work exclusively on designing from now on because that's what makes me happy."

"I see," said Bartlett, himself not sounding very happy. They parked in front of their large, elegant, three story home on the cliff side and went inside. Pamela put some lights on in the downstairs sitting room and went behind the wet bar to open a bottle of white wine, remembering Michael Flagg's suggestion with enthusiasm.

"If me not working at the store is a deal breaker for this marriage, so be it, Ambrose. The same thought has run my head again and again all spring long: Did I marry a rich man to be a shop girl? To put in long, exhausting retail management hours every day and night? Is this not an insulting and absurd waste of my talents and energies? Any well-trained clerk can okay a check and mark down an inventory. You don't need me there to do those things."

"Maybe I just like having you around," he suggested with a surprisingly affectionate smile.

"Really?"

"I'm going to miss you," he said.

Pamela swirled her wine in a glass and tasted it.

"Then build me a studio at the store," she said suddenly.

"Go on," he said.

"You can use the attic where the alterations ladies work. There are only two of them now. If the space were to be remodeled and sectioned off I could share it with them. Of course you'd have to put in skylights and a luxurious bathroom for all of us ladies. And they could use a lovely sofa or two to take an afternoon break on. They're both over sixty-five, you know, the dears. I'd like a lounging area too. And it could be private enough that you could come visit me in it. What do you think? I would be happy to work within reach of you, Ambrose."

"I think it could be easily done," he said without equivocation.

"Really? You would do that for me?"

"I will."

The first meeting of The Venus Club served as the catalyst to several much more heated interactions in and around Random Point the following week.

For example, Polyxena Guzman could never regard Ambrose Bartlett in the same light as before she had heard several women discuss him in damning terms the previous night at The Venus Club dinner. Bartlett appeared at the gym mid morning to try to lose some tension in the course of his appointed work out with Polyxena, who personally trained a few clients. Bartlett had been working out with her for the last six months, principally concentrating on sculpting his lean frame. He'd never had a personal trainer before and admitted to himself at least that it was partially Polyxena's flaxen haired beauty and shapely form that had induced him to put himself in her hands.

That day she upped all his reps and multiplied all his most brutal lifts. She seemed to enjoy his groans of protest when he complained and merely insisted with her calm, catlike smile, that it was good for him and he would surely feel the benefits if he followed her prescribed routines to the letter. Halfway through the workout, she let drop the reason for her sternness that day, saying to him as he executed pushups with her lushly distributed hundred and thirty pound bulk seated on his back, "They were talking about you at the dinner last night."

"What dinner?"

"The one all we ladies of the scene were invited to last night. The Venus Club."

"I didn't know."

"Your wives were there."

"Together?"

"Oh yes, and others you had offended besides."

"...offended?" he panted, finally lowering himself to the floor and waiting for her to dismount him, which she did in the laziest manner imaginable. He scrambled to his feet and she looked up at him with a mocking smile.

"You're a cross bear, aren't you? They all seemed to say so."

"Really!" he huffed, dashing the perspiration from his eyes and running his hands through his short straight black hair.

"Even that delicious young college girl who *isn't* one of your wives."

"You mean Amanda was talking about me, too?"

"She was asked to recount an incident and did so."

Ambrose felt his face grow even warmer.

"It made me feel glad to think that I would have charge of you today," said Polyxena, consulting her chart of exercises for him. "I think we'll switch over to the pool now. You could use some cooling off and I want to work on your butterfly."

She assigned him twenty laps of crawls first, pacing up and down the pool, lovely as always in her white wrap cotton spa dress. Her legs were bare and beautiful, and her full bottom thrust up jauntily by her white platform clogs. She corrected his strokes severely, but with a crooked, naughty smile, to communicate feminist scorn at his bad reputation with female submissives. He cooled off and noticed. He especially noticed how shapely Polyxena's bottom looked, clad in only thin bikinis under the dress. Ambrose wondered why the smart gym owner didn't shop more in his store. She had the body to wear good clothes to advantage. Doubtless she was a smart spender, this shrewd businesswoman, he reflected. Well, he didn't mind her giving him a hard work out, but wasn't tempted to go sub to Polyxena. He had heard she was an ex-dom from Holland before she bought the Random Point gym. He was sure she'd look extraordinarily good in leather or latex, but he wasn't about to give it up to a woman. But if she were of a mind to go submissive to *him*, he could quickly become interested in Polyxena. Her bottom was magnificent and she had the look of a young Maria Schell. She was altogether a divine young woman, whose physical perfections were somehow enhanced by the image of the wealthy and successful entrepreneur she embodied. Here was a lady who was his peer, almost his female counterpart. Ambrose wondered as he stroked up and down the pool whether she was actually flirting with him today.

Chapter Eight

A Surprising Proposition

Michael Flagg crossed paths with his ex-lover Jane Eliot the next afternoon. They ran into each other in the lobby of the gym, each having completed a workout, freshly showered and dressed in summer clothes. Jane had a day off from work at the Gay and Lesbian Community Services Center and was spending it entertaining herself. Lissome yet curvaceous in her beige cotton circle skirt dress, her legs bare and her pretty feet thrust into brown clogs, the thirty something brunette had the peach blossom complexion of a coed.

"Jane has no vices and takes very good care of herself," Michael thought approvingly, exchanging light hugs with the lovely woman he had jilted seven years before in order to give rein to his sexually dominant impulses with the willing women of Random Point.

Jane looked up at Michael, who was still every bit the Celtic warrior god at forty, with shoulders, chest and waist off the cover of a bodice ripper. The bracing sight of Michael Flagg in a tee shirt and levis on a hot summer day suddenly awakened the slumbering heterosexual in Jane Eliot and she paused with her hand on his arm.

"You look like you're leaving," she said, "me too. Let me take you to lunch."

"Really?" he smiled, his blue eyes darting across her face searchingly.

"Don't you want to hear what everyone talked about at dinner last night?" Jane asked.

"You'd tell me?" he held the door open for her and they emerged into the sun dappled parking lot.

"Why not?" Jane laughed, looking very pretty with her dark hair pulled back on the nape of her neck in a tortoise shell barrette, with soft bangs falling over her brow. She wore and needed no make up, so rosy and velvety was her complexion. She was of medium height, with regular, pleasing features and brown eyes fringed with thick, dark lashes. Her mouth was especially inviting as was her graceful throat.

"You look good today, ex-girlfriend," Michael said candidly, handing her into the passenger side of his late model SUV. "Where should we go?"

"The Cottage Inn," said Jane.

"Nice!" Michael said and proceeded to drive them to a small four star B&B that had recently opened off the road between Woodbridge and Random Point. In a very few minutes they were being ushered into a wood paneled dining room where several tables and booths were filled with summer trade. After placing their orders for iced tea and sandwiches, Michael smiled lazily at her, inwardly rejoicing at her good natured acceptance of the way in which their lives had diverged upon moving to Random Point.

"Well, none of them could stop talking about you. It was Michael Flagg this and Michael Flagg that all night long. Did you know that all the women in this town are in love with you?"

"Stop!" Michael grinned.

"I'm serious," said Jane, her eyes sparkling with flirtation. "And it brought back memories."

"I hope there were some nice ones," he said. "It seemed like we both worked too hard and played too little when we lived in Boston."

"We didn't play at all. Because I was an uptight bitch."

"You *were* a bit of a feminazi back then."

"Is that why you never ever tried to get me into the scene?"

"Yes. I was afraid of you."

"You weren't afraid to sodomize me."

"Jane, you remember that?" Michael was frankly amazed at the turn of the conversation and tried to dismiss the mad idea that she seemed to be almost coming on to him.

"How could I forget it? You did it all the time. I realize now that's what you did to get your BDSM fix instead of spanking me."

"I'm sorry," he said ruefully.

"Don't be sorry, I liked it! In fact, I kind of miss it," she admitted. "Not sodomy necessarily, though that was pretty hot, but sex with a big, strong, muscular man." She looked at him meaningfully.

Michael realized what was happening with some amazement. Jane Eliot was making a pass at him.

"But, you *are* happy with Marnie, right?" Michael said, earnestly trying to understand his former fiancée's objective at this instant.

"I am!" Jane asserted, the twinkle still in her soft brown eyes. "But the way those women were talking about you last night suddenly enlightened me to the fact that you are hot to an epic degree, which I never fully grasped before. They honestly made me regret I had never let you spank me. Because that would have been great foreplay for us and then the sex might have been even better."

"Jane are you thinking of being unfaithful to Marnie, *with me?*" Michael asked bluntly.

"Is that an option?" Jane replied brightly, as their daintily arranged platters arrived.

Michael put in an order for a bottle of red wine.

"Let me think about that," pondered Michael, as he regarded the young woman across the booth. He had jilted her and she had accepted the insult with extraordinary grace and philosophical humility. She had stayed in Random Point, opted for an interim job with Hugo Sands at his antiques shop and under his tutelage, had learned how to dress, wear heels, take a spanking and be seductive. Oddly enough, without being anything more than bi-curious, she had wound up the pampered significant other of the heiress Marnie Price, a tall, stunning, blonde girl jock who liked to drink beer, go to hockey games and make love to other women. Jane labored as a social worker during the week, counseling and assisting disenfranchised women, teen runaways, troubled gays and the gender conflicted. But she went home to an Architectural Digest-profiled house on the cliff, richly decorated by her lover, Marnie Price. Michael had assumed that Jane had gone over to the other side for good.

"Jane, you shouldn't tempt me. You know I'm married with a brat now," he said casually.

"I know that you are more madly in love with Marguerite than ever. It shows in your face whenever you're together. And the baby is a prodigy of beauty. But damn it, Michael, when was the last time I asked you for anything? You owe me one just for the magnificent way in which I handled you throwing me over."

"Well, let's think about it while we drink a glass of wine," said Michael with happy resignation. She had very neatly stated her case, levering just the right amount of guilt against the feeble crisis of conscience he was experiencing on contemplating cheating on his wife.

They both ate lightly and sipped their wine slowly, staring at each other over the table.

"I like that dress," said Michael, his eyes going from the well rounded outline of her bosom down to her slim waist, girded by a thick brown belt. "You never used to wear dresses when we were going out. Did you?"

"Didn't you ever want to spank me for that?" she asked merrily.

"Honestly, I did hate those shapeless jogging suits," he replied.

"And didn't you also want to spank me when I went on and on about women's issues, as though you, as a metropolitan police detective were unaware of them?"

"I agreed with you on the issues," he corrected her. "And I always valued you as a woman."

"I know. You were always respectful and never tried to exert your will over mine. Not even once."

"I don't think you've ever been to my house," he said.

"Oh that's right, you and Marguerite both kept your houses. How does that work?"

"We mainly live in her house in the village but we use my house when we want to make some noise without stressing out the nanny. It's worked out well."

"Is anyone there now?"

"No. Marguerite is at the bookstore today."

"I'd love to see your house."

Michael settled their bill and drove Jane to his house in the woods, a spacious eight room lodge with timbered ceilings and planked floors, a fireplace and a quantity of large, commodious wooden furniture, suitable to a big, tall man. Michael showed Jane around, stopping in the palm green, black and stainless steel kitchen.

"The kitchen that would have been mine," she mused, inspecting the ebony cabinets and marble countertops with admiration. "Very nice."

"Come on Jane, I've been in Marnie's kitchen, it's bigger than this whole house."

Jane just smiled at him.

"What kind of crazy mood are you in today?" he asked, still baffled by her sudden appetite for flirtation.

"I am in a crazy mood," she admitted, standing before him and reaching up to put her arms around his neck. The next instant she was pressing against him. Then feeling something between them, she dropped one hand down to his fly and squeezed the bar of iron that had begun to press against his jeans. "I used to own this," she said, tracing the outline of his cock up and down with her fingers. "It used to be all for me," she reminded him.

"Jane, you're being very naughty," he murmured, lifting her chin with one finger and kissing her lightly on her parted lips.

"Then spank me. I permit you to do so," she encouraged him, going so far as to turn around and bend over the countertop, presenting her full-skirted bottom to him. The next thing she knew, he had seized her by the wrist and pinned it her waist with one hand while pulling up her skirt with the other. This operation revealed her slim, oval cheeked bottom displayed to advantage in a pair of tight, sheer white nylon panties. Six smart slaps, administered to either cheek brought the pinkness to her white skin instantaneously. Jane caught her breath in a manner than indicated interest and excitement.

"Hugo used to spank me much harder than that," she informed him helpfully.

"Jane, stop being bad. You're confusing me," he ordered, administering six more spanks, this time harder. These made her gasp, but she didn't attempt to rise, and instead merely undulated her bottom at him provocatively.

"Doesn't it hurt?" he asked, rubbing her bottom through her nylon briefs.

"Mmmmm, a little," she murmured, wriggling as he caressed her.

The intervening seven years seemed to melt away and Michael wondered how he ever could have thought of abandoning this beautiful, passionate girl? Letting go of her wrist he pulled the panties down to the backs of her knees and regarded her bare, faintly reddened bottom with mounting excitement. She drummed on the shiny wooden floor with her clogs, seemingly impatient for the spanking to recommence.

"Why didn't you show me this side of you before?" he flared with irritation, spanking her vigorously six or seven times on each buttock.

"I didn't know it existed," she protested breathlessly, rocking with the smacks but not attempting to avoid them. Then Michael's fingers strayed between her thighs to brush against her moist, parted labia. Penetrating her with first one and then two fingertips, he discovered that she had become fully lubricated.

Normally, he would have taken her from behind, but there was something so piquant and unusual in this situation that he knew he had to see her face while he possessed her, just to make sure this was really happening, and the way she wanted it to. He turned her around right side up and lifted her up onto the countertop, yanking her panties all the way off. Jane undid the button on his jeans, pulled down his zipper and allowed his oversized erection to pop out of his fly like an obscene jack in the box.

"Oh my god, I didn't forget how big you were, but it's a still a shock after all this time," said Jane, stroking the flagpole she now confronted with her long, slim, nimble fingers. Then giving him one mischievous look, she took his breath away by dropping her head and pressing her lips to his mushroom cap. An instant later, she had taken him into her mouth and closed her lips around his shaft, feathering the back of it with the tip of her tongue.

The skin of his large, flawless, circumcised cock was as smooth as she remembered it, but she realized with a start that this was the *first* time she had ever tasted it. At that moment of acute surprise, Michael also realized he had never seen Jane's face from this angle before. The sensation felt so ticklishly novel coming from her that he knew he would ejaculate from sheer surprise if he let her go on with what she was doing a moment longer, especially as she had just begun to actually deep throat him. "Jane, what are you doing?" he let her go on for a few seconds more, then pulled her up. "You should let me do that to *you*," he said, taking her face between his hands and kissing her lips. She grinned, remembering how good he was at oral sex.

"Let that remain Marnie's province," she replied, watching with interest as he produced one of the Rough Rider condoms he still perpetually carried in his pocket and sheathed his cock.

"Don't bother putting that on. You owe me a baby too, don't you?" she casually asked, allowing him to push her back down on the counter while he positioned his penis at the entry to her velvety pink portal, now glistening with excitement.

"You're adorable," he said, not taking her last comment seriously, but delicately reaching down to spread her wide with his fingers to ease the entry of his cock, pausing on the way to press his thumb down on her pulsating clitoris gently but insistently. Her legs went up around his waist and her arms around his neck as she willingly accepted him inside her and felt him penetrate her inch by rigid inch.

"I really miss this!" Jane confessed as he rammed his rod home, first once and then repeatedly, rocking Jane and the table with every plunge. She wrapped her legs around his waist and her arms around his neck, so tightly that he was able to stand up with her in his arms without disengaging his cock from her pussy and carry her into his bedroom. There he pulled out just long enough to place her in the middle of the big oaken bed, in the all fours position, before getting up behind her and reinserting his penis into her vagina from behind. Now he was able to thrust in and out of her slick channel while holding her by the waist with a perfectly unobstructed view of her bare bottom undulating above his plunging cock. Wetting one finger in her own essence, he began to explore her tiny bottom hole, finally inserting it into her anus to the knuckle. Jane groaned and squeezed him two ways, his shaft with her pussy and his finger with her bottom, which brought her to the crest of a resounding climax and then over the edge. As Michael felt her come, he accelerated his penetration of her pussy to a dizzying velocity, until a minute or two later, he also expired in a blissful effusion of sperm.

After they had restored themselves to a semi decent state they tumbled on the bed together in each other's arms, drinking in each other's scent and caressing one another's face and waist, arms and thighs. Finally they simply lay drowsing in each other's arms, neither saying a word yet both wondering if this would or should ever happen again.

Chapter Nine

Further Entanglements

The next week was crowded with social activity for Amanda, who had made new friends at the Venus Club. Polyxena Guzman invited Amanda to a private supper at The Owl in Woodbridge one night after yoga at her gym. Amanda was fascinated by Polyxena and pressed her for stories about her years as a mistress in the Hague. Learning that Amanda was to depart for Europe in a few weeks, Polyxena furnished the names and numbers of scene friends in London, Amsterdam and Paris, should Amanda feel the urge to visit an old world dungeon. Amanda was intrigued but instinctively knew that Colby was not the right boyfriend with whom to foray into the world of black leather and clear latex. Colby liked a skirt to flip up or a pair of tight jeans to dust off, and whether a woman wore a five inch heel or a moc made no difference to him as long as her bosom was pretty and set off to ogling perfection in a clinging top. Not that he probably wouldn't enjoy strapping her down to a bondage bed but she would never dream of giving up that much submission to her pet jock.

Amanda found herself dividing most of her free time not to pre reading her course books for the upcoming semester, as she had planned, but between outings with Pamela and seemingly spontaneous encounters with Raphael Price that inevitably ended with their going to bed together. The art gallery owner seemed to have an uncanny sense of where Amanda would choose to have lunch or go for her afternoon break or evening stroll, and simply be there in time to invite her to spend some portion of the rest of the evening with him. And she was beginning to become quite comfortable in the circle of Raphael's wiry, muscular arms each night.

Several days after the Venus Club dinner, Pascal Robbins came bristling into the shop, hungry for another taste of Amanda while knowing he neither deserved or was likely to get one. She was dressed that morning in a sleeveless and full-skirted white and yellow cotton gingham sundress with a wide belt of the same material encircling her tiny waist. She wore white platform sandals with toe bows and ankle straps on her slender feet, the toes of which had been painted dark red to match her shiny red, short, well shaped fingernails. Today even her lipstick was dark red but her barest fringe of blonde hair was still as short as ever it could be and the fresh sight of it affronted Pascal Robbins' critical gaze. He looked like he wanted to spank her again.

Then the bell of the front door tinkled and Raphael came in.

Amanda had confided something of the awkward situation between herself and Pascal Robbins to her new lover, Raphael Price. Raphael knew Pascal well enough to feature a showing of his work at the opening of his gallery and like Amanda, Raphael knew that Pascal had a beautiful wife of his own. Therefore, Raphael was shocked when Amanda told him that Pascal had kissed her, omitting the spanking portion of the event. Amanda was, however, careful to stress how much she had formerly enjoyed working with Mr. Robbins and how willing she was to continue in a professional relationship with him.

"Something about me inflames his cool heart," said Amanda to Raphael with one of her quick insights. Raphael had promised himself to run sharp interference between the inappropriately amorous photographer and his new protégée if necessary and soon found an opportunity to execute this move with characteristic style.

"Mr. Robbins has been wanting to photograph me," Amanda explained to Raphael to break the sudden tension, "but we can't seem to think of a motif that will match my new short hair."

"If you don't mind getting up early," said Raphael to Pascal, "the light is perfect on my beach at about six am. And Amanda in a wet suit would kill."

Raphael's beach was a curving quarter mile of beige sand on the other side of the woods between his house and the ocean. Amanda's eyes opened wide with admiration of Raphael's suddenly inspired idea, visualizing a spread in Skin Two.

Pascal agreed to the proposed shoot immediately, delighted with the idea and happy to diffuse the obvious tension between himself and Amanda.

They met on the following morning on the beach, Raphael playing quiet chaperone with thermoses of hot coffee and fresh rolls to nibble on. The water was cold enough to make Amanda appreciate the wet suit as she posed in and out of the waves. During the shoot, Pascal obtained scores of beautiful shots of Amanda in glistening, skin tight black rubber and completely forgot the momentary pique he had felt at Raphael for interposing his ridiculously handsome person between himself and the girl.

"He certainly has a way of smoothing out problems," Amanda observed to herself, both admiring and aspiring to possess such easy finesse.

After the shoot, while Amanda was showering upstairs in his house, Raphael began preparing breakfast for two in classic metro-sexual style, planning to offer his summer goddess fresh ground espresso with steamed milk along with macadamia nut pancakes, strawberries and heavy cream.

Amanda was luxuriating in the artfully designed and tiled master shower, with its six shower heads drenching her from above and either side with streams of varying intensity and texture. Having already put in several hours of work that morning (albeit while splashing in the waves of the chilly Atlantic on that balmy day) she felt entitled to surrender herself to the sensuality of a hydro erotic orgasm and positioned her lightly fleeced blonde pubic mound opposite one of the gushing spouts while another hit her around mid bottom from behind. She was just beginning to climb towards a tingling climax when she heard her phone's ring tone, the first sixteen notes of *For Whom The Bell Tolls* by Metallica. As she had been expecting a call from Colby, Amanda aborted mission climax and stepped out of the shower box to pick her phone up off the closest vanity.

"Hi!" she said to Colby, recognizing his number and grabbing a terry robe to wrap herself in.

"Hey Babe!" her lover greeted her enthusiastically, in a deep voice, typically raspy from yelling at sports screens in bars. "You'll never guess where I am."

"Really? Where?" she asked, her heart jumping a little.

"I'm downstairs in front of your front door."

"What?" Now her heart fell through the planked wooden floor under her bare feet.

"I got done with all my bookkeeping work for my parents early so I came back," he explained merrily. "Come let me in."

"That's great, Colby. But I'm not at home," Amanda said, trying to sound calm and casual. "I've been doing a shoot at the beach. But I'm done now. Wait for me where you are and I'll be there in about ten minutes."

Amanda rang off before Colby could say another word and jumped into her clothes as fast as she could. Then she flew downstairs and into the kitchen, looking at Raphael's beautiful repast with a guilty and stricken expression.

"My boyfriend's returned unexpectedly. He's waiting at Hugo's for me. I have to run. And… I can't see you anymore!" Amanda cried, pausing to throw her arms around Raphael's neck and hug him warmly. Then she pressed her lips against his deeply before pulling away. "You won't be mad at me, will you?"

"No, Amanda, of course, I won't. I'll adore you until the end of time and I'll always be your friend," he promised, kissing both her hands before letting her go.

Amanda arrived home five minutes later, still dewy from her shower, and fresh as the morning in her favorite summer outfit of khaki capris, a white shirt and cork platform sandals. Colby was slightly taken aback by the radical appearance of her shorn head, adorned by the shortest ash blonde fringe. But his keen eye also noticed the all over blush that seemed to suffuse her fair face and throat at the sight of him. He took her in his arms, kissed her lips and buried his face in her smooth, fragrant shoulder, rapturously breathing in the scent of Amanda. His hand went up to the back of her head to cradle then ruffle its fine, pale tresses. Colby was dressed in cargo shorts and a white t-shirt, his feet thrust into walking sandals and the rucksack at his feet still tagged with the initials of Logan airport.

"Babe, your hair is shorter than mine," he marveled, pulling away to look at her with a grin. "It's cute, though."

Amanda could see he was not lying, for in point of fact, her bold new haircut was very becoming to a girl with a head as remarkably beautiful as Amanda's. Her wide eyes, wide mouth, high cheek bones, straight nose and shapely chin made this shortest of all haircuts, short of a buzz, possible to carry off with classically feminine charm. Also, her breasts looked like ripe summer fruit straining against the thin white cotton button down shirt. "But why are you so red?" he asked her, looking her up and down while holding her by the shoulders.

"I'm just overwhelmed at seeing you so unexpectedly," she replied, letting them into the house and looking around quickly in case Raphael had left some incriminating item behind him on his last visit.

"Should I have called you from the airport?" he demanded, suddenly realizing how presumptuous he had been in simply showing up, which behavior was based only on the theory that Amanda loved him.

"Well, yes, but it worked out fine," she smiled, leading him upstairs to her bedroom to install him there.

"Hugo and Laura won't be back until the week we leave for Europe," said Amanda. "You can stay here with me every night."

"If you get sick of me I can spend some time with my buds in Boston," said Colby, gratified at the warmth of her reception.

"I won't. Oh Colby, I'm so happy that you're here! You can help with some of the New Rod Quarterly work Hugo gave me."

"Let me handle the female personal ads," he suggested. Amanda ignored this and bundled him off to the shower after his long plane ride.

Naturally, the perspicacious Anthony Newton was well aware of his leading lady's proclivity for spanking, having heard from Susan, who knew Phoebe's photographer husband Pascal Robbins pretty well, that his lovely wife, who sang and acted dazzlingly enough to have landed the role of Lily Vanessi in Newton's summer revival of *Kiss Me*

Kate, was *into it* and always had been. This was one of the reasons the composer had been interested in casting the petite beauty in this particular play with its exuberant spanking scene. And he also had fun matching her up with the Petruchio he thought most likely to get the spanking right and thus ignite Phoebe's ardor for her role to an even higher degree. The actor he had chosen, Baldwin Rosemead, was a tall, broad shouldered, bullet-headed, blue-eyed Englishman, 32 year old, with a booming laugh and big hands. He would do very nicely.

As the production was being filmed for future broadcast, the company rehearsed for weeks. This allowed for the famous spanking scene to be practiced again and again, affording Newton numerous opportunities to observe Phoebe being spanked.

One night, after rehearsal, when everyone but Anthony and Phoebe had gone home, they had decided to run through Kate's *"I Am Ashamed That Women Are So Simple"* song, with Anthony at the piano. Phoebe was clad in a white knit top and a rose cotton a-line wrap skirt, her tiny feet in sage green platform sandals that exposed doll toes painted sand pink. Her mid length chestnut brown hair clustered on her shoulders framed her charming face. She was small but mighty, with a rich, contralto voice and the shape of a miniature goddess. Anthony liked petite woman. His Susan was very small. But Phoebe was even shorter than Susan, by several inches and somewhat rounder. Phoebe's bottom looked lusciously plump under her little skirts and dresses. Anthony didn't think he'd ever seen her in jeans, which rather endeared her to him.

They finished the song and Anthony gave Phoebe a present for good luck. It was a gold charm bracelet, already fringed by an acorn, a pineapple, a teakettle, a camera, a heart and a high heel. But even as she was admiring the gift he had clasped on her wrist, he began to critique her comportment during the rehearsal.

"Really, Phoebe, I would think you could react a little more indignantly to the spanking. It almost seemed as though you were enjoying it," said Newton, poker faced. Phoebe immediately flushed the color of her skirt.

"Should I... struggle?" she asked tentatively.

"Of course you should. The character of Lily Vanessi does not get treated like this."

"I assumed that it was not the first time Fred had spanked her," said Phoebe.

"Perhaps not, but Lily would remain steadfastly indignant, I think."

"Baldwin Rosemead is terrifying large. I go all limp like a kitten getting picked up by the scruff of its neck."

"Phoebe, you're so submissive," Anthony teased her. "That's a real turn on to me. Would you go all limp for me?"

"God yes!" she cried, her eyes shining at him.

"You're so naughty. What about your husband? He looks pretty strict."

Phoebe shrugged. "Maybe I know something about him that would surprise him into shutting the hell up," said she.

"What do you know? Dish!"

"It has to do with Amanda Sands, that pretty coed who does a bit of modeling on the side. He's photographed her a few times. He fancies turning her into one of his book creatures. He wouldn't care if she left Harvard to go pose for silly pictures for him. Well, she revealed to us girls the other night at The Venus Club, that my Pascal inappropriately spanked her. He was piqued because she had cut her beautiful hair off."

"What made him even think of spanking her, I wonder?" mused Newton, aware that Pascal Robbins was not in the scene.

"Because I've turned a naturally bossy, chauvinistic male into a bedroom dom. But his main character flaw is that he doesn't leave it in the bedroom. Here we have a case of him knowing a girl is a spankee by preference, and him using this knowledge to take an inexcusable liberty with her for reasons I don't fully understand but which I suspect involves a sexual outcome."

"Shocking," commiserated Newton, his heart leaping at the possibilities of consoling the wronged wife.

"Hope Lawrence advised me to look at the entire situation as money in the bank," she said, gazing deeply into his eyes with a naughty smile in her own.

Chapter Ten

Colby and Amanda Take Pamela in Hand

"You were smart to come back," Hope Lawrence told Colby Hodge the following morning at the polished wooden counter of the coffee bar at Marguerite Alexander's bookshop as she prepared a breakfast of cappuccinos and croissants for him to take back to Amanda, who was just opening up the antiques shop across the street that temperate June morning. Colby asked her why she thought so. "Because she's been besieged," Hope replied.

"Guys are after her?" Colby asked the stunning blonde barista as he watched her arrange the carton of food. Hope just looked at him. "I suppose she's been sampling?" he asked.

Hope shrugged with a smile.

He put down some cash for the snacks and said, "She's such a little slut, but what can I do? I'm lucky to have her on any terms and she knows it."

"That's a very proper attitude," Hope commended him. "So was coming back. You're the one she's been missing."

Colby reached out for her delicate hand and kissed it before departing with a pleasant sensation of having been completely accepted into the clique of players so comfortably ensconced in Random Point.

He found Amanda dressed in a white sleeveless blouse, a cherry red cotton circle skirt and navy espadrilles turning on lights in the main room of the shop. As he laid out their food and drink on one of the glass counters, under which cameos rested in blue velvet drawers, she slipped a thick, unabridged paperback version of Don Quixote into his hands, saying, "Will you read this aloud to me this summer? I want to take a class in the Spanish version of it next semester and I think it will help to read it in English first."

"Sure," said Colby, for he had always wanted to read it himself.

After they ate their little meal, Colby began to read to her and Amanda curled up in one of the large rocking chairs for sale on the floor to listen, supremely happy at the current arrangement. Now she no longer had to be alone in the shop all day or alone in her bed at night. She had her constant companion to walk with her, swim with her, watch old movies, cook, eat and make love. She had the proper partner to go out on dates with in company with the other scene couples in the village. Colby and she would be welcome at Hope and David's cottage for evening barbeques and scrabble games, at Michael's bar for dancing and darts, at Anthony and Susan's for swimming and billiards.

The only people Amanda thought it prudent to keep Colby well away from was Ambrose Bartlett, Raphael Price and Pascal Robbins, the three local men who still wanted her. Raphael would not be problematical. He was supremely diplomatic and since he'd enjoyed her favors for a couple of days running, no doubt pleasantly sated and highly unlikely to press for additional favors now that he knew her boyfriend was in town. She would inform Pamela no later than that very morning that Colby had returned and trusted her friend would casually pass the information onto her husband, possibly with relish.

Pamela knew that Ambrose admired Amanda greatly and perhaps on some cynical level was enjoying the fact that Amanda would always be out of his reach from now on, in spite of the liberties he had once taken with her. At this point, Pamela was only aware of the session given in trade for the shooting location around Christmas of the previous year and not the subsequent encounter that had provided Amanda with the means with which to lushly augment her month abroad budget. But she still suspected her husband of lusting wildly after the leggy blonde Harvard coed and liked the idea of him knowing that Amanda's muscular and handsome young boyfriend would be in attendance on her friend for the rest of the summer.

Amanda did think that Pascal Robbins would be sure to clash with Colby sooner or later if they met. And almost the moment that this thought occurred to her, the handsome photographer sauntered into the shop calling her name. Cool and immaculate in a summer suit and white shirt, and with his usual cameras slung around his neck, Robbins looked like a GQ ad, which immediately put Colby's muscular back up. The soon to be Harvard sophomore eyed the sophisticated older man with deep suspicion as Amanda introduced them, blushing hard as she did.

"So, I've got the photos we took on the beach. Thought you might like to see them," Pascal said to Amanda, after shaking Colby's hand affably. Colby said, "Hi," but not warmly, instantly sensing a dangerous rival. Amanda wasn't flushed to the crown of her pixie cut for no reason. Pascal handed Amanda a CD, which she slipped into a laptop that was open on the counter. She and Colby had planned to use this device to finalize the hotel bookings for their upcoming trip later in the afternoon.

Amanda opened the disc and dozens of small photo icons popped up before them. Pascal leaned over and quickly set the shots up in slide show format and all three of them began to view the photos Pascal had taken of Amanda in the wetsuit, in and out of the water on Raphael Price's beach the previous day. Many of the photos were stunning, the new haircut revealing Amanda's fine bone structure and drawing the attention to her magnetic blue eyes, which appeared to look a bit too dreamily back into the camera for Colby's satisfaction. It bothered him that Amanda should gaze at Pascal Robbins with such provocative and alluring expressions on her face. Then there was Amanda's magnificent body in the skin-tight wet suit. The full bosom, tiny waist, womanly hips, jutting bottom and long, strong, elegantly turned legs caught the eye even before one began to focus on the striking face above.

"You see," said Pascal, "I told you you could take editorial photos."

Amanda was well pleased with the results of the shoot.

"I could have wrung your neck for cutting your hair," continued Pascal, "but you were smart to do it. It makes your features pop and gives you the edginess you needed."

Colby wished Amanda had introduced him as her boyfriend. She'd just said, "My friend, Colby."

"Do you like them?" Amanda asked Colby.

"They're fantastic," her lover admitted candidly.

"Colby doesn't think I should devote much more time to modeling," Amanda told Pascal, "and I think he may be right."

Colby beamed at Amanda.

"Nonsense," growled Pascal; "You won't be a teenager forever. Work it while you've got it."

"With all due respect," said Colby, "getting into Harvard wasn't easy. Amanda can't be running off to photo shoots every other day. She has to study."

"I can't be a conscientious student and a full time model at the same time," said Amanda. "A little shoot now and then while I'm on vacation or a local gig on the weekend is fine, but modeling is uncomfortable and inconvenient and I like being comfortable and cozy."

Colby was proud of Amanda and all of his potential hostility against the photographer melted away.

Pascal sighed, "I can't argue with anything you've said. But I still want to shoot you some more."

Robbins departed on this agreeable note and Amanda and Colby took one more look at the photos from the beach.

"Babe, your body rocks," Colby said, putting his arms around her waist from behind and nuzzling her neck as his newest erection pressed through his khaki shorts and her skirt and panties to nestle against her bottom.

"That man wants me," Amanda told him, pushing back against him until his rod was between her cheeks through their clothes.

"But, he hasn't had you, right?"

"No."

"That's why he wants to keep shooting you, to get another chance," Colby wisely concluded, deftly pushing up Amanda's skirt and now pressing his manhood against her white cotton bikinis.

"Yes, and he has the prettiest wife imaginable," Amanda said, rocking back against him. "And she's into spanking too."

"Really?"

"I met her last week at The Venus Club dinner. I offered her and all the other ladies there the use of your lap if they ever wanted to get spanked by a hunky young Harvard jock."

"You... what?" Colby turned her around to look into her merry blue eyes.

"Honestly, I did. This village is full of submissive beauties. But I don't know if any of them have ever been topped by a nineteen year old. Maybe Marguerite has. She's done everything. And maybe Susan Ross, because she's still so young herself. But the rest are with men in their thirties and forties."

"Amanda, you little tease," said Colby, not believing a word she said, but using her impertinent suggestion as an excuse to turn her under his arm while bending her over the counter. Pushing up her skirt again, he laid ten smacks across her white cotton panties with the palm of his big hand. Squealing and shifting her hips, Amanda presented an adorable target area, which he continued to spank with a lazy rhythm until the tinkling of the bell on the outer door, announcing a new visitor to the shop caused them to guiltily spring apart and hastily set themselves to rights.

The visitor was Pamela, fresh and cool in a pale, pearly pink, raw silk a-line v-neck sheath and four inch heeled pearl gray t-straps. She carried an envelope purse in the same gray leather under her arm and the sunglasses she removed upon entering the shop were rose-toned. Her shiny, jet-black bob framed her beautiful oval face to perfection and she looked much more like 21 than 28 that summer afternoon.

"Pamela, this is my boyfriend Colby," said Amanda, "I don't think you've ever met."

Colby and Pamela said, "Hi" to each other and shook hands, each giving the other a thorough head to toe scan with a steadily widening smile.

115

"So you're the one who triumphed over all the rest," said Pamela, surveying the good looking, broad shouldered, six foot two blond boy admiringly. "I can see why now."

"Yes, yes, he's very cute, but I'd rather he not know that," said Amanda to her friend.

"Amanda," said Pamela, reluctantly drawing her eyes away from admiring Colby's long, muscular torso under the tucked out shirt and cargo shorts, "can you walk in a show at the store on Saturday?"

"What, does that old geezer who owns it want another crack at Amanda?" Colby asked without regard for discretion.

"Colby please," cried Amanda, in shock, "you're talking about Pamela's husband!"

"Oh my god, you're married to that relic?" Colby gasped.

"Yes," said Pamela good-naturedly.

"Why would you want Amanda anywhere near the store? You know she was his 'ho last year, right?"

"Colby!" Amanda cried again, stricken with horror at this admission. It was the last little bit of the story that Pamela didn't know, until that moment. "How could you say such things?" Amanda said, flushing pink instantly.

"Really?" Pamela looked at Amanda. "Ambrose paid you for sex?" Amanda dropped her eyes and nodded, "Just once."

"Don't feel badly," said Pamela, touching Amanda's shoulder gently with her perfectly manicured natural colored fingertips. "Men like that are hard to resist when they start throwing money at you."

"He wanted to prove to me he was halfway human after that awful scene we had when he spanked me to tears," Amanda said in Bartlett's defense, "and it was before you were married."

"But not before you started dating me, you little slut," Colby snorted.

"Oh shut up, you crass chowder head!" Amanda stamped her foot at him. Pamela smiled, unaccountably untroubled that her husband had tasted the sweetness of Amanda's eighteen-year-old body. Ambrose Bartlett was a piece of work that needed careful management, while Amanda Sands was her new best friend. Pamela wished nothing to disturb the new sense of comfort and satisfaction she had recently found in obtaining a genuinely close girl friend.

"It's all right, Amanda," Pamela reiterated. "Ambrose is making all of his bad behavior up to me this summer. I've been relieved of duty at the boutique and he's building me a stunning studio to work in at the store. I'm going to be 100% free to design clothes and market my line from now on. So everything is quite all right."

Amanda hugged Pamela with her arms around the brunette's slim waist. Colby thought they made an adorable picture and was glad a second later that his shorts were so baggy.

"Pamela I was just telling this Neanderthal that I offered his services to all the ladies at the Venus Club the other night and he didn't believe me."

"Oh, she did," Pamela confirmed.

"I don't understand," he laughed. "But it sounds incredibly hot."

"Who was at the dinner who might be made the better for an over the knee encounter with a jock?" Amanda wondered.

"Let's draw up a list," suggested Pamela with an unusual degree of merriment, producing a pen and tiny, gold chased note book from her flat purse and placing them on the countertop where Amanda had been thrust face down and spanked by not only Colby that day but Pascal Robbins the previous week. Pamela said the names out loud as she wrote, "Marguerite Flagg, Susan Ross, Allison Albrecht, Paula Taylor, Phoebe Robbins, Polyxena Guzman, Damaris Random, Jane Eliot, Hope Lawrence and me, Pamela Bartlett."

"Let's take them one by one, starting with Marguerite," said Amanda academically, then turning to Colby and explaining, "that gorgeous redhead with the hourglass body who owns the bookstore."

"She writes those great spanking novels," said Colby, "I'd never have the nerve to approach someone like her."

"We'll set it up for you," said Amanda confidently.

"But maybe not with Marguerite," said Pamela with an indulgent smile, "she recently married the love of her life and had a baby."

"Maybe not this year. But let's not rule it out," said Amanda helpfully.

Colby felt mercilessly teased and was enjoyed it immensely. Looking at this robust and handsome youth, Pamela herself felt happy, young and free. And the longer she gazed at Colby, the more charmed with him she became.

"Have you really thought this through?" she asked Amanda. "I mean, here you have this fresh and studly boy to call your own, you've barely used him at all and now you're proposing to throw other ladies at him? Is that wise, Amanda?"

"It's probably idiotic, but what do I know? I'm young," Amanda gaily replied. "Now what about Susan Ross?"

"Oh, she'd do it on a dare, she's a little slut," said Pamela.

"Would you like to spank Susan?" Amanda asked Colby.

"Didn't you tell me she belongs to someone big?" Colby asked.

"Anthony Newton," Amanda replied, "but he doesn't own her."

"No, Mr. Newton gives her free rein," Pamela corroborated.

"So Susan is a distinct possibility," said Amanda, putting a check next to Susan's name. "What about Allison Albrecht?"

"She's just gotten engaged to Freddie Johanson. I don't think she's a good candidate," Pamela replied.

"Paula Taylor?"

"She's a recent newlywed too," said Pamela, feeling a slight pang, as Paula's husband Sloan was her own former lover, a fine young man she had neglected, mistreated and finally lost through her own contrariness.

"Phoebe Robbins?" Amanda asked.

"Ah, Phoebe..." Pamela mused.

"The wife of that photographer who shot me yesterday," Amanda explained to Colby. "She's in the scene, her husband isn't. She's going to star in that production of *Kiss Me Kate* that Anthony Newton is directing this summer."

"She is in the scene, but I don't think anyone but her husband has ever had her over his knee. You don't have the time to do the ground work necessary to interest her in you right now," Pamela explained to Colby. "But perhaps when you return to Random Point in August."

"I'll put a half check next to her name and we'll come back to her later in the summer," said Amanda, "now what about Polyxera Guzman? The owner of the gym and spa."

"The blonde with the bod who's always in the pool?" Colby asked, as he had seen the Dutch gym owner doing laps the last time he'd visited the Random Point club and had paused to watch for a moment or two.

"That's the one," said Amanda. "and she admitted at the dinner the other night that she has no man at the moment."

"Yes, but that kind of woman, you don't just play with," Pamela pointed out. "She's the type who uses spanking for foreplay alone. So your man would have to satisfy her afterwards."

"In that case, no check," said Amanda firmly. A playful spanking scene was one thing, but the thought of Colby making love to a beautiful older woman was quite another. Colby sighed.

"Damaris Random?" asked Amanda.

"Never, she's completely committed to William," Pamela said with certainty. She knew her petite Puerto Rican pistol of a partner well enough to vouch for her loyalty to her husband. "She was a little wild in her past and is trying to behave beautifully now," Pamela explained to Colby. "But I'm sure she would find you very hot."

"Jane Eliot?" Amanda asked.

"I don't believe I know her well enough to say," Pamela mused. "She used to be engaged to Michael Flagg, but she's been Marnie Price's girlfriend for years."

"If she used to date Michael and she's been with a girl all this time, she may be longing for a man's hand by now," said Amanda.

"I just don't think you have enough time before you leave for Europe to cultivate a female conundrum like Jane Eliot," Pamela observed. "But as you heard at the dinner, Hugo was the one who introduced her to the scene so I think she'd be well disposed towards becoming friends with his daughter."

"We'll put a half check next to Jane's name then," said Amanda. "Now what about Hope Spencer Lawrence?"

Colby was more interested in this prospect then the rest because he had already spoken to Hope on several occasions, spent a little time

119

around her, found her spectacularly attractive and after their conversation that morning, knew her to be his friend.

"Oh, sure, but you'd have to pay her," said Pamela confidently. Everyone knew that Hope sessioned now and then but that she was still passionately in love with her husband.

"Well, I guess that just leaves you, Pamela," said Amanda, eyeing her brunette friend thoughtfully.

Pamela looked at her and laughed, "Me?"

"Why not?" said Amanda. "You're a bad girl."

"You think I'd let a schoolboy spank me?" Pamela pretended haughtiness but found it impossible not to smile at the two tall, fair-haired, blue-eyed children who seemed to be suggesting that she allow them to make her their plaything.

"Why not?" persisted Amanda, "you're wayward and Colby is sober."

"Of course I am, it's only eleven a.m.," Colby backed Amanda up helpfully.

"What in the world do you mean, I'm wayward?" Pamela demanded.

"Pamela has an eating disorder and body dysmorphia," Amanda explained to Colby.

"I do not!" the dress designer protested weakly.

"How many times have you weighed yourself today?" Amanda demanded.

Pamela hesitated a moment before admitting, "…Twice."

"She's weighed herself twice and it's not even noon," Amanda noted. "And how much did you weigh?"

"One thirteen," Pamela said, a delicate blush creeping over her cheeks.

"You see what I mean?" Amanda asked Colby, who knew nothing of what women weighed but who nodded intelligently.

"Damn it, Amanda, I've gained three pounds in ten days, what more do you want from me?" Pamela cried. "If I get any fatter I won't be able to fit in any of my clothes."

"You see, she thinks that's fat," Amanda pointed out to Colby. "What have you eaten today?" Amanda demanded remorselessly.

"I had some coffee," admitted Pamela with a sigh.

"We need to feed this skinny bitch and get her up to at least 115 by the end of the summer," Amanda told her boyfriend. "You're meeting us for lunch at The Ball and Feather," she continued to Pamela. "I'm ordering for you and if you don't eat it all, Colby's going to spank you," Amanda decided bluntly, looking at Pamela over folded arms.

"You're mad," Pamela told Amanda, with a lightness of heart she was experiencing for the first time in years. Was she really going to let these two perverse babies top her? They reminded her of Logan and Kathy, two cousins who had been her playmates in third grade. Kathy had a playhouse in her backyard and in it, she and her little boy cousin Logan had played mommy and daddy with Pamela, spanking her according to their whim the entire summer. And Pamela had adored them for it.

"What time?" she added, turning to leave them.

"One p.m.," Amanda told her briskly. Pamela gave Colby a slightly mischievous wink as she strode out the door in her elegant heels.

"What just happened?" Colby asked Amanda with a pounding heart. "Did that stunning girl just say that I could spank her?"

"Of course she did," Amanda assured him serenely. "She's going to be our plaything. You saw how the thought made her smile. It sliced years off her age."

Chapter Eleven

Pamela's Playmates

Amanda hung up the out to lunch sign at one and she and Colby quickly walked across the tiny village to the Ball and Feather Inn, where they encountered Anthony Newton and Susan Ross just finishing their lunch in the club room. Newton motioned them over to their booth and they sat down with the composer and his girlfriend.

"Pamela's meeting us for lunch," Amanda confided, "and if she doesn't clean her plate, Colby's going to spank her."

"I approve of that," said Newton, "that girl's weight scares me."

"Does she really starve herself to stay that way?" Susan asked.

"Not anymore," said Amanda confidently. "I'm in the process of reorienting her. And Colby's going to help me."

Susan looked at Colby with interest.

"You're right, Amanda, Pamela needs attention," Susan said, smiling dreamily at Colby. Big, tall boys into spanking were very charming to her and she liked the way Amanda's sweetheart held himself modestly back in deference to Amanda and herself.

"Let me get this straight," Newton said, his dark eyes alight with amusement as he checked the doorway to make sure Pamela had not yet arrived, "you two got Pamela Bartlett to consent to let you double top her?"

Now Colby blinked, not expecting such blunt B&D phraseology to fall so lightly from the lips of a celebrity.

"Yes," said Amanda, "isn't it amazing? Aren't I a natural? I won't even be nineteen for two more months and I'm bossing around a beautiful twenty-eight-year-old!"

"The apple doesn't fall far from the tree," Susan observed correctly.

"You're right," Amanda laughed, "it's in my blood so I shouldn't claim any special abilities."

"Pamela used to have a huge crush on Hugo," added Susan. "She must have transferred it to you. I've never known her to really warm up to another girl before."

"What do you think we should do with her?" Amanda asked candidly as a waitress cleared the table and brought menus. Anthony and Susan were getting up to leave. Susan, who was spending her weekends and vacation days in Random Point that summer was returning to New York that evening to finish out the work week at the advertising agency where she worked as an illustrator. Newton was eager to return to the house to continue with the *Kiss Me Kate* rehearsals.

"Why don't you use my consulting room?" Newton suggested casually as he signed his guest check. "I mean for when you devastate Pamela Bartlett."

"Consulting room?" Amanda said, surprised.

"Examining room too," said Susan. "Fully equipped with everything. Including a doctor's coat and a nurse's uniform."

Colby's eyes widened. Amanda's wide, full mouth curved into an extremely naughty smile. "You mean..." she couldn't quite put her thoughts into words acceptable for a dining room.

"Here you go," said Newton, flipping a small gold key into the air for Amanda to catch. "It's the suite at the third floor top of the back stairs. Check it out first and see if it suits you." The composer shook Colby's hand and wished him luck with a grin, then strode out. Amanda caught Susan's hand as she turned to follow him.

"Why is he spoiling me so?" Amanda demanded, delighted by the loan of a private playroom in which to enact the most voluptuous fantasy she had ever dreamed up.

"Because you make people smile," Susan told her, blowing them a kiss before following her lover out the door.

"What else just happened?" Colby asked the instant they were alone.

"We can play doctor with Pamela," Amanda informed him hastily, as that young woman had just entered the dining room. "But don't say anything yet. And stop blushing!" Colby was indeed aware of the blood having rushed to his cheeks at the mention of nurse's uniforms and equipment. Of course he too had long cherished such perverse fantasies, but how could they know? Or was it possible that all spanking people were anal?

"Poor Pamela," said Amanda, surveying the menu. "I can tell you right now, you're never going to be able to finish everything I order you for lunch today."

"I will," Pamela threatened, "if only to thwart you two sick children."

Amanda smiled sweetly at Pamela and squeezing Colby's thigh through his shorts under the table ordered an Italian salad for the three of them to share and three slabs of vegetable lasagna with butternut béchamel sauce. When the large portions of layered pasta arrived Pamela gazed at hers in dismay.

"Watch this," said Amanda, "just to prove I'm not a mommy dearest," as she neatly sliced Pamela's hunk of lasagna in half and flipped one of the halves onto Colby's plate. "There, now you can relax and enjoy yourself." Amanda filled in the rest of Pamela's plate with the aromatic salad and raised her glass to her friend, saying, "To better eating." Pamela clinked her glass of white wine against Amanda's water glass and Colby's ale mug (for he was either still very good at not getting carded or routinely carried fake I.D.) and delicately sipped the light, chilled liquid. In point of fact, Pamela was very hungry that afternoon, but deliberately left a quarter of the reduced lasagna portion uneaten at the end of the meal. At which point, Amanda looked at Colby with a sad shake of her head, saying, "I told you she was incorrigible."

"What time should I meet you and what should I wear?" Pamela asked, signing their luncheon check as she rose with her purse under her arm.

Amanda grinned at Colby. "What *should* she wear?" she asked her lover. It was the first time his opinion had been asked bearing on any part of this scheme and he beamed at her. "Keeping in mind," added

Amanda, "that whatever she is wearing will certainly come off in due course."

"Something to convey innocence," Colby replied with sudden decision, "With white panties."

"Yes!" Amanda cried approvingly. "Not a lady, but a girl should climb those stairs to the consulting room. At let's say seven sharp."

"I understand," said Pamela, and clip clopped out of the dining room without a backward glance but a secret smile on her lips. It was summer and she felt both indolent and excitable. The evening promised an erotic adventure and she hadn't had enough of those lately.

Pamela arrived at Anthony Newton's house on the Cliffside at seven sharp, in a sleeveless white cotton dress with a short collar, a slim belt and a short pleated skirt that stopped midway down her long thigh line. Like all of Pamela's clothing, the dress was beautifully tailored to flatter her lithe form, drawing attention to her tiny waist and slim legs. The dark haired girl's curves were but slight, yet charming and she had flawlessly accessorized the innocent yet sophisticated look with a pair of high heeled, peep toed, sling backed, lace up sand colored suede oxfords with ribbon tied insteps. She carried a small matching purse containing only a lipstick, her I.D. and car keys.

The front door was opened to Pamela by Anthony Newton's personal assistant, Dennis, the English boy who had been part of Newton's household for the last seven years.

"Hi Dennis," said Pamela, "I think Amanda and Colby are waiting for me. Will you show me up?"

"Of course, Mrs. Bartlett, follow me," said Dennis, conducting her through the elegant foyer of the mansion and down several halls toward the back of the house. Pamela could hear the mellifluous sounds of Phoebe Casper and her co star Baldwin Rosemead singing the *"So In Love"* duet from *Kiss Me Kate* in the music salon on the second floor to the accompaniment of Newton's piano. Dennis led Pamela through the dining room, kitchen and panty before they reached a wooden stairwell at the back of the house, where he left her, saying, "They're on the third floor."

Pamela thanked him and quickly climbed the stairs, hastening to the meeting with a pleasantly beating heart.

Amanda was waiting at the top of the stairs, provocatively clad in a form fitting white zip front nurse's dress, which had come from Susan's wardrobe and which was a great deal shorter on Amanda than it was on petite Susan Ross, exposing a generous expanse of yoga toned, golden tanned thigh. Amanda had found a few afternoons to sunbathe on the balcony of Susan's bedroom in the cliff house even in the short amount of time she'd been in Random Point and the results were sensational. On her feet she wore 4" high-heeled white platform pumps.

"Come in, Mrs. Bartlett," said Amanda pleasantly, ushering Pamela into the sage green consultation room. "Do sit down," Amanda invited Pamela to occupy a brass riveted cordovan leather chair opposite the large red mahogany desk. "How are you this evening, Mrs. Bartlett?" Amanda asked, taking up a pen and clipboard and consulting a paper with notes fastened to it.

"I feel fatigued, restless, bored and excited all at the same time," Pamela confessed abstractly, while taking in all the refined details of the study with her critical designer's eye. Like every other part of Anthony Newton's house, this room was beautifully furnished and elegantly finished. Leather bound medical tomes lined the walls behind the large desk and there was no end of detailed crown molding and soft, golden lamplight to lull the patient into a state of pampered receptivity.

"An obvious case of Spring Fever," Amanda notated serenely, then added severely, "But giving into a chronic eating disorder isn't helping the situation."

"I do not have an eating disorder!" Pamela insisted stubbornly.

"Well, let's call it unhealthy eating habits," Amanda replied firmly, to which Pamela could but subside with a pout. "The doctor would like to see you increase your weight to at least 120 pounds by the end of the summer."

"I think that I can do that," Pamela admitted truthfully.

"You're not afraid anymore?" Amanda asked. Pamela shook her head.

Amanda smiled, "I'm so happy to hear that Mrs. Bartlett. If you don't mind waiting a moment, I'll send the doctor in."

"But you'll stay during the consultation, won't you, Nurse?" Pamela cried, suddenly fearful of being left in the hands of a very young man who might or might not know what he was about.

"Not for the consultation, but I'll be assisting during the examination and subsequent treatment," Amanda assured Pamela, with an irrepressible twinkle in her clear blue eyes.

"That's good to know," Pamela replied and continued sitting up straight. Just before exiting, Amanda dropped the needle on an old fashioned LP in a phonograph on a tall console in the corner of the room. Immediately a slow and soft rendition of Erik Satie's first Gnossienne filled the quiet room, the undertone of the antique record s crackle adding to the dreamlike quality of the entire situation.

As Amanda went out, Colby came in. The tall, fair-haired young man was clad in a white shirt and burgundy tie under a white coat with cuffed gray trousers and black oxfords.

"Good evening, Mrs. Bartlett," said Colby, extending his hand cordially to her across the desk before he sat down. "Thank you for coming to see us."

Pamela nodded and smiled faintly in reply, aware of the young man holding her slim hand in his big one an extra moment before releasing it. She met his eyes and felt instantly warmed by the gaze he returned, which was full of admiration and excitement. He looked down at a file on the desk before him for a moment before speaking, then smiled at her and said, "I see here you've recently stopped taking a certain drug."

"Yes, I'd been taking it for years."

"And how do you feel?"

"Better," said Pamela honestly, for it had been days since she had to deliberately remember to untense her shoulders.

"You know, Mrs. Bartlett, there are all sorts of theories about how to break an addiction. As you know, here at the clinic we consider a physical detox to be most efficacious. But we might also attempt to induce a complete emotional catharsis as well."

"Oh? And what does that entail?" Pamela asked.

Colby opened the desk draw, took out a small, oval leather paddle and placed it on the green desk blotter in front of him. Pamela sat back in her chair. "Don't be alarmed, Mrs. Bartlett. Paddling is an aspect of the treatment that most patients find invigorating."

Colby came around the desk and taking her lightly by the hand, pulled her out of her chair. "Do you consent to put yourself in my hands, Mrs. Bartlett?" he asked her, taking both her hands in his and looking into her dark eyes.

"Of course," she replied, smiling gravely back at him.

"I'm so glad," he replied and in the most unprofessional manner possible, leaned down to lightly kiss her full, red lips. Pamela blinked her long lashes at him in surprise, but in the next instant found herself winding her slim arms around his neck and surrendering her mouth to his in a long, deep kiss. Breaking apart at the same moment, each felt their faces grow warm.

"Are you ready?" he asked. She nodded. "In that case, please bend over the desk," he said, turning her to face it and then gently pressing her into place. Colby smoothed her pleated skirt down over her small, trim bottom and looking at the paddle, decided to leave it where it was for the moment. "Give me your hand," he said, reaching for one of her wrists and pulling her arm into the small of her back.

At that moment, Amanda returned to the room and observing what was about to take place, stayed Colby's arm for just the amount of time it took to fold back Pamela's skirt and reveal her slim cheeks clad in sheer, white lace trimmed French cut briefs. The view of Pamela's nether quarters and long, smooth, graceful legs now greatly improved, Colby thanked his nurse and began to spank their patient's upturned backside in a leisurely manner, with a slow, deliberate rhythm, neither softly or hard, but somewhere exactly in the middle. To Pamela, the large, friendly hand coming down on her panty clad bottom felt perfectly good. It was obvious to her from the outset that the young man possessed a natural aptitude for administering corporal punishment that had no doubt been honed by his adventures with Amanda Sands. This was the kind of attention that was calculated to stimulate the nerve endings rather than mortify the flesh they animated. The result was a subtle sway to Pamela's slim hips and a flirtatious roll of her small, round orbs, to communicate her readiness to receive and react to more.

"Shall we check the color, Doctor?" Amanda asked at length, pulling Pamela's panties down to mid thigh to reveal an even field of pinkness spread from cheek to cheek, every inch of skin surface fully infused with the luscious color. A light-olive skinned girl, with pinky undertones, Pamela tended to stain rose rather than magenta when thoroughly spanked and the hue became her dainty and elegant bottom beautifully. Amanda regarded her lover's handiwork with serene approval, delighted that he had spread his smacks so uniformly across and up and down the small target area that was Pamela's backside.

"It's very pretty," said Amanda, lightly pressing her white hand against Pamela's right cheek. "But it should be much warmer. It should be hot."

"I agree," said Colby. Pamela turned to look over her shoulder at Amanda, whose sexy head to toe look mesmerized her. The white nurse's uniform clung to Amanda's full bosom, slim waist and jutting buttocks like powdered sugar on Turkish delight, the zip front allowing for maximum cleavage exposure and the white fetish pumps on Amanda's graceful feet continually drawing the connoisseur's gaze down to the eighteen-year-old's high insteps, trim ankles and lusciously formed calves and thighs.

"I love your outfit," said Pamela to Amanda.

Amanda smiled and whispered in Pamela's ear, "I love your bottom." To prove this avowal, Amanda began to massage her stylish friend's spanked bottom, slowly and with great appreciation of the resiliency of Pamela's slightly rounded cheeks. "Although," Amanda remarked to Colby, who had paused to watch, "I'd like to see a much plumper version of this area in particular the next time we have Mrs. Bartlett in this position." Amanda gave Pamela a few light pats and then surprised her friend by pulling her panties back up, pulling her skirt back down and gently helping her up from the desk. "Come on, young lady," said Amanda, taking Pamela by the hand, "it's time to go into the examining room and continue with the more purifying portions of your treatment."

Without forgetting to bring the paddle, Colby Hodge followed the two young women into the adjoining room, which was decorated in a lighter, apple green, with white wood and enameled cabinetry and furniture surrounding the central focal point, the examining table. Long paned windows, slightly ajar reflected the soft atmosphere of a late summer sunset on Cape Cod, with a pink and blue sky above and the sound of waves crashing into the rocks of the cove below. Amanda directed Pamela to a wooden changing screen painted with a reproduction of the Botticelli Venus and asked her to undress then she returned to Colby who was quietly locking the door.

"Things are about to get crazy beyond your wildest dreams," Amanda whispered to her boyfriend merrily, pulling him up to one of the white cabinets filled with real and quasi-medical equipment. "All right," said Amanda, "here we go," and then started grabbing items from behind the glass doors and tossing them into a stainless steel basin she found on one of the shelves. Colby watched with fascination as Amanda unerringly chose two pair of clear latex gloves, an old fashioned glass thermometer, a bottle of lubricant, a rubber anal torpedo douche, a vulcanite enema bulb, a number of long, straight, curved and ripply application tips up to four inches in length, a classic clear enema bag and hose, and as an afterthought, Amanda grabbed a vibrating wand.

"Are you serious?" Colby asked her.

"It's all right, she's already consented."

Pamela emerged from behind the screen in a white push up bra trimmed with lace and the matching panties pulled back up. She had also left on her extremely sexy shoes. Glancing into the equipment filled basin, Pamela drew back in startled surprise.

"All that, for me?" she cried, her hand to her white throat.

"You want to feel completely clean and fresh when you leave us, don't you?" Amanda replied reasonably. "Of course, you will be somewhat lighter as well. That is always the effect of a thorough purge." Amanda had no personal experience to back up this contention, but she had gathered such information from her holistic mother over the years and felt no compunction about using it to tame Pamela to her will ever more completely.

Pamela, who was not quite the neurotic people generally assumed her to be, regarding her weight, had always wondered about the efficacy of enemas to spot reduce, but had never quite gotten together the resolve to buy the equipment and try it herself, and she was quite looking forward to that part of the adventure. For the rest, she was even more vastly intrigued.

Amanda summoned Pamela to an old fashioned scale and weighed her, noting the figure on a chart on a clipboard. "One twelve, not one thirteen. You lied to us," Amanda said crisply.

"Your scale may be wrong," said Pamela, pleased by the outcome but knowing that she had not lied.

"You are wrong to argue," Amanda said severely. "Dr. Hodge hates a stubborn girl," she warned. "Come with me," Amanda said, taking Pamela by the hand and leading her to the examination table. "Face down, please," said Amanda, summarily turning her patient to face the table, bending her over, lifting her legs and placing her firmly in position. "She's so light," Amanda said to Colby over her shoulder. "So naughty to let herself get this thin!" And Amanda couldn't resist bestowing one smart spank to Pamela's slim but still prettily jutting bottom, now so appealingly upturned in the French cut briefs. Pamela looked at Amanda with an arched brow, not surprised to see this dominant streak in the much younger girl emerge all at once, but interested to see where it would go.

As for Amanda, all the restraint she had shown in seducing her vanilla roommate Alicia the previous winter, all the politically correct delicacy and mildly Sapphic love techniques she had practiced to give her non scene girlfriend a well behaved orgasm, were but a pale expression of her true polymorphous perversity, which it took a genuine creature of the scene like herself to coax into vibrant life. Pamela was designed by nature and honed by her own self will to be the plaything of others, to be beautiful and receptive and to a certain extent, passive, while those who knew what to do with her, did it.

Colby had watched with fascination as Amanda took control of the fashionable young matron. When Amanda smacked Pamela, the effect was to endow him with an instantaneous erection that he knew would keep himself and the girls company for however long they remained in that sweet, secluded chamber. Amanda gave Colby one look over her shoulder to motion him over to the table before she reached under the waist of Pamela's panties to pull them down. The rose pink had already begun to fade from the brunette's sculpted cheeks, but Amanda's small handprint, just inflicted, rather caught the attention. "Feel how warm she is," Amanda invited Colby. Both of them ran their hands over Pamela's bare bottom, massaging it slowly.

"It's time for your examination," said Amanda, putting on gloves and handing Colby a pair. Pamela shuddered and buried her face in her folded arms. Amanda pulled the panties down to Pamela's mid thigh and divided her bottom cheeks to their view. "Tight and cute, as we knew it would be," said Amanda, pressing the orbs even further apart. Pamela squirmed in embarrassment. "Lie still, Mrs. Bartlett, the doctor needs to inspect you thoroughly," Amanda ordered, fully exposing Pamela's fundament.

"Please, spare me this indignity," Pamela leaned up suddenly and fixed Amanda with her velvety brown gaze. Amanda folded her arms and looked sternly back at her friend.

"What's this? Trying to wriggle out of your disciplinary anal spanking therapy?" Amanda demanded, straight-faced.

"But it's so embarrassing and how can I be sure you two aren't just pranksters operating on the orders of some fraternity or sorority? How do I know you're true perverts?"

"Oh, rest assured Mrs. Bartlett, no Greek house would have us," said Amanda, "and as to perverts, of course we are. How can you doubt it?" Amanda cried. "But I'm too self conscious to submit myself to the kind of ordeal you're about to bear so bravely and Colby respects me too much to force me. And then here you are, the perfect toy for two twisted children to amuse themselves with. So why not just relax and enjoy the ride?" Amanda pushed Pamela back down onto the table, taking off one glove momentarily to pinch Pamela's earlobe between thumb and forefinger, warning Pamela not to argue with them any more but to be instead, a perfect angel for the rest of the night.

Colby went to the head of the table and sat on a stool so that he was eye to eye with Pamela. "Don't worry, Mrs. Bartlett," he assured her, "I can control that crazy bitch if necessary. I'm here for you."

Amanda grinned at Colby over Pamela's sleek, dark haired head and motioned him back to the opposite side of the table. Taking Pamela by the waist she nodded towards the black oval leather paddle they had brought in. "You'd better remind her that she's here to learn some self control and discipline," said Amanda. Colby took the paddle in his hand and began to spank Pamela's exposed bottom cheeks, bringing up a fresh rose tinge almost immediately. He noticed that by increasing his tempo and applying a bit more force, that he could easily make the brunette gasp, catch her breath and whimper. Amanda watched in fascination as Pamela's skin grew rosier under the firm, fast falling paddle swats. Pamela buried her face in her arms and half sobbed into them.

"Are you going to behave and let me take your temperature?" Amanda finally asked, staying Colby's vigorous arm.

"Yes," Pamela murmured. Re-donning the gloves, Amanda anointed the patient's anus with KY jelly and inserted the rectal thermometer into it. Happening to look up into a mirror opposite the table, Amanda couldn't help but notice that a blush was creeping over her face from neck to brow and couldn't help feeling a crazy throbbing in her own sex as she began to invade Pamela's most private recess. She didn't dare look down at Colby's midsection, for she knew a raging erection would be tenting his trousers under the doctor's jacket, so instead she began to compound her own painful excitement by twirling the thermometer around and pushing it in ever deeper. Then she went to the side sink to prepare the first course of the treatment, a small warm water douche in a rubber bulb with a long, thick nozzle. Colby guarded their patient while she did this, massaging Pamela's warm bottom.

Amanda came back, read the temperature as normal, wiped the thermometer with alcohol and set it aside. Pulling off Pamela's panties entirely, Amanda ordered her to get up on her hands and knees in the all fours position with her legs apart.

"She interrupted us while we were examining her before," Amanda reminded Colby while once more deliberately pressing Pamela's bottom open to their view. "She's lucky we can only go so far today," said Amanda conversationally. "I was looking at a website that sells anal speculums."

Colby was amazed but helpfully dabbed a few more drops of pearly lubricant between Pamela's cheeks as Amanda brought him the one-pint douche. "Just relax," he told Pamela, patting her lightly. "It's for your own good."

"And you don't even have to worry about this first one, Mrs. Bartlett," Amanda assured her, holding Pamela open for the nozzle. "because this is just a quick preliminary cleanse and you'll be allowed to void immediately in that lovely private W.C. down the corridor as soon as you like."

Colby gently inserted the tip of the four-inch nozzle into Pamela's bottom as she shuddered and squirmed in response. Amanda deftly unhooked the brunette's bra and removed it, leaving her friend clad in only her high vamp heels. Pamela's bosom was of modest proportions but well rounded and tipped with pretty, rosy nipples. In the doggy position her breasts hung down voluptuously and Amanda again discarded her gloves to squeeze them both somewhat firmly. The doctor lingered over inserting the nozzle, gently twisting it this way and that as his patient gasped and sobbed in shame.

"I can't even imagine what it must be like to have such warm, almost hot water, rushing into my bottom, all at once," said Amanda, nodding to Colby, who began compressing the bolus slowly, sending the jet through the tube in Pamela's rectum and directly into her colon. Amanda held Pamela in position by her slender waist as the water gushed into the brunette's uptilted bottom. Once the bulb was empty, the doctor slowly withdrew the nozzle and set the apparatus aside, taking up a soft white cloth to pat the few stray drops from her cheeks.

"Don't move," he said, running one palm across her bottom while slipping the other under her slightly distended stomach and coming to rest atop her small triangle of dark public curls and just above it, her hidden g-spot.

"Don't touch me there or I'll come this very moment," Pamela cried, pulling back from his deft fingertips, which had begun to massage her lower abdomen. Colby looked at Amanda, who grinned again.

"Don't you dare even think of coming yet," cried Amanda, "we're just getting started here."

"Then let me go," Pamela returned, trying to make her mind a blank and not think about all the ticklish sensations which were simultaneously causing her to teeter on the edge of a climax. The nozzle, the warm water, the feeling of fullness, the residual sting still radiating from her spanked bottom cheeks, all converged to set her painfully athrob. She suddenly knew what men with erections felt like when they couldn't get relief in a timely fashion. She craved more penetration, more spanking, more spreading, more humiliation and then the ultimate release. They allowed her to depart and see to her immediate needs in the water closet.

As soon as she was out of earshot, Colby said, "Wow."

"I know. Isn't she compliant? Could you have invented a sluttier slut?"

"Do you think she's really digging this?"

"Can you doubt it?"

"Why does she let you dominate her like this? Isn't she something like ten years older than you?"

"I'm not sure but she let Hugo dominate the hell out of her too. Maybe there's something about our DNA she responds to," said Amanda gaily, laying out the equipment for Pamela's next course. Then she lifted her head and listened, saying, "You hear that?"

Colby listened and said, "Sounds like she's taking a shower."

"Damn, that's just like her, so compulsive," said Amanda impatiently. Indeed, Pamela had found a that a door opened up from the water closet into a shower stall lined in deco tile and had decided not to return to her perfect young friends in a less than scrupulously pristine state.

"She'll be a few minutes then," Colby pointed, out pressing Amanda's hand to the front of his trousers. "Couldn't we fool around?"

"Well…" Amanda hesitated but a moment, then bent over the exam table, pulling up the back of her short skirt as she did, which though brief had totally concealed the dainty white lace garter belt and panty combination which wrapped Amanda's perfectly shapely bottom.

surmounting her long, show girl legs glamorously hosed in nude nylon stockings. Colby wasted no time in yanking her tiny panties down and then his zipper, before thrusting his fully erect and wildly virile penis in between her slick, pink labia.

"No!" she cried, pulling back. "Rubber!"

"Sorry, dammit!" he cried, fumbling a condom out of its foil wrapper and rolling it onto his erection as rapidly as was ever done in the history of teen sex on Cape Cod.

"Take it easy," she cried, pulling back as he tried to cram his extremely healthy cock into her rather tight pussy all at once. "She'll be at least five minutes," Amanda laughed, now pushing back against him and concentrating on opening up to him. Colby fastened his hands to her small waist and plunged into his girl to the hilt, then commenced to piston his engorged organ in and out at a spark inducing velocity. She let him find his rhythm and rocked with it, pulling one of his hands around and pressing it against her lower abdomen, in the same place that Pamela was so intent on not being touched, lest the sensation trigger an over hasty orgasm. With the image of Pamela's bottom bared, spanked and filled still lingering in both their minds and the incessant pile driving of Colby's cock causing each of their grinding and throbbing genitals to feel electrified with excitement, both Amanda and Colby managed to complete their random act of lust in the creamiest possible way and yet dispose of all the evidence before Pamela's shy and languid return to them, wrapped in a white Turkish bath sheet.

"Let's take a break," said Amanda, feeling she needed a few moments to compose herself before taking control of Pamela again. She turned to Colby and said, "I'm going down stairs to get us something cool to drink. Please feed Pamela drugs and save some for me." With this she thrust the purse she had brought with her at Colby and disappeared.

"Drugs?" asked Pamela, with a curious smile. "I thought this was about my getting off drugs."

"She means the organic kind," said Colby, finding a small glass pipe and a bag of bud in Amanda's purse. "So you can relax more," he added helpfully, filling a bowl and passing it to her.

"Finally, someone gives *me* some weed!" Pamela cried, delighted to light up. She passed it back to him with lowered eyes, suddenly remembering all she had been subjected to by the very young man, who was eyeing her with something like adoration.

"If you force me to go through with that," she motioned to the rubber bag and long hose, "I'll cry."

"I can't wait to see that," he confessed honestly.

"I've never endured anything so humiliating," she added, taking a second hit and feeling a new type of euphoria overwhelm her senses.

Amanda returned carrying a tray with three crystal glasses and a half carafe of pink lemonade. They sipped the cool drink and looked at each other with interest. Amanda's pulse had returned to normal and she felt eager to return to their perverse play-acting. Colby refilled the pipe and handed it to her and in a moment, each of them had mentally returned to the mood of dreamy semi decadence in which they had enacted the last scene.

Seeing the sun had gone down, Amanda pulled the curtains to add an additional degree of seclusion to the examining room.

"Please get up on the table again," Amanda petitioned Pamela, pulling the towel from the willowy brunette's warm, freshly showered body. Both Amanda and her lover drank in the grace and beauty of Pamela's nude form with admiration. "Even her feet are pretty," said Amanda, helping Pamela back into the all fours position and firmly separating Pamela's knees. Amanda allowed her fingertip to trail down the back of Pamela's right foot from toes to heel. Pamela jerked her foot back convulsively, crying, "No, I beg you, don't tickle me!" Amanda grabbed Pamela's foot firmly back between both her hands and gave it one kiss before repositioning it on the table. "She's lucky we're not into tickling," said Amanda to Colby.

"I'd take a caning first," said Pamela.

Amanda came around in front of Pamela and first showing Pamela her fingertip, slowly and deliberately ran it up and down Pamela's bare right arm. Pamela shivered and squirmed, but didn't pull away as she had done when Amanda had touched her foot. Amanda feathered her fingertip across Pamela's throat, down between her small, round, cherry nippled breasts and continued to trace a straight line with it down to Pamela's waist. Pamela was stunned by all the nuances of seduction Amanda seemed to have learned by the tender age of eighteen, an age at which she herself had barely learned how to masturbate.

Satisfied that Pamela had been returned to the same state of arousal achieved before their break, Amanda filled the clear hot water bag and screwed a four inch textured nozzle onto the end of its long white hose. Colby donned a fresh pair of latex gloves and relubricated Pamela's anus, digitally penetrating her to the knuckle. This action elicited a squeak of surprise but Pamela also felt Amanda's light hands on her waist, holding her in place for this intrusive procedure.

Hanging the enema bag on a rolling c stand, Colby brought the apparatus to the side of the table and lubricated the long nozzle with care. "Are you ready, Mrs. Bartlett?" he asked. Amanda shifted her grasp on Pamela to where she held one cheek in each hand and gently spread them. Pamela sobbed with emotion and protested that she was not.

"Yes, you are," said Amanda, separating her bottom cheeks a little more to afford Colby complete access to the tiny, glistening portal.

"She needs more spanking," Colby suggested. "Her color is practically gone." In so saying, he laid aside the nozzle, pulled off his rubber gloves and went around to Pamela's left side. On Pamela's right side, Amanda once again took possession of the slender brunette's waist, to hold her in place. Then Colby began to apply the palm of his hand smartly to either cheek, continuing to spank her until each oval orb had been stained a dark rose. Pamela panted and bucked to and fro under the swats but submitted without protest, feeling her bottom grow warmer and warmer and her pussy throb ever more insistently every moment. Unlike her two devilish young friends, Pamela had not yet come but had been on the brink of the most sensational climax of her life for the last half hour.

"All right, I think she'll let us proceed without arguing this time," Colby finally concluded the impromptu punishment.

"And she looks so much prettier now," Amanda said with feeling, primordially aroused by the deep coral coloration that contrasted so sharply with the light olive tones of Pamela's skin. Once again

Amanda took Pamela's bottom in her hands and opened it for the nozzle, which this time Colby inserted without hesitation, but not quickly. As expected, Pamela immediately lost whatever composure had remained to her, squirming, blushing and stammering half hearted protests to her pleasant tormentors. After the nozzle was fully inserted, Amanda allowed Pamela's bottom to close around the hose and instructed her friend to assume the knee to toe position, dropping her bosom to the table and arching her backside up higher to provide the perfect tilt for a very warm hydrotherapeutic infusion. "Well give her about half to three quarters of the bag," said Amanda to Colby, "then we'll insert an anal retention plug into her bottom. I can't wait to see how her tummy looks in various positions, all distended and full. And if she doesn't cooperate, we'll put her over your knee and punish her until she does."

Colby wasn't surprised at the effect Amanda's words had upon his so recently exercised organ, finding himself in sudden possession of a new erection. Pamela hid her face behind her arms but thrust her bottom well up to present the most accident proof angle for the operation. Colby released the clamp and the warm water began to flow down the hose and into Pamela's bottom. Pamela emitted a small groan of shock and embarrassed emotion as the sensation of being filled in this most intimate of ways redoubled the tingle in her sex and vibrated ticklishly through her entire body. While Colby administered the enema, Amanda efficiently unwrapped and lubricated a slim, flexible, blue, tapered plastic anal probe, about four inches long, and an inch thick at its widest, with a soft, t-shaped handle for easy insertion and removal and a vibrating bullet lodged in the base activated by a push button action.

Once the bag was three quarters empty, Colby snapped the clamp shut and slowly eased the nozzle out of Pamela's rectum while Amanda kept her hand on Pamela's back to make sure she continued to keep her head down and her bottom up. Patting her bottom dry of a few drops of water, Colby took up the ingeniously fashioned butt plug and carefully but firmly thrust it into Pamela's bottom to the hilt. Pamela moaned and sobbed with shame.

"Shake your little tail like a bunny," Amanda ordered, giving Pamela two smart smacks on her upturned cheeks. Pamela obeyed with another sob. "Oh god that looks obscene," Amanda said, momentarily pressing her own throbbing Venus mound through her clothes to calm the turmoil within her own tingling sex. "Now young lady," Amanda said to Pamela, "get back up in the doggy position so we can examine how full your little belly is." Pamela obeyed and submitted to both Amanda and Colby stroking and squeezing her full stomach, which now looked larger than it had ever done in her entire life. It was still a small tummy by any standards, but lushly voluptuous by Pamela standards and she flushed in shame as they looked at her and commented without restraint.

"How cute is that," said Amanda, lingering over massaging Pamela's stomach and allowing her fingers to trail now and then just far enough back to graze the top of the brunette's neatly trimmed pubic mound. "Don't she look sexy with a slightly distended belly, Colby?"

"She looks as naughty as a Weimar republic flapper," he replied, with admiration. "Being forced to retain her enema."

"She has been naughty, what with all the speed and the unauthorized fasting," said Amanda. "Therefore the punishment and humiliation will continue. Let's put her on her back."

"Oh no, god no!" Pamela protested, but weakly as they pulled her limbs out flat and forced her first face down on the leather table and then rolled her over on her back, taking care not to dislodge the anal probe still separating yet sealing closed her bottom cheeks. At the touch of a button, the upper half of the exam table tilted up elevating Pamela's into an angled sitting position. Amanda went behind the head of the table and pulled Pamela's wrists up above her head and pinned them under one hand. This caused the brunette's perky bosom to arch ever higher. Amanda looked at Colby and said, "I'd say we have a good ten minutes before our patient begins to feel any appreciable discomfort."

"How do you know that?" Pamela demanded. Amanda tucked Pamela's hands under her head before coming around to the side of the table and hold a conversation with her friend.

"I don't know it. I'm just guessing, based on Marguerite Alexander stories I've read," said Amanda, going to the bottom of the table and deliberately spreading Pamela's slender ankles as far apart as possible. Then she handed Colby a fresh glove. "If we spanked her Venus Mound and at the same time digitally penetrated her vagina while activating the vibrator in the anal probe, how long do you think it would take for Mrs. Bartlett to climax?" she asked.

"If we're very slow and deliberate about administering the treatment," Colby said, easing his gloved and lubricated middle finger into Pamela's already slick and throbbing slit, "we might be able to get her to last ... I'm going to say three minutes."

"Don't move," Amanda warned Pamela. "Keep your hands behind your head and you'll soon feel something to your advantage." Exchanging one meaningful glance with Pamela, Amanda dropped her eyes to her friend's trim mound and pressed her palm against it. Then she gently squeezed Pamela's unnaturally full stomach, eliciting a groan from her friend.

"You look sexy with a little round stomach," Amanda told Pamela, but transferred her attention back to Pamela's Venus Mound, which she began to lightly spank with her palm. Pamela writhed in ticklish, humiliated excitement under their hands as Colby inserted another finger into her pussy and began to piston it quickly back and forth, rather emulating the rhythm with which he had just taken Amanda. "Bend your knees up Pamela and give doctor access to that naughty butt plug. Time to turn that on."

Colby pressed the button without ceasing to manipulate her vagina while Amanda stopped spanking Pamela's mound, but pressed the heel of her hand down on it firmly instead, including in her action her aroused friend's swollen clitoris. With this extreme confluence of stimulation bombarding the full compliment of her sexual organs, both inside and out, Pamela was helpless to resist a climactic crescendo within seconds of the anal vibrator being turned on. She collapsed limp between their hands after tingling for what seemed like minutes on end.

"Such a good little patient," said Amanda, taking Colby by the hand and leading him towards the door. "We'll be downstairs when you're ready." And so saying, they left their erotically bedazzled friend to tend to every natural and hygienic need in total privacy.

In the outer office, Colby took off the doctor's coat and slipped on the well-cut jacket that matched his trousers. Amanda rarely saw him dressed like a grown up and she grinned in appreciation at the jock who had become a sexual sophisticate overnight. Amanda took him with her to Susan Ross's suite on the third floor of the house, where she had found the nurse's outfit. Exchanging the white uniform for the crisp cotton, double breasted navy wrap dress she had brought, Amanda regarded herself in a full length mirror with satisfaction. In a fresh pair of burgundy platform pumps she had brought to change into, she was six feet tall. With legs that went on forever and a lily waist, her long throat and full bosom, there was no quality of feminine allure Amanda did not possess in abundance, not the least of which was her lovely, smiling face, surmounted by her current short, feathery cap of ash blonde hair.

"Yes, you are all that," Colby said, coming up behind her and locking his arms around her waist while burying his face in her neck and shoulders. "What I'm trying to figure out is why you're being so good to me."

"Well," she said, looking into his eyes in the mirror over her shoulder, "for one thing, I love you."

"I'm beginning to really believe that," he replied, kissing her throat. "I'm just not sure why."

"You got me through Economics last year and you'll get me through Statistics this year," she said practically. "You never try to stop me from bossing you around. And you didn't hold it against me when you found out what I did with Mr. Bartlett. So why wouldn't I share the sublime treasure that is Pamela with you?"

"I just never dreamed you were so open minded on top of being so perverted. I mean, in spite of what you told Pamela, we never even discussed half those things we did tonight. How did you know that I was so into them?"

"You had Pretty Peaches and Water Power in with your DVD's at the dorm."

"They were not in with my DVD's, they were buried at the bottom of my sock drawer."

"Oh, were they?"

"When did you even start thinking about things of that nature?" Colby asked.

"When I started reading Marguerite's stories in the New Rod Quarterlies I found when I was about thirteen."

"Is that where you picked up the bisexuality too?"

"Yes, I think so. But it's only just started to surface. I played with Alicia a little bit last year, but only mildly. Nothing like this."

"Someday at the end of the 21st century, when I'm in that orbiting old age home in space, I'll be sitting on the moon porch with a smile on my face because I'll be remembering the gift you gave me tonight. Thank you, Amanda." Colby kissed her lightly on the lips and they went downstairs together.

Chapter Twelve

Secrets

Within the hour, Amanda, Colby and Pamela, (pleasantly exhausted but curiously refreshed from her several treatments and subsequent showers), were quietly and intimately disporting themselves in the billiard room on the first floor while sharing a bottle of wine that Dennis had cheerfully provided them with. Colby had just broken the pool balls and was leaning over to take his first shot, still in his suit but now minus the tie and with his broad shoulders nicely filling out the jacket, looking more mid-twenties than nineteen, when Pascal Robbins breezed by the open door on his way out of the house. Spotting his two favorite models in the salon, he paused to visit with them. The men shook hands, eyeing each other coolly.

Amanda was immediately glad of this fresh meeting between Pascal and Colby, as what could cool the older man's ardor for her faster than to see her with her handsome, athletic young lover at her side? But Amanda greatly underestimated the magnitude of attraction she held for the photographer. For Pascal's part, he was instantly aware of a chill settling over his heart as he noticed the obvious attachment between Amanda and her boyfriend, as well as the affectionate glances bestowed on the blond boy by his own former model Pamela Bartlett. Not that he had ever been much attracted to the slender brunette, even while they had traveled together on and off for a year. But it rather annoyed him that both young women should seem to dote so much on this kid. In fact, the more he looked at Pamela, the more he realized how relaxed she was in the company of these two attractive children, displaying a degree of comfort and ease she had never done with him alone. What had the boy done to win Pamela over so soon, Pascal wondered to himself as he accepted a glass of wine and joined them in the pool game. He had come to pick his wife up but had just been told that Phoebe would need to keep rehearsing on the floor above with Anthony Newton and her co-star, for at least another hour before she could go home.

The trio told him that they were just going over to Michael Flagg's tavern for a late night snack and invited Pascal to join them. He agreed at once and after they finished their game, drove over with Pamela in her smart, expensive sedan while Amanda and Colby drove over in Colby's jeep.

"You're looking remarkably well tonight, Pamela," said Pascal when she got behind the wheel with an abstracted smile on her face. Pamela did not often smile in repose and it suddenly occurred to Pascal that perhaps she had been naughty recently, and possibly even with the two beautiful children. This sent another pang of something like jealousy through his heart and he threw her a sharp, sidelong glance as he opened the window and lit a cigarette. "What the hell have you three been up to?" he asked suspiciously.

"That would be telling," she replied, with a deepening smile and a toss of her shiny black bob.

"So what's Amanda's boyfriend like?" Pascal asked.

"He goes to Harvard."

"Jock?"

"I believe the young man does play hockey."

"What do you think of him?"

"He's a darling man," said Pamela without hesitation, for Colby's handling of her body, her sex and her sensibilities had been flawless.

"So, are you enjoying married life?" Pascal felt it time to change the subject because the more he thought about Amanda and her popular boyfriend, the more aggravated he felt.

"I'm not sure yet," she replied. "For a while it seemed like no improvement at all. But Ambrose has recently made some concessions that reassured me all may yet be well."

"What's he doing tonight?"

Pamela shrugged as she carefully drove down the Cliff Road and into the village. "He rarely tells me what he does between the time the store closes and I see him at home. Businesses dinners would account for some of the time."

"He's probably at the gym," said Pascal. "I've run into him there three times this week."

"Is that so?" Pamela looked at the photographer briefly with interest, recalling the sudden image of the goddess Polyxena Guzman seated at the table during the Venus Club dinner in the ivory tulle tea dress, with her magnificent bosom half exposed and gleamingly well rounded.

"He's in pretty good shape, so it must be taking," Pascal observed.

"At any rate, at least he's *trying* to quit smoking," Pamela said, eyeing Pascal in a way that caused him to stub out his cigarette with a guilty look. "I'm surprised Phoebe lets you continue to kill yourself with those things."

"Phoebe knows better that to try and tell me what to do," said Pascal with a shrug.

"Oh, that's right, you boss *her* around," Pamela smiled.

"It's more like I just ignore her good advice. She found that out when she tried to turn me vegan."

"You do boss her around though. Don't try to pretend otherwise. She trembles at your every frown."

Pascal looked pleased at this. "That's because she knows I'll spank her," he said.

"You know Amanda spilled the beans about you spanking her at the Venus Club dinner."

"What?" Pascal's heart missed a beat.

"Amanda told everyone how you spanked her without leave. Phoebe heard it all."

Pascal didn't say another word until they got out of the car in front of Michael's tavern. Phoebe knew something like that and yet hadn't said a word nor behaved a whit differently. What did it mean? What young wife could possibly refrain from bringing up an infraction of this magnitude, unless she herself had something significant to hide? His mind made this leap effortlessly. Phoebe was saving this up and waiting for just the right moment to throw it back in his face. Which meant, she must be up to something herself, some flirtation with another man. Could it be her charming new patron, Anthony Newton? Or her handsome leading man? One of the other tops in a village crammed with tops? Pascal's mind was reeling and his heart pounding as he went into the bar with Pamela to join Amanda and Colby, already seated in a booth.

Dru Baxter came from behind the bar to take their order.

"You're working here too?" Amanda asked the good-looking college boy who spent his days helping Hope at the coffee bar in the bookshop.

"More tourists than usual this year," answered Dru with a smile, "so Michael asked me to put in a few nights a week. Hi Pamela."

Pamela stared up at him in bemusement, still floating from her strangely erotic experiences at the hands of the children, but suddenly remembering how exciting it had been to feel this boy's strong arms around her waist the night she had met him here when they had danced.

"Hi Dru," she replied, his name slowly coming back to her as they gazed into each other's eyes, his radiating pleasure and excitement at seeing her again. Pascal moodily ordered a whiskey and went out on the back patio to smoke a cigarette. Amanda and Colby ordered burgers, fries and cokes, then leaving Pamela to study the limited bar menu at length, wandered over to the juke box to study Michael's interesting play list of alt, punk and metal.

"May I help you choose?" Dru asked, sliding into the booth seat beside her. "I know what fancy ladies like."

"Nothing too heavy, or too light," said Pamela, looking fondly across the room at her persecutors.

"I'd take the roast turkey sandwich with lemon caper mayonnaise, lettuce and tomato on a baguette."

"Sounds good."

"Before things get too hectic," Dru began in a rush, but not haphazardly, "I have to tell you something. I've been thinking about you night and day ever since that night."

Pamela blinked back at him in surprise.

"Is it true you're even in the scene?" he demanded, his blue eyes alight with excitement. Pamela nodded and looked back at him with even greater interest. Was this boy really coming onto her?

"But," she began slowly, not sure she wanted to close this door at once, "you know that I'm married."

"I know," he said softly, but took her hand under the table and lightly squeezed. "I don't care. I want to be alone with you and make love to you."

"Really?" she didn't attempt to remove her hand from his.

"Why are you surprised?"

"Well, I'm so much older than you, besides being married," she said gently.

"I like that it's been awhile since you've been with a younger guy. It gives me an advantage. I think you'd find me sensitive and well, long lasting."

Pamela laughed, "You're so bad. Of course I'm not going to even consider such an outrageous proposition. Now please go and put our orders in!"

Dru got up. "Think about it?" he asked, and left to obey her final injunction. A few minutes later, after freshening her hair and makeup in the bathroom, Pamela once again encountered Dru as she returned to the booth. Turning from the bar, the tray of drinks he held aloft in one hand wobbled as he came to a quick stop before her. She looked at him thoughtfully before slowly proceeding back to her seat. He darted ahead of her to place the drink at her table. Quickly checking to make sure that Amanda and Colby were still engaged choosing songs and seeing that Pascal had found a seat at the bar, opposite Michael Flagg, to whom he had begun to confide certain revelations, in exchange for advice, Dru once again demanded Pamela's attention with a longing and passionate look that lingered not on her body but her face.

"I'm in the scene too," he confided. "Give me the chance and I'll give you the best scene of your life."

"Really?" she smiled up at him. "You?"

Pamela enjoyed her late night snack while sipping a glass of white wine and gazing around Michael's tavern in contentment. Colby and

Amanda chattered beside her in the booth, discussing the merits of all the songs they had chosen to play. Closer to the bar, locals and summer trace drank endless pitchers of beer and shouted relentlessly at the baseball games running on all the screens. Out on the dance floor of the clubroom, nicely tanned to recklessly sunburned young people were eyeing each other with a view towards hooking up. Or so mused Pamela, apparently relishing her food in a world of her own, but really thinking most intently about Dru Baxter's proposition.

When the blond boy returned to freshen drinks and clear away dishes, she detained him with a slim white hand on his arm. "When do you get off?" she asked softly.

"Ten," he replied, radiant with pleasure at her asking.

"I'll wait outside for you and maybe take you somewhere fun," said Pamela impulsively, for she knew she couldn't let this crazy night end just yet. She needed to do one more outrageous thing.

Pamela told Amanda and Colby she was going home, kissing them both. Then going up to Pascal at the bar she asked him if he could find his own ride back to Anthony's later as she would be leaving shortly and not going in the same direction. The photographer turned from his whiskey to gaze suspiciously at his former model. "What are you up to tonight?" he asked. Pamela blushed, because she was in fact, about to commit the supreme act of conjugal disrespect, but there was no need for Pascal to know any of that.

"Good night," said Pamela with a catlike smile and leisurely strolled outside into the soft summer air. Strolling up the lane, Pamela called her husband. It was about a quarter to ten. As it turned out, Ambrose had been working out at the gym and was just about to shower. Then he had promised to have a drink with a buddy before going home. Therefore she was not to expect him at home until half past eleven, which information increased the up tilt of her Cheshire grin.

Walking up and down before the tavern, Pamela once again mentally flashed on the fair image of Polyxena Guzman in her classic white bathing suit. "Oh my god, he's courting that Dutch slut!" Pamela thought, rather amazed that her busy man was doing it again.

At ten p.m. Dru emerged from the back of the tavern and joined her on the gravel drive. She pulled him towards her car and he got in beside her.

"Where are we going?" he asked.

"Somewhere you'll like," she replied, and drove directly to the *Damaris* shop in the village. She led him in through the back with her key and up the stairs to the studio. The long, sky lit room was equipped with both bright and soft lights, and Pamela turned on the latter. In addition to drawing boards, computer stations, cutting tables and dress forms, the studio was furnished with a complete set of comfortable, well upholstered furniture, including club chairs and a long, wide futon. Pamela deliberately dropped the back down to create a bed sized platform, upon which she casually fell, disposing her still crisp white pleated skirt about her and crossing her beautifully shod feet. Dru fell to his knees before her.

"Be my mistress?" he implored her.

"What does that even mean?" she asked, ruffling his blond hair under her hand and then lifting his chin. "You're very handsome, young man, so I will listen," she promised him, placing the lightest of kisses on his finely sculpted lips.

"It means I'll worship you and be your adoring slave," he promised, kissing the palm of her hand reverently.

"And what would I do with a slave?" she smiled indulgently.

"Let him serve you," he said, placing his fingers on the hem of her skirt. She watched and didn't stop him when he slowly began to push the skirt up, exposing her long, slim white thighs, inch by inch and only stopping when he came to her white panties. Pamela watched him in great interest without attempting to interfere. Smoothly placing the palm of his hand against her Venus Mound through the scrap of nylon, Dru applied pressure and rotation to his grasp on her sex. Feeling suddenly safe, warm and in trustworthy hands, Pamela allowed herself to actually sink fully back on the sofa bed and for the second time that night, place her hands behind her head while things were done to her.

Elated by her tacit acceptance of his initial advances, Dru hastened to pull her panties entirely off and place his mouth where his hand had just been. She entwined her fingers in his hair but found that he needed no guidance in finding the exact spot just above her clitoris, where she most enjoyed the stimulation of a tongue. Taking one of his hands, she wordlessly placed it between her thighs. Without hesitation he introduced his middle finger into her velvety recesses and began to pump it in and out. She was very wet and her hips thrashed in ticklish abandon under the double fronted assault. After allowing Dru to frig and lick her halfway to orgasm, she sat up, pulled him up and bluntly said, "Have you got a condom?"

In an instant a large Trojan foil appeared in Dru's hand. His face was a study in thrilled disbelief while a jumbo penis jumped out of his jeans the moment he had lowered his zipper.

"Tell me how," he asked, rolling the rubber down over the large mushroom cap of his long, pink, circumcised cock, which was rather thinner than thick, the perfect size for anal sex, Pamela thought. Tossing him one provocative look, she got up on all fours and turned her back to him, flipping her skirt up herself. Dru got up behind her and eased his engorged member into her pussy with great dexterity, holding her open with his fingers, finding just the right angle and invading her creamy depths with the loving care of a man who is determined to make a brilliant first impression on a woman he plans to both win and keep. Without being told, he brought one hand around to place sensitive fingers against her pussy mound and clit, traveling back and forth from it to her g spot, and pausing to squeeze her now freshly flat belly with intuitive expertise. Under these educated manipulations and with the other exotic events of the evening still uppermost in her mind, Pamela did not need longer than five minutes to give in to the second cascading climax of the night. Dru was not far behind her in releasing the pent up passion he'd been nurturing for Pamela since dancing with her on that other perfect night at Michael's bar.

"I'm sorry I can't linger," said Pamela, briskly putting herself back together a few minutes later. "But my husband will be expecting me at home."

"Of course," said Dru, making himself respectable again.

"But it was very nice," she said with a smile.

"I loved it," he replied softly.

"Did you really mean what you said about being my slave?" she asked, brushing her short, shiny bob in a mirror.

"Oh yes!" he cried.

"I'll be needing to go to Boston one day this week. I have to check out things at the other store there. I could use some one to come along and help me carry things."

"I have Tuesdays and Wednesdays free," he said.

"Would you like to join me on Tuesday, then?" she asked. His heart leapt at the thought of them staying overnight in Boston together.

"I would love it!" he replied, seizing her around her small waist, lifting her off her feet and swinging her around. Pamela laughed, flushed, dizzy and basking in Dru's unequivocal admiration.

Then she looked at him seriously and said, "This will be our secret."

Chapter Thirteen

Ambrose Courts Polyxena

Meanwhile, Polyxena, who had just closed the gym for the night, was not surprised to find Ambrose Bartlett waiting for her in the parking lot, leaning against his sleek, silver car. Fresh from his workout and shower, smartly brushed, smoothly groomed and immaculate in a black polo shirt and khaki trousers, Bartlett looked good to Polyxena and she smiled at him.

"Hello. Are you waiting for me?" she asked, opening the door of her Volvo SUV with the touch of a button on her key.

"I was going to ask you if you felt like getting a snack and drink," he said, with a complete lack of self-consciousness.

"You think I go out with married men?" she asked with amusement.

"Why not?" he replied, thinking not of his marital status but how snugly the simple cotton sundress she had on clung to her full bosom, trim waist and swelling hips.

"Why do you think I'm so easy?" she asked, remembering how he had swatted her bottom as she bent over to pick up some pool weights as he was heading for the locker room.

"I don't," he protested, opening her car door for her.

"Yes, you do. You slapped my bottom."

"I couldn't resist. Why have a bottom like that if you don't want it slapped?"

She got behind her wheel but paused to look at him.

"Where did you want to go for this snack?" she asked.

"The Ball and Feather."

"Well, I am hungry," she mused. "All right. I'll meet you there," she said, slamming her door shut and starting her engine. Ambrose jumped into his car and followed her into the village of Random Point, and directly to the inn. The dining room connected to the bar was still open and innkeeper Connie seated Polyxena and Ambrose in a red leather booth.

"When I'm hungry, I eat," Polyxena informed Bartlett, "I don't pick like a little bird. Okay?"

Bartlett looked at her quizzically. "Sure, why wouldn't it be?" he asked, smiling at her with his chin on his hand.

"According to your wives, you weigh their portions. Or weigh them. This obsession with the skinny seems to have lost you your first wife. Am I right?"

"Goddamn, are we back to that Venus Club dinner?"

"Yes." Polyxena then turned to Connie and ordered a rib eye steak and pan roasted potatoes along with a glass of merlot. Bartlett did the same.

"Your body is perfect."

"Perfect, is it?" Polyxena laughed. "Oh, you must really want to get my knickers off tonight!"

"Tell me about your life in Holland, as a mistress. I don't think I've ever met a mistress before."

A slight cloud came over Polyxena's brow as she saw herself in a dungeon, day after day, night after night, the scores of slaves, the bonds, the gags, the lips upon her shoes and toes, the bald heads shining up at her as she towered above their kneeling forms in her corsets and five inch stiletto heeled boots, the preponderance of pancake flat, no longer young, male buttocks, striped from her floggers and canes. She shook her head to clear it of these images and smiled upon him lazily.

"I was popular," she admitted, "but I'm happier doing what I'm doing now."

"I'm not surprised, you've made a tremendous success of the gym. But did you always do the topping? Or once in a while did someone get to top you?"

"Oh, I started in a dungeon as a submissive," she readily admitted. "But in Europe," she continued, "the submissives don't have it so nice as here."

"What do you mean?"

"It's more a slave culture there, not domestic or romantic discipline, like here. From what I'm seeing in this town's sub-rosa B&D clique, all the submissive women are leading independent lives. No one asks permission to do anything, and none of them do any naked scrubbing on their hands and knees."

"You got that right," he agreed wistfully. "In this part of the world, the subs train the doms." Then he thoughtfully added, "But at any rate, they're all too busy with actual jobs to be slaves. Pamela routinely works twelve hour days."

"Is that what she's doing right now, working?"

"It's possible. But she's also got a new friend this summer, Amanda Sands. They've been inseparable the past few weeks, so I expect she's with her."

"That's true, they've been into the gym together at least every other day."

"No one can stay away from your gym. It's your magnetic presence."

Polyxena looked at him cynically. "You must really want me badly," she marveled.

"You know damn well we all want you."

"Then why does no one approach me," she mused.

"Don't they?"

"Not often."

"Maybe they're thrown by the ex-mistress pedigree."

"And then also, most are married," she reminded him.

"I know, but even married people play a little in our scene, as I understand it."

"Do they?"

"Certainly. What do you think happens at parties?"

"People take license to do crazy things," Polyxena reflected as their salads came and they fell to eating.

Presently Bartlett said, "You said you started as a slave in a dungeon over there? Did you not like the things they put you through?"

"I hated it. I just gritted my teeth and got through it, to learn. They insist upon that over there."

"So you didn't like any of it?"

"Oh, I'm not saying I couldn't enjoy a beautiful laced leather body bag or a nice, stimulating spanking, but the usual requirements were far beyond that."

Bartlett asked, "Ball gags and suspension bondage?"

"Oh yes, all that and more, much more. Dildos every where, sexual servitude, clamps, needles, hot wax, two quart enemas."

"And you gave in to all of that?"

"What did I know? They tell you everyone starts that way," Polyxena replied, somewhat resentfully.

"Why don't you let me pay you for a session? I promise to spoil you rotten and make you come."

"Oh that's right, you're the big spender too," Polyxena grinned. "They talked about all of the fancy clothes you send them. They're onto you, you know. They know you've hooked them with dresses and shoes."

"I just like to see ladies look pretty," he replied innocently.

"Tell me something," Polyxena said, before turning to the perfectly grilled steak that had just been placed before her, "how can you afford to spoil so many women? You have to pay something for the clothes you give away. I would fear a situation like in that novel *L'assomoir*. Gervais stocks her shop with expensive chocolates, then eats them all up so there is no stock to sell to the customers. How do you manage to hold onto whatever slim profits are to be had these days?"

"It's a fair question," said Bartlett, delighted by the way her mind worked. She was a shrewd businesswoman who never dreamed of reducing her profits by showering her favorites with free services. "The answer is that I'm doing better than ever. The wealthy are buying up luxury goods at record speed and I sell the highest end merchandise on the Cape. My pets don't receive couture as presents, only nice, smart, ready to wear, and I can well afford to disperse those items on a whim."

"I don't need to be paid for a session," Polyxena surprised him by saying. "I am also doing well."

Ambrose sighed, "So I'm going to have to charm the pants off you instead?"

"You're doing a pretty good job at the moment," she assured him, beginning her second glass of wine.

Knowing he had gained a significant amount of ground in his siege of Polyxena, Bartlett left it at that for the evening. They finished their pleasant dinner, each got into their respective cars and drove home mildly flushed and prepared to spend the night thinking about each other.

Chapter Fourteen

A Shocking Discovery

After finishing their late night snack at Michael's tavern, Amanda and Colby gave the somewhat inebriated Pascal Robbins a lift back to Anthony Newton's house and dropped him off in front. Pascal had arranged to call Phoebe on her cell phone as soon as he arrived so that she could come downstairs and be driven home. Robbins was about to do just that when he noticed that the front door was slightly ajar. Several minutes before, Dennis had heard the plaintive mew of a stray cat he had been feeding for the past few days and had left the door open while he went into the pantry to find some kibble to present it with. A rather dreadful plan formed in the mind of the jealous husband, to creep up the stairs and eavesdrop at the door behind which Phoebe was currently ensconced with the Broadway composer, in order to uncover any adulterous behavior that might be underway. The lithe photographer ran up the main staircase and lightly made his way towards the music room, where he knew they customarily rehearsed.

As luck, or perhaps misfortune, would have it, the French doors were slightly ajar, and while Pascal couldn't see the forms of his wife and her maestro at the piano in 3D, his heart contracted painfully as he saw their reflection together in one of the many elegant gilt mirrors which lined the room and faced the slightly open door. The image that flashed before his eyes but momentarily was enough to give any husband a mortal pang, as it clearly showed his lovely Phoebe, in one of her usual full skirted, portrait collar sundresses, locked in Newton's arms, her head thrown back while his lips grazed her white throat. Pascal's was so shocked that his knees almost went out from under him. For the scene that he was witnessing was no slap and tickle horseplay, but rather a classic clinch right off the cover of a bodice ripper. Phoebe was letting another man kiss her and press her against him. Her bottom sat upon the lap of another man and her eyes were shut in rapture as the other man's lips devoured her throat and earlobes.

Pascal half ran -- half jumped down the stairs and rushed outside into the balmy night air. Walking a little way down the driveway, he put in his call to Phoebe, to let her know he had arrived and was downstairs waiting for her. She answered the phone immediately and breathlessly and promised to be down directly. Pascal got into his own SUV and was shocked by the wild-eyed image that met his gaze in the mirror. There was no way he could pretend not to be upset. In the back of his mind he remembered, Phoebe knew that he had laid hands on Amanda. But she didn't know about the subsequent kiss, a kiss which, in any case, had been but a pale suggestion of a kiss compared to what he had seen in the mirror, Phoebe half dragged across Newton's lap, bosom heaving, face dreamy with delight. She was letting Newton make genuine, romantic love to her! In some sense it would have felt better to Pascal to have caught her with her skirt up over the composer's knee, or even roughly bent over a table, but the melting desire on Phoebe's face as Newton gently ravished her in true Hollywood style, was seriously disturbing.

"And yet, wasn't I just as bad with Amanda?" Pascal thought. "Don't I long to take advantage of one unguarded moment with Amanda to undo her?" These were uncomfortable thoughts and he got out of the car again to pace and smoke a cigarette while he waited. What should he say, what should he do? Whatever he did, it had to be between himself and Phoebe alone. He didn't think of confronting Newton. Too much depended on Newton's patronage to get huffy with him because his wife was a slut. They made movies out of Newton's musicals. Phoebe could be on the verge of the career she deserved. And he was much too fond of his wife to interfere in such a way so as to injure that career. The summer would eventually end, Newton would go back to New York and they to Boston. But could he really continue to live with a woman who was in love with another man? Because that was exactly what her body language implied.

The next moment Phoebe came out of the house and hurried to join him, her cheeks flushed and her eyes wide with apprehension. He looked at her coldly. She stopped short. "Pascal, what is it?"

"You know damn well what it is," he replied.

"Really?" she returned, surprisingly acerbic for all her being flustered, "maybe *I* know things as well!"

"What the hell do you mean by that?"

"I don't know what you know, but I know you're not as good as you expect me to be!" she accused.

"Why, what have you heard?"

"That you laid hands on Amanda Sands."

"Nonsense. I gave the little brat a few swats for cutting her hair," he replied indignantly, waiting the moment or two he knew would produce the riposte, "And you kissed her too!" if Phoebe also had command of this vital fact. Instead she folded her arms, looked at him and said, "You spanked a beautiful girl who you know is into it. If that isn't making a pass, tell me what is, Pascal."

"No, it was not making a pass," he replied with heat. "It was making a point. After all, she's my model. At any rate, what I did doesn't even come close to ... adultery!"

"There's been no adultery," Phoebe returned, on the brink of tears.

"I saw you in another man's arms, Phoebe," Pascal said angrily. "Explain your way out of that if you can!"

"I can't," she said, hanging her head in shame. "I...I..." she hesitated.

"You what?" he snapped.

"I'm in love with Mr. Newton!" the words rang out in the still night air with awful clarity. Pascal was floored by the passionate conviction in Phoebe's avowal.

"...What?"

"It's true and I'm very sorry," she confessed. "I have a mad, overwhelming crush on Mr. Newton and I can't think of anything else."

"Phoebe, do you know how this hurts me?" Pascal demanded, his righteous indignation suddenly replaced by stunned resignation. Mere licentiousness he could address with the back of a hairbrush, but if

Phoebe were truly in love with another man, could there be any reason to return to the same house with her tonight?

"I know, Pascal, I know. But the emotion is too powerful to suppress any longer. I couldn't hide it from Mr. Newton any longer and now it wouldn't be fair to try and hide it from you."

"So you're saying that you no longer love me? You want to break up?" he asked, stupefied at the way this evening was turning out.

"No. I love you. Of course I still love you. But I'm in the throes of a wild infatuation and I'm going to give it its head."

"Over my dead body you will," Pascal said with sudden determination. "Get it the car."

"Why? What are you going to do?" she fell back a step, her hand to her throat.

"I'm taking my little slut of a wife home and beating the hell out of her," Pascal said, tossing her into the front seat and driving off with her.

"Seriously?" Phoebe looked at him, her voluptuous bosom heaving above the scalloped trim of her dainty sundress.

"Certainly! And I'll enjoy it too," he replied with satisfaction. The gauntlet was down and there was no way he was giving his woman up to another man without a fight. Perversely, the frankness with which she had described her new passion fired his blood rather than cooled it towards her. He strongly sensed she was about to show her absolute independence from him by offering to leave him without demur and he found that more interesting in Phoebe than if she had begged him to let her stay.

Both of them jumped at a sudden flash of lightning and the subsequent crack of thunder that rent the air. Looking out the window Phoebe noticed that a cloudbank had moved in over the Cape and as Pascal threw the car in gear and drove off, it began to rain hard and fast.

"What about poor Susan?" Pascal snapped at his wife. "We're only staying at her house for the summer," he reminded her. "How do you think she'd feel if she knew about what you've been up to with her man?"

Phoebe looked a little stricken at being reminded of Anthony's pleasant, cheerful young companion of the last seven years. "Aren't you betraying her as well as me?" he pressed his advantage to inflict the maximum amount of guilt.

"Perhaps, to an insignificant degree," Phoebe answered thoughtfully. "But everyone says that she pleases herself and Anthony doesn't watch her very closely."

"That's interesting because I get the feeling she's almost a wife to him."

"She is, but not a monogamous one."

"You know this for a fact?"

"No, from inference. A lot of the women in this town have had love affairs with each other's men. It seems to be common knowledge and it doesn't seem to bother any of them."

"How terribly European!" he snapped. "Is that what you're doing? Has it gone that far?" he demanded.

"No," she replied and followed him into Susan's house just as it began to pour even harder.

She stopped in the foyer and looked at him as he locked the door behind them.

"So if it's not an affair, what is it?" he asked.

"A heart pounding crush that's gotten out of control on my side and the gracious response of a charming man on Mr. Newton's," she answered candidly, in spite of the very real fear of the promised thrashing. Phoebe would submit to being slapped, but if he dared to give her a black eye, she would have to leave him.

"Oh, you're saying it's all down to you? Newton isn't personally invested in seducing you?"

Phoebe shook her head.

"Right!" he snorted in disbelief.

"Tonight...I practically flung myself into his arms."

"Phoebe, how could you?"

"I couldn't help myself."

"Do you want me to leave?"

"No!" she returned emphatically.

"No? Then I'm baffled. What do you expect me to do?"

"Just ignore it if you can. It'll all blow over soon," she promised.

"You've got to be kidding me. You think I'm going to just ignore you going out on me?"

"I haven't gone out on you."

"Not yet, but that man isn't indifferent to you. He's crazy about you. Anyone can see that."

"Pascal, my head is spinning. I need to go to bed," she said in a rush and ran upstairs to the suite on the third floor they had been occupying all summer.

Phoebe wanted to hide her face, listen to the rain and think about Anthony Newton kissing her, not answer endless questions or endure more scolding. This was the most magical summer of her life, what with the plum role and the opportunity to work under her idol. Falling in love with the maestro was as inevitable as morning fog rolling in off the ocean. It wasn't fair of Pascal to torment her like this when she was luxuriating in the first illegitimate passion of her hitherto faultlessly virtuous but nonetheless artistic life. If she was to be a true diva, she had to *live!*

Pascal didn't follow her directly, but stopped in the downstairs sitting room to pour himself a brandy, which he downed while pacing and reflecting on the best course of action to pursue. It rather disconcerted him that Phoebe wasn't more upset by the enormity of her transgression. She had expressed almost no guilt or remorse and had certainly not promised to abandon her new fixation or even reevaluate her behavior. She was, in fact, being very naughty.

Susan's house was sat atop a gentle hill at the edge of the village, opposite a very old graveyard. Pascal looked out the parlor window at the rain sleeting down on the small stones and black ironwork fence as he tried to figure out what he wanted to do. It was true that he was terribly distressed by the thought of his wife being in love with another man, and not just regular besottment, full scale hero worship mixed with the rarified spice of being a part of this millionaire genius' esoteric fetish world. With all of her waking thoughts given over to Anthony Newton, could there be any quality emotion left for him? Perhaps he could recapture her heart. Perhaps he had never lost it. But was now the moment to try, when she was completely caught up in the excitement and glamour of being Newton's protégée? Both pride and common sense dictated that he leave now and not return to Phoebe until the Newton adventure had worn itself out. But somehow, perversely, and inexplicably, Pascal didn't feel like leaving Phoebe even for an hour.

Why should he abandon the field? He was Phoebe's husband and wished to continue so. It was obvious that Phoebe herself was momentarily beyond reason, but he was beginning to think that to confront Newton might in fact be the best possible way to head off the inevitable. Newton was a civilized man who would most likely respond to a petition from Pascal to leave his wife alone with his usual sensitivity and tact. This would certainly not jeopardize her role in the cast of his show.

Have resolved to visit Newton the following day and make his case, Pascal felt every inclination to go upstairs and spend the night beside Phoebe as usual. But he also knew his honor demanded he do something to express his displeasure to his wife.

He found Phoebe, in a sheer white cotton gown already under the covers with the lights off. She turned her eyes towards him as he entered the room, enough cloud filtered moonlight coming in through the many tall windows for each to see the other clearly.

"You don't think you're getting away with what you did tonight without being punished, do you?" he asked, sitting on the bed, pulling back the cover and drawing her across his lap. Without pausing to pull up the hem of her nightgown he brought the palm of his hand down on her plump, Italian batiste covered buttocks with all the vigor of a righteously indignant spouse. "Did you dream I wouldn't spank the living day lights out of you for coming onto another man when you're my wife?" Again and again his hard hand came down, faster and faster, as Phoebe helplessly thrashed and squirmed to get free, crying out with pain and shock as she got the hardest spanking of her life from her man.

"Don't you dare," he warned, recentering her on his lap, folding her arm to her waist and pinning it under one hand by the wrist. "I don't even know what sort of punishment unfaithful wives get in your world," he said, pausing to let her catch her breath, "but I don't have time to read up on it now." Then two more increasingly uncomfortable minutes passed for Phoebe. "You made a marriage vow, now keep it," he advised her sternly, winding up the windmill of swats he'd been visiting on her belabored and radiant backside.

"You brute!" she cried, jumping up and stamping her tiny foot at him, her hands unconsciously pressed to her bottom. Sobbing uncontrollably, tears streaming from her eyes, she fled to the bathroom, locking the door behind her. Once there she quickly dried her tears and looked at herself in the mirror. Pulling up her gown she examined the reflection of her magenta stained cheeks. She was fair enough to always turn this most electric shade of pink when severely spanked. The moment he'd released her the dreadful pain began to fade, but the memory of her complete helplessness under the assault brought fresh tears to her eyes. This had been a punishment indeed, for Phoebe had been thinking not of discipline but love that very night. She'd received not one, but a garland of kisses from Anthony Newton, from her earlobes to her throat to her lips, while she had been clasped in his arms. When a girl receives such expressions of regard from her very idol, she has reached the zenith of romantic nirvana, and it is rather rude to be yanked back down to earth from this supernatural plane by being smacked awake by one's outraged husband.

"Should artistes even have husbands?" she wondered aloud, brushing her long, chestnut brown hair in the mirror. "Am I not a free spirit? But as yet untried?"

Pascal went into the adjoining dressing room, exchanged his clothes for a light cotton robe and grabbing his extra toothbrush from a traveling case, went to the next closest bathroom to brush his teeth. They were completely alone in the house so it wouldn't be causing a scandal for him to find somewhere else to sleep other than the marital bed that night. As he had spanked her very hard, he contemplated this and in the end thought it a sound plan. This placed him in the small bedroom next to their suite.

When Phoebe heard these various doors open and close within ten minutes, she realized that Pascal had taken himself to another apartment and returned to theirs. Jumping into bed she pulled the covers up over her head and exhausted from all the emotions of the day, fell fast asleep.

The next morning Phoebe awoke early, as usual, showered and walked into the village to buy provisions for breakfast. When she returned, bearing fresh apple crumb muffins, blueberries, eggs and cheese for their breakfast, Pascal had already gone, without leaving the usual note. She had not been surprised at him choosing to sleep apart from her the previous night. Any other course of action would have been intolerably awkward, given the degree of umbrage he had taken at her behavior. Were they to lie side by side and for the first time not touch? Turn their backs on each other and pout all the night long? Better to cool off. Each needed time to ponder how they really felt about the disclosures of the previous night.

Pascal awoke convinced that the simple strategy he had already formulated to deal with the problem was to confront its cause. So he went directly to Newton's house and sent his name up with Dennis.

Anthony received his guest in the dining room where he was breakfasting alone with the New York Times open on a laptop in front of him. Accepting a seat at the table and allowing Dennis to pour him a cup of coffee before departing, Pascal came right to the point of his visit.

"Thanks for seeing me this early. I know you're busy," Pascal said politely because his relationship with Newton went back several years and had always been the most cordial. "I know about you and Phoebe and I'm not happy about it."

Anthony thought, "Wow, that was fast!" and wondered what had made her confess to her husband so quickly after their first kiss.

"I saw you kissing her last night," Pascal said.

Seldom at a loss for words, Newton found himself speechless on the present occasion. Did one say, "Sorry?" for example. It seemed polite, yet inadequate. And yet, did this affronted husband really hold the moral high ground when Newton knew so much about Pascal's interest in Amanda?

Finally Newton said, "I'm sorry. The truth is Phoebe has a sort of crush on me and I'm finding her hard to resist. But I've thought of a way to turn this around. Do you want to hear it?"

"Sure," Pascal replied cautiously.

"Ladies don't bottle up strong emotions, they act on them. If you don't let her get this out of her system, she'll become even more obsessed and that wouldn't be good for any of us."

"Go on," said Pascal.

"Before I tell you my idea there is a vital piece of information I possess that may change your attitude toward Phoebe to a certain degree."

"Oh? What's that?"

"I know you kissed Amanda Sands. Amanda told Susan and Susan told me. Phoebe doesn't know it though. And she never needs to."

Pascal instantly grasped Newton's implication. If Phoebe did know that he, Pascal, was just as bad as she was, how could he ever reproach her with throwing herself at Newton? Checkmate.

"What do you propose?" Pascal asked.

"Let Phoebe have a little fling with me. I guarantee to fall far below her expectations in every meaningful way. She'll realize that you've always been the one and return to you a chastened wife."

"By fling you mean, go all the way?"

"Not exactly, it would be more like taking her to a scary Boston dungeon and putting her through some real B&D. It's not her scene so she'll come back and tell you she was all wrong about me."

Pascal considered the proposition, his chin on his hand. So he knew about the kiss, as did Susan and no doubt Pamela. But still Phoebe didn't know and that was what counted. For the moment she did know, he would lose every shred of credibility as a trustworthy partner, just as she had done with him last night.

"I hate to say this, but it's a pretty good plan," said Pascal. They shook on it and he went home.

Pascal Robbins obviously had no idea of how sexual activities could become in a dungeon. His imagination went to stocks and St. Andrew's Crosses, both of which Phoebe had expressed a horror of in previous discussions they had held about BDSM. Whereas Anthony was thinking of bondage beds and spanking benches, birches and floggers, with mirrors in front and behind, so that Phoebe could see herself being undone from every voluptuous angle. Anthony Newton was only human. He'd felt a strong attraction for Phoebe for several years now and there was no doubt she was painfully in love with him. He'd naturally noticed the brief looks of anxiety that flitted across Susan's face when Phoebe's name was mentioned. She felt what was going on. But it was summer and Phoebe looked so luscious in tight sundresses with her creamy cleavage and round buttocks straining against the print cottons trimmed with lace. Phoebe was a delicious dessert sub, pink, white and fresh, almost innocent and yet overflowing with artistic accomplishments. He loved that she could sing to him as he played. He rather loved her in general. So it had to happen. Of course it had to happen. Better to have neutralized Pascal in advance. How much he would stick to the plan of disillusioning Phoebe he had not yet decided. He had co-opted the noble notion from a dozen screwball comedies in which it had always backfired. But Pascal needn't know that.

Arriving home, Pascal could no longer avoid entering the master bedroom as he needed to change his clothes. When he did so the first thing he heard was Phoebe's mellifluous voice gaily singing Cole Porter's *"What Shall I Do?"* in the bathtub. It was one of Phoebe's favorite songs and he'd heard her sing it many times before. Now it cut like a knife with its jaunty lyrics about a girl who *"loves not one, but two"* Apollo Belvederes. She certainly sounded insouciant for a girl who had been spanked to tears by her husband the previous night. Even choosing to sing that particular song on this particular day seemed a stinging insult to Pascal, who was paradoxically incensed and inflamed by her apparent indifference to his emotions.

As for Phoebe, all she had though about all night, luxuriating alone in the plush guest bed, was the fact that Anthony Newton had kissed her. In the grip of the most intense passion she had felt since the early days of her romance with Pascal, Phoebe was selfishly excluding her husband from her thoughts completely that morning.

As she looked in the mirror while drying herself she saw that nine hours later, her bottom still continued to blush. It had been a very hard spanking. But he had caught her nearly being unfaithful, so she supposed it had been fully merited, that once.

Coming out of the bathroom in a peach dressing gown, with her hair down on her shoulders, she started at Pascal digging through drawers for a fresh shirt and underwear. His chin came up when he saw her.

"Good morning," he said guardedly.

"Hello," she replied coolly.

"You okay?" he asked brusquely.

"Do you really care?" she asked, turning and pulling up the back of her robe so he could see how red she still was. "It's not supposed to be red ten hours later!" she cried.

Pascal smiled for the first time that morning, took his clothes and went into his own dressing room to change.

Chapter Fifteen

The Bostonians

That Tuesday morning dawned slightly foggy, yet warm, promising a golden day to come. Pamela awaited Dru at the shop at seven am and had him load a half dozen packed garment bags into the trunk of her car, which already contained an overnight bag.

"We might stay overnight, do you want to run home and pack a few things?" Pamela asked.

"I do have a bag in my car," he said, blushing, as he'd hopefully anticipated this eventuality.

"Get it then," she said, blushing back, with a merry shake of her shiny black bob. She looked as sharp and fresh as a page from Marie Clare that morning in a fitted white shirt with three quarter sleeves, a straight khaki skirt and dark brown stack heeled pumps.

In a few minutes they were off down the road to Boston, Pamela behind the wheel and Dru in the front seat beside her, the balmy perfumed breeze rushing in through the open windows of the sedan infusing them with that certain sensation of summer bliss mostly keenly felt by the young. Dru was speechless with happiness as he returned Pamela's carefree smile.

"So who is Dru Baxter?" she asked without removing her gaze from the road.

"What do you mean?" he laughed.

"Well, all I know of you is that you work at Marguerite's coffee bar when you're home from college and that somehow, several years back, when you were barely eighteen, if that, you managed to get into one of Hugo's parties with your then girlfriend, Gigi. Whatever became of her, by the way?" Pamela asked.

"She's been at Radcliffe, but she's in Europe for the summer," he replied.

"How did you two manage to crash that party anyway?" Pamela asked.

"We were both at Braemar at the time and we both liked to hang out at Marguerite's bookstore. She has all those great books up in the top gallery. I was there so often that eventually she offered me a job as stock boy during weekends and holidays. Well, the more I was around Marguerite and Hope at the shop, the more I realized that there's a genuine spanking scene in Random Point and of course I wanted in. Gigi and I had been playing spanking games all year, with me spanking her, traditional style. But I might as well admit, at that point in time, I fancied myself a switch and was wild to have a submissive experience with an older woman."

"Go on," said Pamela encouragingly.

"Well, Marguerite was kind enough to give me a scene that I'll never forget and Hope continues to mesmerize me, but I haven't yet found a spankable girlfriend to replace Gigi."

"I'm a bit confused. What is your current orientation? You offered to be my slave, but what does that even mean?"

"Only that I'd love to serve you, in any way I can," he replied cheerfully.

"I don't think that I could ever do what Marguerite did to you," Pamela warned. "I've never had the slightest desire to spank a man."

"No, nor should you," said Dru, daring to place a small kiss on her smooth cheek. "You should always use a crop or a flogger. You're far too elegant to merely spank."

"That's not what I meant," she grinned.

"I know, Pamela. And I agree. You and you alone should be the object of attention and adoration."

"You know you're very charming," she smiled at him and drove on.

They arrived in Bay Back by mid morning and stopped for lunch on Boylston Street. Pamela had never felt a sharper or more healthy appetite than during the past week or so and guiltlessly allowed herself a cup of corn chowder and a dish of ravioli stuffed with summer squash and ricotta. Dru ordered the grilled eggplant, goat cheese and greens and they shared all the dishes between them, including the soup from the same spoon. They needed no spirits to feel intoxicated with each other's easy, cheerful, stress free company. After their meal they proceeded to the *Damaris* store, just a few blocks away, and Dru carried in Pamela's newest samples for the manager to see.

After conducting about an hour of business at the store, Pamela led Dru on a walking tour of all her favorite Back Bay shops, loading him with any purchases she could not do without as they continued to get to know each other.

"So, where did you leave it with your Gigi?" Pamela asked Dru while waiting to be brought shoes to try on in an elegant Newbury Street salon.

"She's not my Gigi anymore. We broke up."

Pamela promptly decided on the shoes, purchased them and whisked Dru back out onto the street as rapidly as possible, eager to hear about the interesting conclusion of the achingly young scene romance.

"Why did you break up?" she asked as they continued along the sun-splashed pavement on the warm, lovely day.

"I guess I can be totally honest with you," he said with a shy smile.

"Of course you can," Pamela assured him. "After all, we've been as close as two people can get already."

"Yes!" Dru replied, taking one of her hands and kissing it gratefully, for the fact that this stunningly stylish Venus had allowed him the ultimate liberty continued to astonish him with joy.

"Well, Gigi is a total alpha girl and can be a little bitch. I let her walk all over me because she's so damned cute and she seriously gave it up to me all the time, plus let me spank her. But when she found out I'd gone sub to Marguerite, who she knew I had a crush on, it pretty much ruined me as a top in her eyes. I lost my credibility. That party at Hugo's was the beginning of the end for me and her. Hugo and Marguerite were mildly pissed that we'd gotten in and made it a condition that we would both have to submit to spankings if we wanted to be allowed to stay. Some of the prettiest ladies took me in another room and initiated me into domestic discipline."

"And you liked it?" Pamela asked, with a twinkle in her dark eyes

"I have to admit, it was too much fun," he grinned. "But the punishment was that I fell in Gigi's eyes."

"What happened next?"

"What happened next was that in my immaturity, I tried to prove I still had it in me to top her and wound up coming on way too strong. She resented it and walked out on me that night. I haven't been with her since."

"And now you're at Vassar," Pamela stated. Dru looked appropriately pleased and embarrassed at once at that fact. "Where there is no shortage of alpha girls. What's going on with that?"

"I'm not saying I haven't had a few encounters this year," Dru said, "but none have taken so far."

"Because you obviously need a scene girl," Pamela said.

"Do you think so?"

"Well, maybe not. Maybe you'd be just as happy serving a vanilla beauty who is virtually unconscious of your proclivities and merely thinks you gallant."

"I could live with that," he replied.

"So you thought you'd practice a bit with me beforehand?" she teased him.

"That sounds awful put like that," he protested.

"Oh, look at where we are," said Pamela, looking up at the awning of a discreet boutique hotel called the Jewel. "I just remembered something. Let's go in."

Dru was amazed to realize that Pamela was picking up the key to a room she had booked for their use that day. They walked upstairs to a beautifully furnished third floor suite and locked themselves in for the next three hours, only pausing to order up sandwiches and coffee in the late afternoon.

As the sun began to go down, Pamela began to think about whether she wished to return to Random Point that night. Then she got a text from Amanda stating that she and Colby were also in Boston that night and asking whether they should all get together.

Pamela looked at Dru, who was finishing getting dressed after a shower in the lavishly appointed bathroom that connected to the suite.

"Shall we meet Amanda and Colby and continue our evening with them?" Pamela asked.

"That sounds great!" Dru replied enthusiastically, for this meant that they would surely spend the night in town, a night during which he could actually sleep with Pamela.

Keeping their activities conveniently anchored in Back Bay, the four friends beguiled the early part of the evening at a performance of a Molière play, which lightened their already buoyant mood even further. Pamela realized with a start that her new group of much younger friends were infusing a sense of fun into her day to day existence that had never been there before, even during her own somewhat fretful youth. And then, the majority of her lovers in recent years had been slightly to significantly older men. Sloan Taylor had been youthful and lovable but still in his thirties. Pascal, whom she had traveled with for a year, was in his thirties. Hugo was in his forties when Pamela developed her crush on him. Ambrose was just over forty as well. All of these men were handsome and appealing, skillfully and effortlessly dominant, confident to a fault and being around them was charming. But it wasn't the same as being with a group of beautiful Ivy League brats with perverse sex on their minds all the summer day.

After the play they stopped at a small café for pizza. Then Amanda suggested that they all repair to Hugo's apartment, a few blocks away, where she and Colby were spending the night. Pamela had been there once before, when she had worked for Hugo and engaged in a brief dalliance with him. They had gone to Boston for the day and wound up playing at the flat for an hour before returning to Random Point. This was at the height of her passion for Hugo and the interlude had represented rather a highlight in their very brief erotic relationship.

Dru was the only one who hadn't been to Hugo's yet and he duly admired the opulently tasteful décor as Amanda invited them to be seated in the front parlor while she went to fetch a bottle of wine. Colby went along to open it.

Pamela lay back on a sofa and kicked her pumps off. Without being bidden, Dru took one of her long, slender, nylon stockinged feet between his hands and began to gently massage it. She looked at him in surprise but presently shut her eyes in exquisite enjoyment, for she'd been on the four-inch heels all day. When Amanda returned, Pamela opened her eyes like a lazy cat and said, "Weed?"

"Of course, my princess," said Amanda with a grin, going directly to the cabinet where Hugo kept his stash. After a few companionable minutes of wine sipping and pipe filling, the company became even more relaxed. Amanda sat in the bay window seat and looked from one to the other of them thoughtfully. "So here we are, four people in the scene, alone together," she said, adding, "It's almost enough for a party."

Pamela looked at Dru and smiled, saying, "Yes."

"Colby and I have never been to one so far," said Amanda, "what are they like?" Colby was seated on the sofa and Amanda was seated on the floor between his legs, tightly wrapped in an autumn leaf print jersey halter dress, her long legs bare and her pretty feet mounted on russet wedge sandals.

"They're like being in a fairy tale or dream," said Pamela unexpectedly. "You never know who will be behind a door, a monster or a prince, or what will happen if you let it close behind you."

"I've only been to that one so far, that Hugo gave," said Dru, "but I agree completely, the atmosphere feels other worldly, as if you've entered your own fantasy landscape. And anything can happen there."

"Let's get back to the 'we have enough for a party' concept," said Colby practically, his hands carelessly ruffling Amanda's fringe of short blonde hair and pinching her earlobes, which made her squirm between his legs and continuously bat his hands away, though not so firmly as to discourage him from continuing with these attentions.

"I'll bet I know what two young men would do with two girls like us if they could," said Amanda to Pamela, "tie us up naked on a bed and take turns strapping us."

This imagined proposition drew a gasp from Dru and an enthusiastic nod of approval from Colby, which Amanda glimpsed when she grinned up at him over her shoulder.

"Are you quite sure they wouldn't rather watch *me* spank *you*?" Pamela replied, sliding her feet back into her heels.

"Oh my god, she's right, that's even better," thought Colby in instantaneous admiration of the endlessly creative Mrs. Bartlett, but waited for Amanda's reaction before commenting.

"Really?" asked Amanda, looking at Pamela with wonder.

Pamela shrugged, "From what I know of men in the scene, that's the way their minds work," she offered as though she had no personal feelings invested in the subject but was merely taking a scientific interest in its exploration.

"Is this true, young men?" Amanda demanded.

"If it is," said Colby staunchly, "it's only because you're so ludicrously bossy with Pamela as a general rule."

"I'm so glad someone finally noticed," laughed Pamela, at which Amanda pouted.

"If I've been bossy with Pamela it's because she needs someone to correct her bad behavior patterns. It's not my fault that at eighteen I'm more mature and sensible than Pamela is at twenty eight."

"She's absolutely right," said Pamela, "and yet it rankles."

"But I like bossing Pamela around," Amanda protested.

"You like bossing everyone around," Colby pointed out.

"What about all the time and energy I expend improving your lives?" demanded Amanda. "For that alone you owe me the tribute of obedience to my will."

"What if I agreed to let you film it for your clips store?" Pamela shocked Amanda by suggesting, forgetting her up and coming reputation as a fashion designer and even that she and Damaris were going to show their line for the first time at fashion week in September, in favor of seeing herself, in the perfect outfit she had on, domming her exquisite teenaged girlfriend on film.

These words galvanized Amanda into action. As she wasn't Hugo's daughter for nothing, she jumped up and ran straight to the storage closet in the back of the flat where Hugo kept his spare video equipment, pulling Colby by the hand after her. Having a great beauty like Pamela offer herself for a video clip was a once in a lifetime opportunity for a beginner director of fetish erotica and Amanda was too intelligent to allow it to vanish without being fully exploited. The question was, should she herself finally break her own taboo and let her on-screen spanking be given on her bare skin?

Choosing the Roman shaded bay window as the background, they set up the straight-backed chair and arranged a few lights to effectively illuminate the set. Colby was sent to fetch Amanda's video camera from the car and the boys agreed as to who was to get the wide and medium shots and who the close-ups, arranging for a few silent signals between them for when it might be convenient to switch up the angles. Amanda gave directions while sharing a few more pipes with Pamela, which interesting diversion served the dual purpose of both relaxing and energizing them for the play-acting to come. Amanda examined Pamela's hands and declared her fingers unacceptably bony for administering a spanking to a bottom as peachy as her own. So she supplied Pamela with a brown oval leather paddle as well as a small ebony hairbrush.

"We'll stick to panties only," said Amanda to Pamela at the last moment, "to protect your reputation as much as mine."

"Agreed!" said Pamela, hugging Amanda affectionately. "And don't worry, I won't hurt you."

"The hell with that, Pamela," said Amanda thinking like a producer, "since it's going to be over clothes you need to make it even harder. Get a reaction out of me."

"This is gonna be great," Colby couldn't help confiding to a Dru who had been virtually stunned into silence by the curiously exciting turn the evening had taken.

"Shut up, you Neanderthal," said Amanda, "I forbid you to enjoy this more than only slightly." Then she turned to Pamela and said, "You'll have to improvise and direct yourself. Let's go for ten minutes."

"Right," said Pamela, touching up her lipstick and smoothing down her already faultlessly smooth bob in a mirror. Then with the two implements in one hand and Amanda's wrist in the other, Pamela stood at the doorway of the room and waited until both Colby and Dru had turned their cameras in her direction and refocused for a wide shot.

"Colby and Dru, when I say roll, track us closely as we walk into the set. Pamela, move more slowly and deliberately than you normally would, give the boys plenty of time to get us completely in frame before you make any abrupt changes," said Amanda remembering all the editing problems she might have avoided on her first few shoots had she put these simple instructions in practice then. "Okay, guys, start rolling," said Amanda presently. When she saw both their red lights glowing, Amanda nodded at Pamela. Pamela paused only to place the lightest of kisses on Amanda's wide, beautiful mouth, then led her blonde friend into the set with crisp determination, but pacing her firm steps slowly enough for the inexperienced cameramen to easily track her progress into the room. Before sitting down Pamela drew Amanda to the properly positioned chair and set her standing to one side of it, advising Amanda, "Don't even think of running away," in a clear, bell like tone of command. Then Pamela gracefully took the seat and carefully laid the hairbrush and paddle on a small, round table within reach. Pamela took her time in smoothing down her straight skirt and adjusting the angle of the chair with minute precision, remembering to give the cameras that moment to ready themselves for the pull over. Then she looked up at Amanda, took her by the wrist and jerked her straight across her immaculate lap.

Smoothing down the snug fitting skirt of Amanda's crimson, gold and burnt orange print dress, Pamela presented Dru with a rear angle head to toe shot while Colby covered their faces and torsos in a medium wide shot. A bit of skill was required between the boys to avoid entering each other's shots, but each had watched enough properly filmed spanking videos to be able to operate their cameras with instinctive skill.

Now all that was left to do was to enjoy the action that was about to unfold. For Colby it was a perfect spanking fantasy dream come true, for Amanda had been relentlessly bossing him around since the day they met and nothing had changed since he'd begun to vigorously and regularly spank her. Her firm, resilient, yoga trained buttocks took so well to spanking that discipline inspired little to no fear in her. But the humiliation of being turned over the knee of another lady and one who she, Amanda was accustomed to dominating almost completely, supplied the extra fillip of emotion one sought in a really memorable scene. Then there was the thrill of capturing this exquisite moment for all time on film. He wouldn't have to visualize this event to relive it, he could watch it. For some time he'd wanted to contribute to Amanda's spanking video library but was as yet unwilling to reveal himself before the camera, not knowing what career he would eventually choose and feeling far less cavalier about provable indiscretions than Amanda apparently was; this was the perfect opportunity to be a part of her creative fetish life at no personal risk.

Dru was thrilled for slightly different reasons, having to do with his sudden and flaming desire for Pamela, whom he worshipped as a goddess, melded with his attraction for spanking. And while he wasn't sorry that this sort of discipline would not be part of their personal relationship, he was happy to vicariously enjoy Pamela's punishment techniques as a useful voyeur. Pamela had been completely correct, heterosexual men and boys *did* enjoy seeing women spank girls on the most elemental, hard-wired level.

"Give me your hand," Pamela ordered, pulling Amanda's wrist into the small of her back and trapping it under her own. "And please behave unless you want to be leg locked," Pamela added, taking up the hair brush and briskly touching up Amanda's cotton wrapped bottom with six hard smacks to each jutting, upthrust cheek. This initial assault was so rapid, sharp and unexpected that Amanda squeaked and squirmed in surprise. "How dare you spank me that hard without a warm up?" Amanda cried. "It's dreadful etiquette and I object!"

"I got your attention, so objection overruled," replied Pamela coolly, letting go of Amanda's wrist and laying aside the hair brush. "Arch up so I can raise your skirt," Pamela ordered.

"So soon?"

Pamela picked up the hairbrush again and again applied it vigorously to Amanda's skirted bottom.

"Arch up?" Pamela repeated. This time Amanda complied, pouting.

After delicately lifting the print skirt to Amanda's tiny waist, Pamela pushed Amanda back down across her lap and regarded Amanda's luxuriously pantied bottom. Instantly recognizing the Loire brand of silk satin lingerie from Paris, which in all of the commonwealth, could only be purchased at her husband's store and then at a great price, Pamela realized that the lace trimmed tap pants were yet another expression of Ambrose Bartlett's admiration for her new best friend. Pamela took Amanda by her earlobe, decorated only by a tiny coral earring, and turned Amanda's head up. "Where does a young lady your age come by such expensive undergarments?" Spank! The palm of Pamela's hand came down on a pure silk satin covered bottom cheek with a resounding clap. "Are you being a little slut of an ivy league call girl again?" Pamela demanded, continuing to spank Amanda through the rich material that gleamed like a golden pearl across the crests of Amanda's jutting cheeks.

Amanda thought to herself, "Bitch is coming a little too close to the truth in this scenario," but she also knew that she had no one but herself to blame for that. The panties *had* come as a gift from Ambrose Bartlett. He was always sending her pretties, though he'd had no physical contact with her in many months.

"I can't help it if men spoil me," Amanda replied without concern. Pamela sighed and picked up the small wooden paddle.

"You can help it and you know very well how. Stop making yourself available to them. Show a little dignity and pride in your femininity!" Pamela scolded, then made matters very much worse for Amanda by pulling the panty seat in towards her crack, thus exposing as much bare buttock as a thong bikini. This move had not been discussed but Amanda didn't feel it the proper time to fight for three inches of modestly. Her genitals were still properly covered, and that was no doubt sufficient to keep her safely tucked into the glamour rather than the explicit category of bottom erotica. Thus exposing her victim to the maximum degree she dared, Pamela proceeded to paddle Amanda soundly, presently causing Amanda to vigorously struggle to get free, which resulted in the promised leg lock, and a searing finale that brought genuine tears gushing from Amanda's eyes and down her face.

"Cut," she said, before collapsing in a heap at Pamela's feet. Then, without getting up or dashing her tears away, Amanda quickly instructed Colby to run and get the still camera in her purse and come back to take some publicity shots. Colby rapidly obeyed her command while Amanda told Dru to readjust the lights a little brighter. When all was to her liking, Amanda and Pamela began to pose for stills, first with Amanda at Pamela's feet and then with her back across her lap. After both a smart hair brush spanking and a brisk follow up paddling, Amanda's white bottom was blushing hot pink from cheek to cheek and none of this luscious color was allowed to be lost to the camera. Even as young and inexperienced as she was, Amanda knew that accidental explosions of artistic creativity never occur in the same way twice. She might never have this combination of talent and enthusiasm together in one room again and was determined to wring every molecule of perpetuity out of it.

Finally, the work was done. They opened another bottle of wine and passed around another pipe, congratulating each other on how well it had gone. And then Amanda realized that of course it would have to be she herself who proposed to take the event to another level. Everyone else in the room was too polite and well behaved. These two hard spanking boys were far too modest and grateful to even consider the raunchily sexual ideas that were rapidly flashing through Amanda's brain.

"I have to admit," Amanda suddenly said, "even though I never fantasize about getting spanking by other ladies, that was hot."

"Even though it was hard enough to make you cry?" Pamela demanded.

"Only because I love you so," Amanda replied. "And you look so fantastically dominant in that straight skirt and blouse."

"Yes, that was hot," agreed Colby.

"Oh god, yes!" Dru concurred, exchanging a smile with Pamela.

"Pamela, conference in the kitchen," said Amanda, pulling Pamela from the room by the hand.

When the two girls were alone Amanda said, "It's a hot summer night and two handsome, strapping blond boys stand before us. We may never be in this exact situation again, all of us so sexy and relaxed, all of us in the scene, all of us buzzed from a beautiful day. Don't we owe it to ourselves and those two pretty boys to take this all the way?"

"What are you proposing?"

"Let's let them have their way with us, right now."

"Really?"

"Let's see what they'll do with a little authority."

"Just a minute, let me get this straight, are you suggesting we give ourselves to them, together, tonight, in the very next room?"

"I was thinking the bedroom might work better," mused Amanda, drawing Pamela out of the kitchen and down the hall into the master bedroom.

"Amanda, what's got into you?" Pamela demanded, her hands on her slender hips as she watched Amanda root around in a magnificent red wood armoire. "You're being so outrageous lately. I don't know what to make of it. Is this what it's all been leading up to, group sex?"

"Pamela, we have two blond, blue eyed, 19 year old Greek gods at our disposal. And we're about one good whipping a piece away from ultimate subspace," said Amanda serenely, producing two velvet blindfolds, trimmed with pearls, one in white and the other black. "These will provide that touch of elegant anonymity that those profligate Venetians were so smug about inventing."

Pamela took the black domino from Amanda's hand and gazed at it thoughtfully. She was feeling very relaxed. The day had been full and eventful. Dru had been utterly charming and running into Amanda and Colby an unexpected pleasure. The play had been deliciously witty and gaily sexy, the perfect entertainment in every way. The snack on the way home had enhanced Pamela's feeling of well being, which was then finished off with the successfully filmed spanking sequence and a bit of good wine and fine herb. She knew the boys had been fascinated by her somewhat harsh treatment of Amanda and this gave her rather a thrill. There was no denying the fact that there was a definite correlation between Pamela's beginning to eat in a healthy manner and an upsurge in her feelings of personal strength and self-confidence. Feeling physically stronger seemed to provide certain side benefits, including a freshly awakened sexuality. And here were the two strapping boys…

"Does this mean we're going to switch lovers?" Pamela persisted in asking as Amanda found figured silk robes in the wardrobe, one white and one burgundy.

"I don't know, we'll be blindfolded," said Amanda, quickly stripping off her clothes down to her golden satin bra and panties and knotting the white silk robe around her waist. She took her shoes off and waited until Pamela had put the other robe on over her ivory and cream lace push up bra and panty combination. She too left her shoes behind as she padded back to the sitting room, with the black blindfold in her hand.

The boys had been quietly speculating about what was yet to come when Amanda and Pamela reentered the room, attractively and intimately arrayed in the paper-thin robes and pretty bare feet.

"We're placing ourselves in your hands," said Amanda, first placing Pamela's blindfold over her friend's eyes, then donning her own. "So, carry on."

Colby stared at Amanda dumbfounded, then exchanged a look with Dru, who shrugged back at him in return.

"What the hell, Amanda?" Colby sputtered, this plea for elucidation coming straight from his analytical brain. In spite of all the unexpected opportunities she had been offhandedly tossing his way since her ultimate surrender to him the previous winter, he would never forget the torments of politically correct scene etiquette she had subjected him to while she made up her mind as to whether or not he would be worthy to occasionally, consensually and with her desires placed first and foremost, top her.

Amanda patiently removed her blindfold and said, "What don't you understand about my offer, Colby?"

"Everything, Amanda," he barked back. Slightly ruffled, but still determined to carry through with her plan, Amanda deliberately filled another pipe and passed it around between them. Pamela had kept her blindfold on and looked like a tall, beautiful baby doll, waiting to be hypnotized. She obediently pulled on the pipe when Amanda placed it between her lips and then smiled. Leaving everything to Amanda was always the best decision, Pamela had found. Only see in how many positive ways her life had changed since Amanda had persuaded her to bob her hair.

"What are the three cardinal rules of sex in the scene?" Amanda asked the two young men. Again, Colby and Dru looked at each other doubtfully.

"There are only three?" Dru asked, with interest, but otherwise content to gaze at Pamela, in her bare feet and beautiful robe, blindfolded in velvet and pearls and waiting passively for... what?

"There may be more," said Amanda, "but the big three are as follows: respect the mercy word, things can go from front to back but not from back to front and the most important of all, no glove, no love."

Pamela unconsciously turned her head towards Amanda's clear, mellifluous voice. So her blonde friend was honestly and truly thinking of having sex with these boys, here and now! Pamela's full, red mouth curved into a naughty smile.

"Now do you understand?" asked Amanda, meeting Colby's eyes with a serious expression belied by laughing eyes. "Provide us with sensations and leave us with impressions. Pamela needs inspiration and me, I'm just a little slut."

He looked at her for a long moment, then stepped up to her and decisively pulled the blindfold down over her eyes again.

"We understand," said Colby, remembering that there were many toys with which to tease and punish girls in the closets of the bedroom, also a drawer full of condoms and lube. "Let's go in the other room," he said, taking Amanda by the hand and motioning Dru to follow with Pamela.

"Face down on the bed, girls," said Colby, as he and Dru guided them to the large, four-poster covered in the richest velvet counterpane. After arranging both women face down, side by side, across the middle of bed crosswise, their heads only a few inches apart, with the blindfolds still tightly affixed to their heads, Colby began digging around in cabinets and trunks until he found two small, whippy canes, two substantial, multi thonged leather floggers mounted on braided handles and two medium weight harness leather straps. Dividing these items equally with Dru he then pulled his new friend out of them room to confer with him out of earshot of the girls. Taking Dru halfway down the hall, Colby quickly shared his several thoughts.

"Amanda's an exacting little ball buster," Colby said to Dru, "so we can't fuck this up. All the moves have to be smooth. Aim perfectly, you get me?"

"Should I even be touching Amanda?" Dru asked politely, happy to take part in any facet of the play to follow but eager not to appear too forward.

"I think that's the general idea, dude," Colby informed him, with a grin. "Otherwise, why the continuation of the double date on this level?"

"How far are we going to go?" Dru asked.

"You heard what she said about rubbers. We're taking this all the way. You with Amanda, me with Pamela. Only we're going to be super sparing with our dialog from here on in, so they have to guess who's doing who."

"And you're okay with that?" Dru asked in wonder. This whole situation developing practically overnight with Pamela was the most unusual case of spontaneous combustion that Dru had experienced since Marguerite Alexander had made him her temporary protégé several years back. With Pamela everything was brand new and unexpected. But he was given to understand that Colby and Amanda were officially going out together and had pledged their mutual love. Could Colby really bear to hand Amanda over to a stranger for full on sex without feeling the slightest twinge of jealousy? It was very hard to grasp.

"What can I do?" asked Colby, "my girlfriend is obviously a super freak. Who am I to judge?"

Dru grinned at Colby and they shook hands before returning to the bedroom, where Amanda and Pamela were turned on their sides and quietly conversing with each other, still blindfolded. Without saying a word, Dru gently pushed them both back into position, flat down on the bed, with their faces turned towards each other. Colby motioned to the girls' sashes and he and Dru, gently rolled them slightly over to

185

pull the bows loose and then remove the silk robes from their lithe
bodies. The boys paused for a moment to look at the girls face down in
their exquisite lingerie. Then each taking the girl who belonged to the
other, both Dru and Colby busied themselves in unhooking the girls'
bras and removing them and then pulling the girls' panties down and
completely off.

Now both young women lay naked, side-by-side, attractive bosom
profiles evident whenever they reared their heads up or twisted from
side to side. Amanda's breasts were full and Pamela's small, but each
delightfully rose tipped. The four pertly erect nipples painted a portrait
of arousal universally understood by artists of erotica for millennia.

Colby took up one of the floggers, measured the length of its
lashes with his extended arm, held the lash tips together in one hand,
then carefully but firmly unleashed them across Pamela's slim,
upturned bottom. It was a smart beginning to an even smarter flogging
and Dru was not far behind Colby in imitating this exact same action,
only with Amanda's jutting, muscular and well-rounded bottom as the
target of the strap that he had chosen to employ.

Colby had only ever flogged Amanda once before, but had made
the most of that first opportunity, learning all he could about proper
technique through seriously studying her responses. Previous to that he
had visited a B&D club in Boston to learn exactly how to use a variety
of implements right after he turned eighteen. He seriously wanted to
spank women well, to be the sort of player they remember with a smile
rather than a shudder. Meanwhile he liked the way Pamela caught her
breath every time a fresh stroke took her by surprise. Concentrating on
Pamela's small, twitching bottom, Colby barely had time to steal a
peek at what Dru was doing to Amanda with his strap.

Instead of starting sharply, as Pamela had done, Dru concentrated
on a slower progression from light to hard swats, making sure to aim
the thin but heavy strap carefully, so as not to wrap it around
Amanda's smooth, white hips or strike at her pink womanhood that
was beginning to peep out now and then as the slashes of the strap
caused her to jerk her thighs from side to side. The double punishment
continued for some minutes, with the young ladies getting more used
to the rhythm of the leather coming down on their exposed bottoms

and both beginning to sink lightly into that ecstatic province known as subspace.

Once the still blindfolded beauties were both radiantly rosy from the corporal discipline, and perhaps panting and whimpering a little more than was strictly seemly in two properly punished girls, Colby signaled to Dru to pause. Then he decisively picked Pamela up and bodily reversed her position on the bed, so that she was now lying head to toe beside Amanda. Next he pulled her up by the hips and arranged her on all fours. Taking his cue from Colby, Dru did the same with Amanda. Now both girls were posed in the doggy style position, their heads arched with curiosity as they awaited any possible command.

Colby and Dru drank in the erotic beauty of the two nudes before them in complete enchantment. They even looked at each other and grinned, as much as to say, "What did we do to get this lucky?" And so far the girls had been as compliant as lambs.

Shifting their position so as to throw the girls off balance, Colby finally broke the enchanted silence, telling them sternly, "It's a little late for modesty, ladies. The both of you, spread your legs now."

Regarding Amanda's pretty coral, pink and blonde fringed sex as something like a dessert tray item, Dru prepared to pay homage to Amanda's feminine charms with his mouth, taking her completely by surprise with his darting tongue. Pulling back instinctively, she shook her head with a pout of resistance.

"She's indifferent to head," Colby explained, stripping off his clothes without embarrassment and reaching for his condom and his lube. "She's contrary like that. You'll have to spank her some more to get her to submit."

"No!" said Amanda stubbornly. But Dru like the idea of spanking her more and briskly applied the palm of his hand to Amanda's cheeks, holding her about the waist under one arm. "All right!" she cried at length. Dru spread her thighs again and took a long, deep taste of Amanda's eighteen-year-old sweetness, taking care to lave her rapidly swelling clitoris with long, loving swipes of his tongue. But sensing her embarrassment at being thus devoured, Dru spared her further torments by switching from licking and probing her with his tongue, to spreading her wide open with his fingers and examining every facet of her perfect sex with his eyes and fingertips. The longer he held her spread apart for such inspection, the more Amanda squirmed in ticklish humiliation and uninhibited arousal.

Within five minutes, the young men had worked the young women up into a keen state of receptivity, spanking and caressing them until both girls were feverishly slick and fragrant with their own excitement. And Amanda had been absolutely correct in her supposition that the two athletic nineteen-year-old boys were eminently capable of delivering to Pamela and herself the thrill of their lives. As each boy had already come once that day, albeit hours before, there was no question of a good, long, hard, satisfying pump ride for both Pamela and Amanda.

Traditional submissives, Pamela and Amanda shared an affinity for this position and let themselves be taken from behind with breathless abandon. There being no question that the boys would eventually come, their focus was first and foremost of getting the girls off. Colby knew Amanda's secret, it was having her g spot pressed with the tips of his fingers while penetrating her to the hilt. But he didn't know Pamela's secret, so he tried a few experiments. First he reached around and began to pinch her nipples while thrusting deep inside her. Pamela squirmed and squeaked, but didn't pull her small bosom away. Feeling he was onto something good, Colby continued to play with her breasts, squeezing and pinching as hard as he dared, because she seemed to like this very much. Then he remembered the night in Anthony Newton's examining room and how anal Pamela had been, so he switched his focus to the brunette's delicate rear portal and began to digitally penetrate her in addition to continuing to possess her forcefully from behind. Pamela's whimpers and gasps increased to a satisfying degree after this refinement had been added.

Dru, meanwhile, found Amanda's key pressure points with remarkable acuity and kept his long, thin fingers drumming against her Venus mound and lower abdomen as he continued pistoning into her slick, clenching pink velvet vise. Even if Colby hadn't called out the advice about her attitude towards receiving oral tribute from across the bed, Amanda would have known that it was not Colby making love to her at that moment. Dru's masculine attributes were similar but not identical to Colby's. Amanda thought Dru's penis just as lengthy but slimmer than Colby's and markedly more circumspect. He responded to the most minute of Amanda's bodily responses like a man who really knew how to pay attention to the woman he was with, reassuring Amanda that she had done well to include him in the present adventure.

Flipping off her blindfold at last, Amanda gazed up into Colby's face, which loomed above Pamela's upturned bottom as her lover rammed his manhood home into her best friend's vagina. Noticing Amanda looking at him, Colby gazed directly and unsmilingly back into Amanda's eyes while deliberately tightening his possessive grasp on the lissome fashion designer's exquisitely small waist. Amanda gasped, unexpectedly thrilled by the seriousness of his expression. A grin, laugh or even a smile would have completely destroyed the mood of the scene. Because a sexual encounter this exotic was no laughing matter. Her mini orgasm was rapidly succeeded by a full-scale climax that set her throbbing, half sobbing and gasping for breath.

As soon as Dru felt Amanda let go, he allowed himself his own ecstatic release. Amanda turned to smile at him, he leaned down to kiss her lightly on the lips and then they began the somewhat awkward rubber-clad disengagement process, ending with separate trips to separate bathrooms to restore themselves to decency.

Colby stole the few extra intimate minutes alone with Pamela to quickly and efficiently bring her to a whimpering climax and then dragged out his own pleasure a good ten minutes longer before ejaculating deeply but safely in the pulsating recesses of Pamela's innermost sex. Pamela had unreservedly relished Colby's thick, hard, splendid cock generating heat, light and liquid within her. These young boys had mastered techniques it took most men twenty years to come by and Pamela was duly impressed.

The morning after the Back Bay bacchanalia that had taken both Colby Hodge and Dru Baxter so completely by surprise, Pamela and Dru enjoyed a very early breakfast at their exquisite boutique hotel and then got back on the road to Cape Cod, each feeling relaxed and warm in each other's easy company. Meanwhile, Amanda and Colby awoke in each other's arms, made love, prepared a small, fresh breakfast of coffee, fruit and buttered bread, showered, set Hugo's flat to rights and departed by mid morning to also return to Random Point.

While all of this was going on, Pamela scarcely gave a thought to her husband, Ambrose Bartlett, who himself was waking up on a large platform bed in the lighthouse, with Polyxena Guzman. Wrapped in a sheer, white cotton night gown, she pressed back against him, her voluptuous buttocks right in front of his groin while his hand clasped around her small waist, drew her even closer. She awoke at the same moment he did and rubbed back against him in the pale morning light, fresh ocean air blowing in through all the windows, which were partially opened. Then she sprung out of bed and pattered off to the bathroom in bare feet, affording only the briefest glimpse of her curvaceous form under the tight white sleeveless gown. He heard her brushing her teeth and when she reappeared her white blonde hair looked freshly brushed. All vestiges of sleepiness were gone and Ambrose reflected that she was obviously one of those obnoxiously cheerful morning people. He sighed, rolled over and covered his head with the bedclothes.

"You don't have to move, I'll bring you some coffee," she told him with a laugh, lest he think she was going to immediately begin playing the personal trainer with him and demand a set or two of morning push ups. He raised the coverlet and watched her migrate to the kitchenette area of the loft, which had been magnificently retrofitted for a first class cook when William Random had bought and remodeled the hundred-year-old edifice that overlooked one of the village's prettiest coves. Once the lighthouse had been gutted and remodeled for extreme yuppie habitation, with an elevator, hardwood floors, leaded windows and Italian plumbing, the architect-contractor realized that he could charge anything he wanted in rent for the location, and did so without remorse.

In a few minutes Polyxena was back with a tray of aromatic coffee, steamed milk and the two large blueberry muffins they had not been able to eat at the inn the previous night when he had taken her to dinner. Ambrose Bartlett had no idea that Pamela had gone to Boston for anything other than business with anyone other than herself. Just the mere fact of her going at that moment had given him the idea that the time had come to press his suit with the glamorous immigrant.

He had taken Polyxena to a new inn with a highly rated kitchen and had plied her with gourmet food far too luxurious to be served in large portions, which left her satisfied, yet wanting more. He did not talk about Pamela or the state of business in Random Point, but instead questioned her for hours, in minute detail, about her experiences in Europe, first as an employee in and then as the owner of a dungeon. Anecdotes from the world of BDSM were endlessly fascinating to him and as he rightly supposed, this type of talk was equally stimulating to Polyxena, who didn't normally talk about herself at such length or so frankly but found she did not mind doing so in this instance.

The truth was that she had gotten fed up waiting for Dieter Brandt to return to her as it was obvious that he was never going to. And here she was at age 36, at the absolute peak of her beauty, going about day to day admired, but untouched. It was nothing to do with sensations. She adored her Hitachi wand and had an orgasm every day. But she missed the feel of a man's arms around her, along with his companionship. She missed hugs and kisses and lap bouncing sex, along with sharing meals together and even the occasional vacation. She knew it was absurd to begin a love affair with another woman's man, but here was Ambrose Bartlett, the only man at the moment who was avidly pursuing her. Bartlett was the man whose face lit up more than any other when she strolled into the exercise room. Bartlett was the man who was always leaving a cupcake or a sprig of violets or an antique matchbox on her desk, a tiny gift each day or two, to remind her that he was thinking about her all the time. Bartlett was the most eager of her trainees, putting out the most effort in his work outs, determined to fashion the most interesting male body she could desire to play with in her spare time. He had even made a solemn promise to her that he had quit cigarettes for good, giving her his gold cigarette case for a keepsake. It was an antique from the 1920's, inlaid with onyx and worth quite a few thousand dollars. Naturally Polyxena had had it appraised. She was a very practical girl.

So she had invited him back to the lighthouse and had given him everything he had thought of asking for without demure. A light but tantalizing dinner and a half bottle of champagne had put her in the perfect mood to be seduced and he had followed through with every particular of suave sensitivity he could muster or remember from attentively reading all the novels of Marguerite Alexander. What he hadn't done was spank her. He really hadn't dared. Not yet. Because in the case of this sophisticated former mistress, he really rather wanted her to *ask for it*, in one way or another, before taking the risk.

Polyxena sat on the bed with her legs crossed, nibbling at a muffin and sipping coffee while smiling at him.

"So how come you didn't spank me last night?" she teased him, in her very slight Dutch accent, "I thought you're the big spanking guy."

"You were being a perfect angel, so how could I?" he replied, brushing a tendril of pale hair off her face. Her light blue eyes twinkled back at him.

"Oh, so you noticed how good I am!" she laughed approvingly, finding it difficult to see why the other girls had so many complaints to make about Bartlett.

"You're too good," he advised her pointedly. "You have to be a little naughty if you want to get spanked."

"Let me think, maybe I'll come into your store without panties later today," she suggested.

"If you do, I might have to pull up your skirt and check."

Savoring a juicy blueberry, she looked at him in a such a way that he took the coffee cup out of her hands, put it down, pulled her straight across his lap and spanked her through the sheer white cotton gown, swatting her six or eight times on alternating cheeks, which each began to instantly redden under his large, hard palm. She squirmed, but not to get away, to grind a little deeper against his throbbing morning erection.

Pulling up the back of her gown, he bared her luscious bottom, already pink from his hand against the creamiest, whitest skin he had ever beheld. "Maybe you are naughty enough to be spanked first thing in the morning," he decided, delivering another dozen smacks to each upturned orb before probing between her thighs with nimble fingers, to discover her sopping wet. Turning her over and pulling her up to the pillow beside him, he straddled her and took her for the second time in ten hours, putting what they both felt to be an official stamp on their brand new love affair. The moment he was in her, he tilted her chin up with his hand and told her, "Look at me, young lady." Her eyes fluttered open and he looked down at her seriously. She felt an unexpected thrill being made to look into his eyes all the while he was plunging deep inside her velvet glove. He let go of her chin and clasped one of her hands in his own, squeezing it. Then he pinched her ear lobes and her nipples, stroked her throat and hair, kissed her face and shoulders, in short, made love to her in every subtle way even while he was taking her deeply and hard. In the end she felt adored and in the end, she gave it up, her rapid gasps and inward shudders proving to Bartlett beyond any doubt, that he had touched every button correctly and the exact number of times to earn the title of lover to Polyxena Guzman.

Since he always kept a complete change of clothes in his car, Ambrose Bartlett was able to go directly from the lighthouse to Bartlett's that morning without stopping home. Meanwhile, Pamela drove into Random Point around ten a.m., dropped Dru Baxter off at his house in the village and proceeded home directly.

Pamela stopped in the kitchen, said hello to the cleaning ladies, started a pot of coffee and ran upstairs to change her clothes before going into Bartlett's to check on the progress of the remodeling of the alterations department into her own design atelier. As Pamela passed through the master bedroom on the way to her walk in closet she noticed that the bed was made and the room fully set to rights. This puzzled her and she ran downstairs again.

"You haven't done the upstairs yet, have you Corazon?" Pamela asked one of the girls casually.

"No Miss," replied the small, Latina housemaid cheerfully. Pamela thoughtfully waited until the coffee was ready, poured herself a cup, added milk and took it back upstairs with her. When she got back into the bedroom she stared at the bed. If the girls hadn't been up yet then there could be only one reason the bed was already made, and that was that it hadn't been slept in by her husband the previous night. Interesting!

Pamela donned a putty colored jumpsuit with a stand up collar, ¾ sleeves, a nipped waist, pegged legs and pockets.

"So who was he with?" she wondered.

Chapter Sixteen

Polyxena Goes Shopping

Ambrose Bartlett was sitting behind his desk reading some paper correspondence and glancing from time to time up at the bank of security cameras that lined one wall of his executive office at Bartlett's department store when he noticed that Polyxena Guzman was in Designer Sportswear. It was the first time he had ever seen her in his store and his heart contracted in excitement at this sudden appearance. She was in a white cotton wrap dress and clogs. He knew the outfit well. Like all of her dresses, it accentuated her small waist, ample bosom and rounded hips superbly. As she swished those lush yet gym pampered hips around the mark down racks he contemplated going out to meet her. He was on his feet before thinking twice about it, checking the elegant fit of the Tom Ford suit he had pulled out of the back of his car to put on for the first time that morning before he left the lighthouse. Looking back at his monitors once more his heart jumped a little as Polyxena held an exciting Betty Page dress up to her form in front of a mirror. But she put the dress back at once. Ambrose scowled. How like her to be practical. As if she could not think of one single place to wear a dress with a crinoline petticoat to. He had no patience to wait for the elevator and took the stairs down to two.

Polyxena was not surprised to see Bartlett pop up before her as she crossed the circular plush carpet that the various salons branched off from on her way to lingerie.

"Hello," he said. "About time you came in and spent a little money," he commented dryly.

"A hunna eighty dollars for a sundress?" she asked incredulously, in the accent that charmed him so.

"I saw the photos from the Venus Club dinner," Ambrose said, leading her by the hand into lingerie. "You had on a beautiful sundress. I'd like to see you dressed like that more often."

When they entered the lingerie salon the tall, smartly dressed, voluptuous, forty something female manager of that department came forward and greeted them with a smile.

"Good morning Mr. Bartlett, may I be of some assistance?" she asked, smiling affably at Polyxena.

"Yes, Miss Karson, bring us half a dozen day dresses from Betty Page in an 8. Put them in Executive One," said Bartlett, specifying one of the fitting rooms not equipped with a security camera. Then he walked Polyxena through lingerie, suggesting silk gown sets and delicately embroidered gauzy cotton negligees from Italy. Before entering the fitting room she looked at him and arched her fine eyebrows. "Come in with me and tell me how they look," she said. He came in, locked the door behind him and swept Polyxena into his arms. She surrendered her lips to his. A moment later he was amazed to feel her slip down to her knees before him. He saw her hands go to his trouser zipper in equal astonishment.

"I missed you already," she explained, "have you missed me too?" she added teasingly, pulling down the zipper.

"I have," he replied, lightly stroking her pale blonde hair back from her brow. His cock had jumped to attention the moment he had seen her on the monitor in his office, now it jumped out of his pants at her with full enthusiasm. She laughed in gratified surprise and flashing him the naughtiest smile he had ever seen on her beautiful face, enclosed the bulbous mushroom cap of his fully erect penis between her rose petal soft lips and began to demonstrate her considerable skill at tonguing, feathering, tenderly kissing and voraciously sucking the correspondingly responsive organ of a virile lover. Both turned to look at the pornographic image of the luscious blonde down on her knees to the well-groomed executive, with half to three quarters of a large sized penis in her mouth and out of her mouth, in her throat and down her throat at any given moment, her prettily manicured hands wrapped around the base, until she freed one to gently begin squeezing his balls.

"Stop it, honey, she'll be back in a minute," Bartlett warned, coming closer and closer to climax under Polyxena's dungeon-honed ministrations. He remembered what she had said about every Dutch mistress in the club where she got her experience, having to train first as a submissive and serve every sexual need of the clients in the process. Was that where she learned to give head like this? And was she in fact beaten until she had gotten it right?

"Come for me," she said, pulling her lips away from his cock only long enough to say this.

"I don't think…" he began to protest.

"And then fuck these bullshit fripperies and take me to jewelry," she said, straight faced, her blue eyes alight with laughter. Bartlett smiled in return, ruffled her hair again and pushed her head back down on his cock. Now she was speaking his language, offering him a rich, rare treat at a price he understood. He wanted very much to give her jewelry, to give her anything to bind her to him.

"All right, get ready," he warned her, trying to time his orgasm so that she could pull away as soon as it started. She looked up and nodded her head, fastening her lips even more tightly around his cock and bracing herself for the hot deluge that he presently discharged against one of her inner cheeks inside her mouth. Nor did she release his pulsating organ until she had swallowed his entire load of semen.

Fearing the return of the department manager with the dresses he had ordered, Bartlett hastily stuffed his still hard but now drained penis into his pants and zipped himself back to respectability. He helped her to her feet and hugged her to his chest. "You didn't have to do that," he said. "But it was fantastic."

There was a knock at the door and Miss Karson brought in the dresses and hung them up about the large, luxurious dressing room, then discreetly disappeared.

"I'm not trying those things on," Polyxena said, fixing her lipstick in the mirror.

"Never mind, I'll bring them over to the lighthouse and you can try them on for me later," he said, escorting her out of the fitting room. He took her down to the basement in an elevator and led her to a nondescript storage room that he opened with a key. Inside of this room were boxes, shelves and a safe, which he keyed a combination into.

"I can't give you anything from jewelry that's already been out because there's a chance that Pamela will have seen it and will recognize it if she sees it on you," Bartlett explained to Polyxena, as he withdrew several blue velvet jeweler's cases. "But these pieces haven't been checked into inventory yet, so you can pick from these."

He opened the blue velvet cases on some of the boxes and revealed necklaces made of gold, diamonds and pearls.

"Which should I choose?" Polyxena asked, delighted that the wholesale price tags on the various pieces ran in the five to ten thousand dollar range. The long neglected beauty beamed with pleasure at the tribute.

Bartlett chose a heavy, solid gold chain with a pearl and diamond pineapple pendant and fastened it around Polyxena's bare white throat.

"This one is perfect because you can wear it every day. It's casual and fun but still luxe."

"I didn't really come in today to shake you down," said Polyxena, catching a reflection of herself in the gleaming and glittering necklace in a small mirror. "I really did miss you."

"Thank you," he said, catching her hand and kissing it. "You're a fine woman. Don't think I don't know that."

"When will I see you again?" she asked as they went back up to the first floor in the freight elevator. It let them out near the door to the employee entrance and the parking lot behind the store.

"As soon as you like," he said, unable to suppress the happiness he felt at being loved. He walked her out to her car in the parking lot.

"Really? Won't you be expected home at a certain time by your wife?"

"Pamela's showing at fashion week in September. She'll be in her studio night and day until then working with Damaris to get their collection ready."

"Oh yes, and then there's the boyfriend," said Polyxena.

"Boyfriend?" Ambrose asked, as his heart seemed to skip a beat.

"I think she has one."

"No!" Bartlett was floored.

"I saw her drive into the village this morning with a cute blond boy in her car. The way they were looking at each other and talking, it seemed to me they were more than just friends."

"Blond boy?" Bartlett tried to remember if he'd seen any blond boys buzzing around Pamela lately, or ever. Come to think of it, she'd been dancing with a blond boy who looked barely college aged, when he'd found her at Michael's bar the other night. Boyfriend? Of Pamela? Really? "Wow," he said, "that's interesting. I didn't know that. If anything I thought she was in love with Amanda!"

Ambrose Bartlett wandered back to his office and sat at his desk, staring out the window at the perfect blue sky. Then, not five minutes later, Pamela walked in. The next thing he knew, she was sitting on his knee, her arms around his neck.

"How are you?" she asked, looking deeply into his dark eyes. He smiled back at her.

"Never better, honey. How was Boston?"

Pamela saw that he really had never been better. Quitting smoking and spending two hours a day at the gym both exercising and relaxing had taken ten years off his face in less than a month. His color that morning, was in fact not dissimilar to that of the flushed boy she'd woken up with several hours before in Back Bay. She knew why Dru Baxter had been flushed and wondered if the same event had actuated her husband's heightened color.

"Really good," she said. "That hotel was first rate." She got up off his lap and he got up as well.

"Want to see the progress on your new atelier?" he asked and led her off to the new design suite that was being remodeled for her use on the top floor of Bartlett's.

"Is that your new Tom Ford suit?" Pamela asked; "The one that's been in your trunk for months?"

Bartlett's heart skipped another beat but he casually replied, "Yes, I forgot I even had it."

"It looks good but you've lost some weight. Give me the jacket and I'll take it in for you," she said. He looked at her with interest as he handed her the jacket.

"Really? You'd do that yourself?" he asked. She looked at him as though he were mad.

Pamela gasped with appreciation when she saw how far the redecoration had advanced in transforming the previous drab industrial green attic alterations department into a luxuriously appointed ultra modern high tech design studio. The adjoining bathrooms had been redone to Scandinavian standards of excellence and a pretty lounge for the seamstresses to take their breaks in had been completed. The last room, Pamela's private office lounge, was now being fitted with an inlaid tiled drop ceiling, heavy wooden paneling, smart furniture and a hardwood floor. Pamela could see that her husband had spared no expense in creating an ideal workspace for her and hugged him with genuine gratitude. But she came away disturbed by the faintest scent of a perfume not her own lingering about his lapels. This of course meant nothing. He might have stopped at seven perfume counters on the way into the store and been exposed to random sample sprays. Pamela marked the scent made a mental notation to sniff around Polyxena Guzman the next time she went to the spa and see if her scent matched the faint sachet that she had detected on her husband's suit.

"And I have a present for you as well," he said, reaching into an inner pocket to produce a plain, printed invoice from Chipper Knight advertising. Pamela glanced down at the details and a delighted smile spread across her face as she read the short hand notations that indicated Bartlett had purchased five color pages in the October edition of Vogue to feature whatever apparel from their collection Pamela and Damaris might choose to advertise.

"You only have a few days to make the deadline for the photos," he said. "Why don't you have Pascal Robbins shoot them with Amanda while they're both here?"

"That's a very good idea," Pamela agreed, instantly in favor of anything that involved her new best friend.

Chapter Seventeen

Caned in Cambridge

Pascal Robbins was so captivated by the idea of spending two whole days shooting Amanda Sands that he barely noticed Phoebe telling him she was taking the train into Boston to get her hair done and visit her corsetiere. Phoebe Casper Robbins had become addicted to corsetry during her first Summer in Random Point several years before and had been having custom cinches and other one piece garments made for her at the rate of one every six months, at a tiny shop in Back Bay. But this was not the real reason she was going to spend the night in Boston.

Upon debarking at the station, Phoebe followed the instructions she had been given by Anthony Newton and hailed a cab to The Marlowe hotel overlooking the Charles. Anthony was waiting in the bar for her, immaculately suited and unhurriedly consulting a wine list, which he then ordered from. Flushing with excitement, guilt and embarrassment, Phoebe slid into the upholstered banquet opposite him with a radiant smile and heaving bosom, demi-exposed to perfection in a clinging cotton summer dress.

"I've never done anything this naughty before," Phoebe confided, reaching for his hand under the table. He squeezed her hand in his and leaned over to kiss her lightly on the lips.

"I know," he said. "You're so innocent, it's scary. Susan Ross knew more than you when she was eighteen."

"Would she be terribly hurt if she knew we were meeting like this?" Phoebe asked, suddenly distressed at the thought of Susan Ross.

"No, certainly not," Anthony assured her. "We have a more or less open relationship. Not to say that she'd be thrilled, but I've never restricted her very much and she knows that I'll pursue a passion every now and then."

"Is that what I'm going to be, a passion?" Phoebe asked, entranced. He lightly squeezed her knee through her skirt under the table.

"You already are," he replied. "Why else would I have taken on this whole *Kiss Me Kate* project?"

The white wine arrived, was uncorked and poured for them by the young waiter, who went about these tasks unpretentiously and without interrupting their conversation. Anthony clinked glasses with Phoebe, saying, "To many future shows, together."

"Is that all?" she asked doubtfully, sipping the cold wine slowly.

"Phoebe, of course I *want* you," he said, pinching her earlobe between two fingers, just above her tiny pearl earring. She shuddered, a deeper blush creeping across her cheeks.

"For you to say that you want me makes me happier than I've ever been in my entire life," she said sincerely, for Phoebe was at that moment in the throes of the deepest infatuation with her director. She thought about Anthony every moment of the day.

"What did you tell Pascal you were doing today?" he asked.

"That I was having a corset fitting. He doesn't realize that when you have a custom corset made, it's going to fit. Normally they're sent to me. Today I'm picking my new one up."

"How delightful," said Anthony, "I'll come with you. Women in corsets knock me out. You can wear it out, under your clothes. It'll be fun seeing how everyone stares at your figure. Then we can go have lunch and you can suffer because you're still in your corset. Then we'll keep you in your corset ever so much longer, so that by the time we get back to the room, you're ready to be ripped out of it."

Phoebe was unutterably thrilled by his proposals. Not only did her idol seem perfectly engaged by the idea of squiring her around Boston all day and tucking her into his own bed that night, but he looked relaxed and happy about it, as if spending this much time together alone was the most natural thing in the world to him, as if he was as much in love with her as she was with him. For Phoebe it was an extraordinary dream come true. She had known for several years that

Newton was fond of her, but she had thought it to be in an abstract way, as one is of a charming younger relative, kitten or puppy. She had never expected her romantic overtures towards him to be received so openheartedly. Newton seemed to genuinely like her on top of being open to a sexual dalliance. It was almost too much pleasure to bear.

And yet on the way to the corset shop, he brought her back down to earth by once again mentioning Pascal. They were walking down a Back Bay street, having agreed to a pick up point with Dennis in the Bentley, when Anthony said, "How are thing between you and Pascal at the moment?"

Phoebe frowned and shook her head, as though the thought of her handsome and sexy but also bossy, disagreeable and barely trustworthy husband was rather unpleasant.

"He's very angry at me. I don't think he'll ever really forgive me. I should leave him. Or tell him to leave me."

"Oh, don't do that," Anthony said, though mildly. "You make such a handsome couple."

"That's true, we take a nice photograph together. But he doesn't deserve me," said Phoebe sagely, openly strolling along with her hand in Newton's.

"What man deserves any woman? But you do still love him, don't you?"

"I suppose so," she said softly. "But as dreadful as this sounds, I love you more."

"Oh, honey, that's sweet," said Anthony, squeezing her hand. "But at the same time, very naughty. You're really coming out of your shell this year."

"I can't help it. I see all the women around me in Random Point, and they're living their lives to the full. While here am I – probably as pretty as I'll ever be, and faced with a once in a lifetime opportunity to give myself to someone I dream about every night. If I didn't throw myself at you this summer I wouldn't be human."

"Silly, I've been flirting with you ever since we first met," Anthony said.

"But would you have acted on your impulse if I hadn't made the first move?" she persisted.

"I wouldn't exactly have called it a move," he grinned. "It was more like a significant look and a wistful sigh."

They entered the tiny corsetiere's shop that was like the inside of a French chocolate box, it smelled so sweet and looked so dainty. The narrow main room was lined with drawers and cases carefully crammed with custom sewn silk satin foundation garments suitable for both theatrical performances and intimate interludes, along with every day cotton reptide cinches and holiday velvet corselets in every rich color from burgundy to gold. One dressing room, one mirror and one chair for a visitor to occupy while waiting filled out the front of the shop, which was presided over that day by a sprightly twenty five year old with tight black spiral curls half way down her back and the kind of waist a corset shop wants to promote, suitably drawn in several inches more by a classic pale blue brocade Victorian cinch worn over a thin white cotton chemise. She was Violet, the owner's daughter and recognized Phoebe at once, having waited on her before. She brought out a finely worked lavender and gold threaded embroidered corselet for Phoebe's inspection. This was a long line one-piece garment, with a built in push up bra swathed by a fichu of lavender chiffon and meant to be worn with a matching g-string. She had very much hoped to be wearing full seated panties the first time Anthony spanked her and this thought gave her a moment's worry in the midst of her admiration for the stunning girdle.

Anthony encouraged her to try on the corset before they left the shop and got her to open the curtain and allow him to see her in it before she put her clothes back on. He even tightened her laces himself, accustomed to this pleasant task from the early days of his courtship of Susan and simultaneous trysts with Marguerite Alexander, who always promoted and extolled the wearing of custom corsetry to new ladies coming into the scene. Phoebe knew she would be wearing the new garment for Anthony that day and had chosen a complimentary pair of ultra high vamp gold platform stilettos with ankle straps, back zippers and four and a half inch heels. He had noticed the shoes right away and how they took her fitted lilac cotton dress to another level of sexiness, but paired with the full-length corset, they were sublime.

Phoebe asked Violet to remove the garter straps from the corset hem for the moment as she didn't plan to wear stockings with peep toe sandals and Anthony nodded, "Quite right." It was summer after all. He insisted she keep the corset on and wear it back to the hotel. She agreed and closed the curtain back up to put on her dress again. With the corset pulling her waist in two more inches, the dress floated about her waist until she pulled the belt tight. The resulting silhouette was magnificent. Phoebe was not a tall girl, and she was also quite bosomy and ample hipped, but her waist was nipped, her shoulders graceful, her feet tiny and her legs well turned and shapely. Like his Susan Ross, Phoebe was loveably small.

Even though tightly cinched, Phoebe suddenly felt ravenously hungry and begged Anthony to feed her well and as soon as ever he could. Rather fortuitously, the first café they passed on the way back to meet Dennis at the rendezvous corner, was vegetarian in addition to being gourmet, and Phoebe pulled him inside with the greatest pleasure. In a few minutes they were sitting in the window and presently enjoyed savory dishes of mushroom risotto, along with fresh cucumber and tomato salads and a bottle of chilled white wine. She loved that Anthony wasn't forever going out for cigarettes like Pascal, who cared far too little for good food as a consequence of having tobacco battered taste buds.

Before the check came Anthony called Dennis and readjusted the meet up point to save Phoebe walking any more on the extremely high heels. She hadn't complained but he'd been around fashionable women long enough to be constantly aware of such logistics. They exited the restaurant and stepped into the Bentley waiting for them at the curb, which then transported them back to the beautiful suite overlooking The Charles.

Phoebe was amazed to see a baby grand in the living room of the suite. Anthony said they would practice all her numbers later if she liked. He showed her to a private bedroom where Dennis had already placed the small valise she had gotten off the train with. A moment later, his hands were on her waist and his lips on her silken white throat. The playing and fore-playing would come later, but at that perfect summer afternoon moment, both of them felt full to bursting with desire and tacitly agreed that the sex simply could not be put off another instant.

He pushed her back on the bed, pushed up her skirt, pulled off the g-string and leaving her still tightly laced into the heavily boned corset, fucked her just the way she wanted it, hard, fast and to the hilt until she expired in his arms, irritated to a frenzy of clitoral excitement by her new lover thrusting his impressively virile cock into a pussy slick and receptive with amatory desire, hero worship and love.

Phoebe radiated joy and satisfaction as she lay against her new lover under the coverlet they had pulled up over their bodies. Anthony had stripped down to his skin but Phoebe was still in the corset and heels fifteen minutes after their first sexual encounter, luxuriating in the thrilling experience of being held close by him. His well-exercised, trim body was redolent of sandalwood soap and his heartbeat was slow under her ear pressed against his chest. Pascal's heart raced all the time, she was sure due to the many cigarettes, cups of coffee and shots of alcohol he consumed every day. Anthony might be a dozen or more years older than her husband, yet he seemed both better conditioned and healthier. Phoebe wondered with a start whether she was actually beginning to dislike Pascal. She had never been aware of thinking of him in such a critical light before. Indeed, the very act of mentally comparing Pascal to another man and Pascal falling short seemed like a radical departure in her attitude towards the man she had chosen as her mate. Would it, could it, ever be the same between her and her husband again?

Anthony drew her close and buried his face in her chestnut brown hair. "I haven't just jumped a girl's bones like that since college," he apologized. "Usually I'm all about the seduction." But Phoebe wasn't paying attention. She'd just been thinking, "If I get pregnant I'll keep it." She had naturally noticed him pull out before ejaculating against her smooth white thigh but there might have been a drop that escaped before he did.

She turned her back to him so he could unlace her corset. When she was finally released a few moments later, her entire torso seemed to ecstatically vibrate. "So pretty," he said, caressing her satiny curves from full bosom to slim waist to rounded hips. Phoebe's stomach was flat and her pubic triangle adorned with tight, soft brown curls. Then his hands went to her bottom, slightly plump and creamy white. He patted her lightly, in a way that seemed to promise, "Later."

They dozed in each other's arms for about an hour, then went to their respective luxe bathrooms and showered. Anthony had promised to take her to a real dungeon, with bondage furniture and esoteric equipment. She had never been out on a date with a scene player before and had expressed an interest in "going on all the rides" the B&D salon to which he planned to conduct her could offer. Anthony wasn't sure of what she meant by that but certainly knew how to fasten a girl to a whipping post and smarten her up with a flogger.

He looked into her room as she was getting dressed and said, "Put on something comfortable this time, Phoebe, we'll take a little walk then catch that Molière play."

Phoebe was once again charmed by Anthony's instincts. How much better and more dramatic their encounter in the dungeon would be if it occurred after dark and after an interval of protracted longing. In addition, she loved Molière and relished the thought of sitting beside her lover in a theatre, laughing together and perhaps holding hands or even touching each other more intimately in the dark. Here was foreplay of the most elegant stamp, intellectual as well as physical.

Phoebe placed her tiny feet in white platform espadrilles with ribbon ties, donned pristine white on white nylon lingerie and over that slipped a fitted, a line, zip front white cotton sundress with a navy piped sailor collar. She came out carrying a navy cardigan over her arm and a small white handbag. She had pulled her long, full head of light brown hair back into a high ponytail and it suited her heart shaped face.

"You'll need a bigger purse than that," he said matter of factly.

"What for?"

"The chocolate."

Deeply intrigued, Phoebe exchanged her tiny clutch for a white shoulder bag large enough to accommodate several boxes of after eight mints. But Newton had something even better in store for her.

Once again, Dennis dropped them off a number of blocks from their final destination, a playhouse on Boylston Street, so that they could take another stroll through Back Bay streets on that golden, waning afternoon. After they had walked a few blocks, they came upon a chocolate shop that might have been the first cousin of the corset shop they had visited earlier for the sense of luxurious indulgence it communicated. The very scent of the air within the shop was madly intoxicating. Phoebe looked at her new best friend with even deeper respect. He obviously planned to make amends for depriving her of foreplay before their initial engagement by seducing her with chocolate all afternoon.

Anthony ordered them both tiny cups of drinking chocolate, which were thick with heavy cream and infused with chili. These were so rich that Phoebe began immediately to perspire, in spite of the frostily air-cooled interior of the shop. He let Phoebe choose truffles and pralines for them both and had her tuck the pink box into her purse. As they still had thirty minutes to get the six blocks to the playhouse, they walked without any great haste, looking into windows as they went and discussing everything they saw.

"You know, Phoebe," said Anthony, lightly taking her hand as they walked, "I was just thinking, you told me that your husband has spanked you and not badly at that. If we proceed with our original plan, which is that you bring home marks from another man, Pascal being the old fashioned type, wouldn't that ruin spanking for him?"

"I hope it does. The last time he laid hands on me it was perfectly awful. I cried!!"

"Seriously? He spanked you that hard?"

"Yes, just the other day. After he saw us together. I gave him a very dangerous tool when I told him I was into it." she reported gravely.

"Phoebe, I have a good idea. I think you should tell Pascal that I only wanted you for sex, and the sex we wound up having was bad, and because I let you down, you're over me. He'll believe you."

"Tell me again what you told him when you talked?" Phoebe asked.

"I said I'd give you a horrible scene that would give you a disgust of me and send you back to him."

"And why would you do this for him again?"

"Because I want him to think I'm not in love with you."

"Well, no one ever said you were in love with me."

"I'll say it now, I am in love with you," he told her with a kiss.

"So now you're suggesting that instead of returning to Pascal with crass whip marks to prove I'm off you, I instead confide the details of an awkward encounter…?"

"… which ended in ignominious disappointment for the both of us!" Anthony helpfully suggested to his new paramour.

"And make him promise never to reveal these details to another living soul?"

"I don't care about that," Anthony replied cheerfully.

"So you're willing to be thought impotent in order to preserve the feelings of my unworthy husband?"

"To preserve his feelings for you, in case you should suddenly realize that he's the one you made your vows with for a reason. I'm just saying, Phoebe, let's be sensible and not put your comfortable marriage at risk."

"I'll think about it and give you my answer later," she said, reaching into her purse and pulling out a hazelnut truffle to thoughtfully bite into. "I'll tell you in the dungeon."

At the play, Anthony and Phoebe laughed without restraint, consumed numerous liquor truffles and after he draped his jacket over their laps, pressed and squeezed each other through their clothes from time to time. He found her wet under her panties and she found him to be so hard through his trousers that she whispered naughtily in his ear, "My hand is ready, may it do him ease," quoting from Katerina's final soliloquy.

After the performance, he took her to his favorite restaurant, where he had called ahead for a private room and informed the chef of Phoebe's vegan preferences. Once more Phoebe thought of how badly

Pascal compared to Anthony in sheer sensitivity to her needs. Her husband barely credited Phoebe's health conscious requirements the status of an eccentricity. While Anthony was happy to forego meat while dining in her company, fully agreeing that it would be best to do so always. The truth was that Anthony was simply more thoughtful, agreeable, sensitive and savvy than her husband in every way. Phoebe sighed once in regret for her ever-diminishing regard for her man and then addressed the beautifully prepared vegetarian fare with an extremely keen appetite.

Having completed their meal, they took another walk around Back Bay, this time hand in hand. It was another warm, clear, starry night, the air perfumed by summer blossoms.

"I never looked for a dungeon in Boston before," Anthony told her, "and I had a hell of a time finding anything suitable. Commercial ones don't exist here, due to zoning, but there are a handful of mistresses who rent out their play spaces and I think the best one of them is in Cambridge, pretty close to our hotel."

"Should we go back to the suite so I can change into something sexier?" she asked, looking down at her flats doubtfully.

"You can change in the car on the way," he said. "I have some things for you," he told her, then called Dennis to come and pick them up.

They strolled along Newberry Street until Anthony's driver caught them up. Once back in the Bentley Anthony opened the four variously sized boxes Dennis had placed in the back seat on his employer's instructions. Anthony unerringly handed her the smallest box, which bore the logo of *Damaris* and contained a black satin bustier with garters attached, a pair of sheer black bikini panties, and a pair of black tinted pure silk seamed stockings. Phoebe inspected everything with delight and took great care in handling the delicate hose. The back of the sedan was roomy enough, but changing clothes in it would still be an awkward operation and Phoebe seemed skeptical that it could be accomplished at all.

"Come on, I'll help you," he said, untying her lacing espadrilles and placing them out of the way. Used to changing clothes quickly back stage, Phoebe shrugged and entered into the spirit of the game, reaching under her skirt and pulling her pantyhose down and off. Anthony took them from her and tossed them into the same compartment he'd placed her shoes in. She quickly unbuttoned her shirt and pulled it off. Anthony took it. Then she unzipped her skirt and slipped that off as well. Anthony took this too and placed it with her blouse to one side. He admired her in her tailored white cotton bra and panty outfit for a moment. "That's so cute," he said, "but it's too good girl for a dungeon. Put this on," he said, making her turn her back to him, unhooking her bra and replacing it with the bustier, which had a long row of hooks down the back. He fastened all the hooks quickly. "Fits you like a glove, nice!" he remarked, of the becomingly tight foundation garment he'd just put her in.

"How did you know my size?"

"Oh, Pamela shopped for me."

"You told her what we were doing?" Phoebe was shocked. Pamela was too close a friend of Pascal's for this not to seem worrisome.

"No, I just said I wanted to give my leading lady presents for good luck in the play. She has no reason to think anything of that."

Phoebe was a little embarrassed to switch the white panties for the black ones in front of Anthony, even though he had already had her and they were officially lovers. "Go on!!" he urged her, grinning at her sudden shyness. She pouted and insisted he close his eyes while she engaged in this slightly awkward operation. He folded his arms and leveled a stern look at her. "Phoebe, you know how impatient I am. Don't keep me waiting." She didn't want to receive her first spanking from Anthony in the Bentley with Dennis listening on the other side of the partition, so she complied with the order to swap pants.

"Very nice!" he said. "I like it when girls obey me the first time."

While Phoebe pulled on the delicate hose ever so gently, Anthony produced a stunning pair of black velvet, snub nosed fetish pumps with five-inch heels and a small shoehorn. Phoebe's eyes widened in appreciation at the shoes and immediately slipped them on. Her shapely legs and slender ankles, set off to perfection by the elegant heels, were irresistibly seductive.

"Now for the dress," he said, opening the biggest box to pull out a sleeveless, double breasted cherry red leather halter dress with a row of black buttons up the front. Phoebe slipped her arms into the garment and quickly buttoned it up. The fit could not have been more snug, hugging her womanly curves from bosom to knee.

"I never had a dress like this before," she confided. "It smells heavenly."

"I love the way you dress, but you could go a little edgier now and then," Anthony said. "You have the figure for it."

"The way you spoil girls, how can we help falling in love with you?" she grinned.

The final box was long and slim, containing a pair of black elbow length, silk lined, lambskin gloves with buttons that finished the outfit on a richly fetishistic note. Phoebe carefully put them on then wrapped her arms around Anthony's neck and kissed him on the lips. His arms went around her waist and he hugged her against him for a moment before letting her go.

"Looks like we've arrived," he told her, as Dennis pulled up to a small Beaux Arts style apartment building on a street near Porter Square. Anthony led Phoebe into an immaculate and empty foyer at the end of which they found a small elevator that took them slowly up to the sixth floor. Turning right down a carpeted corridor as he had been instructed, Anthony pulled Phoebe by the hand behind him to an apartment door with the number 6A embossed in gold upon its dark wood. Only one bell ring was necessary to summon a tall, attractive, pale brunette in her late 30's to the door. She was wearing a long sleeved white blouse and a black leather hobble skirt that clung becomingly to her shapely hips and thigh lines, with black fishnet hose and stiletto booties.

"Mistress Sophia?" Newton asked, pleasantly extending his hand to shake her elegant, slim one.

"Yes, how are you? Come in please. Everything is ready," said the lady in the accent of a native Bostonian. She led them down a smartly painted and thickly carpeted hall to a large room at the end, where she left them alone without another word. Anthony had settled everything with her over the phone in advance and she knew better than to waste the time of a gentleman who had projected the air, when they spoke, of not being likely to need a tour of the facilities or a course in the use of the equipment. Moreover, he had sent Dennis to Sophia earlier that day with the basic payment in advance with the promise of a generous tip if everything was to his employer's liking that evening.

When the door closed behind them Anthony recognized all the familiar furnishings of the working dungeon: spanking benches, horses, whipping post, stocks, St. Andrew's Cross, a rather intriguing looking sling for suspension and two bondage beds, of different height. There was also an exam table, a changing screen and an enormous black lacquered chest of drawers filled with toys and a number of mirrors. The windows had been curtained in slate blue velvet and the curtains had been drawn. The floor was made of shiny parquet and the walls had been painted a smoky blue gray. The lighting of the room was low and indirect, more golden toned than white. Anthony almost wished it were a little brighter. He wanted to be able to see exactly how red she became. Then he noticed that there were fat russet colored wax candles in big sconces running around the upper walls and picked up a box of matches to light them. Now there was exactly the right amount of ambient light in the dungeon and he regarded a suddenly shy Phoebe over folded arms, even able to detect the beginnings of a blush creeping across her face as she paced around the room taking everything in.

"So tell me, Phoebe," Newton said, casually peeling off his jacket and rolling up his sleeves to his elbows, "do you see yourself as my girlfriend or my submissive?"

She was started by the question but liked it very much.

"Couldn't I be your submissive girlfriend?" she asked.

"I've found that when they're girlfriends, they don't stay submissive for long," he replied.

"In that case, why can't I just be your slave?" she replied, astonishing him by dropping to her knees before him and reaching for his zipper.

"Don't be naughty," he scolded, slapping her hand and pulling her up to her feet. She held her hand to her cheek as though she were about to cry.

"Why not?" she asked, "I adore you. I want to be your slave!" she stamped her very small foot.

"How can you be a slave when you won't obey me in the only thing I ever asked of you?"

"What thing?" she cried.

"Sparing your husband the humiliation of being well and truly cuckolded by a man more powerful than himself."

"Why should he be spared anything?" she wondered aloud. "That selfish schtunk!" she folded her arms stubbornly.

"I don't think he's as bad as all that, Phoebe," Anthony insisted. "He came to me like a gentleman and asked me – in all sincerity – to leave his wife alone. He didn't threaten or even curse. He was, well, nice about it. And I convinced him to look the other way while you sowed this one little wild oat. But he only consented based on my promise that I'd do my best to cure you of this crush you have on me."

"But it's not a crush."

"Yes it is."

"I know it is, but now that we've made love, it's so much more."

"I know, Phoebe, we're genuinely simpatico. You know the words to all the songs I play and I'm happy playing for you. You could be my muse, my go-to girl for productions until the end of time. And we could use that very reality to cloak an ongoing relationship. But unless we're discreet, these fun and games will hurt two people we love."

"It's too late, he already knows I love you."

"He knows you think you do. You can go home to him tomorrow and tell him you were mistaken. You're an actress, this is something even an ordinary girl could do, blindfolded. Actress, real girl, both possess the training to protect a male ego and maintain harmony in the house."

"I'm tired of catering to his ego. He isn't worthy of that much kindness and care," Phoebe stubbornly insisted.

"All right. Let's change the subject," said Newton crisply. "Just stand there," he placed her in the middle of the room. "and let me look at you." He paced around her, his chin on his hand, contemplating her radiant, blushing beauty in the rich, expensive leather outfit that fit every part of her so becomingly. She clasped her hands behind her back and lowered her eyes, feeling her heart contract in excitement at the sudden change in his tone from beseeching to commanding.

"I need a minute to take this all in," he mused aloud. "I'm not used to thinking of Phoebe Casper Robbins as a sex object. Usually when I play with a girl for the first time in this way, I've just met her moments before, off an introduction. For you, I already feel so much. And yet, until just the other day, when you gave me that look, I hadn't even planned to try to touch you, for years. And now you say you want to be my slave…"

"I do!" she cried, meeting his eyes with a twinkle in her own.

"Very well then," he said, looking at her and wondering how to keep her in the pretty dress for a bit longer yet still make an impression on her through the heavy leather. "Go and bend over that table," he instructed, pointing her to a leather padded, waist high bondage bed. "Right at the end. Put your head down on your arms and keep your legs together. For now," he told her, searching in a cabinet for an oblong hard wood paddle, about a half-inch thick. Returning to her, having found a suitable sorority type paddle, Anthony placed one hand in the small of her back and lay the paddle across the exact middle of her petitely voluptuous buttocks, still well clothed in the skirt of cherry red leather. As the position caused her skirt to ride up and reveal the tops of her black, seamed stockings, Anthony observed just how sculpturally rounded both her thighs and bottom cheeks were, actually somewhat plump, which he hadn't guessed at before, having never seen her in jeans or even capris.

"Just a moment," he said, flipping open his phone and with one hand adroitly photographing the paddle laid across Phoebe's skirt.

"What…what are you doing? Taking a picture?" she cried, starting up and looking back.

"I'm documenting your ordeal so you can complain of my obsessive voyeurism to Pascal," Anthony informed her, pocketing the phone and swinging the paddle against Phoebe's seat in a swat that was punctuated by a resounding crack and a subsequent cry of shock and pain from the startled girl. Anthony pushed her back down on the table and swung from the other side, again causing her to cry out and this time do a little dance on her high-heeled shoes. "And then you can explain that it's how I overcompensate for being unable to perform," said Newton, getting ready to deliver a third crisp swat with the paddle.

"Ha!" said Phoebe. "I would never tell a lie like that, no matter how hard you beat me."

"Really? We'll see."

"I have a cell phone too and I'll just take a picture of your hard-on," she threatened.

"I see you're not taking this seriously," Anthony said with regret. "Even though I'm trying to save your marriage. You know you haven't called Pascal once today. And you're not going home tonight. He's going to figure out what's going on and confront you the second you get home."

"I don't care. And it doesn't matter anyway. He loves Amanda and he got to photograph her today, with me not around. He's barely noticing I'm gone."

"That's not true," Anthony said, and aroused her attention with three or four heavy swats of the wooden paddle, each of which seemed to take her breath away, though she had stopped crying out. "Let's see the effect," he said, pushing her skirt up to her waist and happily noting the dark pink swathes of color that decorated her creamy white bottom so ill protected by her sheer black panties. This time he got his photo before she even knew he had gotten his phone out. But when she heard the click of him saving it she turned and smiled at him, touched to her romantic core that he was saving a personal album of naughty French postcards commemorating their first play date. Nor had she the slightest intention of complaining to her husband about it.

Pulling her up off the table, Anthony led her to the whipping post and turning her to face it, pulled her arms up over her head and cuffed them around it. The halter cut of her dress exposed her upper back completely and that creamy little expanse of skin was his next target. He went and chose a flogger and found her staring at her reflection in a facing mirror when he returned.

"Your bottom will match the color of that dress when I'm through with you tonight," Anthony promised, wrapping all her long brown hair around her neck to hang down upon her bosom. "But first, this!" He began to smartly fan Phoebe's bare upper back with the many lashes of the medium weight whip. The sting of the flogger roused her from her narcissistic reverie in the mirror and she began to yip and squirm. Dialing back the severity a few degrees, Anthony continued to smarten her up with the whip, pinkening her back from shoulder to shoulder.

Remembering that it was still summer and that Phoebe would be wearing sundresses all week, Anthony stopped flogging her back and gave it a rub to disperse the sudden redness that spread all over it. The gentle touch of his hand melted Phoebe, who sighed and began to all but hump the post.

Taking her down, Anthony briskly undid the front of her dress and slipped her out of it. The sight of luscious little Phoebe in the black bustier made him smile. Now he turned her to the mirror to look at herself again. Phoebe thought what perfect taste Pamela had to choose this for her. The black velvet fetish pumps made her feel at least five six and that made her feel like a whole new young woman.

Sitting down on the lower bondage bed, Anthony took Phoebe over his knee for the first time. "Give me your hand," he said, reaching for her wrist, which he then held to her waist. "Phoebe?" Anthony asked, smoothing down her sheer panties across her small, yet plump, round cheeks.

"Yes, Anthony?"

"I don't approve of the flippant way in which you're conducting your first extramarital affair," he advised her, smacking her over her panties until she jumped on his lap, kicked her legs up high and tried to squirm away with every ounce of strength she could muster. He held her fast across surprisingly muscular thighs. "You should be worrying about being caught, trying to fend off embarrassing questions, acting on your husband when you're together, to distract him from the truth. Instead, you're acting like you don't even care. Where's the fun in that?"

"I'm glad I don't care. If I cared, I'd be conflicted. I'd feel guilty. Wouldn't I?" she retorted, freeing her hand to rub her bottom.

"You should feel guilty and conflicted."

"Why?"

"It'll help you accept your punishments."

"I'll accept anything from you," she vowed.

He pulled her panties down to bare her already rose hued bottom.

"I never thought you'd be naughty enough to really need to be spanked, but here you are."

Anthony began to spank her bare bottom, holding her fast by the waist, rapidly, rhythmically and with all the indignation he could facsimilate. But it was no use. She was in a world of her own. If she felt pain, her brain wasn't processing it. Instead, she felt herself floating on waves of pure emotional bliss. At last her let her go. Her buttocks were blazing pink. He turned her around on his lap and she clung to him, her arms around his neck as he took her in his arms.

"Oh please," she said, as she broke away at last, "can't we do it here and now?"

"I'd love to do it here and now," he agreed, looking around for the perfect height bench to bend her over.

"Come over here, bad girl," he told her, taking her summarily by the earlobe and leading her to the altar of their second sexual encounter. "face down to hide your lack of shame." He made her lie over the edge of the bench, arranged her to his satisfaction, pulled her panties off completely, and getting behind her forced her thighs apart with his hands. Her pussy was glistening with excitement, which he enhanced by delicately spreading her wide open with his fingers and holding her apart while she realized he was minutely inspecting every pink and coral petal of her femininity.

"I wonder if you're really ready," he mused, teasing her with one fingertip at the opening of her vagina while holding her spread with his other hand. She wriggled and bounced from side to side, groaning with frustration at the delay.

"I am! I am!" she cried impatiently.

This time he penetrated her slowly and began to piston into her in a leisurely fashion, holding her by the waist and rocking her, but slightly, with every thrust. No lubricant was needed for Phoebe was slick and entirely open to him. He began to amuse himself, first by pulling at her velvety earlobe, then by capturing both her wrists under one of his hands on the small of her back, then by punctuating every forth or fifth plunge with a matching smack on one of her still glowing cheeks.

Spotting her little purse a few inches from where her head rested on the leather paddled bench she was bent over, Anthony got an idea.

"Is your phone in that bag?" he asked her.

"...yes," she replied, reluctantly pulling herself back from her reverie of sensation.

"Get it out and call your husband."

"What, now?" she cried, leaning up on her elbows, then her palms to look back at him in amazement. He smiled at her and pushed her back down.

"Yes, call him while I'm fucking you and tell him that you missed the last train and will be staying in town overnight. But sound distressed about it and add how much you miss him."

"But..." she began to search for the right words to protest this bizarre command.

"Go on and do as your master says," Anthony recommended, prompting her to action with several more smacks while never ceasing to slide his penis in and out of her as calmly as before.

Phoebe thought it ironic that Anthony wished her to pretend him incapable of satisfying a woman when he clearly possessed the control of a seasoned porn star but knew it was a lie she could not let loose in the world. She put through the call to her husband without further argument.

Chapter Eighteen

Pascal Takes His Chance

Pascal Robbins was sitting over dinner at The Ball and Feather Inn with Pamela and Amanda when the phone in his pocket vibrated. He had spent the day shooting Amanda in the woods around Random Point. It had not been an intimate shoot, there being Pamela and Damaris in attendance, along with the art director from Chipper Knight and a make up artist from Bartlett's. But now all the hectic activity of the day was past and the several assistants to the shoot had departed, leaving one of the designers, the photographer and model alone to replenish their energies with a fine meal with good wine to match.

The girls heard Pascal say, "Oh, hi honey, how are you?" He listened for a moment, then replied, "The shoot went well. We're just having dinner... Oh, really? ...Okay, I'll see you tomorrow then. Bye." He put his phone away and told Pamela and Amanda, "That was Phoebe. She missed the train and will be staying in Boston tonight." Pascal knocked back the remainder of his martini and added, "She's with Anthony Newton."

Pamela and Amanda looked at each other blankly then back at the man. "Did she say so?" Pamela finally asked.

"No. She's pretending she's staying with her friend Julia. But she's with him. I know it."

"How do you know it?" Amanda cried.

"I know he's in Boston today."

"How?" Pamela asked.

Pascal shrugged, "Oh, I've been keeping tabs on him since I found out Phoebe is in love with him."

"Tabs?" Amanda asked.

"It isn't hard," said Pascal. "It's easy to see a big Bentley driving in and out of this tiny village. Plus, he always stops at Hope's counter for coffee on the way in and out of town and I always hit that same counter mid morning. She tells me all about everyone who's been in and out and what they're up to."

Pamela thought, "Note to file, keep not trusting that blonde girl."

"How do you know she's in love with him?" Pamela asked.

"She told me flat out that she is. Said she had to, and I quote: 'Give it its head,' whether I liked it or not."

"Oh my god, does that mean she's leaving you?" Pamela asked.

"I don't know if it'll end that way," he replied, flagging down Connie, the innkeeper, to ask for another cocktail. "Maybe I'm the one who's supposed to do the leaving."

"She actually told you she's in love with another man?" Amanda asked, feeling shocked and terribly sorry for Pascal Robbins all at once. Anthony Newton would be a formidable rival for any man.

"She did and without remorse," he insisted.

It seemed so dramatically conclusive to make such an announcement to one's husband, especially a husband as sensitive and volatile as Pascal Robbins. Didn't Phoebe realize that these were words one could never take back? Amanda looked sidewise at Pascal who was almost smiling at her perplexity. In a blink Amanda's nimble understanding jumped to the next paragraph in the book of Pascal Robbins, where she learned that Phoebe's decision to give in to a Bohemian passion with a fellow artist polyamorously freed him to do the same thing... with her!

"What are you going to do?" Pamela asked.

"What can I do? I've already beaten her. It didn't make the slightest impression on her," he admitted.

Amanda and Pamela looked at each other again.

"You know what I mean," he told them. "I turned her over my knee."

Pamela smiled and said to Amanda, "He's so sexy, isn't he? I can't believe Phoebe would even look at another man."

"Well, what are you going to say to her when she gets back?" Amanda asked.

"I don't know."

"Are you hurt?" she pressed him, both pleased by and suspicious of his candor.

"Yes, very," he replied, leaning his chin on his hand and gazing into her blue eyes with his suddenly more soulful brown ones. Pamela noticed that Amanda had drank almost a whole glass of wine at this point and felt this accounted for her friend's newfound compassion for the apparently forlorn photographer.

"Phoebe is very naughty," Pamela said, "but you don't want to overreact. You'll never find another quite like her."

Pamela wasn't able to linger much longer over dinner. Although they had all had quite a long workday, she needed to return to the design studio and check on the progress that had been made that day by the sewing team. Also, Dru Baxter was meeting her there at exactly ten thirty p.m. for a quick but urgent tryst which he had begged for in a sweet text to her earlier that day. Making Pascal promise to see Amanda home, Pamela departed, thanking both her companions for a successful shoot day. Amanda had even received another check to add to her European shopping spree fund in return for her day's modeling labor.

"Ask me in?" Pascal said to Amanda as he pulled up to Hugo's house.

Amanda looked at him with hesitation, saying, "Do you promise not to rape me?" For while she was feeling slightly more charitable to the urban wolf than she might have done had she not drank the generous portion of wine, the liberties he had already taken with her were never far from her mind when he swam into view.

"How can you say such a thing?" he demanded. "No wonder I want to spank you."

Amanda folded her arms and looked at him.

"Of course I won't rape you!" he sputtered. Amanda relaxed and then nodded for him to follow her.

While Amanda gathered the cats for their evening meal and then let them all out into the woods behind Hugo's house, Pascal asked if she would offer him a nightcap. In one way and another, Pascal felt that women had been outsmarting him all month, but he could still figure out how to throw a college girl off balance. And that was where alcohol came in. She was already a little tipsy and she already felt somewhat sorry for him. If he couldn't cinch this deal, he wasn't worth the name Photographer.

Pascal stood opening the bottle of wine she had thrust into his hands upon entering the kitchen, admiring Amanda's tall, slender form. She was perfectly dressed, as usual, this time in a white shirt, beige wrap skirt and beige flats with black leather accents. He thought how she was meant to be his present muse.

"Colby's parents sent my father a case of that," Amanda informed Pascal, lest he forget that Amanda's beefcake boyfriend would be returning to her side the following day.

Pascal set aside the open wine bottle and looked for some glasses.

"I don't want any," she said.

"Are you sure?"

"You really want me at your mercy, don't you, Mr. Robbins?" she laughed at him.

"Would you please stop calling me Mr. Robbins?"

"I don't mind smoking a pipe, though," she said, searching in a kitchen cabinet for one of Hugo's stashes. Pascal liked that idea just as much as her drinking with him. The point was to break down her resistance, and he recalled from his own college days, that weed usually got the job done as efficiently as alcohol, less the hang over.

"You said you'd let me shoot you nude, why don't we do it now?" he suddenly suggested.

"Are you kidding? We've been shooting all day, and I just stuffed myself with food," she laughed.

"Who cares? We're alone, my cameras and lights are in the car, we could be done before you know it." He knocked back the first glass of wine quickly. "That is good," he said, thrusting the empty glass towards her for a refill.

Amanda said, "You drink like someone out of 1960," but refilled his glass, gratified by his admiration of Colby's family vineyard.

"Come on, Amanda, don't you want to add another five hundred bucks to your Euro shopping excursion fund?"

"Five hundred for my first nude photos ever?" she cried. "I don't think so!"

"What then? It's the standard rate for a short glamour shoot," he replied honestly enough and it was twice what he had paid her for the wet suit shots at the beach. Amanda had also made five hundred dollars shooting fashion stills for Pamela and Damaris that day.

"I don't doubt that, but after all, this is me we're talking about. Those photos might be valuable some day."

"Well, what do you want?" he asked, mentally deciding he would go to a thousand if necessary, so much did he believe that getting Amanda naked would inevitably lead to him taking her to bed that night. Amanda smoked a bowl, offered him the bong, which he refused, then took it back and drew at the pipe again, looking at him. Then she exhaled and looked at him again, seeing a tense, interesting and exciting man, whom she didn't trust in the slightest but felt herself increasingly drawn to.

"A verbal contract," she replied.

"Who's going to witness it?" he asked.

"This," said, getting out her phone, setting it to video mode and standing beside Pascal, holding it away from them at arm's length to record the statement, "Pascal Robbins herewith agrees to pay me, Amanda Sands, five hundred dollars for my first nude photo shoot ever with the following stipulations: One: That it be tasteful and artistic rather than explicit; Two: That any profit Mr. Robbins realizes on the sale of any of the photos taken today over and above one thousand dollars, be split evenly with me, Amanda Sands; and Three: That Amanda Sands will have a choice of ten of the photos to do whatever she wants with for the rest of her life. State your name and that you agree on this date of June 22nd, 20__." Pascal immediately did as she asked to cinch the deal, his heart contracting with joy at the prospect of seeing Amanda before him without a stitch of clothing on most likely within the hour. She sent the video to Hugo's phone and saved a copy on her own.

"Very well," said Amanda, "get your cameras and lights and meet me upstairs in Hugo's attic." She then ran up to her room to wash her face, brush her teeth and apply a touch of lipstick and mascara. She found herself momentarily wondering what to wear when she remembered that she was presently to wear nothing at all. She smiled at herself in the mirror and realized that she was no longer exhausted But what about him, she wondered. Surely that almost middle aged, cigarette smoking, near lush was tired after a day that had begun at six a.m. She grinned and thought, "He must want me very badly. He must feel he absolutely has to have me tonight. Tomorrow Colby and Phoebe will return. In a few weeks I'll be gone. It'll be ages before he gets another chance like this with me."

She walked up the back stairs to the attic dungeon slowly, pondering, "How far should I let him go? Should I let him go nowhere at all? He promised he wouldn't ravish me. He gave me his word, so I'm safe. And yet, he's very handsome." Suddenly she felt sleepy and she realized she was indeed still exhausted on top of being stoned. "The way it works is, if we stay up all night talking until sunrise, Pascal will finish the bottle of wine and go home unsatisfied. But if I weaken and beg to be tucked into bed, it'll all be over in moments." She opened the dungeon door and switched on a few low lights. "Of course," she continued to muse, "I could let him take his photos and then just send him home." But she would probably do no such thing. She didn't like sleeping alone in Hugo's large, creaking old house.

Pascal was back with her momentarily and efficiently began plugging in his two lights while assessing the room's capabilities with a practiced eye.

"I have an idea," said Amanda, stepping in front of a bondage bed, "that this should be my pedestal." Then still fully clothed, she adopted a series of poses she felt might display her charms to advantage. She curled up on one side and brought her wrists in front of her. "We could put me in cuffs," Amanda said, "and I could hold my wrists in front of me, like this, or behind me, like this," she pulled her arms back behind her at the small of her back, and arched both her head and torso backwards. "You could get some good breast shots with me in this position and I could sort of cheat my legs together."

Pascal didn't mind Amanda's art directing her own shoot, she had obviously studied her angles, knew what it would take to maintain her modesty and seemed to have some very good instincts for dramatic poses. Once she had communicated her thoughts, and observed him quickly placing his lights and metering the area she had proposed, she stepped behind a painted screen and disrobed. A minute later she appeared before him totally nude without bothering to try to cover her breasts or fleecy blonde triangle of pubic hair. Instead she unself-consciously began to search in one of the armoires for the leather cuffs she wanted to wear. Hugo's equipment being very well organized, she found two pair of cuffs with boat hooks already attached within seconds and brought them back to the bench.

"Here, help me get these on," she said, thrusting the wristlets into his hands. He buckled each of her wrists into one of the cuffs. She then sat on the bench to wrap the remaining pair of cuffs around her ankles. Then, while still sitting down, she linked the anklets together with a boat hook. Sweeping her now tethered feet back up to the bench and curling them behind her she lay on her side and hooked her wristlets together and placed her hands facing each other in front of her muff as she lay facing him. "Do I look helpless?" she asked.

"Not really," he replied.

"Tell me the exact moment I begin to look like that girl in *The Seventh Seal* just before they took her to be burned at the stake," Amanda said and then attempted to facsimilate that expression of abject terror tinged with profound resignation. Pascal was extremely familiar with the character and film Amanda referenced and had to admit, the hair cut was almost identical to that of the doomed fourteen century Swedish waif, but his model still looked anything but helpless.

"I like the way you look," he told her, "you look sexy and hot."

Amanda posed in the cuffs, twisting her body every way she thought might look appealing, holding Pascal's lens with her eyes in every shot. She had played with cuffs a good deal with her high school boyfriend and with her hands behind her back was even able to hook her wrists to her ankles and present Pascal with a simple hogtie. Lying flat on her stomach while lifting her head and chest, she revealed to the photographer before her the full upper mounds of her bosom while her bent knees and legs shaded her jutting buttocks. She saved her most insolent and daring expressions for the hogtie, knowing that all the portions of her body he most wanted to see fully exposed were modestly concealed in this position.

Finally abandoning the cuffs – she was able to undo all the fastenings herself in a few moments – Amanda switched from bondage poses to yoga positions, giving a small and slightly broken twist of her own invention to each one. Amanda had been thinking about posing nude for over a year and had already worked out all of her best angles so that all Pascal had to do was move around her and snap shots.

"Now just for the sake of the photos, pretend you really want me," Pascal advised, as they came to the end of the shoot.

"How can I tell if I really want you until you take off *your* clothes?" she surprised him by saying.

"Seriously?" he put his camera aside.

"I'm just asking, what are you offering that I might want? I mean, given the fact that my 19 year old boyfriend is a muscular jock." She stretched and for the first time allowed her thighs to part ever so slightly to reveal a slash of pinkness amidst the blonde curls.

"Experience?" he suggested casually.

"Really? You consider yourself a virtuoso?"

"Amanda, don't be crude. It isn't like you."

"Why am I crude? You're the one who set this whole shoot up to get a shot at fucking me. Can you even begin to deny that?"

"No, but you needn't express it in that vulgar manner," he admonished her, taking down his lights and winding up the cables.

"You're a calculating wolf who planned to get a young girl completely drunk and then take shameless advantage of her," Amanda went on, still making no move to get dressed.

"Can I help it if I'm crazy about you?" he replied unapologetically.

"Yes, of course you can, any decent married man would," she ruthlessly replied.

"Look, I don't make a habit of cheating on my wife. In fact, I've never done it before."

"And how about going after girls who are half your age? Have you never done that before either?"

"No, actually, I haven't. I'm never drawn to my models."

"I see. You're really better than that. It's just me as an individual who brings it out of you."

"Exactly," he said with his easy smile.

"Suppose I did let you have me, just this once, would you have to brag to Phoebe? If you did, it would surely get out. And then every lady in the Venus Club would think I'm a total slut."

"What the hell is The Venus Club?"

"You took our picture that day."

"Anyway, I don't kiss and tell, you're the one who tells things to people," he said with mild reproach.

"If anything did happen between me and you, kissing wouldn't enter into it. You smoke and drink too much," she replied, unconsciously placing her hands on her curvy hips as she set the rules for the possible projected engagement. Even as she did so, she inwardly fretted that perhaps she was being too bossy and harsh with this very engaging male who was also the brilliant photographer who had already brought her beauty to the fore several times, once well enough to land her on a billboard in Harvard Square. And yet, as with most of the other men and boys in her love life to date, it appeared she was fated to take control.

Pascal looked at her intently for a moment, then sighed and returned to his packing up. The fact that she had not put her clothes back on yet was encouraging, but her words rejected him almost contemptuously. This comparing him to her jocular boyfriend was just the sort of needling that made him want to spank her again.

Amanda hesitated before speaking again, taking a stroll around the attic while she thought about her options.

"Why haven't you taken your clothes off yet?" she asked conversationally. "After all, I invited you to."

"I usually leave that for last," he admitted, taking the opportunity to sweep her up and down with an appreciative gaze.

"I can tell you're very thin, your clothes just hang on you," she observed critically. "No doubt this is due to all your smoking and drinking and poor nutritional habits. Which naturally results in a total disinterest in exercise."

"I play racquet ball once a week," he shrugged, knowing that all she said was correct.

"That's true, I have seen you at the gym now and then," she granted, still strolling around the dungeon while he watched her. "And your dissolute lifestyle has yet to show itself in your face. But honestly, how virile can an almost forty year old man be who treats his body the way you do?"

"I haven't had any complaints," he said, beginning to realize that the more insulting she became, the farther away she wandered from the pile of clothes she'd left behind the screen.

"Are you saying that in spite of your dissipation that you can still deliver a long lasting, rock-hard erection?"

"Why don't we see?" he asked, pleasantly conscious of that exact entity, which had suddenly and earnestly jumped to life behind his zipper.

"I actually love kissing as foreplay, so I'll make you a deal, Mr. Robbins," she said, coming back to him and standing before him. "If you quit smoking cigarettes, the next time I'm in a position to entertain you, I'll let you make love to me."

"What's this you're saying now? You'll let me have you if I quit smoking?" he replied in amazement. "Aren't you the most managing female who ever lived?"

Now, at last, Amanda decided to go back behind the screen and put her clothes on. From which location she said, "Maybe I just care about you, Mr. Robbins. If you think about it, you'll derive multiple benefits from making the commitment. You know, Anthony Newton doesn't smoke and he takes very good care of himself. He's older than you by maybe as many as ten years, but his glowing good health gives him the advantage."

"That and talent and maybe ninety million dollars," said Pascal wistfully.

She came out, tying the wrap skirt around her small waist.

"How about a hug to send me on my way?" he asked. She graciously put her arms around his neck and pressed her front against his. Both were instantly conscious of her womanly bosom crushed against his chest and her lower abdomen pressed against his pants front. He kissed her behind her ear and upon the back of her slender neck. Holding her in his arms, he let his right hand fall upon the crest of her buttocks. "Can't I even spank you for being such a ball buster?" he asked, lightly patting her bottom.

"All right," she said, "but just a little bit."

Pascal didn't wait for a more elaborate invitation, but sat down on the bondage bed, pulled Amanda straight across his lap and administered twelve or thirteen crisp smacks to the seat of her cotton skirt while holding her fast to his lap with an arm thrown across her trim waist. Each swat was full bodied and resonant, delivered to impart the type of heat that takes many minutes to dissipate. The last few, especially vigorous spanks caused Amanda to squeak and in the end, begin to kick. But as soon as he had begun, Pascal seemed to let her go. Amanda jumped up and looked at him, with something of a sparkle in her eyes, her hand going back to her bottom to rub it. It had been a harder spanking than the one he had given her in the shop, which was, in Pascal's view, only proper after she had as much as accused him of being a weakling, not to mention teasing him so much over the last hour.

Amanda walked him down to the front door and opened it to let him out into the blossom heavy summer night air.

"Will you do it for me?" she asked on parting.

"What do you think, Little Miss Bossy?" he replied with a grin, taking out his half pack of Marlboro reds and putting them into her hand.

Chapter Nineteen

Marion Craig

Amanda would have been struck dumb with wonder to learn what her lover was doing in Boston on the day of Amanda's two photo shoots instead of knocking around town with his buddies as he had told her he would. For at noon sharp that same day, he might have been observed entering a sleekly modern and obviously exclusive Cambridge apartment building in a light weight fawn colored suit, with the air of a young businessman with an extremely important appointment to keep during this particular lunch hour.

She was waiting for him in the lobby, a slim, smartly dressed, impeccably groomed brunette in her early thirties, with an impatient look in her arresting brown eyes. In a way she reminded him of Pamela, plus five or six years, even down to the tension she seemed to hold in those slender shoulders, but this woman, Marion Craig, radiated a kind of intensity he hadn't encountered before. She looked him up and down in an appraising manner he might have enjoyed from a girl his own age but not so much from this lady. There was almost something insulting in the once over that preceded their handshake, even though she followed up the look with what passed for a warm smile for Marion. Colby looked even better in person in the nicely tailored suit than in the photo he had emailed her, which didn't quite capture the fact that he was 6'2, broad shouldered and athletically built.

Going up in the elevator she continued to look at him with appreciation, as though congratulating herself on her excellent judgment in planning this encounter. Colby smiled at her with relaxed affability, the urgency of the young go-getter dropping away from him as he remembered exactly why this attorney had agreed to meet him at her apartment on her lunch hour. If you didn't count Amanda, and you didn't, because he had met her as a classmate, this was his first actual play date with a grown up lady. How he had found Ms. Marion Craig was while helping Amanda edit The New Rod Quarterly the previous week. He had asked to be allowed to handle the personal ads and she had given him the current folder. On going over the new ads for that week, Colby could not fail to notice Marion Craig's terse request for a good looking male disciplinarian in Boston, promising to provide the same with a shapely bottom that was in much need of strict correction. A photo illustrated email exchange had followed, rapidly heating to a point where some sort of action had to be decided upon. The result was this meeting, where Colby had arrived with the express purpose of spanking her and if her follow up correspondence didn't lie, going much further than that. A few weeks before, the notion of topping a sophisticated older woman might have aroused sensations of confusion and insecurity in the soon to be college sophomore, but since the experience with Pamela and Amanda, Colby had become imbued with a new confidence. After all, he had proven capable of pleasing both Amanda Sands and Pamela Bartlett, passing every test they had thrown at him and managing to offend no one in the process. From what he had observed so far, he had no fear of encountering an excess of sensibility in Marion Craig. Nor did she prove this instinct wrong the moment they were alone in her stylish apartment.

Marion looked at her expensive watch and said, "You look a lot better than I expected. That's a very nice suit." She had a sexy voice, a little hoarse, a regular Mrs. Robinson voice.

"Thanks. I like the way you look too," he replied, wondering what she had expected.

"You look like you're competent to handle this," she went on, lighting a cigarette. "And I do appreciate your discretion. You haven't mentioned allowance so far. I'd like to be out of here in forty minutes. I think this should be enough." Marion handed Colby an envelope full of hundred dollar bills.

Colby stared at Marion and then at the unsealed envelope she'd put into his hand, wondering at how she could have misunderstood his overtures to her so completely, wanting to laugh aloud but also wanting to see how far he could take this thing. He remembered Amanda challenging him to state that he could turn down big bucks from a woman who needed to be serviced with spanking and sex. There was a practical side of Colby Hodge that wanted very much to keep whatever was in the envelope for the upcoming trip to Europe, imagining dazzling Amanda one night with a stunning suite at a four star hotel. But charge a pretty lady? In addition to being unchivalrous, it also seemed undignified. How can you take the moral high ground with a spoiled, demanding bitch when she is paying you? All of these thoughts flashed through Colby's mind in the half second before he thrust the envelope back into Marion's hands. "You made a mistake," he said, amiably enough.

"Really?" she looked cynically at him. "You're not a male prostitute? You're still going with the Harvard boy story?"

"It's not a story," he said, taking out his student id card and showing it to her. She stepped back in surprise.

"Colby Hodge is a real name?"

"Yes."

"So you just came because you're young and horny?" she asked him bluntly.

"Sure, but I also want to spank you," he answered cheerfully, taking off his jacket and rolling up his sleeves. "And don't worry, I can have you back on the pavement in twenty six minutes."

Marion looked at him doubtfully. He had seated himself on one of her sleek, minimalist sofas and was emptying his pockets of change, keys and condoms. When she approached him tentatively, he reached out, grabbed her wrist and yanked her down across his broad thighs. She caught her breath but didn't have long to wait for the first smack to fall juicily on the seat of a pencil skirt tight enough to greatly enhance the allure of her small but shapely bottom. He felt right away that it was a hard, gym toned backside under his hand and noted the just barely audible pants that followed each crack of his palm on her skirted rear. Holding her tightly by the waist, he warmed her up for a couple of minutes like this before trying to figure out how to get the snug garment up or off most expediently.

233

"Get up and get that suit off," he said at length. "And you'd better have real panties on, not some silly thong," he added for good measure, realizing he hadn't been the slightest bit authoritative with this dreamer who had poured out her desires for rough sex after even rougher spanking in a series of trenchant emails to him the previous day and night.

"You're only 19," she charged, shrugging out of her jacket and unzipping her skirt negligently, "what do you know about real panties?" Sure enough, she had on the world's plainest black bra and a black thong. Her breasts were small and well shaped. He turned her around to look at her bottom, which was especially attractive, possibly her best feature.

"The penalty for coming to a date with a spanking guy wearing a thong is that you don't get to keep it on," Colby said, yanking her thong down and making her step out of it, whereupon he was startled to see a silky triangle of pale reddish curls surmount her Venus mound, for her straight, fine, almost shoulder length hair was dark brown. "What, you're a natural redhead? And you dye your hair brown?" he demanded. Marion shrugged carelessly. "I love redheads," he scolded, pulling her back down across his lap and continuing to spank her vigorously. "You know, you might be too perverse for your own good," he told her, unceremoniously unhooking her bra, pulling it off and tossing it aside. "Let's talk about this whole meeting a male prostitute off Craig's list gambit," he said, pausing to let her catch her breath.

"It wasn't Craig's List, it was Hugo Sands' magazine," she reminded him.

"Still, you were taking a big risk with your "I want rough sex" and your envelopes full of pelf. Don't you realize there are maniacs out there? You're just lucky I intercepted your crazy ad and answered it myself instead of printing it. I'm only a temporary assistant editor at the Rod but even I know what should never go into print."

"I love that you're being so protective of me, but does this mean I don't get the rough sex?" she turned to ask him.

"Oh, you'll get it," he told her, pushing her off his lap and standing up to unzip his trousers. "Stay there," he ordered, when she'd scrambled to her knees. "And just blow me," he added, presenting her with a formidable hard-on. She looked up at him with an arched brow and the first genuine smile he had seen light her dark brown eyes. Then she proceeded to engulf his mushroom cap with her lips and lave his shaft with her tongue all the way down to its base. Marion's fellatio was so good that he had to stop her before a full minute had elapsed lest she bring him off too soon. "All right, that's enough, you proved you're as much of a slut as your letters promised. Let's move on," he said, lifting her to her feet and taking her by the wrist over to a bar with several bar stools, one of which he bent her over directly. "I hope you're wet," he said, parting her thighs and beginning to probe her with several fingers, "because I didn't bring any lube." She was wet.

"I have lube," she suggested, craning her head around to catch his gaze, while pushing back against his fingers.

"Okay, go get it," he ordered, pulling her up and giving her another sharp smack on her small, jutting buttocks to speed her departure. Marion ran off to another room and returned shortly with a bottle of lubricant. Colby smiled, took it from her, put it aside and bent her back over the barstool. Since she had already proven herself capable of taking the entire length of his cock down her throat, he had no fear of not being able to cram the whole thing into her narrow vaginal canal, but did her the courtesy of generously lubricating his condom sheathed shaft before plowing into her tight but flexible and responsive pussy with one long, hard, deeply penetrating thrust that elicited a cry of pained surprise from the leggy brunette. Colby saw in the facing mirror that Marion did have stunningly shapely legs. Her face was also turned to the mirror and it looked very pretty as the shock of the first thrust began to fade and the college boy began to fuck her deeply and rhythmically, holding her fast by the waist. Then, noticing that she kept her eyes on her own face in the mirror, he reached out and grabbed her hair into a ponytail in his hand, holding it close to her head, skillfully, without hurting her, but forcefully, to let her know that he was completely in control. Colby turned out towards the mirror, so she could actually see his cock sliding in and out, in and out, as he'd seen the porn stars do in their video clips, to reveal the great length of their organs. He saw Marion become mesmerized by the hard, pink thrusting tool she could so easily watch from the angle she reposed at. Now he let go of her hair, and pulling both her wrists back to capture them under one hand on the small of her back, Colby used his other hand to reach forward and pinch the erect nipples of her breasts. At this point she began to say, "Ogod! Yes! Do that more!"

Instead, he pulled out completely, drizzled a goodly amount of lubricant up and down her bottom crack and placing one of her own hands on each of her cheeks, ordered her to spread herself open for him. When she hesitated slightly, he slapped her at least a dozen times, hard, reddening each globe of her bottom from thigh to hip.

"All right!" she cried, "I'll do it!"

"You'd better fucking do it. Your lunch hour is half over and you still haven't come for me yet," he observed somewhat sternly. Marion would never know quite how much it turned him on to have her obey this command with the girlish timidity she was still able to muster, in spite of her obvious sophistication. Seeing her open and receptive, feeling himself as hard as he had ever been and making sure the lubricant had been lavishly applied to the bulbous knob of his penis, he carefully but firmly began to force it through her tiny anal portal, pushing her hands aside in a moment to get a proper grip on her waist as he thrust his cock all the way home up her rectal canal. Once again, she rather screamed at the first thrust in, but before one tear could fall, became quickly acclimatized to the length and girth of his meaty organ pumping into her backside and soon began to push back against his thrusts, opening herself to the greatest degree possible to accommodate him and ride this perfect act of anal mastery to the orgasm she knew she was only seconds from achieving. And when she enjoyed that release there was no mistaking her satisfaction, for she was quite the loudest climaxer he'd ever made come. As she wrung his cock out like a wash cloth with her convulsing anal ring, Colby knew he'd done exactly what she'd brought him there to do, and so he then allowed himself to orgasm ecstatically inside her, which act bound them together in a state of electrifying bliss for about a minute more.

When Marion disappeared into the bathroom to repair herself, Colby did the same in a different bathroom, pausing to look at his watch and note that a mere twenty four minutes had passed since they'd come upstairs. They met again in the foyer and the most calculating and remote woman he'd ever met surprised him by putting her arms around his waist and laying her head against his chest while whispering, "That was perfect. Thank you."

He said, "You're welcome," and held tilted her chin up to kiss her softly on the mouth. Her face was a very beautiful one.

"Can I call you again?" she asked hopefully.

"Of course!" he replied without hesitation. "Maybe we can have lunch or dinner next time too."

"Really? You'd want to?"

"Sure I would. You're a fascinating lady."

"Me?" she smiled at him as though fully relaxed for the first time in days perhaps, and lit the inevitable cigarette.

They walked out to the elevator. Since no one else was around to hear their conversation, Colby said, "What I can't understand is why someone as sexy and good looking as you would ever think you had to pay for a man's attention."

"Well, I wouldn't pay for just any man," she smiled. "But once you'd sent me your photo, combined with telling me what you're into, I knew I had to try you. As far as the allowance goes, I just figured it would uncomplicate things and enable me to get exactly what I wanted from you."

"I'll be back in the city some time soon," he said, as they emerged onto the street. "If you feel ... tense again, call me."

"I will Colby Hodge," she said with a grin as his ridiculous name passed her lips. She put out her hand to shake his. He squeezed hers, drew her to him once more and gave her another kiss before they parted, each with a smile that was slow to fade.

Chapter Twenty

Phoebe Fibs, Pascal Persists
and Amanda Acquiesces

Amanda opened the antiques shop a little earlier the following morning and stationed herself at the front window in order to observe Pascal Robbins' moment of arrival at the bookstore for his morning espresso, for she knew she had to speak to him as soon as possible in order to correct any and all errors she may have made the previous night after the long and exhausting shoot day had left her brain dead. She saw him arrive at ten sharp and immediately put up the "Back in fifteen minutes" sign, locked the front door and ran across to the bookshop.

Pascal was already seated before Hope at the coffee counter and Amanda tapped him lightly on the shoulder. He turned to smile at her, taking in her fresh, cool appearance in her navy wrap dress and tan ribbon tie wedge espadrille sandals.

"Hi honey," he said warmly.

"Can I talk to you for a minute?" she asked, pulling on his sleeve. He followed her to a small wooden booth and Hope nodded to Amanda to indicate she would bring her usual cappuccino directly.

"So, I haven't had a cigarette since I saw you," he smiled. "Are you ready to give it up to me?"

"Oh, Mr. Robbins, you're not really going to hold a girl to a promise made when she was dizzy with exhaustion, are you?" she asked.

"Yes, I am," he replied pleasantly.

"Well, we can talk about that… later," she said, then plunged on, "but what I really felt I had to ask was whether you intended to share your suspicions about Phoebe and Mr. Newton with Susan Ross?"

Pascal looked at her thoughtfully, then replied, "No, why would I?"

"Oh, good!" Amanda breathed, relieved. "You see I happen to know that Susan is still madly in love with Mr. Newton and I wouldn't want to see her heart broken over something that may not have even happened."

"Don't worry," said Pascal, "she won't hear anything from me."

"Thank you!"

Hope brought Amanda her coffee and Amanda drank it with pleasure, noticing for the first time that Mr. Robbins did indeed no longer reek of stale tobacco. He had an altogether fresher look that morning than she had ever seen in him and a more attractive sparkle in his eyes.

"You really haven't smoked today?" she asked with a grin.

"Not at all. And I just had my car detailed. Took all my suits to the cleaners too."

"I'm so glad, for your sake," she told him, glancing at her wristwatch and realizing it was time to return to work. He got up too, leaving enough cash on the table for Hope. Pascal walked Amanda over to her father's shop.

"You don't honestly think I'm going to let you wriggle out of the bargain, do you, Amanda?" he asked as she opened the door to the shop and reversed the sign.

"Of course I do, Mr. Robbins, because you're a gentleman," Amanda serenely replied, favoring him with a smile as delightful as the balmy June morning air. He followed her into the shop, closed the door behind him and leaned against it, looking at her.

"So you're saying you were teasing me last night?" he asked. Amanda looked at him with a flutter in her tummy.

"If I was it was because you pushed a tired girl too far with your "Lets take nude photos at ten p.m.' brainstorm," she replied with some spirit.

"Look, I'll let you out of the bargain on one condition," he offered, affably. "That I get to spank you again, for being such a cocktease."

"But you already spanked me quite well," she pointed out. "I could feel it for an hour."

"I'll bet it was snowy white again in seconds."

"No, it stayed quite pink for some time," she said, her cheeks flushing the same shade as she recalled the sensation. She looked so adorable at that moment that he had to kiss her. He did so quickly and then let her go.

"All right," he said gallantly, "I'll take that kiss as my forfeit." And a moment later, he was gone to the station to meet Phoebe's train.

As the bell tinkled with his departure, Amanda stood in the doorway looking thoughtfully after him. He looked back once before climbing into his SUV and waved a cheerful goodbye.

Phoebe Robbins' heart was also fluttering as she beheld her husband leaning against the door of his car awaiting her with folded arms. Affecting a demeanor of severity he hardly felt after his most recent soft and flirtatious exchange with Amanda, Pascal frowned heavily at his petite partner while taking her luggage to stow in the trunk.

"Well, how was Boston?" he asked, bristling with ill suppressed indignation at what he knew to have been a idyllic romantic getaway with the idol of her heart.

"Hot and humid," she replied, getting into the car.

"Really? What did you wind up doing last night?"

"I saw a Molière play," Phoebe replied, unhappy to the point of near tears to think of having another quarrel in the car.

"With Julia?" he prodded, throwing the car in gear and beginning the short drive to the other end of the village where they were spending the summer in Susan's house. Phoebe looked down at her hands folded in the skirt of her pale green cotton summer dress.

"No," she replied softly.

"With someone else?"

"Yes."

"So, you spent the night with someone else," he stated bluntly.

"Yes."

"Phoebe, do you want a divorce?" he demanded.

"No!" she cried. "Honestly, Pascal. It didn't … go well last night," she cried, somewhat shamefacedly.

"Really?" he looked at her cynically. "In what way did it not go well?"

"I'd rather not say," she murmured, squirming on a bottom that Anthony Newton had finally found the resolve to cane stringently that morning, leaving six perfectly spaced red weals across it.

Pascal didn't say another word until they had arrived at the house. He carried her bags inside and they went upstairs together. Once in their suite he opened a few windows to let in the sweet morning air, slightly tangy from the nearby coast.

"Something is different," she said suddenly. "You smell different, the car smelled different and our room smells different. Have you stopped smoking?"

"Yes, as a matter of fact. I have."

"Oh darling, that's wonderful!" she said, sincerely beaming her approval.

"Humph!" he said, sliding into the window seat, putting up his feet and looking at her. "As though you care about your old husband!"

"Pascal, don't say that. I care about you very much. I love you."

"You seem to love a lot of people."

"No, I love you."

"What happened last night?" he demanded.

"Nothing," she said, adding sadly. "Or, almost nothing."

"Are you saying that you didn't have sex with Anthony Newton last night?"

She looked down and with difficulty replied, "Something happened with his health a few years ago, and he isn't … potent anymore." She didn't trust herself to meet his eyes but turning around and lifting her skirt, added dramatically, "So he makes an impression this way." She was wearing sandals without hose that day and a skimpy pair of white cotton bikinis, which she pulled to one side to exhibit her deep red marks from the caning, the skin slightly raised and swollen where they neatly lined her bottom. Pascal's eyes widened and he came close to touch her skin and feel the ridge that each mark made across her creamy peachy pink skin.

"Are you saying he's a sadist?" Pascal asked, recoiling at the marking and yet on some level inwardly glad that his would-be unfaithful wife had been dealt some real pain in the course of her adventure.

"He did seem to enjoy hurting me," she replied, as though of a bitter memory.

"What are you going to do for that?" he asked, gingerly touching her again. She winced as his fingertips grazed the soon to be welts. He took his hand away and she let her skirt drop back down.

"I don't know. I suppose I'll go to the organic pharmacy and get some arnica," she mused.

"So are you saying that it's over?" he demanded.

"I'm saying that it never began."

"Well, suppose he wants to... to beat you again? He pretty much owns you because of this show and every subsequent one, doesn't he?"

"No. That will never happen again," she vowed. "That kind of pain is way beyond anything I'm interested in."

This was the first bit of truth she had uttered that morning to her husband. The thrashing was a last minute inspiration that Anthony had gotten her to consent to, just so she'd have some sort of tangible proof of dissatisfaction with her celebrity lover to display to her mate. Phoebe had no idea that a caning could hurt so much but it happened so quickly that six strokes had harshly fallen before she could remember to scream "mercy" instead of just simply scream. He'd held her down across a table in the suite to administer the caning and followed through with steely determination, for her own good.

Phoebe cried for five whole minutes and cast him the most reproachful looks she could muster, beholding her reflection in a mirror with horror as the red marks swelled before her eyes.

"You didn't say you were going to be brutal!" she protested. "I think I need an ice pack and at once!"

"No!" he urged, pulling her into his arms and holding her close while similarly gazing at her exposed bottom in the mirror with surprised appreciation of his own neat handiwork. "You want those marks looking as angry as possible when you show Pascal, so he'll believe you've been through a ghastly ordeal."

"Well, it has been ghastly!" she cried, feeling terribly sorry for herself.

"I'm sorry Phoebe," he spoke against her ear as he held her. "But those marks are surest way to make him believe you're over me."

She pulled away from him, dabbing her eyes with a lace-trimmed handkerchief. "Are you sure you don't want me to actually be over you?" she asked.

"I am sure of that," he smiled, pulling her back into his arms and kissing her until she forgave him.

"Will you make me an ice pack?" she asked, a little abashed, a little meek and with just a little twinkle in her soft brown eyes as she looked at her husband affectionately. He nodded solemnly and went to the wet bar to fulfill her request.

When he came back she was lying in bed in an ivory satin quilted wrapper under the comforter. On seeing him appear she turned on her side and taking the tea cloth wrapped ice pack, put it under the covers against her punished cheeks. She looked very pretty with her long brown hair down on her shoulders and the top of the dressing gown parted to expose her creamy cleavage.

"Will you nurse me back to health?" she asked, reaching her arms up to go around his neck and pulling him down to the bed. "Mmmm, you smell so good today," she told him, breathing in the pleasant scent of his clean skin instead of stale tobacco for the first time in their entire relationship.

Everything that day seemed to conspire to throw Amanda in Pascal's path. Colby arrived back in Random Point mid morning and kept her company in the shop until lunchtime, when he went across to Hope's coffee counter to buy sandwiches to bring back to the shop. He brought the food back to Amanda in Hugo's editorial office, where she was answering New Rod Quarterly email at his computer station. Then he went into the connecting galley to start some coffee brewing. Amanda heard Colby's phone ring while he was there.

When he came back into the office she noticed him texting a reply. "That was my friend in P.Town," Colby said, "you want to go to a clambake tonight?"

"Colby you know I don't like seafood," Amanda said, not looking up from typing. Colby did know that.

"Seriously? Not even clams? They're so delicious. Especially when you dig them yourself."

Amanda shivered with distaste. She looked up and said, "Colby, you know both my parents are vegan. We never had fish in the house. The first time I smelled it I almost died. No, you go on to your clambake, I'll be fine."

"Are you sure, Babe?" he asked, already texting an answer to his friend that he'd be there at dusk.

"Of course. For one thing, it's Friday night. I think Susan Ross is going to be back and if so, I can meet her for dinner," said Amanda, helpfully.

By the time Amanda closed the shop at six, Colby was long gone. Just as she was putting up the Closed sign, Pascal Robbins pulled up to the front of the shop and got out to greet her.

"Is he becoming obsessed with me?" Amanda wondered, vaguely smiling at him, and concluding, "He can't seem to keep away from me today."

"Hi," she said, holding the door open for him to enter, as he seemed to want to. He had an 8" x 10" craft envelope under his arm.

"Hi Amanda. I've got your check for last night and you need to sign a model's release," he said, opening the envelope on the back counter. She followed him and noticed a disc in a jewel case marked "Amanda Pix" beside the model's release. She took a pen from Pascal and looked the document over. He had modified his usual boilerplate to include the provision she had mentioned the night before. She folded the five hundred dollar check and put it in the pocket of her skirt.

"Thank you," she said.

"Do you want to see the photos?"

"Now?"

"Why not? Don't you have a laptop handy?" he asked. She invited him back to Hugo's office and put the disc into his computer. Soon the photos were jumping up on her screen. She looked at them critically and could not help but be pleased.

"I'll bring these to Susan tonight. She can use some of the poses for her cartoons," said Amanda, particularly enjoying the effect of the poses where she had her wrists behind her back, pulling back her shoulders and thrusting her full breasts up at the perfect angle to reveal their rounded perfection. "You've done an amazing job, as usual," she credited him. "You captured ever pose I wanted just the way I wanted it. These are provocative without being sleazy."

"Go for a walk with me?" he asked.

"Okay," she agreed, and shut up the shop. They left by the back and began to walk along the brook that ran behind the street the shop was on. There were still several hours of golden sunlight left in the day and the air was redolent of blossoms, alive with birds in the trees above and buzzing with insects. It all made Pascal feel young and on the brink of an adventure and had the same effect on Amanda, who felt it even more intensely.

"Did Phoebe get home okay?" Amanda asked.

"Yes, I picked her up myself."

"Well?"

"She admitted she was with Anthony Newton last night but she's pretending they're not really having an affair," he disclosed casually, as thought it had all ceased to matter. "They've obviously decided it's the best way to keep me on ice, while they decide how to proceed."

"How did you react?" Amanda asked.

"I pretended to believe her. I even accepted the "guilt" edged mercy sex she threw me as soon as we got home."

"What makes you think it was mercy sex?" Amanda laughed.

"Because she never tried that hard to please me before."

Amanda was curious to hear the details of the encounter but refrained from asking.

"You should have heard the story she told about Newton not being able to get it up anymore," Pascal continued; "She showed me six adorable cane marks as proof of his impotence-driven sadism."

"That does sound like a big fib," said Amanda, having been given to understand from Susan Ross that her master was a vigorous cocksman. "Did you say there were marks?"

"Phoebe was well marked," said Pascal, "and I was secretly glad. He would had to have caned her pretty hard to raise those kind of welts and as far as I'm concerned, the little slut deserved it. I just wish I had the intestinal fortitude to beat her that hard myself."

"Don't you?" Amanda asked doubtfully, having felt his hard hand on her bottom only the previous night.

"No, of course I don't. Though I will admit that the marks on Phoebe's bottom turned me on."

They walked on for some minutes in silence, until they came to a clearing in the woods with a white stone summer house, open on all sides, with a roof supported by columns all around. They entered it and walked around inside, finally sitting down. Amanda put her feet up on the seat in front of her and hugged her knees to her chest. Pascal stretched out on his back and looked up at the sun beginning to set in a rosy glow against the still blue sky.

"They're patronizing me, Phoebe and him," said Pascal, "with this story about him letting her down sexually."

"You think they made the whole thing up to help you not lose face?" Amanda asked.

"Oh, I'm sure of it. And I'll bet it was his idea. For her part, Phoebe couldn't care less about saving my feelings anymore. *He* wants me to think she's over him but in reality, she's over me."

"Please don't say that, Mr. Robbins. You can't be right. You should see how beautifully she blushed when you unexpectedly showed up at the Venus Club that evening," Amanda pointed out.

"It's all right, Amanda. I'm not as backward as they think I am," he replied. "I haven't gotten this old without learning something about human nature."

"What do you mean?" asked Amanda.

"I mean I understand what Phoebe's going through. Suddenly she's experiencing emotions that mirror those she usually portrays on stage. No one could expect a passionate young actress not to rack up a couple of major love affairs while at the height of her beauty and powers."

"So, it doesn't make you mad?"

"No, I'm not mad," Pascal sighed. "After all, she mercy fucked me, like I said."

Amanda liked that he seemed to appreciate Phoebe's gesture rather than resent it. There was a bristling quality to Pascal Robbins that seemed somehow softened by his first official cuckolding. Even knowing him as little as she did, Amanda might have expected a much more angry and violent response to his wife's blatant escapade with another man the previous night, but clearly the photographer's libido had risen to the fore, to dominate even his masculine pride.

"Beside," Pascal added, confirming her evaluation, "I'm so in love with you that it's been taking my mind off the whole situation."

"Mr. Robbins, don't talk like that," Amanda cried. "You know I have a boyfriend."

"Why do you persist in calling me Mr. Robbins?"

"I pay you this respect to continually reinforce the inappropriateness of you lusting after me."

"It is inappropriate," Pascal admitted, "but not illegal."

"Instead of me, you should be focusing on winning your wife back," Amanda told him, while trying to repress a sudden impulse she had to lean down and kiss the upside down face that almost leaned against her hip.

"It's too soon for that," Pascal said. "Her head is too full of him right now."

"How come you suddenly know all these things?" Amanda asked, amazed at his calm and no doubt accurate analysis of his wife's state of mind.

"I'm just applying logic," he explained.

"Damn," thought Amanda, "when men apply logic I always wind up in bed with them." She looked down at Pascal again. Even upside down, he was handsome. And Colby would be away at his clam dig most of the night. The sun began to set in a blaze of pink and blue and the temperature dropped a degree. Amanda pulled on a beige cardigan and looked at him again. In the next madly impulsive moment, she had gone from sitting cross-legged on the cool marble bench seat beside him to stretching her body full length atop his and was now pressing her lips to Pascal's with her arms locked around his neck. His arms went up around her waist to pull her down hard against him as his tongue entered her mouth. This time there was no stale cigarette essence remaining to put her off and she lay grinding against him, groin to groin as they kissed and hugged.

Getting a different idea as true dusk began to fall, Amanda sat up on her knees, straddling him and reached down to tug on his zipper. He understood he was about to receive a once in a lifetime gift and hastened to free his erect and fully energized penis from his trousers. Amanda pulled her little bikinis to one side and guided his mushroom cap against her moist labia.

"Are you wet enough?" he asked as she reached down to perfectly position him against her slit.

"Let me just rub against it for a few seconds," she said, sitting on his shaft and allowing her labia to fold around it as she moved back and forth by inches. "Let me get it slick," she said, lying on his chest and whispering in his ear, with her limber knees fully bent on either side of his torso with her calves flat on the bench. After achieving the desired result, Amanda sat up on him and let him fill her completely, her full navy cotton skirt modestly shrouding what soon developed into deeply penetrating intercourse. Amanda lightly bounced up and down, up and down, the summer breeze ruffling her tiny fringe of blonde hair and adding extraordinary buoyancy to their first real sexual encounter. Pascal maneuvered himself into a sitting position with his back against the high stone bench, in order to be able to hold her by the waist and assist in the pumping up and down until they found their perfect rhythm.

A runner ran by on the brook side path to their right in a flash of motion, but slowly enough for Amanda to recognize Raphael Price. To the casual observer, Amanda was simply sitting on Pascal's lap, facing him, with her legs tucked under her on either side of his lap. But the full spread skirt and Amanda being who she was, caused the runner to grin and make the shame on you sign with his fingers as he darted by.

"Who was that?" Pascal asked, "Did they see us?"

"It was Raphael Price and of course he saw us," Amanda cried, but continued to rub up against him in a way that caused just the right amount of friction to trigger a classic clitoral climax before too many more seconds had passed.

"Let me put a condom on," he said with some urgency.

"Give it to me," Amanda said, pulling off him, while still throbbing from her orgasm, and taking the foil wrapped safety device he offered her, expertly rolled it down over his cock and then sat back down on it, letting it fill her all at once with a powerful thrust. "Now, go!" she said and let him set the rhythm with his hands on her waist. He jumped her up and down on his rampant organ perhaps twenty times before expiring in wash of ecstatic sensation deep inside her still spasmodically convulsing velvet glove.

A few minutes later, having put themselves back together, they started back to the shop. Walking through the woods beside the brook, they held hands. But they broke apart before emerging onto Shadow Lane where their cars were parked.

"There's a party at the Cliff house tomorrow night," said Amanda, "Let's hook up there and hang out together. Where Phoebe can see us."

"Really?" Pascal needed no more than moment to see where she was going with this. Until a few days ago the last thing he would have wanted would have been for Phoebe to realize just how passionate he had become about Amanda. But now that she'd come out so boldly about cuckolding him, there didn't seem much point in trying to hold onto the moral high ground. She'd obviously stopped caring about what he thought of her. Maybe it was his turn to stop caring about what she thought of him. He naturally imagined that Amanda's primary motivation in sparking a flame of possessive jealousy in Phoebe's bosom was to distract Pascal from his relentless pursuit of herself. Reawakening Phoebe's interest in Pascal would be the most elegant way to cut him loose while at the same time allowing her to neatly hand him back to his wife. "You honestly think she'll care or even notice?"

Amanda just looked at him with a confident smile, as much as to say, "Look at me, what wife would feel disinterested with me around her man?"

Chapter Twenty-one

Paddled by Proxy

There *was* to be a clambake in Provincetown that night and several of Colby's friends would be there, but Colby never had any intention of attending it and had in fact returned to Boston to meet Marion Craig again. When his phone had rung while he was with Amanda in the shop that afternoon, it was a text message from Marion that read: "Ann Rice Beauty me tonight?" To which he had rapidly replied, "What time?" To which she had responded, "After six, my place."

Then he had gone back into Amanda and told the lie about the clambake, knowing she would never agree to accompany him thence. Colby then went back out to his car on the pretext of getting something to call Marion. She picked up her phone on the first ring, saying tensely, "Yes?"

"What do you mean by 'Ann Rice Beauty' me?" he demanded.

"What do you think I mean?" she rather growled.

"Crawling around double plugged while I cane you?" he ventured, because that was what he primarily remembered from the Ann Rice *Beauty* book he had read and hugely enjoyed at age twelve or thirteen. It wasn't something he was ever going to be allowed to do with Amanda.

"Yes!" Marion hissed, obviously exhaling cigarette smoke. Colby imagined her looking at herself in a mirror while she talked to him, and narcissistically approving her own trim thigh line and small waist. "Make me your whore tonight."

"Oh don't worry, I will!" said Colby, suddenly getting a diabolical idea.

He left for Boston by mid afternoon, with a plan to stop by his friend Ben's house. Ben was one of his hockey buddies and a fellow history buff, probably pre-law, as Colby planned to be. He was living and working in Boston over the summer and due to being shy, and somewhat nerdish, not getting any sex from girls his own age, no less sophisticated older women. But Colby knew that Ben was as fascinated by fancy ladies as he himself was, because they had discussed fetishism at length one night over many pitchers of beer.

He found Ben in an Allston apartment he shared with four other classmates watching a baseball game with a few of his roommates. Colby dragged Ben out of the jock ridden flat and down to the street, saying to his friend on the way, "Remember what we were talking about the other night when we both got so fucked up on microbrews? Well, guess who I just met? A B&D call girl, right here in Boston."

"Seriously?"

"I've already sessioned with her. She gives Harvard boys discounts, fifty per cent off. You can spank the hell out of her skinny, fashion forward ass for two fifty and she'll probably throw in a hand job. She's good looking too."

"How old is she? Do you think she owns a panty girdle?"

"Early 30's. She might, but definitely Spanx. That's the same thing, right?"

"Not exactly, panty girdles were much more endearingly awkward and unbreathable."

"This babe will let you breathe in any part of her, I guarantee that. She's a thrill seeker and a bit of a slut. Act the slightest bit toppy with her and she'll give everything up to you."

"Will you introduce me to her?" Ben said, after a moment's mental calculation as to the state of his checking account. Yes, he had at least two seventy in there. This was going to happen!

"Yes, I'll take you to her right now if you want."

"Give me five minutes to shower and put something better on," he said, racing back upstairs. Colby waited in his car, texting Marion, "Bringing a friend for you to entertain. Put a girdle on. He's paying you two fifty to take a damned good spanking. Don't let me down."

A minute later Marion texted back: "Long line, panty, corset, teddy, corselet or cinch?"

Colby laughed, texting back, "Panty, you crazy bitch. And have the ballgame on your biggest TV so I have something to do while I wait."

She texted back, "Is he cute?"

He replied, "He's 6'3", fit and good people."

She wrote back, "Hope he's not too good, I only want to whore for mean, handsome bastards."

Colby chuckled and put his phone away. Ben arrived back at the car in clean jeans, a plaid summer shirt tucked in under a thick leather belt and high collared ankle boots instead of his usual trainers. He'd slicked his straight brown hair back from his brow and replaced his glasses with contacts. All of this being done, he still wasn't exactly good looking, but he had good skin, looked healthy, clean cut and youthfully masculine. Ben was, in fact, good enough for Colby to pimp Marion to and Marion was perhaps a little too good to be an awkward boy like Ben's first BDSM fling, hence the allowance requirement. Always very much the economist at heart, Colby liked things neat, tidy and in perfect balance if possible.

Colby drove Ben over to Marion's and escorted him up, using the key codes she had given him to use the elevator. Marion was standing in the open doorway of her condo ready to admit them, dressed in a severe pencil skirt, white blouse and 6" fetish pumps, her hair pulled back into a topknot, her lips a slash of burgundy against her olive toned skin. Colby was charmed that she had contrived to look like a Domination Directory ad for it would surely comfort Ben that he had locked onto a real player.

Marion smiled at Colby but took Ben by the hand and immediately led him into another room, closing the door behind them. Colby wandered into Marion's den, where she had tuned her state of the art TV to the ballgame for him and provided an ice bucket full of bottles of popular local ale to match. Colby smiled. After a few minutes of dead silence, he suddenly began to hear the sound of a rapidly administered spanking coming from Marion's guest bedroom. Colby guessed that was where she kept her toys and fetish wardrobe. A lady as affluent and stylish as Marion would have to own a corset or two, a leather cat suit, one or two leather cocktail dresses, leather pants, to say nothing of shoes and boots. Colby never would have thought of such things had Amanda not hammered them into his head while they lay in bed together at night discussing the scene and the larger fetish world, as both were fascinated to realize that they were at its very epicenter, being young, vigorous and of late, so very active. Not that Colby planned for Amanda to ever discover his secret Boston sweetheart.

The spanking went on a very long time. Colby was impressed. It seemed that Ben was really into spanking. He realized he had done Ben a big favor. Deciding to save the beers for later, Colby went out again and took a walk around the immediate neighborhood, his blood on fire with the notion of being able to go back and simply take that woman, the moment he felt like it, with no preambles. He strolled in the warm summer sun for another half hour, buying Marion some flowers. As he was returning to her building he saw Ben emerging into the hazy sunlight of the fading afternoon. He went across the street to meet him.

"Hey, didn't I tell you that lady rocked?" Colby laughed, seeing from Ben's relaxed and happy face that he had enjoyed himself in a way he had only dreamt of in the past.

"She was delightful," Ben confided, then adding confidentially, "I think she's really into it. I couldn't spank her hard enough. She kept wanting more."

"Yeah, she's a crazy bitch," Colby agreed, but in an undertone, with respect to the discretion of the fashionable neighborhood. "Well, can you find your own way back, buddy?"

"Oh sure, I'll jump on the train," Ben assured him. "Thanks again!"

When Colby went back up to Marion's she was waiting for him in her bedroom, in a diaphanous negligee and marabou trimmed gold slippers. The sheer white robe had the desired effect on Colby, especially when she turned around to display her slim oval bottom, stained dark rose red from thigh to hip. Then she fell back on her bed on her back, looking at him while she took her topknot down. He straddled her and sat back on his legs, looking down at her.

"Women get paid for doing this?" she asked wonderingly.

"You made my friend really happy. He thinks you may be into it," Colby said.

"That was too easy. I thought you'd take me out and really make me whore for you on the street," she said, looking up at him in all seriousness.

"Do you want a good beating?" he asked, looking around for something to tie her wrists with.

"Make me do some lowlife."

"You really are a crazy bitch," Colby said, pulling the tie sash out of the belt loops of her robe, doubling it and looping it around her wrists, after pulling them up above her head. "You think I'm going to get into dangerous shit with you on the streets so you can get your thrills?" He tapped her lightly on the cheek, then, when he saw how this made her catch her breath, slapped her across the face just a little harder. "You want to get us both arrested? Or do you want another pimp to come after me for impinging on his turf? Or how about if some psycho picks you up and does you some serious harm?" Marion turned her face the other way and squeezed her eyes shut, as though bracing for another slap. Colby slapped her face a few times. Her eyes shot open and sparkled with excitement.

"And here am I," Colby complained, pulling down his zipper, "fulfilling your request to be whored out, in the nicest possible way, and all you can do is complain that I didn't degrade you enough." Now he pulled aside her robe, pushed her thighs apart and nudged his fully extended organ into what appeared to be his newest personal possession, Marion's ever so welcoming vagina. "If I fuck you hard, like Ben didn't, maybe you'll be satisfied." Marion gasped as he plunged in to the hilt but arched to meet the thrust with eyes shut and a rapturous look of abandon on a face that was softened by desire and no longer holding any tension at all. Trapping her bound wrists under one large hand, Colby completed the act of possession in a couple of minutes, pulling out just in time to shower her small bosom and flat stomach with his essence.

"Why didn't you come on my face?" she asked after he had untied her wrists.

"You know, you have a terrible self image," Colby scolded, rumpling her smooth brown hair. "I should spank you for that. Maybe next time."

"You want there to be a next time?" she asked wryly, assuming her ivy league stud would be tiring of her at any moment. He took the hand he'd just freed and kissed it, saying, "Silly."

He didn't have much dressing to do but buckling his belt gave him an idea and he unbuckled it again and snapped it out of its loops, saying, "On second thought, I have some parting words for you. Roll over!" Very much taken by surprise, she hesitated but a moment before obeying.

"I want your word of honor that you'll never talk a strange man into pimping you again, least of all on the street. And I'm going to strap that small sized backside of yours until I get it," Colby promised severely and pulling up her filmy robe to fully expose her bottom, which was still dark rose from Ben's large hand falling across it hundreds of times, began to lay the strap on with vigorous indignation. "I like you and I won't have you putting your crazy bitch ass at risk for a thrill. You want a thrill, you call your kinky college boy. Understand?"

The strapping was delivered with something less than the full strength of his arm, but that was still saying quite a bit and before a minute had elapsed, Marion had begun to sob and cry real tears, begging for mercy and swearing to obey his command to the letter. Colby left well satisfied that he had not only given Marion a scene she would remember for the rest of her life but that he had begun the rescue of her self respect and insured her future safety, at least to the greatest degree that he possibly could considering her proclivity to take risks.

Chapter Twenty-two

Eve of an Eventful Day

Pascal and Amanda emerged onto Shadow Lane as though nothing remarkable had occurred between them in the woods ten minutes before and were about to get into their cars and proceed on their separate ways home when Susan Ross came out of the bookstore and hailed them.

"Hello," she cried cheerily, looking like a picture postcard for summer by the sea, a petite, small waisted girl in a yellow gingham sundress with a long, thick wheat colored ponytail caught up in a blue circle clasp.

"Remember what you promised," Amanda said under her breath to Pascal before Susan was upon them, hugging them both.

"I'm glad I ran into you two, you can help me with my deliveries," Susan said, reaching into a large shoulder bag and pulling out several small, blue velvet jewelry boxes. "Here Amanda, this is for you and were you heading over to the gym tonight?"

"Yes, I thought I would," Amanda said, receiving three boxes into her hands. "What are these?"

"Open one!" said Susan. She also handed Pascal a box, saying, "Would you give this to Phoebe when you see her?"

Pascal smiled his assent and slipped the box into his jacket pocket. Meanwhile Amanda had opened her box to reveal a heavy platinum signet ring with an onyx face upon which gleamed a graceful *September Morn-ish* nymph bending at the knees with her hands on her knees, embossed in platinum.

"Look inside," said Susan. Amanda did so and saw the letters "VC" engraved on the back of the face.

"VC for Venus Club," Susan explained. "Anthony had one made for each of us. I designed the Venus. Do you like her?"

"Oh, she's darling!" Amanda cried. "I'll treasure this for the rest of my life!" She immediately put the ring on and admired it. Pascal did the math of a heavy platinum ring times ten and again felt somewhat overwhelmed by the monetary might of his rival for his wife's affections. And yet, having achieved his long cherished goal of possessing Amanda so painlessly, his mood was too buoyant to allow him to dwell on his all too tenuous grip on his wife's affections. He would sort all of that out later, and it appeared that Amanda was going to help him do so.

"So, please give Polyxena one of these when you see her tonight," Susan said, indicating the second box. "Do you think Pamela is at the shop tonight?" Susan asked.

"No, she's working in her new studio at Bartlett's," said Amanda, "but I'm meeting her for lunch tomorrow and I can deliver this to her."

"Thank you! And don't forget about the pool party tomorrow night," said Susan to both of them, just before getting on her bike to peddle over to the *Damaris* shop and deliver one of the rings to the designer who was busily supervising her sewing team as they continued to assemble the new collection.

Amanda went home to feed the cats and pack a gym bag then proceeded to Polyxena's gym and spa, where she found the comely owner organizing china behind the counter of her new coffee bar. Recessed into a small niche off the front lobby of the gym, the semi circular area had been painted dark green trimmed with gold and furnished with two inset varnished black wooden bench seats and facing tables. Polyxena had tied a green apron over her white spa dress and pulled back her white blonde hair in a green ribbon tie.

"Can I offer you the first drink from my new bar?" Polyxena asked Amanda, who was already pulling the jewelry box out of her pack.

"Thank you," said Amanda. "Something cool, I think." She looked at a short list of coffee and espresso drinks on a small black board placed on an easel to one side of the bar. "An iced mocha latte?"

"You want the lo cal version or the tasty one?" Polyxena asked, setting up two shots of espresso to brew.

"The tasty one, of course," replied Amanda with a grin. Polyxena nodded her approval and added heavy cream, a scoop of bittersweet Dutch processed cocoa bits and a dash of chili and cinnamon to the blender along with ice and the prepared espressos. In a moment Amanda was sipping with pleasure.

"This is magnificent. I must have one to bring Pamela later. I've been fattening her up a bit and if I could get her addicted to these they'd add three pounds in a week," said Amanda.

"You think her husband will stand for her going from a 2 to a 4?" Polyxena wondered, eager for Amanda's opinion of Ambrose Bartlett's attitude towards his wife.

"If you ask me, I don't think he should have any choice in the matter," said Amanda.

"I don't suppose her boyfriend will care much," Polyxena threw out casually.

"Boyfriend?"

"That blond boy who's working at the bookstore this summer. I saw her driving him into town the other morning."

"Oh, you mean Dru?" Amanda looked at Polyxena and sipped her drink while trying to figure out what Polyxena was getting at. "I don't know that he's her boyfriend."

"No? They seemed to have that sort of body language. Now, what is this?" Polyxena asked, as Amanda handed her the ring box.

"Anthony Newton had them made for all of us in the Venus Club. Susan designed the goddess."

Polyxena looked in the box and was pleased to put the ring on at once. Then she frowned. If Pamela was her sister now, was it quite correct to annex her husband away? She looked up and met Amanda's gay blue eyes, feeling a swift jolt of jealousy for the younger woman, who had obviously engaged so much of Ambrose Bartlett's interest the previous winter. Had Amanda not spoken precisely and dramatically of being "broken" by him? It was most disturbing to connect that intensely personal event with her new lover and this stunning eighteen-year-old.

"Do you think Mrs. Pamela loves her husband?" Polyxena abruptly asked Amanda, unconsciously communicating to the intuitive girl that if Pamela did not love her husband, she, Polyxena, certainly did.

"Well," said Amanda, after a moment's hesitation, "to the extent that he's lovable... I think she does."

"That's right, he wasn't very lovable to you, was he?"

"He's a bit of a martinet, but he's okay," said Amanda with a grin. "He's mellowed out a lot lately. He even finally let Pamela quit the boutique at the store. That's all she really wanted, not to have to work behind a counter any more and just devote her time to designing."

"And what about you? Does he still pursue you?"

"Oh no, that's Pascal Robbins' job now," said Amanda, finishing her drink and pulling out some cash to pay for it.

"No, please, it's on the house," said Polyxena, her heart lightened by Amanda's apparent shift in older man interest from Bartlett to Robbins.

Amanda hurried away to the yoga room to take a class and Polyxena went back to arranging her cups and saucers with satisfaction.

Chapter Twenty-three

Two Spankings in a Moonlit Garden

The following evening Anthony Newton was giving a small party for his cast around his recently redecorated swimming pool. A local gourmet caterer had laid out a table of mostly vegetarian hors d'oeuvres with a bartender in attendance at the wet bar to make the players and musicians drinks. By eight o'clock the rehearsal was over and the pool and hot tub were beginning to fill with merry cast members in swimsuits. Being elegantly feted by a celebrity host wasn't a usual occurrence in the lives of the humble rep players and they were determined to relish the experience like Joan Crawford mingling with the haute ton for the first time in a pre-code movie.

Amanda and Pascal met at the Cliff house and went in together. Anthony's performers and stage crew were streaming through the house towards the pool and Pascal and Amanda followed them. When the reached their destination Amanda thought her escort would immediately go up to the bar for a cocktail, but instead he went into one of the cabanas to change into his bathing trunks, still in a pleasant daze as a result of having made love to Amanda the previous day. He hadn't felt so relaxed in months and looked forward to slipping into the hot tub to complete the restorative treatment.

Amanda changed into a white swimsuit and wrap around cover up dress and accepted Dennis' offer to get her a plate of food. She waited at a small patio table where she found Susan Ross, adorably clad in a dark red two piece bathing suit with nautical accents, her tiny feet thrust into white wedge sandals with blue and red trim, already seated with a luscious looking umbrella topped drink before her. They greeted each other with hugs and then, between bites, Amanda began to tell

Susan about the photo shoot she had done with Pascal that had produced so many lovely poses. Photos of well posed B&D models were essential reference tools to a graphic novelist and Susan had recently begun writing and illustrating a new book with a new heroine based on Amanda in appearance.

When Pascal came out and saw Susan he remembered he had the most recent photos he had taken of Amanda on his laptop and fishing it out of his rucksack, set it up on the table where the two girls sat. Anthony Newton and Phoebe Robbins entered together but he left her to begin playing with a complicated sound system he'd recently had installed in the pool building. In a moment a New Order song came on and the composer continued to program a New Wave play list for the rest of the party.

Phoebe located her husband between the two blonde girls but instead of approaching them, took her herself to the bar, where she requested a glass of white wine. Phoebe was dressed in one of the costumes from the play, a lilac cotton sateen skirt over a crinoline paired with a sleeveless white blouse, a wide black belt and black velvet stack heeled pumps that added four inches to her stature. Phoebe was handed champagne, which she drank quickly before strolling casually by the table where Pascal sat. It did seem to Phoebe, as she approached, that the youthfully goddess like Amanda, in a sheer white wrap dress that showed her bikini clad form underneath, was sitting almost on top of Pascal, or rather seeming to, as she hung on his shoulder while reviewing the photos on the screen. When Phoebe passed behind the company she was able to look over their shoulders and see that the photos on the screen were of an extremely nude Amanda Sands looking like a pinup from a men's magazine, in her leather cuffs pulling her wrists up behind her back or nestling between her knees.

"Do your parents know you're posing for pictures like that?" Phoebe asked bluntly, causing everyone to spring apart.

"Phoebe, she's eighteen," Pascal explained without heat, though with eyebrows slightly raised at her indignation, "and there are no explicit shots."

"Does your boyfriend know?" Phoebe wondered in a low tone that only Amanda caught. Amanda stiffened and moved away from the table, as though she were on her way to a new location and had only been pausing there a moment.

"Speaking of my boyfriend, he may be here any minute and I promised him a wet bathing suit to ogle," said Amanda before taking off her dress and slipping into the pool. Phoebe watched Amanda slide into the water in her miniscule white bikini over folded arms. Seeing her sitting so close to Pascal and draping her arm around his shoulder in an utterly familiar way, had sent a jolt of pure electricity through Phoebe's heart. She went back to the bar for a second glass of wine. Amanda swam a few laps, then got out of the pool dripping wet and remarkably beautiful. Grabbing her cover up, she strolled out into the gardens behind the pool. The air was very balmy and although most of the blossoms had closed for the night, the perfume of roses and lilacs lingered about the hedges and marble seats. A radiant half moon kept appearing and disappearing behind a few, gauzy, scudding clouds and the stars were equally bright. Amanda did, in fact, expect Colby to arrive shortly and was eager to avoid an awkward encounter with the wife of a man she'd just slept with before Colby's eyes.

Lying down on a stone bench flat on her back, Amanda looked up at the stars while trying to calm her pounding heart. Phoebe had looked very volatile just then, which made Amanda realize that her aim of getting Phoebe to refocus on her husband, had been realized.

"I'd like to talk to you," an angry but still mellifluous female voice started Amanda into a sitting position a moment later. It was Phoebe, arms still folded, standing over her.

"All right," said Amanda, pulling her wrap dress back on and knotting it tightly at her waist.

"Why would you pose so provocatively for my husband? After you claimed to be affronted by his spanking you for cutting your hair?"

"I've always wanted some nude shots in my portfolio and Pascal has such good taste. It was an entirely professional arrangement. I signed a release and he paid me a standard fee. And for your information, my father knows all about it and my mother will shortly."

"But not your boyfriend, that hunky jockey top boy you were so cavalier about offering the services of to the other girls at The Venus Club. He won't take it so lightly, you posing like that for Pascal, will he?"

Amanda shrugged, "It depends on the mood he's in. Colby can be unpredictable. But above all, he's pragmatic and I have a check for my posing fee to show that it was all about work for me."

"Are you saying that it was less about work and more about play for my husband?"

"Not exactly, but he did ask me to pose, I didn't ask him to shoot me."

That much was true and Amanda realized that she ought to stop there. Phoebe didn't need to know how far things had gone, she was already sufficiently jealous to reclaim her man on just seeing Amanda touch Pascal's shoulder alone. It was time to terminate this interview before any needless truth escaped her lips involving her husband's relentless pursuit of her and her own extraordinarily weak resolve in resisting him.

"So, he's been running after you, has he?" Phoebe fumed, folding her arms even more tightly.

Amanda considered. The correct answer was yes, but why get Pascal in trouble with his wife when she wanted them back together?

"No, but he's been sad about you preferring Mr. Newton to him."

"Who said that?" Phoebe shot back.

"You did, apparently. He said you did."

"It's not true. I didn't say that at all," Phoebe replied uncertainly.

"He said you were with Mr. Newton in Boston and that you considered him your lover. Something about an Isadora Duncan moment."

"Humph! There isn't much you don't know," Phoebe huffed, pacing about the garden path. "So, who suggested the handcuffs?" she asked.

"I did."

"I see!" Phoebe paced. "Well? Did you seduce him?"

Amanda was taken aback and remembered the interlude in the summerhouse. She had in fact abruptly initiated their sex act by sitting astride Pascal's recumbent form as he lazed on his back in the warm summer dusk.

"No!" Amanda replied emphatically.

"So you're saying you let him take those pictures of you without giving him sex?"

"Yes," Amanda replied honestly, as the sex had occurred on the day *following* the photo shoot.

"I think she's lying," said Colby Hodge, who had noiselessly stolen upon them. He had seen the photos on the way around the pool open on Pascal's laptop where Susan was still admiring them. "And she has a history of making up to older men who can advance her career," said Colby, helpfully stoking the fires of Phoebe's spousal indignation.

"Well, you're wrong," said Amanda stubbornly, sensing that Pascal wasn't likely to contradict her claim to innocence.

"You let your girlfriend do these things?" Phoebe challenged Colby, Amanda thought, quite naughtily. "I heard that you're a spanking man. Why don't you spank the brat?"

"Why don't we both spank her?" Colby suggested enthusiastically, taking hold of Amanda's waist. "I'll hold her down for you, shall I?" And before Amanda knew what she was about she found herself thrust down across her lover's massive thighs as he sat on one end of a marble bench. Holding her in position with one hand, he unbuckled his leather belt with the other and whipped it out of the loops of his khaki trousers. "Here, Mrs. Robbins, you'll need something other than you soft little hand for Amanda's hard butt."

"What?" Amanda cried, "No! This is not acceptable!"

Phoebe accepted the belt with a smile of wonder and doubled it in her small hands. Standing to one side of Colby and behind Amanda's exposed bikini clad rear and long legs, punctuated by white wedge platform sandals, Phoebe had all the room she needed to swing.

"How dare you?" Amanda demanded, craning her head around to glare at Phoebe. "You're the one who should be getting a spanking, for cheating on a perfectly nice husband with someone he can't possibly help but feel inferior to and then mortifying him by admitting it boldfaced. You didn't even have the decency to try to hide your affair!"

Colby casually folded Amanda's right arm back to her waist and pinned it there by the wrist then smacked each of her cheeks through the tiny bikini bottom several times. "Don't be rude and fanciful, Amanda, Mrs. Robbins would never go out on her husband. Can't you see she's a lady?"

Phoebe warmed to Colby and was glad of his substantially masculine presence beside her.

"Maybe I should be the one getting spanked," Phoebe conceded, testing the snap of the strap in the air, "but you happen to be in position and your own boyfriend gave me his belt. So take this for coming onto my husband!" Phoebe took careful aim and delivered a stroke across the centermost portion of Amanda's bottom.

"Wait," said Colby, stopping her, "these are useless anyway," he yanked the bikini bottoms down to Amanda's knees, exposing her slim but rounded tan lined backside. "There, now you can see what you're doing. And you," he warned Amanda, "be still! Let Mrs. Robbins get on with it." He leaned down and whispered in her ear, "Do this for me and I'll forgive you for fucking her husband."

Amanda turned her head to look at him.

"Come on," he said aloud, "be a good girl and take what you've got coming."

Amanda dropped her head and sighed her resignation. Colby nodded to Phoebe, who began to swing the strap against Amanda's resilient cheeks with unexpected enthusiasm, for up until this point no one had ever known her to exhibit the smallest amount of dominance over anything. A singer by profession, falling into a rhythm came naturally to Phoebe while the vigor of her lashes expressed the passionate emotions of a sudden jealous young wife. "Owie," thought Amanda, remembering that she had been openly demonstrative with Pascal in front of his wife in order to force a confrontation between that gentleman and this lady, not this lady and herself. "Why would she even go after me first?" Amanda wondered, thinking this quite perverse.

Phoebe presently discovered that she liked strapping Amanda's beautiful bottom, that Amanda could apparently absorb a great deal of strapping before even beginning to complain and that by leaning against and intermittently holding onto the broad shouldered, straight backed Colby Hodge, she could obtain even better traction for swinging the strap. Even in the moonlight, Colby could observe Amanda's skin shade turn from white to pink to dark magenta as the petite, perfumed brunette beside him worked herself up into a damp and feverish state through her own exertions.

"Good, you're doing great!" Colby encouraged Phoebe unnecessarily, while tightening his grip on Amanda's waist even more securely. "And so are you," he told Amanda cheerfully. "It's good you're not screaming because then everyone would come out and see."

"When we get to Milan," Amanda whispered, "I will buy the sharpest dagger I can find and stab you in your sleep!"

"What was that she said?" Phoebe paused to inquire. "Was she admitting to having slept with my husband?"

"That wouldn't mean a thing, Mrs. Robbins. There was probably no sleeping involved." said Colby to his trusty right hand martinet. "But please continue!"

Amanda began to feel very sorry for herself and tears came into her eyes. Of course she knew that she could stop this thing at any moment simply by revealing just how deliberately Pascal had stalked and (albeit subtly) hounded her until could no longer avoid the inevitable, just to get it out of the way so they could all move on! But admitting such truths would disillusion Phoebe even further about her husband and she might decide to abandon him then and there. And wouldn't it hurt Pascal's feelings to know that she felt he had all but forced his attentions on her with his relentless photo shooting and verbal flirting therewith? For when all was said and done, she found she rather liked Pascal Robbins and fancied he might well be a keeper, to travel through the rest of her life with as a friend. In the end, her stronger urge was to protect her new lover rather than expose him as cad in the eyes of his wife, whom Amanda knew he still loved and who certainly deserved adoration, goddess that she was. Amanda peeked back at her new disciplinarian, seriously aiming each slash of the strap and following through with her whole body when she wasn't clinging to Colby. "Miniature goddess," thought Amanda, with satisfaction, as her buttocks became numb to further pain and the exercise became one of exhausting Phoebe. In a moment, Phoebe handed Colby back his strap.

"Thank you," she said to Amanda, helping her up. "I feel like that got rid of a lot of stress!"

"Well, why stop there?" Amanda challenged, pulling her bikini panties back up. "Let's get rid of all your stress!" And with that, Amanda shoved Colby off the bench, grabbed Phoebe by the forearm and turned the small diva over her own bare, golden thighs.

"What the hell?" Phoebe turned, unable to grasp what was happening. Colby scrambled to his feet, grinning in anticipation of the splendid show about to unfold.

"You have your nerve trying to teach me a lesson, Phoebe Robbins," said Amanda, smacking Phoebe just once through her skirt and crinoline before realizing what a fruitless effort repeating the action would be through so much material, so she briskly folded back both skirt and petticoat, which was no easy task for the many layers of fabric veiling the target area. Presently, Phoebe's pantied and garter belted bottom was revealed, the combination in lilac satin embroidered with green and gold butterflies, the cheeks plump and round, thighs smooth and creamy. "Oh and I don't think we need these," said Amanda, summarily pulling the fancy briefs down to Phoebe's knees. "And as you can see, I don't need anyone to hold you in position for me!" Amanda said with conviction, then taking a really firm hold of Phoebe's waist, began to belabor that young woman's bare bottom with the palm of her hand.

Amanda Sands spanked Phoebe Robbins not only to recover her own dignity but also and probably mainly, to entertain her boyfriend Colby Hodge. She couldn't remember the last time she had spanked another girl apart from childhood playmates she would intrigue into playing spanking games with her. She had dominated Alicia with a bit of light bondage and teasing and she had used Colby to spank Pamela for her. But suddenly something new clicked in her brain and she realized that she needed to begin spanking women. There was just no reason not to, especially when they were so beautiful and as obviously naughty as Phoebe.

"I took it like a lady and didn't make a fuss, so you'd better do the same," Amanda warned Phoebe before visiting a perfect volley of hard spanks down on alternating cheeks. "We won't have much time until other people begin coming out," Amanda warned, "so I have to make this count!" Then she delivered a few dozen stinging smacks at a rapid pace. Phoebe strained to get free and kicked her feet in the dangerous high heels extremely high. Amanda forced her legs back down. "You deserve this so much more than me," Amanda told Phoebe. "Running after Mr. Newton when you know Susan Ross is so attached to him! How do you think she's going to feel when she finds out what you've been up to?"

Phoebe had no answer to this question and bit her knuckle, feeling every smack but much too afraid of attracting unwanted attention to make an outcry. Amanda went on spanking her captive slowly and methodically, connecting fully and deeply every time her palm landed on one of Phoebe's increasingly rosy upturned cheeks.

"I'll end it!" Phoebe suddenly cried. "I will! I know it's wrong."

"You'll stop being in love with Mr. Newton?" Amanda let Phoebe up and the blushing, emotionally over wrought actress hastily set her clothes to rights, looking over her shoulder to make sure no one had observed the last scene.

"Yes," Phoebe said, turning to Amanda and meeting her gaze frankly. "If you'll stop ... feeling sorry for my husband!" Amanda saw that Phoebe had guessed the exact impetus of her brief affair with Pascal Robbins and took Phoebe's small hand to kiss it.

"Thank you, first lady I've ever spanked," said Amanda.

"Come to think of it, you're the first girl I've ever spanked," said Phoebe, embracing Amanda.

"Life is good," thought Colby, taking his turn at embracing Phoebe. Aloud he said, "Mind you keep a sharper eye on your husband from now on or next time I'll spank you myself. I'm getting tired of extracting Amanda from the bony grasp of these elderly Romeos!"

Chapter Twenty-four

Happy Endings

Just about the same time, Ambrose Bartlett was arriving at Pamela's new studio at the top of his store, laden down with petit fours and fruit tarts for his wife and her evening sewing crew, two interns from design school and two of the local community college girls. Pamela looked up from a dress form she was draping with pleasure and surprise, never knowing Ambrose to show her this type of consideration before. The cakes were laid out in the galley adjoining the workroom and Pamela started the various café quality coffee brewers and tea makers to furnish her workers with refreshments forthwith. In a crisp, straight-skirted summer dress that displayed both her slender waist and long leg line to advantage, Pamela looked the image of a stylish professional, her new bob adding a touch of edge and glamour to every look she had been showing that summer.

After preparing an espresso for her husband, she led him into the private retreat he had ordered decorated for the few moments of relaxation her busy days and nights might afford. Here there was a comfortable chair and divan arrangement, a TV console and a recessed napping area with a luxuriously fitted bed.

"I booked us into The Library for fashion week," said Ambrose, handing Pamela a confirmation sheet.

"How perfect!" Pamela cried, clapping her hands. "And thank you for bringing us cake." She then surprised him by biting into a petit four and then actually finishing it.

"You look nice," he said, surveying her critically from head to toe. Her shoes were magnificently high with red soles.

"Thank you. I'm letting myself put on a few pounds, per Amanda's instructions."

"I see you're pleased to let her boss you around," he observed, with a relaxed smile.

"I've needed a girlfriend for so long," Pamela said, by way of explanation.

"And she's just right for you," he agreed. "Youth is fashion's muse."

Pamela said that was true and took his empty cup away from him.

"Pamela, come for a little walk with me, I need to talk to you about something," Ambrose said abruptly, and led the way out of the store through the back exit. They began to stroll down the street that flanked the large parking lot and then proceeded through some of the tree-shaded back streets of Woodbridge.

"Is everything okay?" Pamela asked.

"I think it's fine," he replied, "but I feel like I need to tell you that I've been seeing Polyxena Guzman."

"Oh? Really? Seeing?" Pamela replied, her heart jumping slightly. "Are you saying that you want to break up?"

"No! Absolutely not!" he paused and ran his hand through her short, silky black hair. "No, honey, no." He brought her face towards his and kissed her lightly on the lips. "I'm really enjoying being married to you. And I was hoping you were starting to feel the same way."

"Actually, I am," Pamela replied.

"Polyxena will be my mistress," said Bartlett simply.

"So you're that fond of her, are you? I can understand that, she's a magnificent woman."

"And the strange thing is that it's not about money. She doesn't want any."

"Why is that strange?" Pamela asked. "She's independent and you're attractive. As I understand it, she's been lonely for a man for some time."

"That's true," Ambrose said, not surprised at Pamela's quick, unemotional grasp of the situation.

"And then, you let her dominate you. I've seen it at the gym."

"Well, she's my trainer."

"And a fine one too," said Pamela, with a smile. "I've never seen you looking so well."

"I'm so glad you're not upset, Pamela," said Ambrose. "You're so busy with the line and after fashion week, who knows how much traveling you'll be doing. You'll never miss me the few nights I'm away."

"Of course I'm upset, I'm just suppressing it like I do all of my emotions," Pamela explained.

"Well," he said, "isn't there anything you want to tell *me*?"

Pamela glanced at him, wondering what he could mean. Then she remembered Dru and felt her face go warm. Did he know? She saw by the way he was half smiling that he did.

Pamela shrugged and replied casually, "I'll admit there is a boy in my life. But as soon as the summer is over he'll be off back to school."

"That kid I saw you dancing with?"

"Yes. I've been kind of making him my Boy Friday. He's borderline submissive, so he's been helpful to me this summer."

"It's only right you should have followers and that they be young and beautiful. Amanda has obviously been good for your head."

Pamela took his hand and said, "Let's go back to the studio, go into the retreat, lock the door and take a half hour break on that delicious bed with the thousand count sheets you put in there for me."

Phoebe looked down at Pascal relaxing in the whirlpool all alone, his eyes closed with a pleasant smile on his face. She rustled her petticoats and he opened his eyes to continue smiling up at her.

"Hi honey, why don't you put a swim suit on and get in?" he suggested, patting the water invitingly. She folded her arms and scowled.

"I don't think I'd compare very well to these size 2 glamazons," said the petite actress, eyeing a few of the taller, slimmer girls from the cast of the show who were jumping into the big pool. And of course, she still retained the image of Amanda in her bikini to contrast her own more ample proportions with.

"Don't be silly," her husband urged her. "How often do we get to play in a hot tub?" he asked. "Ask Susan to lend you a swim suit," he said suggested.

"No, I've already had three glasses of wine. I'm afraid I'll pass out in the heat," Phoebe refused.

"You had three glasses? Uh oh!" Pascal said, knowing his wife well enough to be able to predict the coming crash. He jumped out of the Jacuzzi and told her to wait for him while he changed back into his street clothes in one of the cedar lined dressing cubicles provided for this operation. "Phoebe why in the world did you drink so much so fast? You know you don't have the head for it," Pascal said. "Come on, honey, I'll take you home before you get sick." And he led her out to his car.

Phoebe was very happy to be driven home by her husband because her heart was nearly broken by the revelation that he was in love with Amanda Sands. She had been exposed to Amanda's magnetic sexuality full force that night and didn't wonder at Pascal becoming enraptured with the eighteen-year-old.

As soon as they arrived at the house, he pulled her upstairs by the hand and sent her to the dressing room to change into looser garments. When she returned to him in the bedroom she was wrapped in a rose silk dressing gown and her hair was down on her shoulders. He made her get into bed and drink a large glass of water.

"How do you feel?" he asked, stroking her hair back from her brow.

"I think I'll be okay," she said, looking at him thoughtfully. "This is helping," she said, finishing the water. Then she looked down, on the verge of tears.

"What's the matter?" he asked, touching her face delicately.

"The matter is that I'm violently jealous of that beautiful young girl you're in love with."

"First of all, I'm not in love with Amanda and secondly, now you know how I feel!" he said, finally ceasing to be solicitous.

"Oh yes you are. How could you help being?"

"I have been drawn to her," he admitted, "but only as a model to shoot. Because of the proximity, don't you see?"

"It's been the same with Mr. Newton and me," Phoebe eagerly agreed, "it's all because of the proximity."

"Oh? You think that maybe once the summer's over and you're no longer around Anthony Newton every day that you'll be able to be happy with me again?"

"I am happy with you!" Phoebe put her arms around Pascal's waist and lay her head against his chest. He tightened his arms around her. He knew she was only sorry she had strayed because it had caused him to do the same. The fierce sexual jealousy that had invaded her heart that night was the one emotion strong enough to overcome her infatuation with the affable composer and redirect her attention to its proper recipient.

"You're a fickle little slut, but I love you," he observed as he held Phoebe close, thinking of how clever Amanda had been to arrange everything as she had done. She was certainly a managing young female, yet her instincts were always correct. Of course he'd give Amanda up for now. What choice did he have? She'd be off to Europe with her boyfriend in a couple of weeks anyway. But once the school year began, Amanda would be back in Cambridge and once more in his proximity, as he and Phoebe lived in Boston. He would naturally call her for work and she would certainly accept. She'd never turned a job down yet. Then he'd have a second chance to dazzle her and he determined that if it came to pass, that he would be on top next time.

The vigor and enthusiasm with which Colby Hodge attacked his summer associate editorship at the New Rod Quarterly left Amanda breathless with admiration. She looked up from reading one of his brisk and breezy editorials and said, "Maybe I did pick you for a reason, other than your shoulders." And his expertise didn't stop there, he also displayed an easy diplomacy in answering letters that rather dazzled her. She herself labored over letters, never sure of how frank her replies ought to be. Whether consciously or unconsciously, she tended to copy Hugo's gently authoritative editorial style, throwing the odd compliment at the shy and mildly teasing the pompous. But striking the perfect balance between expertise and arrogance was difficult and Amanda spent far too much time going over her responses before submitting them. Colby, on the other hand, dashed off everything without a rewrite or any other edit than a spell check. So light was his touch with advice, remonstrances or jokes, he was never in any danger of giving offence.

As the days of June melted away, Amanda found she had more friends in Random Point now than she had time to spread among. Seeing he was amenable to staying at the shop anchored to the desk in Hugo's office, Amanda began to presume on Colby to allow her to escape for a half hour here and there to visit Hope at the coffee shop, walk over to Damaris' shop and look over what was new, or meet Pamela for a quick sandwich when her friend was able to take a break from working on the collection. If Amanda happened to run into Susan Ross in the street, they might stroll down to the brook, smoke half a joint and fall into a lengthy conversation as they continued to walk in the woods. Once Amanda realized, to her chagrin, that she had left Colby alone at the shop for two and a half hours before returning to him. And yet, when she did come in, he was pounding his keyboard just as violently as when she had left him. He barely looked up when she walked in and didn't even glance at the clock.

All the rest of that day, Colby seemed distracted. They went to a Chinese martial arts movie in Woodbridge that night and when his phone pulsed in his pocket, he went outside to take the call. This puzzled Amanda, as Colby was not normally a slave to his phone. After the movie they strolled to the same ice cream shop where Amanda and Pamela had indulged themselves after getting their hair cut several weeks before. Colby wanted to order a hot fudge sundae but Amanda made him compromise and they walked out with two wafer cones each with a scoop of vanilla fudge. Walking along and slowly licking their cones, they stopped to look in windows and talk about which shops were for the tourists and which for the locals, speculating on how much rent they paid and whether the summer trade was good that year.

"Colby, who called you?"

"Oh, just one of my friends," he said, in a tone that did not ring true.

"You don't usually answer phones in the movies," Amanda observed.

"What can I say, babe? Drug deal," he grinned.

"Seriously, Colby, what's going on?" Amanda asked suddenly. They had both knocked the ball of ice cream into the cone by now and the treats were nearing their delicious end. They walked along in silence for a half block, each of them waiting for Colby to speak.

Finally he said, "I need your advice, Amanda."

"Really? Mine? What about?"

"I've..." he hesitated a moment, then plunged into his confession, "... gotten a little involved with a woman. And when I say woman, I mean a crazy bitch. She's in the scene of course, one of Hugo's readers, good looking, older, hardcore sub, and she's become fixated on me, to the point where she's demanding more of my attention every day."

"When you say a little involved," Amanda asked, "how little are we talking about? Have you just been emailing and talking on the phone?"

"Amanda, be yourself, we're talking about me and a B&D slut, I've already fucked her a number of times, beat the hell out of her too and I've even handed her over to one of my buddies, just to take the edge off, but the lady is insatiable and I feel like I've gotten in over my head. Don't get me wrong, I like her, but I'm not free to satisfy her whenever she needs it. She's just beginning to realize that and it's fucking with her head. I'll be lucky if she doesn't start stalking me."

Amanda said, "Where does she live?"

"Boston."

"Oh, I see. That's why you've been running off to Boston so much lately."

"Yeah," he said, with only the most marginal tinge of abashment, given his recent discovery about Amanda and Pascal.

"How old is she?"

"Early 30's. She's an attorney. She's getting me work at her firm in August when we come back. It'll look good for when I apply to law school."

"And you met her through the magazine? She wrote for advice and you answered, offering hands on assistance?"

"Yes, and you're not going to believe this, she initially thought I was offering to session with her and she brought cash to our first meeting."

"Really? How much?"

"I didn't take it, but five hundred."

"That's impressive," Amanda remarked with admiration.

"The amount or that I didn't take it?"

"Well, both."

"I couldn't take money from a lady," Colby said. "It's just not in me."

"What about the economist in you?" she asked.

"I know, but it just wouldn't be gallant."

"Colby, take me home and hold me. I'm getting a pain in my stomach just thinking about you with another girl."

Colby said, "You just ate your ice cream too fast. But I'll gladly take you home and hold you."

On the way to Hugo's house Amanda asked numerous questions in order to form a complete picture of Colby's possibly fatal attraction. Finally she asked to see Marion's photo. Colby tossed her his phone and told her it was the sixth or seventh shot in his archive. Amanda paged through the candid shots of Colby's friends until she came to a medium shot of a smartly suited brunette with an enigmatic smile on her wide, sexy mouth. She was exactly as Colby had described her, thin and good looking, with undertones of tension rippling behind her cat grin.

A little while later, after the regular evening chores had been dispatched and they were undressing for bed, Colby said, "Did I mention the bitch is neurotic as hell? She almost scares me, what she's into. I'm afraid if I leave her to her own devices she'll hook up with some sadist or actual pimp who will turn her out for real."

"Well, you're not going to leave her to her own devices," Amanda said, slipping in between the sheets completely nude.

"No? You don't think I should break it off cold?"

"No, no, no, that would be dreadful after giving her so much more than a taste of what a good scene can be."

"So, what should I do? I mean, we're going to Europe in a week. I'm afraid she'll get despondent when I'm gone."

"What about this other boy you hooked her up with? Won't he come through for her?"

"I think he'd love to spank her again, but he's too innocent to get into the sex trip she craves. She wants to be used like a whore."

"And, is that what you did with her?" Amanda smiled.

Colby shrugged, "I had to be a little harsh with her, she wouldn't have it any other way."

Amanda reached for Colby's phone on the bedside table, saying, "Can I send her picture to a friend of mine? He lives in Boston, he's single, he's the right age for her and a great top."

"Sure, go right ahead," said Colby enthusiastically.

"I'll tell him if he's interested we can arrange for them to meet. His name is Marty. If they have good chemistry, your worries are over, he'll take her off your hands," she said, typing Marty a message to accompany the photo of Marion Craig. Seconds later her phone pulsed with a reply text from Marty Patmore that read: "Thanks, Amanda, I would love to meet that lady." Amanda showed Colby the text.

"So now you even have Marty's phone number," she said. "You can give it to Marion first thing tomorrow and then let nature take its course."

"So, I assume you're not faulting me for getting involved with this crazy bitch because of your most recent fall from grace with P. Robbins?" said Colby, with curiosity rather than heat.

"The scales are now in perfect balance," she conceded, "but it does pain me to think of you making love to another lady."

"It wasn't anything like making love."

"I know, you treated her like the slut that she is, but that's hot. And the idea of you having hot sex with another woman is twisting my stomach into a knot," Amanda admitted.

"You weren't bothered after that time with Pamela," Colby reminded her.

"I know, but you have to remember, that never happened," she told him with certainty.

"That scene with Mrs. Robbins," Colby began, "you have no idea how perfect that was for me. Thanks, Babe. I owe you all the luggage carrying and silly clothing shopping in Europe that you can stand."

"Thank you," Amanda smiled.

"Thank you, for not climbing all over me for sleazing after another babe," Colby said. "I just couldn't seem to help myself."

"Colby, you were doing what you were supposed to do as a New Rod editor, networking, reaching out. Face it, you're a player now. You pursued and won me, then I let you into those Pamela games, now you're writing a column under a penname with your real photo. Women are asking your advice and more, much more. You've been doing this a week and you already have followers and groupies. You can never go back to being that innocent boy. You're going to be dealing with these crazy bitches for the rest of your life. Just like the men will be chasing me for the rest of mine."

"I figured you'd understand if you ever found out," said Colby. "And since I had money in the bank with you from past indiscretions, I didn't hesitate. But if I thought it really bothered you, I'd drop this whole line of activity overnight."

Amanda took this pledge to mean that Colby continued to worship her as a goddess and finally felt her shoulders relax, for they had been stiff since he'd begun his dazzling admission.

"Let's just take these things as they come," Amanda suggested. "We can't seem to stop them from coming."

"Here, anyway. In Europe, we'll be as one," Colby declared. "I'll probably keep you handcuffed to me the whole time to make sure no one tries to steal you."

Amanda willingly clung to her lover, both excited and alarmed by the calm confidence that seemed to suddenly emanate from Colby Hodge. In measures of sophistication he was catching up with her fast.

Chapter Twenty-five

Full Circle

Ever since his unexpected but extremely pleasant erotic encounter with Jane Eliot the week before, a tiny detail had been nagging at the brain of former detective Michael Flagg and one very warm night, he decided to take a detour on his way over to the bar in order to intercept Jane as she left work at the Gay and Lesbian Services center in Provincetown. With perfect timing he arrived just as she was leaving the building, looking charming in a trim blue summer dress, her hair pulled back in a barrette. Pulling his car up beside hers as she got behind her wheel, he saluted her and asked her if she had a few minutes to chat. Jane did not look surprised at this requested and nodded back with a smile. They both parked and agreed to take a walk around the village.

"How have you been since I saw you last?" he asked.

"Well, and you?" she grinned back.

"Look, I have to ask you something."

"You don't have to. I'll tell you right now, the answer is yes. I did go back and rescue the rubber out of the trash," said Jane. "Remember I said I thought I left my phone and ran back for it?"

"And then what happened?" he asked, though able to guess.

"I went straight to one of my best friends, a lesbian GYN, and got myself inseminated."

"You can do that without permission of the donor?" he asked.

"I told her you were the man who jilted me and she agreed that you owed me that much. Anyway, we don't know if it'll take or not."

"Oh Jane, why?"

"Michael, you were the man I'd picked to be the father of my children. Marnie agrees that you'd be much more likely to provide good genetic material than some strange sperm donor we know nothing about."

"And does she know how you got the sperm?" he sputtered.

"She didn't ask."

"So where do I come into all of this now? And what about Marguerite? She'll know the minute she sees the baby, unless I tell her beforehand, which I'll obviously have to do. Damn it, Jane, this is really going to complicate my life."

"Relax, we don't know if it took yet," said Jane with a serene smile. "But I think that of all people, Marguerite would understand. I gave you up to her without a fight years ago and now I'm taking just a little bit of you back. She can spare it."

"Well, what am I supposed to be to the baby if there is one?"

"You could be its godfather," Jane suggested. "Marnie'll take care of everything else. She'll settle money on any baby of mine the day it's born. We're not getting married or anything radical like that, but she's my girl."

"No, it's too crazy," he protested.

"Oh, but you kind of like the idea. I can see it in your eyes," she laughed. "Now let's go have sex one more time to make sure it'll happen," she stunned him by suggesting. She looked perfectly serious, however and even took his hand. "I'm all on fire just thinking about it," she added truthfully. For although she adored Marnie Price, Jane had never actually stopped being heterosexual and the refresher course in the classic boy girl hook up with Michael the previous week had left her hungry for more. The fresh sight of him and scent of him beside her made it even harder to resist temptation.

"Let me get this straight," he said, "you want to have sex with me again, just to make sure you'll get pregnant?"

"No, because I'm aroused just looking at you and I'd also like to have another spanking."

"Nonsense, you're just saying that, but I don't know why," he remarked, giving her a side-glance.

"Don't you realize it's because I still love you?" she asked.

"Jane, I love you too, but –"

"I'm not trying to break up your marriage," Jane promised and he believed her because above all things, his ex-fiancée was honorable.

"Seriously," he protested, "I was just on my way in to work. We'll talk about this more though."

"Marnie's out of town until next week, come see me after work," Jane invited him breezily, getting into her car.

The morning after the day they returned to Random Point, Laura found herself unable to sleep past seven, in spite of having stayed up late the night before, drinking wine and smoking weed with Amanda, Colby and Hugo. She left Hugo slumbering peacefully and put her head out of the window to breath in the scent of the morning woods.

Amanda and Colby had expressed their gratitude for having been allowed to stay at the house together by preparing a spicy, savory Indian dinner for the newlyweds, by way of contrast to the Mediterranean cuisine they'd been partaking off all month in Italy. After the plates had been cleared away, they continued sitting around the kitchen table as Colby pumped Hugo for juicy scene anecdotes based on publishing the magazine for twenty years. Mindful of still being on his honeymoon, Hugo mentioned only incidents from the pre-Laura era, which his bride noticed and appreciated as a sign of respect.

The wine working quickly on the light drinking Amanda, as soon as Hugo got onto the topic of obsessive female fans, she blurted out that Colby had a crazy bitch of his own who he had been cultivating all month and who was verging on becoming fatally attracted to her boyfriend. Colby flushed at this revelation but considered it a signal that discretion belonged to the sober and countered that he had to do *something* to occupy himself while she, Amanda, was seducing Phoebe's husband! Now it was Amanda's turn to blush with embarrassment, though she staunchly defended her honor, insisting that Mr. Robbins had been pursuing her *relentlessly* and that she had only decided to give in to him after determining beyond a doubt that *his* wife was cheating on *him* with Anthony Newton!

This revelation shocked Hugo and Laura so gravely that Colby decided to lighten the mood by describing the subsequent spankings he'd witnessed Phoebe and Amanda trading in the garden at Anthony's pool party with a fan's enthusiasm. Amanda hid her face in her hands, blushing even more deeply.

"She is a pleasant girl," Laura thought back on their late night with a smile. "Why was I ever afraid of her?"

Laura washed her face, brushed her teeth, dressed in denim capris, a camp shirt and sneakers, put her hair in a ponytail and went downstairs to drink coffee. Then she peddled her bike down Shadow Lane, impelled to discuss the Anthony and Phoebe affair with Marguerite before agreeing with Hugo's plan of "keeping clam" to her sister Susan about it. Laura knew that Marguerite always got up early and taking a chance that her best friend might have spent the night at her husband's cottage a quarter mile down Shadow Lane, as Marguerite sometimes did, Laura proceeded thence.

As she neared Michael's house, Laura noticed that the car parked outside, alongside Michael's, was not Marguerite's, but someone else's vehicle. The next moment, to Laura's astonishment, she saw Jane Eliot emerge from the front door of the house, joined by Michael Flagg, who embraced and kissed the slim brunette, before waving her goodbye as she jumped into her car and gaily drove away. Laura pulled her bike behind a tree to collect her wits as she processed what she'd just seen. One thing was certain, she wasn't going to find Marguerite Alexander Flagg inside that house this a.m.!

Laura peddled back home and found Hugo up, dressed, drinking his first cup of coffee and sorting through hundreds of emails in his den. He looked up from his computer and smiled as she came in, saying, "Well, the shop made some money, the house is in perfect order and the cats are all alive. I think the kids did a pretty good job, don't you?"

"A very good one," she agreed, sitting in the window seat with its open window looking into the back garden that butted up against the woods.

"They're gone," Hugo reported of Amanda and Colby, "they were down the road by five a.m."

"Really?"

"They're off to Europe today."

So they were alone at last, at home for the first time, while married. Now Laura noticed a small jewelry box on Hugo's desk, identical to the one that had contained the Venus Club ring that Amanda had delivered to her the previous day. He followed her gaze and said, "It's another of those rings. Amanda left it with me to decide what to do with."

"Really? Why you?"

"Anthony had it made for Cassandra. He gave it to Amanda to send to her mother, but she doesn't want to."

"Why not?" Laura's heart had begun to thump unpleasantly when Hugo mentioned his former love.

"When a magical object like a ring is received by a believer, it often actuates a journey back to the sender. Amanda thinks the ring will bring her mother back to Random Point."

"Is that something I should be afraid of?" Laura wondered aloud.

"No, of course not."

"Then why is Amanda?"

"I'm not sure," Hugo lied, aware of Amanda's fear that her mother might abandon her worthy stepfather if she once again fell under Hugo's spell.

"Anthony is certainly getting a lot of ideas lately, isn't he?" Laura mused. "It isn't enough he had to annex Pascal Robbins' wife, but now he's set up this new situation with Cassandra that will almost certainly result in her coming to Random Point and wrecking who know how much havoc on our marriage?"

"We don't have to send the ring," Hugo suggested.

Suddenly remembering having seen Jane Eliot leaving Michael Flagg's door only minutes before, Laura reported this event to Hugo in photographic detail, down to the roses in Jane's cheeks as she kissed her erstwhile fiancé goodbye that deliriously fragrant summer morning in the woods.

Hugo marveled at the circumstance his bride had witnessed, wondering what to make of it while flashing back to a mental image of Michael Flagg and Jane Eliot entering his shop for the first time almost eight years before, engaged to be married and on the brink of relocating to Random Point. After leaving his shop, they'd proceeded to the bookstore across the street, where Michael had glimpsed Marguerite for the first time. This was the exact point at which Michael's relationship with Jane ended and his great love affair with Marguerite Alexander began.

"Maybe things are just supposed to come full circle now," reflected Laura, pushing the box containing Cassandra Campi's Venus Club ring back towards her husband. "Send Amanda's mamma her ring."

About the Author

A lifelong enthusiast, Eve Howard has been writing, editing and creating spanking erotica since the 1980's. There are 10 previous volumes in the Shadow Lane series as well as a pictorial publication called *Shadow Lane's The Art of Spanking Volume One*. Eve has also written, directed and produced over 170 spanking videos and has recently returned to the small screen as a performer in some her own productions. Designed to make people feel *good*, rather than guilty about being into spanking, Eve's books suggest an irreverent alternative to the BDSM extremes portrayed in such novels as *The Story of O*. Eve was the editor of the beautifully designed *Stand Corrected* magazine, which raised the bar for spanking publications in the 1990's. And for over 20 years, Eve's company Shadow Lane has been one of the primary social organs of the real-life spanking scene, throwing annual gala events for fellow enthusiasts to come together and celebrate the spicy variation that has preoccupied them for so long. Eve lives with her husband Tony and their two cats in Las Vegas.

Reader Reviews about the Shadow Lane Series

"I've become addicted to the "Random Point" series so much that I can't wait until the next chapter. I've ordered the first two Shadow Lane volumes and have re-read them over and over. I never tire of them. Eve s the only person I know who can make an enema sexy."

"I discovered Shadow Lane about a month ago via AOL. Prior to that time I thought I could write excellent spanking erotica. Then I ordered. "The Problem with Laura." This is just a note to commend Eve Howard's spectacular talent and to say thanks for an incredible erotic experience."

"I have just completed "Return to Random Point" and decided that I had to write about how much I enjoyed it. I have not been so aroused since reading my first discipline novel many years ago, about a girl raised in England and "coming of age" as I believe they put it. More recently I have enjoyed reading Grant Andrews' My Darling Dominatrix and Ann Rice's "Beauty" series. It seems that women, though, have the right touch when it comes to writing about this subject. Eve, especially, knows how to touch that erotic nerve and bring it to a pure, raw sensuality until one feels that he/she is near bursting with lust."

"I, for one, have always loved (and by loved I mean devoured... breathlessly) Eve Howard's novelettes. To read them... especially when I was just 'coming out'... was to feel completely validated. I truly identified with each and every heroine; the feisty, sassy ones, the shy, demure ultra 'subby' ones... the young ones, and the more mature. I loved the gentle yet firm "taken in hand" nature of the romantic variety of spanking D's that Eve always incorporated into the stories. I loved that the plots were not complicated... but, feasible nonetheless. I loved the depictions of sexual escapades after many of the spanking interludes. I appreciated that the girls were cherished and adored by the affably rogue-ish gents... that the submitting was willing and desired... that it wasn't like 'rape.'
    I like the settings... having grown up in New England and living here almost my whole life. I LOVED the idea of the bookstore (which I always find sexy). Then and now. I could cite many passages too, but I fear I've rambled enough. Eve was/is always my favorite spanking author."

www.ingramcontent.com/pod-product-compliance
Lightning Source LLC
Chambersburg PA
CBHW031113030726
47496CB00002BA/518